Charles Harris was born in Rockwell, Iowa in 1945. He has spent almost his entire working life in the forefront of creative departments in most of the world's biggest advertising agencies. He has been an award winning Creative Director with Leo Burnett, J. Walter Thompson, Ted Bates, Foote Cone & Belding and Publicis. He has won global awards as a copywriter for his work in Radio, TV and Print campaigns for clients in Australia, Singapore, Dubai, China, and the UK. He writes The Creativity Works Blog on Typepad.com and although retired from the advertising mainstream, he continues to work as a professional photographer and creative consultant.

He has lived in the UK since 1981 with time out for work in Southeast Asia for several years in the 1990s. He now resides with his wife, Marilyn, in the Hampshire countryside of Southern England. He has a daughter in Oregon and a son in London.

Also by Charles Harris –

ICE ANGELS

CRE8TOR

MISSOURI FALL

The Suns of God

Charles E. Harris

Hannington, Hampshire, England

The Suns of God

ISBN 978-1-84799-788-3

Printed in the United States of America

To all those creative guys and girls who slave through late nights and weekends to make other people wealthy, and to all the altruistic ones who 'just want to make great ads'. As if it's going to make a difference. Anyway --

Imagine what you can do tomorrow – and do it!

Preface

Having had a long and successful career at the creative edge of the advertising industry across the globe, I was often told by people outside the industry how they avoided advertising and 'never bought anything that was advertised'. Unless you live in an as yet undiscovered corner of the Amazon or Papua New Guinea such a claim is frankly impossible.

The extreme opposite viewpoint comes from young immature advertising people who incredulously believe that the ad campaign they are currently creating is going to 'make a real difference' to people's lives. That is equally absurd and pitiful.

'The Suns of God' pokes fun equally at people who make ads and people who don't even know they are the targets of an industry that is creative, fun and ruthless.

You will enjoy the real life advertising stories and case histories that have been woven into the fabric of my fiction, but whatever you do, don't take any of it too seriously! I certainly don't.

Begun in 1977 and tweaked for thirty years until I couldn't cling to the clutter on my desk any longer, the final revisions of this yarn were made in an effort to keep up with the changes of technology that have occurred since 1977. A hopeless task.

The story that I originally told in the genre of science fiction in order to distance it from the true life situations has begun to look like recent history rather than a fun poke into the future.

Sneak Preview

The essence of Oron touched the dull blackness of the tiny asteroid. It was cold. Completely without heat. As he touched it, the pitted surface gave way and the substance of the asteroid disintegrated into countless particles of floating dust. The asteroid was the ash of some long dead star.

Oron felt the presence of another. A moment later his mind was touched by a greeting from the essence he knew as Atos.

"Oron, my friend."

"Atos, your light is dim. Are you grieved?"

"Oron, we are doomed."

"That is not news, it's common knowledge. Entropy is inexorably taking over everything and we're headed for the oblivion that awaits all things at the end of the Universe."

"Are you sure, Oron?"

"That the Universe will end there is no doubt."

"Then yours is a plea for infinity?"

The light source he knew as Atos twinkled with interest but answered with silence.

"Ash is the saddest thing in the Universe, Atos. To think that all the beauty of the stars, the forests and oceans of the planets will one day be turned to ash, and that ash will be the only thing in Universe is for me sadness absolute."

"But as long as we don't have to clean it up, why worry?"

"Look, Atos, I think you ought to take this a bit more seriously..."

"Brighten up! Doom and gloom puts a hole in my soul. I don't need it. But if you must carry on, then I'll be your friend as I always have and hear you out. I take it your trip to the end of the Universe did not go well?""It had about as much suspense as a candle in a hurricane."

7

"It was just like I told you then. Entropy reaching its ultimate conclusion. The last gasping star reduced to pathetic ash. The last spark of energy cashed in trying to heat and light the-"

"Cold vast emptiness of space."

"You cut me off."

"I knew what you were going to say. You've been giving me that speech for the last thirty thousand years, Oron."

"So why did you go and watch it?"

"I didn't think it could be as boring as you said. But it was."

"That's not what's troubling you."

"No, Oron, it isn't. Look, we have four point one six three billion years to reverse things, not a nano-second more."

"Reverse Entropy? You're completely daft. How in the hell do you shove a Universe into reverse?"

"There are already those who are working on it."

"Thinking about it, Atos. *Doing* anything? I doubt it."

"Then we'd better get busy. We have the power, Oron, you and I, all of us -- the power to change the future. It's only the past that cannot be changed."

"That's pretty profound, but --"

"While you're feeling so complacent, I think there's something else you should know."

"What can be worse than the end of the Universe?"

"Well, when I got there, the End had already come and gone."

"What do you mean?"

"I mean that the calculated time for the grand finale has been moved up and none of us were consulted. I made the scheduled time jumps precisely as you instructed, but when I got there, the show was over. The Universe was already gone, caput, phoot, flame out! Entropy is accelerating faster than anyone has realised."

"Think I'd better cancel my holiday in the Sun?"

"No, the end isn't imminent, but as soon as you get back, I think we'd better press the tit for Plan B."

8

Freeze-frame

His eyes were deep blue, but they did not see. His lips were drawn smoothly in a patient expression. Few wrinkles creased his calm and pleasant face.

In his fine dark hair there were a few ice crystals close to the scalp, telltale evidence that adequate moisture had been retained when he had been frozen in 2006.

Through the plexi-glass cover of the cryonic capsule, his form was in full view. His long arms outstretched along his sides, he lay neatly and firmly wrapped in glistening metallic foil. His cold fixed gaze at the ceiling had remained unchanged for a hundred thousand years. It had been his respected wish that his eyes should remain open after death.

Occasionally a thin wisp of liquid nitrogen vapour tumbled across the ceramic contours of his frozen face. Canisters of the liquid gas had kept his body frozen at a constant temperature of -273 degrees Centigrade inside a nearly perfect vacuum. Like a giant thermos bottle, the capsule sealed out the threats of heat, radiation and bacteria.

A hundred thousand years had passed since Mason Jackson had made his first desperate step towards a second chance at life. A victim of lung cancer, Jackson had been given a twelve-month warning by his doctor that death was at hand. It was his misfortune to be living in an age when large portions of the population indulged in the intriguing pastime of smoking the leaves of certain plants that were dried and rolled into small cylinders called cigarettes. Jackson himself didn't partake of such dubious pleasures himself, but it was nonetheless the dirty deal of fate that he expired from the effects of other people's smoke.

When he received the medical report in November of 2004, he was, he felt, quite justly in a state of extreme bladder overload, or more to the point, pissed off. He had suffered badly in his youth from an asthmatic condition and fought off one attack after another, gradually overcoming the condition, bringing it steadily under control, only to be robbed of his breath yet again by uninvited cells raging through his bronchial tubes.

Mason lived and worked in Melbourne, on the continent of Australia on an early human inhabited planet. He was in the prime of middle age, enjoying the fruits of a successful career in advertising. At first devastated, he bounced back and fought the disease with all the strength his mind and body could muster. He tried conventional medicine, and then added homeopathy and meditation. He felt fitter than at any time in his life. Single with an eye for the women, he continued to play the field. He was tall, handsome, alert, tanned, and dying at a rate that accelerated weekly.

One crisp clear July winter morning after a cold swim in his garden pool, Mason's maid brought him the newspaper. It was wet. How it got that way or the fact that it was wet, didn't matter to him anymore. These days news no longer seemed relevant, so he consciously read all the trivia he could find and avoided the news altogether. Laughing at a little cartoon of Mickey Mouse, Mason went on to read the accompanying article about the life of Walt Disney. Disney's vision and creativity had long been admired by Jackson, a creator of modest repute in the parochial circle of admen in the southern Pacific Basin.

Disney died in the mid-1960s, and though it had been initially reported his body was cremated in a private ceremony, there was considerable evidence that his body had actually been turned over to a Cryonic Society for quick-freezing and, hopefully, thawing and rejuvenation at some later date.

Mason's imagination clicked into overdrive. Was this the chance he was looking for? A quick freeze and a shot at a second life? What would he change if he had it to do all over again? He talked avidly about it to his colleagues and friends. He made copious lists, drew up fantastic plans. But nobody took him seriously.

Mason Jackson obtained brochures from several Cryonic Societies in North America and Japan. No such facility was as yet available Down Under. Eventually he rang the President of the New York State Cryonic Society and learned that there were nearly six thousand people who had been quick-frozen and placed in capsules awaiting the fortune of the future.

Replying in a registered letter, the Society President explained how Jackson would go about making the arrangements to have himself cryonically preserved. Mason was amused to read that financial and legal representation was handled by the New York Metropolitan Death Insurance Company of New York City.

The choice was now clear. If Jackson was cremated or buried, there was no hope for the future. When his body was gone, his brain was gone -- his mind was gone and that would be the absolute end of him. Mason's urge to survive was so strong he even considered just having his head preserved, so that perhaps the brain and the mind might be revitalised in some technological miracle of the future. But what was his mind without his body? Why live if you couldn't breathe fresh air, bask in the warmth of the sun, drink fine wine, eat glorious food, climb mountains, and of course, have sex.

Mason Jackson was convinced that if he could be cryonically suspended until they had a cure for lung cancer, then there was a chance to live again and redeem himself as a human being and as a greater creator-- not just as an advertising man, but as an originator of fresh ideas that could make life better for everyone.

Jackson's investigations into cryonic procedures soon revealed significant failings. It seemed that finding a cure for cancer was more likely than developing a cure for the destruction ice would cause in his body. In 2005 the chances of successful cryonic suspension followed by successful thawing were so slim he nearly didn't write the cheque after all. But he did write it. He wanted a chance at a second life, no matter how slim that chance might be. It was far better than no chance at all.

If he was thawed out and found he was blind or handicapped, he could always commit what he called 'self-inflicted euthanasia.' There was always that opt out. And in his dying days, he found he liked to think about death, burrowing into a king of macabre pleasure in knowing that ultimately he possessed the power of life or death over his own person.

Secretly he proceeded with his plans. The New York Cryonic Society had stressed the importance of being quick-frozen immediately after death, whilst the body was still warm and well before rigor mortis had set in. That was why frozen vegetables and fruit were nicer and 'fresher' than tinned ones. Careful preparations had to be made to give the freezing process the optimum chance for success.

All his body fluid had to be removed and replaced. As they explained it, if he was frozen with his normal body fluids intact, billions of tiny ice crystals would form and rupture every capillary in his body, rendering him a helpless haemorrhaging blob when thawed out. Indeed, the Cryonic Society had been experimenting with new types of embalming fluids. Not only did they preserve organic tissues, but as freezing occurred, the fluid did not crystallise, is merely hardened -- without cutting or rupturing the surrounding tissues.

Mason Jackson disappeared from Australia in November of 2005. He left no messages, no clues. His friends and colleagues in Melbourne believed that he had simply become distraught with his terminal illness and probably had drowned his sorrows with a bottle of Dom Perignon and a midnight swim with the sharks in Port Phillip Bay.

12

There was no reason to suspect that any foul play had been involved. His affairs were in order; there was no family to leave his estate to, though several friends named as beneficiaries had considerable difficulty in getting their money when there was no body. In time though, the matter would quietly fade into a forgettable mystery.

Mason Jackson walked into the head office of the New York Metropolitan Death Insurance Company on Lexington Avenue, in the borough of Manhattan, on the morning of November 29. He inquired about the Cryonics Society Investment Fund and was guided to a small office on the 41st floor. An hour later he left the office with the policy holder's copy of the Planned Death and Rejuvenation Policy. The cash outlay was $39, 512. That provided for doctor's fees, the all important embalming and quick-freezing operation, and a seven hundred and fifty year maintenance contract for refilling the liquid nitrogen canisters that would keep him frozen. He felt that advances in medical technology would probably be able to resurrect him within one hundred years, but the extra time made him felt a little better about what he was doing. It also included the price tag of his cryonic capsule at $15,995. Mason put the last of his fading faith into the Society and the Insurance Company.

He knew the whole thing would be out of his hands as soon as the embalming began, but he had seen for himself the perfectly functioning cryonic capsules in the Society's warehouse on Long Island. He had also been shown the carefully wrapped and frozen bodies within them. Maybe he would meet them again.

The Society, in conjunction with the Insurance Company, offered an investment programme that guaranteed financial well-being in the next life. Increments of $5000 were invested in government bonds. At the end of his

13

internment, his original investment plus a return of 5% compounded semi-annually would be credited to the bank of his choice. After a hundred years or so, the interest accumulated would undoubtedly make him a rich man. If the rejuvenation was unsuccessful, the money would be given to the descendants of the 'policy holder' if that was his wish. If no one was eligible to collect the money, it would revert to the Society for research funding.

Mason handed over five hundred thousand dollars, his entire savings, and nominated himself as the sole beneficiary of the investment income, whilst giving the finance director of the fund full authority to invest it on his behalf as he saw fit.

The Planned Death and Resurrection Policy explicitly stated that the policy holder must die on the property of the New York Death Insurance Company. A counsellor suggested that whenever he felt weak, Mason should report to the 41st floor and lie down. Anywhere, it didn't matter.

While he was still feeling up to it, Mason went through a comprehensive battery of tests including IQ, co-ordination, reflex, memory, eyesight, hearing and every other physical reading that would build an accurate record of Mason Jackson the Body, prior to death. They even went so far as to take film of him walking, talking, smiling, and eating and so on. The record was filed in the capsule awaiting his death, as did a bona fide copy of his Planned Death and Resurrection Policy. "Keep it in a safe place" they always say.

Surprisingly, Mason lasted through November and lingered through all of December.

Christmas was particularly unsettling as he had planned to be dead by then, and had no one to spend neither it with nor any money to buy gifts for anyone. The Society's benevolence was forthcoming however. They gave him a cash advance on his Policy so he could splash out on a lavish lunch at the Waldorf Astoria.

Two days into the New Year, 2006, Jackson reported weak and gasping for air to the reception desk on the 41st floor. He didn't make it to the bedroom that had been set up for him. He just fell on the floor and asked for the embalmer. The Cryonic team whisked him into the cold room.

The President of the Society himself came in to send him off. All of Mason's last minute friends were there: the doctors, psychiatrists, embalmers, even the sales rep who took his money and the financial controller who tried desperately hard not to smirk. The band that played at his hearing tests played Henry VIII's classic Greensleeves at Mason's request. Everyone wished him well, reassuring him that he'd made absolutely the right decision.

Then they rolled in a special surprise - his beautiful new cryonic capsule with hydraulic suspension had been waxed and polished!

Mason thanked them all and then begged them to get on with it. The doctors concurred that Jackson's condition was irreversible, and that he would die in the next ten minutes anyway. They shook his hand, tucked the Policy copy into his palm, gave him an injection and sent his body into the peacefulness of the deepest sleep.

His heart beat was light and erratic when the new formula embalming fluid began to drip into his veins. The liquid nitrogen canisters were activated and a boy from the mail room came in to assist with the foil wrapping and insulation. Within the hour Mason Jackson lay comfortably in his capsule, loaded into the spacious boot of a 1998 Chevy station wagon that sped over the Brooklyn Bridge on its way to the Society warehouse on Long Island.

The years passed, and not surprisingly, the New York State Cryonic Society became successful. With the help of the financial expertise of the New York Metropolitan Death Insurance Company, they were able to open branches throughout the world. Of course there were many loud voices of protest and dissent against the whole idea of cryonic preservation. People said the world was already over-populated. And that Man had no right to play God. And that the Society doctors murdered people before they were clinically dead. Mind you, nobody really wanted to die, and more and more people like Mason Jackson took the risk to reach a second life.

A major triumph for the cryonics industry came in August 2074 when a cure for heart disease was approved. Relatives of several preserved individuals (perhaps hoping to collect the insurance money) pressed for a thaw. Fifteen out of twenty-two policy holders were successfully resurrected and cured!

"Freeze. Wait. Regenerate!" became the thing to do.

As the centuries passed, and a cure for cancer could not be found, Jackson's capsule was polished less frequently and the dust began to settle and shroud its identity. Eventually it was forgotten about and lost. Then, in a time so far forward that Mason Jackson could not have dared imagine, hands touched the metal of his capsule, and voices exclaimed excitement at their discovery. "Here's one worth saving!"

Archaeologists carefully removed the ancient metal shape with the cracked and scattered remains of several others for transferral to the Bionic Institute of Primitive Engineering to await further study.

Chinook

For Medical Team 439 at the Pan Quadrant Bionic Institute, it was a pretty routine booking, implementing a thaw on a frozen humanoid. What was unusual however was that they were performing rejuvenation on a man frozen for one hundred thousand years. The case history documentation recounted that the ancient cryonic capsule had first been brought to this part of the Quadrant by a community of doctors fleeing insurance company persecution around the 751st century. The capsule was then acquired by the Life Science Museum under the auspices of Central Thought, the former Central Office of Information. Later, it was interred in the Institutional catacombs when Central Thought abolished the Resurrection Committee in the 900th century. For ten thousand years, a politically nervous central government had ceased resurrection activities.

In past millennia, a hero's welcome awaited the preserved traveller from an earlier epoch. Multi-media coverage of the entire resurrection process provided spectacular entertainment and attracted huge sums of sponsorship revenue. But in these stressful centuries, an additional human being was simply not welcome in the economic equation. Times were tight, planets groaned with heavy populations. Space itself seemed to be filling up. The less said about another mouth to feed the better.

Why this person had been called up from the reserve pool of intelligence was anybody's guess. The doctors scanning the notes understood nothing about the man's origins and could see little reason in rejuvenating him other than the interest of meeting someone fifty thousand years older than anyone they'd ever met before.

The second coming of Mason Jackson was officially a state secret. Team 439 was chosen for the operation because it was small and efficient and would do what they were told with no questions asked. Security was tight but invisible to the Team. Had they been alert to the importance of what they were doing, they probably would have been quietly eliminated. Indeed, when the head of the team, Dr. Loretta Kowalski found out that Jackson was an advertising man, and not a food scientist or a synthetic inventor, she was very uneasy knowing there was more to this than she wanted to know. Dr. Kowalski prayed she wouldn't show her concern to anyone else.

Security could count on her, as long as she kept her thoughts to herself. She for one did not want anyone to know she had anything whatsoever to do with resurrecting an advertising man. "The Computer works in mysterious ways," she thought to herself, resolute about not wanting to know more, not wanting to get involved in something larger than her own life. It was more than her job was worth, but she was already involved.

Dr. Kowalski simply could not get it out of her mind. What value would anyone from the 20th century have here? Why had she been chosen to resurrect him?

Kowalski assembled her team in resurrection room. The capsule had been cleaned, and the synthidium sleeve the archivists at the Bionic Institute had installed was pulled away. Now for the first time, she could look through the discoloured but still transparent shell. Her long thin hands were covered with tight green rubber gloves that squeaked when she ran her fingers across the surface.

Investigating the instrument readings on the cryonic control panel, Kowalski looked to her senior technician for a second opinion. He nodded approval and Kowalski began to turn a small shiny valve on the ancient capsule. A hundred thousand years after the Chevy wagon had taxied Jackson's fresh frozen corpse to the warehouse on Long Island, warm air once again entered his twentieth century environment. Green rubber gloves padded applause as the team congratulated Dr. Kowalski on a job well done. She smiled, made a little bow and left the room.

Scanners showed Jackson's body to be remarkably intact except for massive damage to the lungs. But that would be repaired before resurrection. Sensors indicated the temperature in the body cavity was still minus 273 degrees Centigrade. The resurrection team moved swiftly. Green-gloved hands opened a sliding door underneath the corpse compartment to disconnect and remove the long empty liquid nitrogen canisters. Pairs of eyes studied rows of readings and glowing graphic panels. Every mind was alert, studying data watching for signals.

The temperature inside the body rose past minus 235. The thaw had begun. The body lay quiet, silent, still, blue eyes unblinking, frost twinkling in the eyelashes. Jackson's blue-grey lips looked incapable of ever moving again.

The treatment for the lung cancer that was the official cause of death in 2006 involved the simple administration of an anti-biotic gas that was now pumped in with the warm oxygen. The gas would permeate the smallest cells of Jackson's body, and detergent like, would lift out the cancer virus organisms. As the gas was pumped in with the patient's breathing supply, it would be pumped out through a filtration system that would collect and trap cancer cells and any other unwanted 20th century organisms, automatically storing them in phials for future study or destruction.

Gradually the composition of the atmosphere inside the cryonic capsule would be brought into equilibrium with the air in the resurrection room.

Suddenly Dr. Kowalski returned. Reappraising the resurrection schedule and the bio-data on Jackson's body, she had decided on a change of plan. She had in her hands a plastic bag containing a complete set of new lungs for Jackson.

"Stick these in when you get a chance. Lung cancer is easy enough to cure. but asthma is tough, I suffer myself. He'll appreciate a breath of fresh air after what he's been through." Secretly she hoped the cell structure throughout the body was healthy enough to warrant the price of the silk lungs from the department's organ bank. She also made a note to see if there were any pieces of Jackson she could take from him as payment. But there was nothing he had that they needed.

Almost three hours after the warm air inlet had been opened; the air temperature in the capsule had crept up to a hyper-critical 0 degrees Centigrade. But deep in the heart of the ancient cadaver, the tissues remained hard frozen. Like a steak taken from the freezer to thaw, the outside began to dr_p long before the inner ice lost its granite grip on the tissue.

Thermo sensors now registered minus 20 degrees in the stomach. It was time to hook up the electro-chemical stimulators. The system tested positive. Everything was ready for the next stage. Kowalski ordered the opening of the capsule. The atmosphere inside the capsule now matched the atmosphere outside and there was nothing to gain by having the body covered. The four team members took positions around the capsule where handles were located and began to lift the yellowed plexi-glass cover. It disintegrated, its shattered crystals falling like splintered snow on the silver foil covering the stone cold corpse.

"Never eat yellow snow," one of the masked faces said. The debris made attempts at hygiene superfluous.

For the first time, hands were able to touch the thawing body. Kowalski watched intently as her team ever so delicately removed the silver foil. Like onion-skin, it had deteriorated so badly that it kept tearing into tiny pieces, making it extremely difficult to remove. It was half an hour before all the layers were painstakingly peeled away and the frozen figure of the primitive man lay naked in the midst of the silvery trash.

As he thawed, more and more beads of water -- like sweat -- appeared on his body. The interior temperature edged slowly upward. It reached freezing point, then 10 degrees of warmth. As it approached room temperature, the electrochemical apparatus was activated and the body was warmed from within still further. Each member of the medical team watched the data streams with tense excitement.

An inventory was the next step. Kowalski gave the instructions. It was necessary to check the exact contents of the body against the micro-filmed list enclosed in the capsule on the fateful day in 2006. If there was any discrepancy, well-- it all depended on what was missing. Some things could be replaced.

Sonic probing of the cell structure confirmed that the embalming formula had worked very well. No discernible deterioration could be detected. No ruptured tissues of any kind were apparent. They double checked the inventory and handed the results to Kowalski. She glanced at Mason's luke-warm nudity and impulsively commented, "Put some underwear on this poor bastard." The order was duly carried out.

The time was ripe for the lung surgery. Kowalski made a few fast incisions into Mason's meaty chest. Minutes later, her assistants deftly removed the lumpy leftovers inserted the shiny silk bags and plugged in the new bionics. Kowalski coughed and left the theatre again.

The new lungs though made of fabric, were virtually a copy of those in a champion decathlete. Kowalski yawned with waning interest as she watched the procedure on her view frame in her private lounge. The task of micro-welding the new bits into the old slots fell to Dr. Ethel Jones, a 370-year old former housewife from Gannymede who won the chance to learn micro-surgery as a prize on a quiz show. Dr. Jones had only recently joined Kowalski's crew and was eager to demonstrate her dexterity and newly learned skills.

She was good, very good. Thirteen minutes later, Mason Jackson had better lungs than any Olympic athlete of his century. Now, only one more relatively simple procedure stood between the eternity of death and the spark of life. Kowalski inspected the housewife's laser work on her view frame, grunted approval, and signalled the team to prepare to carry on. She joined them in the resurrection room.

With no ceremony or fanfare of any kind, Dr. Loretta Kowalski leaned over a small control unit and pressed the button that started the disembarking cycle. On her command, a drum lowered from the ceiling and hovered over Jackson. The drum unfolded several needled appendages that reached down to the body, penetrated the skin in a dozen places and started pumping freshly manufactured blood into the veins. Due to certain evolutionary changes occurring in the human species during the hundred thousand years Jackson had been suspended, it was necessary to manufacture the exact blood composition that his body required. Blood of his type and constitution had not been documented since the 117th century. A trolley carrying several litres of the specially manufactured blood was on hand in the event of unforeseen emergencies.

As the new blood was being pumped in, the embalming fluid was being pumped out. It took only sixteen minutes to complete the change from embalming fluid to new blood. Every organ, vein, artery and capillary was flushed free of the ancient residue.

Each member of the medical team was required by law to sign the resurrection certificate authorised by the Resurrection Committee. Dr. Kowalski signed last.

The electric shock that would make Mason Jackson's cells live again was only seconds away.

Staring at the glazed, dead-fish eyes of the man on the table, Dr. Loretta Kowalski threw the switch at 2.31 pm on the afternoon of December 7th, 120006. It was Mason Jackson's 100,061st birthday. And a helluva present.

As the massive shock charged through every cell, the arms twitched, then convulsed in increasingly violent spasms lasting several seconds each. The green-blue irises of his eyes rolled up and disappeared into the sockets. Vacant white bulges protruded from the hollows and melted frost splattered across his crisp clean new undershorts. His whole body then arched into a climatic, fearful final convulsion that left the body quivering with electricity. Or was it Life?

Rebirth

The thick dark hair of his scalp had curled somewhat as it thawed in the moist conditions, but it seemed to straighten out a little as Kowalski threw a new shock deep into the cranium. The head lurched forward, the neck arching in a sudden severe jerk of the spinal cord. A ball of feeling began at the base of the spine and moved up through the spine until it reached the middle of the back behind the heart and lungs.

The chest quaked and trembled, heaving and rippling with the burst of voltage. The robot drum injected adrenalin into the heart. Nutrients were pumped into the veins. The eyes, which had remained open staring at Kowalski, suddenly collapsed closed. Dr. Jones saw it first - sensors had picked up the first heart beat. Then the first breath. Nutrients and adrenalin were instantly increased.

In seconds, an auto-respirator flew down from the ceiling. Whirring like a distant siren it landed on Jackson's chest and gently grasped his torso, massaging the muscles and moving the rib cage in a steady rhythm establishing a stable pattern.

As everyone watched the monitors, the heart gained strength with every beat. Ethel Jones, Organ Welder, viewed the whole scene with immense pride and approval. Metabolism was controlled by the computer as Mason slept the sleep of the living for the first time in a hundred and eighteen thousand years. But until he regained consciousness could he even know he was alive again?

Central Thought provided the computer runs that would keep Jackson alive but it was still necessary for the medical technicians to maintain their vigil over the instruments that kept track of the body's status and the recording equipment documenting the resurrectee's progress. But as the automatics took over, boredom set in and Kowalski's team switched off the lights and left for lunch.

Mason's sleep went deeper and deeper. As his body quietly regained its functions, a re-orientation programme began to tell him what had transpired in the last few hours. He would always treasure these first 'memories' as the most valuable. The programme told how, according to the micro-film report found in his capsule, he had died and was cryonically suspended. And then Central Thought began to tell him what the Universe was like outside his room on that day, December 7th, 120006.

It was several days before the computer chatter stopped. Jackson remained deep in sleep. It was not a coma. He had strange dreams of a world with ten billion people fed by farms on other planets. He also dreamed of a frigid winter in New York City, of foot blistering beaches in Australia, and a parade of advertising campaigns for airlines, banks, burgers, and drinks.

It was December 15th when he awoke. The technicians predicted the awakening twenty-five minutes before hand. Dr. Kowalski was notified floating in her pool aboard her private satellite in time for her to arrive with minutes to spare.

Mason Jackson regained consciousness in perceived privacy. The fact that the walls looked opaque and he was alone in his chamber disguised the fact that the walls were completely transparent from the other side and the team never took their eyes off him. Jackson stirred and began to look about the room, finding little to focus on. After the first forty-eight hours of Resurrection procedure, Kowalski's team moved Jackson to a comfortable bed with clean white linen. A small table stood on the right side of the bed with red rose-like flowers in a blue steel vase. There were no windows but there was a door on the far side of the room that tempted his curiosity. He recalled the story he had been told of his resurrection, but as yet there was no evidence whatsoever that this was not just another room in the offices of the New York Metropolitan Death Insurance Company. However he noticed that his breathing had improved dramatically and there were dressings on his chest that were painful to the touch.

Mason could hear no sound save for the reassuring flow of air in and out of his mouth. For awhile he concentrated on this steadiness, gradually shifting his focus into the space between the breaths. He was aware of thoughts, images from tantalising dreams. He watched them drift up and away. And then the door opened.

Dr. Loretta Kowalski led her team into Jackson's chamber. She smiled broadly as she approached his bed and stared down into his face. He felt disadvantaged to be looked down at. To be without information. To be under someone else's control. He raised himself up. Supported on his right elbow, he turned toward the team.

"Good morning, Mr. Jackson." Dr. Kowalski broke the silence with the warmth of her greeting. Mason noticed she spoke with a peculiar accent. Not quite European, nor Chinese, nor anywhere that he knew. Still it was clipped with efficiency, precise in its articulation, easy to understand and certainly not unpleasant.

"When, when is it really?" Mason asked wryly.

"You have dreamed it is the year 120006."

"I think this is still a dream."

"It is not a dream."

Mason sensed something unearthly about the woman.

"Christ, come on you're having me on. Where's the camera?"

Kowalski found the quaint 20th century language intriguing.

"The cameras are everywhere and nowhere to be seen."

Jackson was intrigued, but felt she was telling the truth. He studied her face. She seemed young, confident and he hoped, understanding.

"Hey, let's lighten up a little okay? I'm not dead am I?" He wondered at the prospect as he uttered the question.

Titters and mutters spread through the team. Loretta Kowalski answered convincingly, "Not any more. You really are quite healthy even though if I may say so, you are extremely fortunate. Time has treated you better than most."

Jackson paused for a moment and looked at each member of the medical team. Then he reached out and touched the red flower. It was soft, velvet, *real.* "Shit, I made it. I actually, really, goddam made it!"

"Yes, Mr. Jackson, you goddam made it, as you would say."

"I was sure we would have blown ourselves up but we didn't do it, did we. It's amazing! This is fantastic. I want to give you a hug."

"In many ways, the whole Universe will probably seem amazing to you. But do calm yourself; your body still needs much rest. You may ask us questions but if you don't mind, we have a few to ask of you too. And it wouldn't be professional to let you hug me."

Heads leaned forward, voices congratulated the new Resurrectee. They tried to answer his questions but with little success.

"Who won Superbowl XL? What's the unemployment rate? What's the pound against the dollar? Did they ever land on Mars? Can I have a pepperoni pizza for lunch?"

An hour later, Kowalski and her exhausted team left Jackson still barking questions. In the next room, they discussed their patient's progress. Was he really the same Mason Jackson who had lived all those tens of thousands of years ago, or was he the product of Central Thought? After a cup of coffee they went back in. Jackson was sitting up and full of life -- and more questions.

"Hey, there's no mirror in this room. Can you bring me one? I'd like to see what I look like after all this time."

"I think that can be arranged. The cryonic process was reasonably kind to you. Of course I can't make you look

younger; I'd have to have approval to refer you to a Re-
maker."

An assistant left hurriedly and returned with a hand
mirror. She gave it to Kowalski to give to Jackson. "Well
what do you think?"

"Pretty much the way I remember myself, really. A few
little creases beginning to appear on the face, but you
wouldn't call me a 'wrinklie'." A few well-placed streaks
of silver amongst his predominantly dark hair gave him a
rather distinguished air.

"Same strong, slightly dimpled chin, cheek bones on the
high side, nice average nose, lively eyes, green. Yeah,
that's me, alright. Not bad. Quite presentable."

"I'm glad to see you're pleased with yourself. We would
like to continue investigating the coherency of your
memory. If it's all right with you that is."

"Of course, I don't mind."

The team worked from prepared questionnaires. Jackson's
memory of his experience up to 2006 was acute and this
was a particularly rewarding aspect of the team's
Resurrection work. His personal history had not been
programmed, reprogrammed or in any way tampered
with. His memories could only have come from a
properly functioning brain. The patient's recovery
prognosis was very positive indeed.

Leadership Hall

Three human forms stood in animated conversation precisely in the middle of the vast inner sanctum of the supreme heads of state. So extreme was the secrecy surrounding the movements of the inner circle of government that few people who entered this vast hall realised where they really were.

There was no way of telling just how large the enclosure was. Its walls were made of energy and not of matter. The flow of forces within it gave it colour and light and beauty of infinitely variable tone, intensity and depth.

There was a fascinating illusion for every visitor that the walls were at the same time both very close and very far away, flowing and ebbing without definition or scale.

The three life forms were the Leaders. The supreme heads of government of the entire inhabited Universe. This particular triumvirate had been continuously in power for the last seventy Universal-years. It was their duty to maintain stability and promote economic growth for a hundred years of elected office. But now, with only thirty years left of their term, the economy was beginning to show the first palpitations of the uncertain future that would immediately ensue with the next change of government.

Already the news media were planting the first important questions: Who would the next Triumvirate be? Which quadrant would they come from? How liberal would current circumstances allow the next regime to become? How much growth could be achieved? Would they increase spending in the sciences? Would they listen more or listen less to the vociferous lobbies on planet conservation? Would they increase spending on terra-forming and new planet construction?

There were always the controversial questions too: What if they were threatened by as yet undiscovered sentient life forms? And what about all the money being wasted on Anti-Entropy research -would a new government finally put a stop to it?

So far, polls proved that nearly all these questions and issues had been dealt with to the satisfaction of the majority in the first seventy years. You couldn't please all the companies all the time, but the consensus agreed that the Leadership had so far not really hurt anyone's income or hopes for a better tomorrow. Indeed, the three Leaders usually passed the scrutiny of the computers of Central Thought, the major decision making machine of the Human Universe.

The Leaders did actually rule, not Central Thought. 'C.T.', as it was popularised, was capable of ruling if anything happened to the Triumvirate, but simply was not allowed to do so. Instead, as a measure of the effectiveness of the government's decision-making process, it was the custom for C.T. to display its judgements with a simple numerical mark. For example, the cumulative score the Triumvirate rated on the subject of defence spending was 7.8 out of a possible 10. Because defence spending was always up, -- even though an outside enemy could not be precisely defined, -- the defence industries probably would have voted 10 out of 10.

On education, C.T. gave them a 9.3; on planet conservation, 5.6; on Anti-Entropy research, 7.4. Not that it made any difference. It didn't -- save for the bookmakers who would take bets on the marks. The Triumvirate ruled and that was that. Sure, they could use, and did use, C.T. as their chief adviser, but they could decide to dismiss its advice in favour of their own human feelings.

This morning's first conversation was about a censorship ruling made on one of the jungle planets. It obviously provided a source of great amusement amongst the Leaders as they flexed their minds into shape before facing the more serious working agenda of the day.

"If Wee Kloan Yu seriously wants his people to think their world is flat, he can but try!" one of the Leaders, Rios, exclaimed.

"He goes too far sometimes." Leader Prime smiled.

"What would it cost to send a Physics Freighter out there and really make his planet flat -- like a coin?" Big-jawed Jarrod enjoyed his own joke.

"That would certainly teach him!" Rios laughed.

"Uh oh", cautioned Catherine Prime, "Time to get to work I'm afraid." She was tall, elegant and moved with the same degree of exceeding grace with which she spoke.

She was born into an ambassadorial family on Sri-Alpha 3 and gained rapid promotion during the last 270 years. Her intelligence and charm had captured the eyes of the public and the High Leaders alike. Now she was one of them.

"Our first appointment today is with Mr Bernard Mucous, Managing Director of the advertising conglomerate Hooke, Ligne & Syncher. Our discussion with him will concern our long term option with regard to the promotion of the Anti-Entropy Programme.

"Mr Mucous' credentials are impeccable. His company has developed many successful campaigns for the Government in the past. Indeed, our current 'Godliness is next to Cleanliness' campaign to save money on litter collection was conceived by a team working under the direct supervision of Mr Mucous.

"This is the credential run-down their computer sent our computer on the status of the company."

The information appeared for each of them just in front of their eyes. A projected image floating toward their foreheads, then permeating the skull quite painlessly to nestle into their awareness and memory. The technology made reading and learning an effortless process.

Uni-date 23.9.120083.

Agency: *Hooke, Ligne & Syncher*

Date established: 1.1.9010
Current Billings: 1200 Million Billion
Current Assets: 3 Million Billion
Media split: News stories   25%
Impulse beams   17%
Outdoor   4%
Vidi-mags   9%
Radio   6%
Direct encounter 11%
Holographic   28%
Employees: 2,000,498
Offices: 6,000
Method of remuneration: Commission with fee system for new product work.
Minimum project income required: 100 Billion
NOTE: All prospective new clients (government offices excepted) must make a submission of financial security to the agency (details available on request).
Statement of the HL&S advertising principles:
        Effective advertising is the product of mature, creative talent and clear analytical thinking. We put the client's interests first. We're totally committed to strong brand positioning and added value creative branding. Our creative work is built around the Big Idea. We believe in campaigns. Not simply ads.
Contact: Mr Bernard Mucous for a list of our clients and other particulars.

This text was followed by a dreamlike experience recalling many of the great ad campaigns the agency had done in the past century. A swirling montage of shiny products, glistening clothes, colourful food and smiling people left the Leaders dizzied, dazzled and barely able to re-awaken in time to see the panel slide back at the far end of the Hall.

Bernard Mucous was escorted in.

The two male Leaders stepped back into the aurora of light and colour. Leader Prime walked forward to meet him. "Welcome Mr Mucous. I am the Director of Marketing and Advertising for Quadrant Four."

"Thank you for this opportunity, Director. Do you mind if I beam this meeting into our company boardroom?"

"I can only permit voice transmission, Mr Mucous. But do proceed. The security system will automatically block out any visual transmission."

Mucous was a little surprised that the security arrangements for what he presumed to be a routine government advertising brief were so severe, but he didn't show it.

"The Supreme Leader of Resources and Trade, advised by Central Thought, has selected your agency for a very difficult assignment, Mr Mucous."

"I'm delighted to hear that, Director. However I should like to point out before we go any further that Hooke, Ligne & Syncher have a minimum charge for work on new products. Of course, in your case you may be happy to hear that as you are already a client with the agency, you will not have to make a submission to win us as your agency."

"Thank god for that!"Leader Prime exclaimed."Advertising agency people are so conservative; I don't think I could face the prospect of presenting to them ever again!

"As for your fees, we are prepared to meet your requirements. And in this case, Mr. Mucous, we would like to add our own incentive clause."

Mucous raised an eyebrow.

"It may interest you further to know that your campaign will have at best a fifty-fifty chance of running, no matter how brilliant your work is. We will pay up whether we run the campaign or not, but to make things really interesting, we will double the fee if the campaign runs and proves effective."

"Very generous and sporting of you, Director!"

His manner didn't go down at all well with her. She had at first been prepared to like this man, having seen his face in the trade press on numerous occasions -- but she had since decided he was too slick, too confident, too used to getting his way.

"Here's your brief then, as it was set out by Central Thought. At this very moment, the exact detail of the briefing document is being fed into the central computer at Hooke, Ligne & Syncher There is absolutely no risk of it going astray.

"The basis of the brief is this: there is a world in our Quadrant called Earth. No doubt your media department can give you some details of the planet, they presumably must have dealt with audiences there at some time - but I confess I don't know of the place myself.   "Earth has been selected because it is so little known - it can easily be isolated by selective media, making it ideal for a test market. The outside world will have little feeling about what happens to the inhabitants should anything go wrong. Not that anything could."

"Your considerations seem well grounded, Director."

"They do not originate with me. The brief comes from higher up than my department. I am merely following instructions. However, Mr. Mucous, I do happen to be in agreement with the aims of the brief.

"But now for the sting in the tail of this project, Mr. Mucous..."

Leader Prime enjoyed pretending to be the Director of Advertising as she walked in a small circle around the fat piggy form of Mucous, himself still slobbering over the generosity of the incentive clause.

"This planet called Earth has a fifty-fifty chance of being used to precipitate major new developments in the issue of Anti-Entropy Research."

"How could a forgotten planet contribute anything?" Mucous probed.

"Call it a sacrifice if you prefer. But Earth and many planets like her could be wholly consumed as a fuel source."

"Astounding! An ad campaign that could really change people's lives! I can't wait to get my teeth into it!" Mucous grinned through his saliva. "Pardoning the Director's superior knowledge, I happen to know something of the solar system Earth orbits within. All nine of the planets are standard planet types. Lumps of rock. Mantles of gas, molten core, the usual things. None of them is a *radiant* energy source."

"I can't fault you on that. But as the Leaders have warned everyone for the last 500 years or so, the radiant sources are not infinite. Very few new suns are forming. Fewer in fact than are burning out. The Universe, Mr Mucous, is in negative growth. Can you understand that? And that is really what this brief is all about. Getting the message into the public mind. If they won't accept energy cutbacks, they'll have to sacrifice something else."

"Their *planets*?"

"It may be necessary."

"Then there is another route?"

"Not according to the findings of any research done to date. But in the future, who knows? Maybe a way to reverse the death of the stars can be found and implemented."

"So the planets...."

"Will be towed away and dumped as fuel on dying suns to provide a few extra years' warmth and light as and when they are needed."

"Will that really do any good?"Mucous gaped, aghast.

"Survival is everything! Think long and hard about it. You may well need to use language like that in your campaign."

"Destroy our own planets for fuel? Is that what our heroic history of technological progress has achieved?"

"Stop whimpering, Mr. Mucous. You sound like a member of the target market. We'll need a very convincing PR and ad campaign to get the people behind us. You must come up with the solution. The people of Earth must be convinced to give up their planet for the benefit of the common good of all humanity. We will make provision for them on housing commission planets already under construction for them.

"I've already promised you that Hook, Ligne etcetera will be well rewarded. And I'll warn you now that the agency chosen by the political Opposition will be using strong, emotionally-based stuff too. They'll probably try to sell this insignificant Earth place as a tourist attraction or something."

"Any more warnings, Director?"

"I would imagine that the Opposition will employ Scratchi and Scratchi-- and that may cause everyone some problems. Otherwise, I've given you the Big Picture as my superiors see it. The fine detail may yield some other troublesome considerations, but understand this, Mr Mucous. You and your agency are now committed to this Failure to respond to our brief in a thoroughly enthusiastic and professional way could result in the ruination of your business and the silencing of everyone around the boardroom of Hooke, Ligne & Syncher We of course do not make threats, but we do carry out orders. Do I make myself perfectly clear?"

"Wha-!" Mucous was flabbergasted, practically spitting out his frustration.

"Come now, Mr. Mucous, I'm sure you can see that this thing is too hot to toss into the wrong hands. You are the right hands. We have every confidence in you and your team."

Leader Prime extended her hand toward Mucous, secretly hoping he didn't have the bad manners to touch it. But he did.

Bernard Mucous didn't know whether he should be proud or pissed off at having been roped in to this mess. Would the Board kick him out when he got back? Or give him a candy-coated cyanide pill?

"How much time have we got on this thing, Director?"

"One hundred uni-days for your strategic thinking. At that point, we would like to see a proper presentation of your work to that point. Final execution is up to you really. Timing will be crucial. Central Thought will give us the answer based on the temperature and pulse of public attitudes. But don't be surprised if the campaign sits on my shelf for several years waiting for the right moment. So, if there are no further questions..."

"May I see an outline of the brief, please?"

"But of course."

The words of the Outline Brief formed in the space in front of Bernard Mucous, he paused to scan it.

Central Government Advertising
Quadrant Four Advertising & Communication Services
Department of Trade & Industry

Outline Brief No. 324087450837545540-1

To: The Management of Hooke, Ligne &Syncher, Certified Practitioners of Advertising and Propaganda.

Issued by: Central Thought (c)

Date: Classified

Present at Initial Briefing:
*The Director of Advertising &Marketing Communication, Quadrant Four.
*The Chairman of H. L. & S. ID number 584-42-5520-5491

Subject: Planet Earth, System Sol - 1, Star Sector 6, Galaxy E-45.

Marketing Objectives:
1. Stimulate economic growth in Sector, Galaxy and Quadrant.
2. Maintain or increase current levels of income for Government.
3. Maintain order and stability of market environment.
   Control market forces.

Advertising Objectives:
1. Establish awareness of Entropy as a problem to be dealt with urgently.
2. Create interest in the problem of Entropy.
3. Establish desire to see the Government doing something about it.
4. Achieve belief in the prescribed Government action as the best way forward.

Target Market Profile:
Primary: Opinion leaders of all sexes and all ages.

The Profile continued. It was too long to go into the detail of it here and now. He'd go through it back at the office. Mucous shook his head. The shock registered deeply on his face as the gravity of the Brief sank in.
"I wish you luck, Mr Mucous."
"Thank you, Madame. I assure you it will be an honour and a privilege for Hooke, Ligne & Syncher to convince the human multitudes of the Universe that Earth and other planets should be destroyed for the common good." The Director of Advertising glided away toward her two eaves-dropping colleagues who had obviously enjoyed seeing the ad-man being grilled.

Bernard Mucous left the Hall with the hottest brief in history.

Alien Creations

Mason Jackson breathed into his hands and rubbed them briskly together, then flicked on the reception monitor. 'Judy, is it just me or has the heating gone off in here?'

Blonde and blue eyed, with a face that never aged past twenty, Judy took it as another cue to spar with him. 'It's you. You're so old your blood can't creep through your veins anymore."

"Is that any way to talk to the boss you've been secretly in love with for sixty years?"

"Give me a break! You still think you can smooth talk your way into my knickers, don't you? I know what you get up to on those business trips of yours."

"I drink Vasectomy Water, I can do what I like" he snapped back.

"The number of times I've had to lie for you -- hang on, visitor landing. It's Miss America, the journalist from Cosmic Campaign megazine, here for your interview I believe."

"I'll be right out; I've just got a screen full of little aliens to shoot down first... pccheeeuw! pccheeeuw! zap-zap! Shit! They got me!"

"Mr. Jackson is involved in intergalactic negotiations at the moment, but he assures me he will be with you right away, Miss America. Can I get you something to drink, or maybe a refreshing gas ampoule to inhale?"

"Mineral water and a whiff of ozone will buzz me beautifully, thank you."

Judy pressed the buttons on the wall and the order was served. Mason breezed in.

"Hi! Miss America, I presume. I'm Mason Jackson, hope you didn't bring Bert Parks with you."

"Merry America, Cosmic Campaign. Who in the stars is Bert Parks?"

"Sorry, old joke, 20th century actually. Come into my inner sanctum. Here, let me take your drink-- like the ozone do you? Clears the head, doesn't it. "

"Just what I needed. I've got a splitting headache."

"Get rid of it with the new Guillotine triple head razor." Jackson nodded toward a Guillotine advertising poster displayed on the wall behind Judy's desk.

"What"?

"I like the old ozone too."

"What a marvellous office, Mr. Jackson."

"This is the inner space home of Alien Creations."

"What is an alien, exactly?"

"Someone with a refreshingly different point of view. Anyway, Miss America, what can I do for you?"

"Please, just call me Merry."

"Do I have to?"

Trying to establish some degree of business-like sanity, she ignored the jibe. "Do you mind if I record our discussion as an interview for my megazine?"

"After waiting two centuries for Cosmic Campaign to interview me, I'd like very much for you to record."

"May we begin then?"

"Yes. Recording?" She released two tiny cameras from her handbag. They flew to opposite ends of the room. They were being manipulated on remote by Merry's producer back at Cosmic HQ.

"Recording."

"To be perfectly honest with you, Miss America, I have very little regard for advertising and marketing journals."

"I'm sorry to hear that. Perhaps today's experience will change your attitude for the better."

"I doubt it. Nothing against you personally, but I know how agencies and advertisers use Cosmic Campaign as an arena to fight their image wars. And I know how much it costs them to get their point of view in your magazine."

"Can you substantiate such an outrageous claim?"

"In several instances. Judy, will you access the corporate files on Scratchies, HL&S, and Ogle Void?"

"I don't think our viewers are really interested."

"No, perhaps not. It certainly isn't news anyway, is it? But they might be interested in knowing that this interview isn't costing me a cent. Not a smidgin of a single credit. This, folks, believe it or not, is a genuine, unrehearsed interview with Alien Creations-- not a single Take Two will be granted."

"It's obvious why we've never interviewed you before."

"I hope so. Until now, Cosmic has been personality hype from the opening colour bars to close. Full of the same wonderful people doing the same wonderful things and winning the same wonderful awards."

"How many awards have you won, Mr. Jackson?"

"Several. But it was long before your time, Miss America. When an award was worth the award."

Then you admit you're passed it?"

"I'll put that down to your immaturity. There was a time when I needed awards. I had them when I needed them. Now I reap re-wards, rather than a-wards."

Miss America adjusted her knobs.

Jackson continued."Why *am* I being interviewed for your gossip-ridden little rag anyway? And the way it's written. Constipated. Up to the eyeballs in opinionated, rumour mongering shit. It could do with a good vowel movement."

He had to hand it to her, Merry America stayed on course regardless of the flak he threw up--

"Let's just get to the fact, Mr. Jackson."

"I suppose you're used to being slagged off, working for Cosmic as you do."

"Mr. Jackson, can we just get on with it?"

"Merry, my apologies. Tell you what, I promise to punch your tough-shit card for you before you leave, okay?"

Merry burst out laughing. "You really are incorrigible! I was warned I'd never get any sense out of you."

"Thanks for laughing. I was afraid you wouldn't. I'll behave now. For a little while anyway.

What is 'have'? Can I be it? Has anyone ever been 'have'?"

"I really wouldn't know, but perhaps we can get on with the interview and discuss that later.

As you may be aware, Cosmic Campaign megazine recently unearthed a lead from a big industrialist that they were running short on materials and energy for the very first time in their company's history. It could be the first sign of the first recession in several thousand years. If that lead turns out to be true, it's going to affect our own industry deeply. It could mean the first cuts in A & P budgets in anyone's memory."

"*I* remember, but that's another story."

"Alien Creations is a small independent."

"Can't get much smaller than a one man band with a personal assistant, I'm afraid."

"We'll forget for the moment that your manufacturing plants employ over fifty-four thousand people--"

"And sixty-two thousand robotic functionaries."

"That aside, your point of view adds another dimension to our coverage."

"Do you know what Pirates are, Miss America?" Jackson blew on his hands, rubbed them and smiled.

"It's archaic, but I do know what it means. My research assistant said you're a cryonic Resurrectee -- full of ancient idiosyncrasies"

"I hope you're not here to discuss the pros and cons of frozen immortality. Judy! Would you turn the heat up some more, I feel an uncomfortable chill coming on."

"On the contrary, Mr. Jackson, I'm far more interested in your Pirates. And I'm sure our Cosmic viewers will be au fait with the term. You must admit though, that of all the people who survived cryonic Resurrection, none of them had the background in persuasive communications that you brought with you. I mean, you've actually met the founders of some of the biggest ad agencies the universe has ever known-- in person!"

"You mean David, Charlie and Maurice, Leo-- yeah. I met 'em."

"So anyway, that's why your point of view is important to our readers."

"I don't disagree for a moment."

Judy appeared at the door."Thought you could use a little charge of ozone."

She disappeared as quickly as she came. Jackson nestled back in his chair to start the story. Merry America leaned forward staring intently at the creator. Her pupils were huge.

"Merry, the Pirates I'm going to tell you about are essentially the financial controllers of private industry who exert enormous influence on government at every level. Basically there are only about fifty thousand people in the industrialised Universe that matter. They are the ones who set policy for government to follow. Because they have a stranglehold on banking and financial services, they will always control the economy. They provide the money for new projects and new thinking. Nothing new happens without their support. Without their support, new thinking, new ideas, new projects, products and services simply get squashed. It has been this way since the first breath of Expansionism. Since long before man could fly, let alone expand his domain across the stars.""Humankind has always expanded."

"Yes, but have we ever improved?"

"Disease was defeated. Life expectancy has been multiplied."

"It's about as good as it can get, wouldn't you agree?"

"Yes, I would say so."

"I thought you would. And everyone else probably thinks so too. But it's a dead end. A trap.

Where do we go from here? Erehwon. Nowhere."

"First you say you're Anti-Expansionist, Anti-Technology, then you admit there's nothing better."

"There must be something better. I just don't know what it is."

"But you're still prepared to stand up on Cosmic Campaign and point the finger at people who have fed you throughout your career. Who are these elite fifty thousand? I take it you have met them. You know at least a few personally--"

"I have met perhaps three thousand. It is a very tight network. And it functions extremely well. Very profitably."

"Will you tell us their names? At least a few? Who is the network leader?"

"Their names are unimportant, though you would certainly be greatly surprised by a few of the faces. If you want to look them up yourself, the names are all published every year in the Fortune Universal Top Million."

"Do you wish you were in the Top Million?"

"I wish I was in the network of the Fifty Thousand. I'd certainly make my opinions known amongst them."

"Well, this is your chance. Even if you're not in the elite Fifty Thou you have this access channel at least. Perhaps I might remind our viewers at this point that it was Mason Jackson who coined the commercial phrase '*Success in business depends on success in communication*' or at least he wishes he had."

"Thanks for the memories, Merry. Look, I'm not anti-big business. I'm certainly not anti-success. It's human nature to climb the Mountain, strive for money, and thirst for power. But as we all know, money isn't always used for the good. And power over others has certainly been abused badly throughout human history. I would just say this to the Fifty Thousand: You've gone just about as far as you can go now. The Universe has been industrialised, civilised, humanised and used every way you can think of. There are no new planets to find. No new energy or mineral resources to discover and exploit. The new frontier no longer exists on the fringe of explored space. It exists in the Mind. It exists at home. There are no excuses; it is time for you to use your money and power for human good."

"You mean they should give their money away? Something akin to what the ancients called socialism?"

"God no. I don't mean that. I just mean that it is time to conserve, recycle and re-assess. It's a simple Law of Matter and Energy. Like the Gaia principle. The Spaceship Earth concept. Now it's the Universe. It's all we've got. We have to learn to make the most of it. The Universe has no more gifts to give."

Even Merry America was stunned to silence. It took her a few heartbeats to pull her voice together.

"This has been Miss Merry America with Alien Creator, Mason Jackson, for Cosmic Campaign."

Fade to black.

Duplicate Brief

Three human forms stood in animated conversation precisely in the middle of the vast inner sanctum of the supreme heads of state. So extreme was the secrecy surrounding the movements of the inner circle of government that few people who entered this vast hall realised where they really were.

Leader Prime held the floor. She was tall, elegant and moved with the same degree of grace with which she spoke. "The first appointment for today is with Mr Mason Jackson, a Creator, who is known to Us for his pioneering work in the field of fantasy products. His contributions to science and industry in that field have done much to make life almost bearable on the Outer Planets.

"In addition, Jackson's one-man company has produced some outstandingly successful advertising campaigns, none of which has ever been for the Government. I need not bore you with the background to our purpose in seeing him as you are well aware of our recent encounter with Mr. Mucous."

"Here then is the credential survey of Jackson's company, Alien Creations Unlimited."

The familiar printout style of C.T. appeared in front of their eyes, floated towards the forehead as they focused onto it, and finally sank through the skull and nestled into the memory.

Uni-date 26.9.12083

Agency:	*Alien Creations Unlimited.*	
Established:	*11921*	
Billings:	*18 Billion above and below the line.*	
Media Split:	*Impulse beams*	*15%*
	Outdoor	*2%*
	Radio	*31%*

Video magazines 33%
Holographics   11%
Direct Encounters

Employees: 2*
Offices: 1
*Mason Jackson, Founder. (C.R.)
Other activities: Alien Fantasy Industries
(Games, Dolls and Experiences)
        Sales: Undisclosed millions of billions
                Employees   54,811
                Factories: 2
                Offices: 1
Method of Remuneration:
        Totally negotiable fee or commission.

Statement of advertising principles

"Most advertising is a waste of people's time.
My professional goal is to produce communication that
helps people make an intelligent purchase decision.
When they experience my communication, they will be
glad for the interruption.
Every product began with an idea. Every advertisement
must capture the original enthusiasm of that product idea
and present it in such a way that people will give a
calculated human response, i.e. they will be persuaded to
Know, Think, Feel, and Believe whatever you want them
to about the Product
Any asshole with half a brain can give you half an idea
and half the answer. Because we look at the whole
problem with our whole brain, we give you the whole
solution. And therefore we are not assholes.
To succeed in business you have to succeed in
communication."

At the end of the info-sheet, the Leaders were treated to a moment of Union with a Wuzy Doll, Jackson's primary contribution to the society of the 121st Century Universe. As always, each experience was completely private and personal. And unlike any other individual's Wuzy encounter.

Jackson had made himself unbelievably wealthy by mass marketing Wuzy. Indeed, the advertising industry often suspected his campaigns of using his patented dream-technology to win sales. But as long as he protected his patent, they had no idea if he used it or not.

"I note with interest that Mr. Jackson has C.R. status." Rios raised the point. And that he has not been under surveillance for quite some time.

"Quite. It *is* unusual for a Cryonic Resurrectee to succeed as he has done, but obviously his background in advertising and marketing was relevant preparation for the commercial way of life prevalent in our era."

"I suggest that this is precisely why C.T. has selected him to tender."

Mason Jackson checked in to the reception desk of the Universal Advertising Centre in a pyramid shaped building in the shadow of the windowless black monolith everyone knew was Leadership Hall.

"Class 10 clearances to see the Marketing and Advertising Director of Quadrant Four", Jackson said proudly to the young man. It wasn't every day you got to see the Government Ad Director of an entire quadrant. The world of advertising and, for that matter, everything else in the Universe, had long ago been divided into four equal sections of the Universal sphere. In theory, each quadrant extended out into space with equal infinity.

Each Quadrant was governed as a Region answerable to the Universal Leaders and Central Thought.

"Proceed to the transporter room. Her secretary will meet you there."

Jackson knew the Marketing Director was an attractive female, he had seen her in vidi-mags. But her name was not known to him, or to anyone else outside her department. Her exact identity was a state secret.

49

Anonymity was a life preserver in the dog-eat-dog world of government and advertising. So many executives had tried to make a name for themselves in this portfolio - and had been found fried by a laser gun - that the idea of dispensing with names altogether had seemed a sensible solution.

The Director's secretary escorted Jackson to the entrance of what appeared to be a vast empty Hall. It felt cold. And dry.

"A hot drink perhaps?" Jackson asked somewhat shyly.

"I don't think you'll be here long enough to drink it," the secretary smiled as she left him on his own.

It was an energy room, the scale of which Jackson had not seen before. A slender female form in an elegant crimson gown stood perhaps 90 metres away in the middle of the place. She wore a black helmet with a glistening visor that reflected a maelstrom of fantastic colours given off by the swirling energy plasma that enclosed the space. It was as if the walls were alive.

Jackson was disappointed when he saw the visor. He had hoped to meet the nameless lady face to face.

"Welcome, Mr Jackson." Her voice was mysteriously close. More like she were only 2 metres away instead of ninety.

He walked swiftly towards her. "Thank you, Director. Do you mind if I record our conversation?"

She liked what she saw and heard. Her strong sixth sense told her he was intelligent, interesting, reliable and sensitive. Any 20th Century man would have delighted at her appraisal. "I expect you to do so. However, I request that it must be an audio recording only. No micro-screens are allowed."

"As you wish. How may I help the Director?" Jackson, in spite of his outstanding commercial success felt humble if not a little awkward talking to a silver bubble. He felt the need to be formal, but an old earthly desire to be casual too. He knew he'd have to break the ice if he was ever going to relax.

A shiver shot across his shoulders tingling the hair on the back of his neck as she walked towards him. The distance closed rapidly. The fascinating amplification of their voices eliminated the need to stand close, but it was only natural after all, to want to have conversation at close quarters.

"The Supreme Leader of Resources and Trade, advised by Central Thought, has selected you for a very difficult brief, Jackson."

"Why don't you just call me Mason? It's less formal, and I would feel a lot more comfortable if you did."

Madame Prime grinned behind her mirrored visor, yes, she liked this Mason Jackson. His courtesy and sincerity were thinking that Jackson an extreme rarity in the advertising game. Her first impressions were honed to ambassadorial sharpness. The hemispheres of her brain were highly adept at relating observations to give an accurate holistic assessment of people, especially men.

"I would be pleased to call you Mason."

"Before we begin, Director, I wish to point out..."

"I know, your fees - always money before business these days."

"All of us must maximise our time."

"Not rich enough yet, Mr. Jackson?"

"It isn't the money, I don't need any more of it, and please call me Mason. Time not money is the most precious commodity there is."

"But you have hundreds of years ahead of you."

"Perhaps, but I have many fantasies yet to experience and many more yet to create. You can buy me away from my pleasures if you're willing to pay the price, as anyone can."

"Everyone has his price."

"I have, may I say, a *negotiable* virtue."

"Then you call yourself an artist?"

51

"A dreamer."

"No matter. You have been chosen and you will be rewarded as you require."

They stood face to visor; Jackson was still a bit unnerved by the fact that her voice sounded exactly the same level as it did when she was ninety metres away.

"I like the trick you do with your voice. An extraordinary act of ventriloquism.'

"I like your curiosity. No doubt you're going to need it. The energy fields here have something to do with the voice throw. I'll have Central Thought send you the rundown on it later if you wish."

Jackson's face reflected in the curving surface of her visor. He looked at himself distorted and ugly in the fish-eye effect. Days later when she looked back on it, Catherine Prime didn't fully understand why she did it, but suddenly the Director slid her visor back.

"There. Is that better?"

Jackson was jolted by the revelation of her face. In a moment it was all things to him-- serene, intelligent, wise, sparkling, and beautiful beyond his usual dreams. He didn't quite know what to say next.

After Jackson had fumbled long enough, she said, "Call me Catherine." Hidden in the swirling energy field, Jarrod and Rios couldn't believe what was happening. Leader Madame Catherine Prime was revealing herself to this total stranger, a man she had never met before. Prime was from a long family line of the most highly respected ambassadors. But her sixth sense was highly evolved, much more than theirs; she should be trusted in her judgements of others. They would not interfere. And yet, this man was a Creator, and one from the 20th Century. It was all most out of the ordinary.

Jackson stumbled a step further as his lips found her name. "Catherine. And a very beautiful name it is too." Even though he was sure it wasn't her real name, he appreciated the implication of her act. He was thinking at a million miles an hour. Why had she shown her face if she had needed to remain anonymous? It was then that Jackson had a deeper intuition -- a knowledge without substance that she was not merely the Advertising Director he had seen in the vids. So who was she? What was she? What was this brief about? What were the higher stakes?

Maybe the Advertising Director he had seen in the vids had been eliminated by a jealous colleague. Could this woman, 'Catherine, have done it? Was she impersonating the real Director? Jackson was repelled by the thought.

Even though he was ruthless in maintaining his own standards of creativity. Cutting out the deadwood wherever he saw it. Polishing and improving his ideas and executions, it just wasn't in him to be ruthless to people and other living things.

He found himself staring into her dark brown eyes.

"Your fee will be doubled if you succeed."

"I haven't said I'd take on the job yet, Director."

"I'm afraid it's far too late to turn back now. Central Thought has not merely selected you, it has committed you."

"Now wait a minute! I don't even know what this job is! I may very well have something a helluva lot better to do! What the hell kind of Government are you people running here anyway?"

"I'll thank you to control yourself, Mr. Jackson"

He'd blown it. Catherine spun and walked away from him. She hoped the other Leaders waiting in the plasma fields would not choose this moment to nose in.

She turned and glared back at Jackson, snapping her visor down defiantly.

"Okay, let's get on with it." Jackson was nobody's fool. He was a Creator. They wanted him here. There must be something about the brief that let the project seek him out. Besides, if he still didn't like it, he could sit on the job for months, maybe even years. There was no hurry. If they didn't like it, they could rewrite the brief and give it to someone else. There was always a way out of things he didn't want to do.

"Your task, Mr Jackson, is to convince the public that the planet Earth should be used as a source of fuel. That is, pushed into a designated sun to assist that sun in burning longer."

"Right. Earth? Is this some kind of joke? I don't find this at all amusing if it is! People live on Earth, do you know that? I lived on Earth, for Christ's sake! Did you know that? Yes. Of course you did- do! That's why you selected me isn't it. Geesh! Why Earth for chrissake?"

"It's all in the comprehensive brief which C.T. is feeding into your office computer at this moment. C.T. has selected Earth for its own reasons. But this particular planet, 414-D/3, is merely the first in a long term plan to optimise the return on useless planets.

"Useless planets? Mercury maybe, Pluto perhaps, Fulham, or Fison, but Earth? People *live* there. Or at least I think they do."

"You are overly sentimental."

"Has the Government lost its humanity?"

"Are you accusing?"

"No, er, I mean yes. I had no idea things were so desperate that we had to start using planets as firewood to keep the suns going and industry turning over! The goddam Pirates have sacked the Universe, and now they want to go back and cannibalise their own efforts, it's madness--this can't be happening and you want me to be a party to it?"

"Mr. Jackson, we are not about to incinerate Earth yet. But the time is coming closer than anyone realises. Central Thought has only recently reported that the Universe is now in a state of negative growth. It may be tens of thousands of years before we have to evacuate inhabited planets. Earth and other planets may be spared. The final recommendations have not been given. But just think of a planet simply as a platform for some designated activity. We build stations every week that are larger than this Earth planet of yours. And who are these alleged Pirates to whom you referred."

"Nothing. A theory of mine, that's all. I meant nothing by it"

"Quite right. Why not just think of it as a responsible first step? C.T. does. The reasons, the feelings - every facet of coming to grips with the problem could not be in better hands, Mr. Jackson. You are a Creator and a known commercial expansionist. The combination is ideally suited for your task."

Jackson became in his own thoughts. His mind searched his memory banks for a postcard-- a view of this planet-- Earth. He hung in space looking down on a blue, green and brown planet swirled with white clouds. The postcard was stowed in the bottom of an old titanium trunk he kept in a vaulted cellar at his vacation home on Omicron.

"Think into the future, Mason. And think back to your fantasy research on the Outer Planets." Catherine was playing another tune on his emotions. "We would like to see you back here in a hundred uni-days with your preliminary strategy. Executions can come later."

"No pressure then. Right, OK. Well you're lucky you're talking to me. The ability to see into the future is uncommonly rare, Madame."

The meeting was over. Leader Prime disappeared into the aurora of colours. Jackson retreated towards the door, his mind still orbiting Earth. Then in the flash of a space gate entry, his mind was orbiting Poltan, a dismal mining planet. He remembered the miserable life of the miners. Short dim days, long dark nights. A planet that would have been beautiful with a bit more heat and light. But their sun was too far away. And Jackson knew the allusion Catherine was making.

As sun after sun faded, even Inner Planets would experience this horrible bleak chill. The dark days would

55

yield nought but a downward spiral of hope and purpose. Men would be driven to despair, even to suicide. But most would do anything to have a second chance.

Foul Airs

A light rang in the corner of his space as Jackson sat down at his desk mumbling incredulously at what the Government was up to. It shimmered for a moment then coalesced as the holo-vision call began. Jackson shivered slightly as he recognized Noddy Hemsley. Like himself, Hemsley had a tiny ad agency with some difficult accounts.

"Mason? Good man, good man! Look, I got a small problem with Willysports."

Hemsley laughed as he coughed and lit up a cigarette. He already had one in the process of burning the edge of the desk behind him.

"They want to project a fashion image of their entire retail operation."

"Shouldn't be hard provided they can back it up with a fashionable experience in-store for shoppers -- you know, give customers confidence that their friends will think they're someone to be reckoned with... the usual creative stance.

"By the way, have you seen the New Willysports?" Noddy burbled.

"No, I don't think I have. Where is it?"

"Same place. But they've redone it inside."

"I was there the other day. Didn't look anything different. Nothing special anyway."

"No, they just did it last night."

"Suppose they did it themselves to save money."

"As a matter of fact they did."

"Is the building still standing?"

"Building hell, that place is a planet."

"Exactly, I can imagine how shoddy it turned out by doing it overnight."

"It's not the greatest but it ain't bad. Besides they want their new fashion image to be done overnight too!"

"Do I hear you right? A store as big as a small planet full of sports gear. They've got an absolutely unique position as the only sports outfit in creation that can offer the concept of a 'Sportsworld' and they decide to change it overnight? Unbelievable. Sounds like Airs again."
"Well, he managed it."
"Jeezo, Noddy, that doesn't mean *I* gotta do it too!"
"But, Mason, I'll lose the account if I don't deliver. Ben Airs will go bananas."
"But he's only the consultant."
"Not anymore, Ben Airs now *runs* Willysports, he owns it lock, stock and gun barrel. Over lunch at the Cafe Royale,
Airs pulled the strings that absorbed the store into Strident Enterprises, along with the Observer Star Video Network. He's more than an enemy consultant; he's a mega-manipulator."
"Bloody hell."
"Ben is a brilliant business man, actually."
"He told you that, himself didn't he? Thought so. Look, Noddy, we're old buddies, and once upon a time I owed you. But not anymore. I've just been asked to save the planet Earth from incineration and my head is blitzed."
"Earth? Where the hell is that? Sounds like they need somebody to design them a new image. You got their number?"
"Look, Noddy, Willysports is already the biggest goddam sport store in the whole goddam universe -- so what's the point? How can I improve the situation for them?"
"Ben's asking for it."
"Ah, yes, so Ben can get bigger and wealthier and lord it over you even more.."
"Do it for me. Please?"
"Why are you doing it, Noddy?"

"I've got bills to pay."

"I'll lend you the money. No, I'll *give* you the money. I'd rather do that than watch you slide into thin Airs."

"Willysports is actually vital to the economy, I'm sure you can see that..."

"Midgalaxy Bank, maybe. Universal Cargo, perhaps. Geesh, what are you doing? Tears! Noddy? Don't cry! I can't handle crying. Stream the data into my banks and I'll make the presentation with you tomorrow morning. Just stop crying for chrissake."

"0900." Noddy sobbed with thanks.

"Mark."

"You and I and Dixon."

"The Media Merlin?"

"I thought you'd ask him for me."

"Of course. Glad to do your job for you, Noddy -- sorry. Don't cry, for Chrissakes!"

"Remember, Mason. It's fashion, fashion, fashion at the worlds of sport!"

"Over and out, Noddy. But be warned, it's my show this time, my show.

"And of course they'll love you too."

"I don't care about that, Mason. I just want to create some great ads and keep the business. But I'll do you a favour and ring Dixon for you."

"Sure, thanks, Noddy."

Noddy disappeared.

"What a goddam lousy business this can be."

The data had been filling the banks for about twenty minutes. Jackson stepped out of the time tube at the Hub of the Universe and walked to the entrance of Willysports and into an unbelievable retail world that descended several hundred floors. There was nothing like it anywhere else. Though the combined presence of the millions of stores in some of the larger competitor chains was larger, this was still a unique one-off experience.

"Let's see how fashionable this place is... for, say, tiddly-winks."

A hostess handed him a welcome card. She looked suitably fashionable, save for her dreary uniform. He spoke into his card. "Tiddly-winks please."

And the card replied, "Come forward to the shafts and jump to the 2002nd floor. A hostess will greet you for a game."

He leapt into the white light of the shafts. There was the familiar first moment fright of freefall... but in what seemed only a few heart-stopping moments, his feet touched lightly onto something solid. He looked down and saw the floor marked 2002. A coloured light blinked a welcome through the white-out. As he started toward it, a young man in a Willysports uniform approached.

"Tiddlywinks, sir?"

Jackson nodded and followed the young man, noting his uniform was festooned with medals and badges devoted to various tiddly-wink championships. Suddenly they entered into a dazzling tiddly-wink casino displaying every conceivable tiddly and wink apparatus.

"Not much call for tiddlywinks these days I'm afraid, sir."

"Yes I rather thought you could do better than this." Jackson teased.

"We just keep this small stock for the chairman and his club friends," the young man gestured toward the central arena "care for a game?"

"I, uh, don't actually play myself," Jackson fumbled."Just looking really. In fact I don't know the difference between the tiddlies and the winks."

"Don't really know myself, actually," the young man whispered in confidence.

Jackson had similar experiences throughout the store. A Willysports ski instructor showed him over ten thousand styles of skis, projected him onto a holographic Megahorn mountain, but finally confessed she'd never actually been skiing in her life.

"I've learned all about it from tapes, though."

Jackson walked into an empty billiard hall the size of a major starbase landing apron. When he picked up a cue stick to make a practice break on a beautiful pure crystal table, an alarm went off! The stick turned red hot in his hand as he explained he didn't know he had done anything wrong.

"You should have waited for one of our billiard champions to appear," the securi-bot chided.

Willysports was intimidating. As a shopping experience it hardly gave you permission to come back for more. As a sports facility, it had tremendous potential. As a retail store, a lot needed to be done. And the brief was to make the place fashionable! Jackson felt it needed not merely a Big Idea, but a Concept. Indeed, nothing short of an immaculate conception would save the day.

When Jackson reached the Chairman's Suite on the top level of Willysports at 8:45 the next morning, fifteen minutes early just in case what happened next would happen. Noddy Hemsley was already there pacing the corridor, chuffing fags and flicking ash on the carpet.

"Great man, great man! Change of plans for Ben. Come on, we're meeting Airs downstairs. Show me the stuff on the way down."

"Sure, it's in here." Jackson wondered where Dixon was. There wasn't going to be any chance to see it. They were just going to make the presentation 'blind'.

"Dixon couldn't make it, so I took those media suggestions Ben Airs made and cabled them into your computer. It should have made the bookings by now."

The lift shafts spilled them out onto the transport level. A big shiny black spheroid sub-light cruiser hovered a few feet away. The door slid noiselessly open and sucked them inside. Ben Airs liked to show how important he was. He dressed for power. And he performed for his clients and suppliers with an air of paramount urgency -- managing by crisis over every trivial detail. He pretended he was so busy he couldn't waste a single minute, not even for greetings or good-byes. He never said hello, not even on the vidi-phone. Every conscious moment was utilised in making deals, analysis and passing judgement on others. People came to Ben Airs. He went to see no one except corporation Chairmen whom he considered as equals.

Grey, grossly overweight and bespectacled, Ben Airs sat on his self importance, his buttocks snuggled into a rhinoplaz sofa with a few media printouts in his hands. The walls were covered with viewing screens plugged into various market and share data listings that changed constantly. The cruiser lurched into a high speed shift.

"Be brief. I have business in Epsilon Pie in 15 minutes. I trust you can find your own way back from there."

"What an outright self-important prick," Jackson thought. "I'm not paying for the goddam cruise-cab to get back to my own craft where the meeting was supposed to have been in the first place!"

Meanwhile, Noddy was grovelling in good form, "No trouble at all, Ben, not to worry."

"Let's see the stuff."

"Mason has the stuff."

"Yes, I have the 'stuff', but I also have a presentation that will take somewhat longer than fifteen minutes."

"Let's just see the stuff and forget the presentation."

"The presentation is integral to the stuff."

"You now have only twelve minutes."

"Is the stuff vital to you?"

"The stuff is essential to Willysport. I've promised my staff we will have the final answer on marketing and advertising today. It's on air tonight. Why are you wasting my time?"

Noddy lit a second fag and burned his fingers as he put it to his mouth next to the first one.

"Noddy, why is this man of yours wasting my precious time!"

"Mr. Airs, you are wasting *all* our time. If you want to see the stuff, you'll have to make more time. You now have scarcely ten minutes to see and appreciate the solution that will keep Willysports happy and commercially successful for the next hundred years." Jackson asserted himself as far he normally was ever prepared to go. But Airs was more difficult than normal.

Blood vessels stood out in relief on Airs' face as he folded his arms in defiance.

Jackson continued staring back at Ben, "After seeing the 'new store' which looks remarkably like the old store, and having experienced the charm and inside knowledge of its staff, and now having been confronted with your countdown to crisis attitude, I am convinced that neither you nor your staff are capable of judging the merit of the work I have prepared on your behalf."

Noddy Hemsley collapsed under the pain of heart attack. A medi-bot, obviously employed by Airs for moments like these, whizzed to his aid, and slid him into a life support unit under the coffee table.

"You presumptuous jackass!" Airs bellowed.

"Temper temper, children. Name calling Mr. Airs? Is it really necessary to degrade yourself so? Now, to the stuff. Only an expert in retail marketing could adequately judge my work..."

"I *am* an expert you dick-head!"

"Oh, really?" Jackson jabbed again. "Of course you could let the shopping public decide for themselves. We've booked airtime in your name for the slots you requested tonight."

"Look, this is your last chance, butt-wipe! Show me the stuff and I'll know immediately whether it's any good or not!"

"Sorry, I don't work that way, Mr. Airs. And I do not work to your somewhat questionable standards, I work to mine."

The sub-light cruiser decelerated. One of the view-screens displayed the approach to Epsilon Pie. Ben Airs turned away from Mason Jackson and punched a button.

"Sheila, get me the Chairman of Willysports on the screen a.s.a.p. I want him to see this jackass I've got with me."

"Sorry, Mr. Airs, the Chairman is indisposed on the 2002nd floor until after lunch. Would you like to leave a message?"

"I'll get back to him later." Then turning to Jackson, "The door is open, if you have any sense you'll leave, and take Hemsley's body with you."

Jackson stood on the landing apron. He beamed a cab call into the ether and waited. The body in the cocoon next to him stirred. Noddy was waking up.

"How'd it go? Did he love the stuff? I knew he would. You really know how to get through to that guy!"

"I don't know how to tell you this, Noddy..."

The cab was entering deep space. Jackson looked at his watch. The cancellation deadline for tonight's commercial broadcasts ticked into history. "Could you pull over at the next rubbish disintegrator, driver? I have an important contribution to make to the field of advertising."

Pirates

'Mail coming up, Mr. Mucous, on band eleven.'
'Thanks, Hilary"

Bernard Mucous swivelled to face the executive mail bag, a 52-inch screen that scanned his correspondence for anything important, and sniffed out junk that might waste his time, but storing it for those afternoons when the boss had had too much lunch and going over correspondence was a good excuse to close the door and fall asleep. If any of the junk mail managed to wake him up, he reckoned it was worth viewing.

"Marketing Image, save that for later, Broadcast Media, scan-scan-scan.

Ah, Cosmic Campaign, this is practically our house magazine let's have a lookie inside--"

The cover of Cosmic Magazine swirled into an animated computer graphic sequence. The titling, in gold Optima, strobed in centre frame before a neon grid graphic squeeze-zoomed top and bottom, sandwiching the words in the middle. Page wipes flicked through item after item. New campaigns, new mergers, new buy-outs, but familiar names on every page.

"Alien Creations? That's a new one on me."

Mucous moved his control mouse to pounce the cursor on the full page article and hold it there while he read the titles and waited for this section of the magazine to flow into live action footage.

'Alien exposes pirates', the female voice said excitedly.

'Hi, I'm Merry America, following yesterday's controversial statements from Mason Jackson, owner of tiny but prosperous Alien Creations Unlimited, we've followed up with another exclusive interview. Jackson is a fascinating man. His background includes cryonic resurrection from 20th century Earth-- where's that? You might say-- and the invention of the Wuzy Doll.

A Creator by anyone's standards, Jackson tells a tale of piracy that has spanned the galaxies and now the Universe itself.

"Who are these Pirates, Mr. Jackson?"

Mucous watched with some interest at the man seated across from the interviewer. He vaguely recognised him, but he was well aware of his company, and he had half a dozen Wuzy Dolls himself scattered in various rooms at home.

"Three thousand of their names are known to me, I couldn't possibly list them for you now. But as I said yesterday, a glance at the Fortune Top One million will give you a solid idea of the people I am talking about."

"So, by 'pirates', you don't actually mean bandits who go out and stop people in cold space and rob them?"

"No, of course not. Those are petty thieves and bandits. And the impact they have on society and civilisation is insignificant. I'm talking about people who have had a devastating impact on the whole of our lives. The very core of the way we live-- the way we work, the way we play, even the reasons we think we have to do those things has been guided for profit by the great pirates of civilisation."

"I'm sure our viewers are familiar with the term pirates, even though it is archaic..."

"Manipulators then. Because that is what they are. The most powerful manipulators in human history. And they can be found at every point in our history. As person-kind has expanded through the universe, so too has the relative strength of the manipulators. To be frank, I'm sorry I ever used the term pirates. It's far too petty and carries too many emotive associations. The people I am referring to are people that really matter. Pirates don't matter; they're just a nuisance factor, especially when they cause insurance policies to go up."

"Can you give us some examples of the power and influence of these fifty thousand manipulators?"

"In the history of my own planet, Earth, it was long thought that presidents, prime ministers and emperors were the great rulers. In more primitive societies, that may well have been the case. A powerful man became king. And with kingship came immense wealth. But as land-owners were surpassed by the merchant class, people did not need wealth to become royal. Nor did they need to become public figures to become powerful. Many people had much more wealth than the people in government. It was this class that used their great influence -- the influence of their money-- to obtain the results they wanted, regardless of who was recognised as the leader of the people."

"Fascinating. Give us some names."

"Venetian families. Machiavelli, Howard Hughes, J. Paul Getty, the Kennedy family -- all in 20th Century Earth history of course..."

"I don't think any of our viewers would know any of those names."

"Then I'll give you some names they will know."

"Please do!"

"Vermeer, Shelton, Suisse, Zamba, Harlesden, Gnuma, Oxonic, even Scratchie could go on a list like that."

"How do you know these names?"

"I do business with them, of course..."

"That doesn't speak very highly of you, then...have you any proof of their 'manipulations'?"

"These people are not what you would call squeaky clean. I dare say I'm not very clean myself-- is anybody clean out there?" Jackson cupped his hands to his mouth and shouted toward the camera.

"But times have got to change. This universe of ours is almost full. Infinite expansion has kept the holders of all the power and money striving at the cutting edge of exploration, discovery and exploitation for a hundred and twenty thousand years plus. Now those days are numbered. Now they have to find new goals. Perhaps now they'll turn on each other. It's happened before when the known limits of the world were reached. It was called war, and it means Chaos. It could well be that we are now headed for Universal chaos."

"Surely that's a ridiculous conjecture!"

"Just remember, folks, you heard it first from Alien Creations. Look, my life has spanned a hundred and one centuries. My travels have taken me to every type of galaxy and human society. I have done business with the Pirates. They import my Wuzy Dolls and they pay a royalty on every one they sell. Getting them to pay me has been satisfaction enough until now."

"Why have you changed your mind?"

"Until now, I have liked the way I live. I think we all do. There is no unemployment. We all make more money every year. We all can afford to have the latest widgets, gidgets and gadgets. Until now."

"Yes?"

"We can't afford it anymore. None of this is affordable. This chair. This stupid magazine we're doing. The screen itself. The cans of head-clearing ozone. None of it! It's all a waste of time. We've reached the end of the path and we don't know where to go. I'm merely suggesting one scenario. But I hope the Fifty Thousand can get their act together and sort something out; otherwise it will be a scramble between them. And you and I and trillions of others will be caught in the crossfire."

"Please, be more specific, Mr. Jackson. I'm sure our audience will find your answer very entertaining."

"Let's take the simplest possible example. Getting from A to B. Planned obsolescence in vehicles is too obvious. Let's be more subtle-- to see if we can wake you up a little. Animals and men once pulled carts across the land in the early history of my planet. Steam was harnessed as a source of power. Then the Pirates got onto it and sold it to civilisation at a comfortable price and a comfortable profit.

Next, motor cars used liquid fossil fuels to drive engines that propelled vehicles. The Pirates who owned the land that held the fossil fuels made a killing and became even more powerful.

But there was not very much of this fuel on my planet. The time came when it ran out. But long before it did, the Pirates developed free hydrogen power and solar power and nuclear power to replace the fossil fuels. But did they let civilisation have it? No! Not until they got top money for every last drop of the stuff. And now my planet hasn't a single drop of fossil fuel."

"But isn't that just progress?"

"You see how we have been manipulated to think so. Why did we even use that precious black gooey liquid as fuel in the first place? Why did we have to use it? Because we were manipulated. Because people with more money than you or I have always paid people like you and I to do things for them so we can buy things we can actually do without."

"Forgive me, Mr. Jackson, but you sound like a repentant ad-man who's simply guilty of having done his best and is looking for someone to blame for his own world going wrong."

"Ahh. My world. And yours. And everybody else's.

"Selling things we don't need? So what would you do, close every ad agency in the universe?"

"No, I'd get them working 24 hours a day to wake people up before it's too late! We have to stop consuming! We have to reverse the upward spiral of spending. Listen, listen to me everybody-- it's not bloody money we're spending, it's our planets, our stars, our galaxies, and our whole goddam universe! We ran out of oil on Earth. And sure as hell, we're going to run out of stars someday too-- solar power isn't free. We're spending the suns faster than they are being naturally recreated. And the viewers of this program are responsible."

The camera angle panned away from an angry, grimacing Mason Jackson to a sweetly smiling Merry America.

"This incredible message of doom and gloom has been brought to you by Cosmic interviews.

Merry America exclusively for Cosmic Campaign Megazine. If you would like to comment on Mr. Jackson's views, contact us now on the following code.

A barcode display appeared centre-frame.

Mucous was as still as a stunned mullet. Then he erupted with rage. "Goddam sonovabitch, who the hell does he think he is? That asshole is as good as dead. I wonder what the viewer-ship figures are like on that story.

"Computer, give me viewer-ship figures on that goddam Alien story, and then have every single byte of it erased from the company copies of Cosmic Campaign, and that means, now!"

"Mr. Mucous, ' the computer voice sang, ' latest figures show one hundred thousand four hundred and thirty-seven viewings up to the last thirty seconds."

"Shit, a thing like that could catch on. That Alien sonovabitch is quite a manipulator himself."

Meanwhile, Merry America thanked Mason Jackson for another excellent interview.

"I won't be around tomorrow, Merry, so no more interviews for awhile."

"Can't handle the fan-mail, eh?"

"It was rather more aggressive than I expected. And after today's tete-a-tete, I think I'll dive for some cover."

"Don't blame you. By the way, do you have any evidence that we're running out of suns? I mean, things could get pretty dark around here if the suns went out."

"Yes, I have it on very good authority."

"Can I quote you on that?"

"Well, I don't really think I should say anything more on the subject."

"I thought you believed in the things you said today."
"Of course I do."
"Then can I quote you?"
"Yeah, okay. I guess so. But I might as well make sure you got the right words, so take this down..."

HL & S

The scene is the pan-cosmic boardroom of Hooke, Ligne and Syncher where the agency heavies are having a top level brainstorm. Lightning strikes first in the form of Bernie Mucous, who kicks the ball into the cerebral arena. Very heavy stuff, this:

"Well, what are we gonna do with this crazy brief from the goddam government?"

The Creative Director smiles out of a vat of white wine, "Give it to the juniors as a copy-test." Chuckles around the room.

The Head of Account Service sees his opening, his first thrust of justification for his presence in this rare meeting of the agency's mega-brains trust.

"Research is the key. I propose that we submit a 2000 page memo explaining that the project failed in consumer testing. Make it an on-going situation."

"Yeah", the Creative Director chimes in again. "We could do it on a computariter, why bother a human brain for this shit?"

Nods of approval all round the room, but Mucous didn't buy it. He moved for control, blowing a thunderhead of smoke above his head with a tobacco-free stogie. Then whooshed a second cloud of the smelly smoke down the length of the table. It got their attention.

"Look, you wankers, this thing is serious. With a capital 'S' for superbucks. The kind of big money we pay you."

"You think so, Bernie? Is there a big fat juicy budget for this?

"I know there is, asshole!"

"Maybe one of our subsidiaries could have a crack at it. I've got a golf tournament coming up and I need to practice my putting."

"No, damn it. Put yourself in the goddam hole for a change. The bottom line is it's gotta stay in here with us.

I will not see our relationship with the Government Advertising and Marketing Department jeopardised. So let's get cracking. Give it our best shot. Whaddya say, Marve?" Bernie fired a searing look of sincerity right between the eyes of the Creative Director, Marvin Fuchwitt.

"Right, Bernie. Let's let 'em have our best shot-- a salvo of the good old V.I.P.S. - Visibility! Identification! Promise and Simplicity! Let's go for the Big Idea!"

This seemed to be the right cue for Wally, the Head of Account Service, to leap back in, "Yeah, we dash out a dozen concepts, zap 'em into half a dozen consumer groups, buy 'em a ticket on an omnibus, cross the 'I's and dot the 'T's, make a recommendation and we're off the hook!"

"Not so fast", Bernie replied, but for once he was ignored.

"It could stay in research for three or four years, you know."

But that sort of attitude made Bernie burn. He really wanted to win this one. "The brief calls for top line ideas in less than a hundred uni-days from now!"

"Okay, so we tailor the research to give us a clear winner on the first round."

"Do we do things like that?" The Finance Director gaped with shock.

"Where have you been, Jerry? This is a persuasive communications company. The best. And if that's what it takes to persuade the client he's on a winner with us, of course we'll do it. Besides with only a hundred days for the job, we don't have time to fart around with more than one round of research."

"The prescription for tunnel-vision is a redundancy notice, isn't it Bernard?"

"The name of the game is profit at the client's expense, not ours." Wally seemed to side completely with Bernie now.

"Will you guys stop thinking about pussy and get your head around this brief! We're not leaving this goddam room 'til we get a bead on this thing!" Bernie snarled, then roared out of his seat and started pacing at one end of the table, scowling up and down at his troops like a drill sergeant.

"Now, have I got your attention? Good. Look and learn. This is Earth", he said, producing a small white ball from his pocket. He tossed it into the air toward the middle of the table. It hung there as he activated a projector inside it. An energy field encircled the ball about 10 centimetres from its surface, effectively forming a spherical back projection screen orbiting the small white ball. When the pictures of Earth's topography came up, they provided the group with a three-dimensional look at a model of the planet about a metre in diameter.

"From where you're seated, this is what the planet would look like if you were in a shuttle craft orbiting about a thousand miles above it. Of course, if you go stand by the door, you'd see Earth pretty much as it looks from its single moon.

"Milton, you're the number cruncher from Media. Fill us in on the place." Bernie sat down, his eyes wandered suspiciously over his minions.

"Not much to tell, really. Third planet from its sun, etcetera and so forth, apparently one of the longest inhabited planets in the Quadrant. It is in fact a natural planet; it doesn't even have an artificial shell around it, although its permanent climate control system is the latest installation of its type.

For some reason there is an enormous amount of traffic between Earth and its moon every day - an exceptionally high proportion of the local population. That's how we buy our media in this market. If there's one place we're guaranteed an audience, it's aboard the shuttle buses between the moon and the mother planet.

74

Impulse beams sell a lot of confectionery on those flights for our clients. Vidi-mags are successful vehicles for selling hard goods. And some of our outdoor poster sites on the moon can be viewed from 1000 kilometres out. Some of the largest in the Quadrant."

"What's the surface of the planet like, Milt?"

"As you can see on the projection, quite varied. Two thirds ocean, as you can see - polar ice caps, fairly even distribution of human exploitation - construction and development common even in the dense jungles and polar regions. The easy-breathe atmosphere recovered from severe pollution a long time back. "

"Summary?"

"My own psycho-graphic analysis, combined with Government demographic statistics summarises the society as culturally deficient, conservative, typically provincial, low to medium tech, little outside tourism despite the curious maintenance of a natural environment with wilderness areas. On the whole, safe, and quite forgettable. It's very much a back-water, frankly."

"And what do you think, Wally?"

"Low-tech generally means high-tack to me, but it looks sort of pretty to me. I guess I'm old-fashioned, but I actually enjoy getting out of artificial environments a few days a year. This one looks quite pleasant. Wouldn't mind trying it out sometime."

"Yes, Marve?"

"Know the Consumer, know who you're talking to. We haven't really defined the target audience yet, but what do we know about the Earthlings? What kind of people are they? What turns them on and gets them going?"

Marve looked at Bernie, so Bernie looks at Milton.

"I'm the numbers man, remember?" He turned to address Marvin. "You'll have to set up your own meet-the-consumer study to answer that fully, but the hard data points to a flat society with no celebrities, a lot of complacency, an acceptance of their way of life and no desire to change it. If anything, they are dedicated, it would seem, to absolute maintenance of the status quo."

"In short, a bunch of deadheads."

"Like I said, low-tech and high-tack."

"Definitely not your upwardly mobile kind of population."

"Technologically they are a living museum, both on Earth and

their solus moon. It's backward alright."

"I disagree." Wally woke up again. "Earth, according to the Archaeologists Handbook of Ancient Sites, is the home of the Library of the Tree of Humankind. And the population of Earth is dedicated to preserving it."

"You mean that's their sole aim in life?"

"As a Society, it would appear so. I see no other. Of course I assume individuals have individual aims...""What? Like high priests of preservation or something? Ridiculous suggestion."

"May I remind you that there is no such thing a bad idea in a brainstorming session?"

"Then why the fuck did you invite Milt?" The acid comment was ignored as they'd all heard it and said it before.

"Look, ff that's all these backward Earth-types do, they deserve to end up on the fuel dump!"

Bernard Mucous raised his voice above the rest. "Wally's right! He always wants to change the goddam product instead of developing a tough creative line that'll sell the product no matter how distasteful the thing may happen to be. But this time, the product is too damned pretty and probably religious to boot. Nobody's gonna want to burn a place that's pretty. And nobody's gonna want to be held responsible for turning a bunch of loony librarians into religious martyrs. We gotta dig up some dirt on this patch of garden and find a way to discredit their goddam library."

"Bernie, don't take this thing so..."

76

"Seriously? I hope that's not what you were going to say, Jerry. I know we're already the biggest goddam ad agency in the Universe, but HL&S was built on doing good ads and sticking with our promises. I promised the nice Government lady we'd do our best. I gave her my word. If you guys don't want to give your best, I'll finish the goddam project on my own!"

"I'm with you," Wally sucked up.

"Me too," Marv boot-licked.

And then all the heads were nodding up and down in common consent, and the brainstorm began in earnest.

"We need a totally integrated umbrella campaign."

"Mainstream activity, plus below-the-line subtlety."

"Since when is activity below-the-line subtle?"

"Search every seg-way."

"Mete out the mnemonics!"

"It's ideal for Direct Mail."

"Lateral thinking. We need lateral thinking on this."

"I'm looking for an opportunity window here."

"This idea has got to work right across the board."

"I can see something Synergistic"

"The man's a fucking genius."

"Cachet. Give it some cachet!"

"We're not selling a goddam perfume here."

"Do you think planet incineration come under the heading of a Distress Purchase?"

"I got it!"

"The man says he's got it, Bernie."

Let's look for a scientific approach."

"Boring, Jerry."

Totally tedious."

"Unilaterally uninspired."

"Then maybe science softened with a little emotional appeal - maybe even a lot of emotion melted over it?"

"Yeah, like 'Do your bit to beat back Entropy', or 'The way of life you save could be your own'."

"Gee, that's original, Marvin."

"Excellent. Not."

"How about a good old-fashioned Energy Saving campaign?"

"You're popping with corn now!" Bernie brightened up considerably.

"How about: 'The energy you save could be your own'?"

"I like it."

"I think it sucks."

"It sucks so much that's why there's a vacuum in space."

"On second thought, I think I *almost* like it."

"I think the Earthlings will love it."

"You do, Bernie? Marve was aghast.

"There's a good basic human appeal to Sloth buried in there."

"Buried how deep?"

"Definitely an Idea in there somewhere. Clever stroke getting the word 'energy' into it in a meaningful and relevant way."

"How about 'Save light, read with a friend.'"

"You don't need light to read by, Wally. And I'm not so sure about such a severe savings angle. It might panic people."

"Yeah, we gotta continue to promote absolute confidence in the Leadership."

"Then let's go for the kids, Bernie!"

"Good approach, Marve. Excellent. Get 'em when they're young so they grow up with the idea."

"And we can use the kids to feed the idea to their parents."

"That's the stuff, Jerry." Bernie encouraged them all forward.

"Brill!"

"We'll get the whole goddam family ecstatic about frying Earth!"

"We need that hook to catch the kids, Marve."

"A hero. They need a hero. Maybe somebody like a Jolly Green Titanthrope."

"No, something gentler, like a Ronald McMarvellous."

"Why not a Little Green Man?"

"Hey, how 'bout an Earthling? It's full of greenies already."

"And who the hell cares?"

"No, I got it, I got it! A *spark* of energy. That's it! Don'tcha see? That's what we want Earth to give us in the end -a spark of energy!""I see him, Bernie. I see our character, our hero, our campaign vehicle, I see, wait for it -- 'Sparky', the energetic friend!"

"Yeah, great! But make it 'Sparky *your* energetic friend'!"

"We'll splash the little bastard everywhere."

"Holos, dolls, games!"

"A new brand of batteries and lights."

"Sparky shirts and hats and thermo wraps."

"And the beauty of it all is this - everything is made possible by the selfless generosity of those wonderful people of wherever it is who sacrificed their planet whatever it's called for the good of all mankind!"

"Sparky will be the symbol of their sacrifice throughout the Universe."

"Maybe we could change the name of Earth to..."

"Shut up, Jerry!"

"I'm glad we're all agreed on my approach, then" Bernie said, reaching for another stogie and completely satisfied that they had the makings of the winning campaign for him and the coffers of HL&S.

"That poor miserable Alien sonofabitch."

"Who? Sparky?"

"No, not Sparky. Forget it. Light my stogie, Marve, and you can be Creative Director for another month."

Departure

"**J**udy!" He had a million things to run through with her. "Judy!

Once more like that and he could audition for Cary Grant tribute night. He went to the computer and called up the brief from Central Thought to take with him. She must be staring in the shop windows again, he thought.

He tried bleeping her pager and got a red light reply that indicated she was indisposed. Tick-tock. Vite vite! Speed of light! Got to get going. Finally, Jackson couldn't wait a moment longer. He left a message on Judy's terminal, trying to be polite but when he played it back he thought it was a bit sarcastic. Too bad. No time to change it.

"Judy, dear, wish you were here so I could yell at you! Where are you when I need you most! Look, I've got to rush off now on that new project I picked up from the Quadrant advertising director. Be watchful! Since my Cosmic interview I've been getting some pretty hostile mail. Keep security and secrecy uppermost. Put my current workload through the Mason Omega program -- it should write everything virtually the same way I would have done it myself.

"Try to make things look like I'm still there. Got that? I could be gone for several weeks. Check for messages from me every day. And keep my access channel open so I can collect messages from you at my end. It's safer for you if you don't know where I am. If you don't know you can't get into any trouble over it, can you?

"Keep an eye on the computer for signs of external input. Especially from Central Thought. If anything comes in from C.T. please put a code message on my access channel with the file channel key so I can get to it safely when I need it.

"I'm heading for the transport centre to board Pan Galaxy Flight 217, I think you should know that much at least in case anything happens, but don't risk beaming anything to me on board.

As always, input from my end during my absence should be locked in and hidden from probes. Oh yes, beware of strangers! Also, change the locks on my data banks and inform me of the new combinations by encoded message. Cancel all my meetings for the next 100 uni-days and set the company on auto-pilot. In other words, you're in charge. If it looks like I've bought the ranch, tell the Government Marketing and Advertising Director of Quadrant Four, she will want to know.

"Sorry I missed you. Your loving employer, Mason.

"P.S. Re: business bits:

> 1. McCosmos is due to get in touch with me for a galactic re-launch of their burger chain. Keep P.P. waiting peacefully for my return.

> 2. Watch Cosmic Campaign for news about the Mmaracan Tourism pitch. It's been too long without a positive word, and I think I must have missed out on the business after all.

> 3. The only other thing that might be wanted when I get back is Guillotine's new triple-head razor launch."Three-heads-are-better-than- two-are-better-than-one and the triple head laser promises to take heads off quicker than anything ever invented. We may have to miss out making a pitch for that one, especially if McCosmos genuinely need attention."

Jackson packed a small synth-hide bag from his wardrobe at the office apartment and entered a telebooth for the instantaneous journey to the spaceport. He bought a return ticket on route 217 to the end of the line with Pan Galaxy. Now all he had to do was wait for the liner to arrive.

He stood on the platform with thousands of other people waiting to catch space hops all over the Quadrant. The screen said he had about 30 minutes to waste. Jackson's mind wandered freely. He wondered about Earth. What life was like there now? It should make a good test market. Probably like all the other planets and artificial environments that Man inhabited throughout the known Universe. Blowing up a planet was no big deal. The spaceline planners did it all the time to clear the path for travel networks. But if they were going to start confiscating inhabited planets, well that was another story. Enough was enough. He wished he could have said something about it in the Cosmic interview and bugger the consequences.

He was no cosmic physicist, but it seemed hopelessly inadequate to him throwing little planets, even big planets on suns to make them burn a little brighter or burn a little longer. There was no way there would ever be enough planets to sustain the process. But this seemed to be the only solution the cosmic thinkers could come up with so far. As yet, there was nothing known or even dreamed of that could supplant or replace suns for heat and light. And life could not survive without them.

Or *could it*?

Jackson suddenly wished he was a scientist instead, working on the leading edge of technology, pioneering new processes. Then there was a new thought: If he could dream a dream - perhaps the scientists could make it come true. And if they couldn't? Was it possible to *live* a dream? Forever?

Several miles above the platform, a huge liner approached, sensors responded, and a window opened just long enough to allow flight 217 to enter the climate control dome, then silently sealed shut again.

Jackson saw the time and headed for a call panel. He decided to put through a last-minute call to Director Prime. He didn't know if it was a fake identity, so he simply asked for the Director of Marketing and Advertising. He hoped that she wasn't too busy to see him. Then he heard her voice, but got no picture.

"I'll try another line, Director, the picture's faulty on this one." he said.

"Security measure, Mr. Jackson. I can see you perfectly, but the security system is blocking your vision from this end...I see you're about to catch a liner."

"Yes. I've decided to go straight to Earth and have a look for myself. Director, I don't want to get involved in your policies, politics and your games of hidden identity, but this brief is sinking into me, it's *effecting* me. And I know it must be very important to you that I come up with the goods. But I cannot promise that my recommendations will be anything like what you expect. This is not a conventional task that can be handled by conventional practices.

It's not a question of putting a product in a package and selling it."

"Mr. Jackson, for someone who doesn't want to get yourself involved in policies and politics, you certainly had a strange way of keeping quiet about the suns dying out. Do not expect any support from this office if you are forced to produce evidence for the severity of the entropy situation."

"Pan Galaxy Flight 217 arriving on platform 4."

"I only have your word on it anyway. I've seen no proof."

"I should also be careful with your accusations against strong and influential people. I cannot save you if one of them decides to have you for lunch. No one can."

"They're calling my flight. I've got to go. Hate to miss connections. Thanks for your support so far. May I contact you later with any questions I may have?"

"That may not be a good idea. But you can try."

Mason thought Catherine's voice was sincere as the whited - out screen blanked to black and the call ended and a huge shadow enveloped the terminal platform.

The enormous synthidium shelled liner lowered to within an inch of the pedestrian surface of Platform Four. Hundreds of window-less doors slid open in unison to admit the three thousand or so waiting space travellers. Jackson was conspicuous by his lack of large luggage. Most people on long journeys such as this took much more than Jackson's little bag. But he needed to travel light, and could rely on hotel services for most of the things he would need. He was used to carrying his brain in his head.

Most of the passengers would choose to sleep for the duration so he didn t expect much socialising-- and that cut down on his wardrobe requirements considerably.

"Mind the doors" the doors said.

He heard the warning, but didn't listen to it. He was halfway through the entry-way when the well-mannered metal beasts closed on him. They shuddered, opened and closed again behind him.

"Do not delay departure by obstructing the doors" they scolded.

How embarrassing! Passengers stared accusingly at him. He'd just delayed everyone's journey by three seconds.

The ship was pretty standard. Bog-boring in fact to anyone who did a lot of travelling. But he was going to a pretty dull destination anyway. Jackson had a business class ticket; 'Clobber Class' Pan Gal once called it. But a new campaign now touted it as 'Clout Class'. It entitled him to every facility on the ship except the Top Class Lounge.

There was virtually no staff. No hostesses like the old days. No waiters either in economy. At least there was no tipping. All the services were automated. Presumably, so the ad campaign promised, Pan Gal still had a real live pilot sleeping somewhere on top of the hull, ever ready to spring into emergency action should the ship's computer awaken him. How comforting.

Most of those travelling cattle class or 'Shoestring' as their baggage labels said, herded themselves straight into the Casino where they all hoped to win enough credits off the Pan Galaxy gaming tables to pay for their entire trip. But more often than not, their pockets emptied or even bank accounts zeroed, they would stumble into the hammock bays and sleep the weeks till landing.

Contrast that with Clout Class. Mason was guided personally by a humanoid escort (Top Class was served by real humans) to the Clout Class Champagne and Oyster Bar where he was offered a sumptuous seafood buffet to accompany a bottle of Moet & Clicquot Vintage 12209. Frank Sinatra hummed in his memory; it was a very good year.

PanGal Flight 217

Aboard Pan Galaxy Flight 217, everything was about as boring as you'd expect. The passage to the Sol System was long by any standards. Nearly twenty uni-days. There were seven jumps to make on the journey which were practically instantaneous, but the sub-jump speeds required in heavy traffic and population areas slowed progress enormously. With so much time on their hands and not much to do in a relatively confined living space, most passengers chose to go under and sleep for days on end.

Jackson was uncomfortable and feeling niggly, roaming the corridors and haunting the lounges and bars. He was the sort of man who loved to travel if he could be at the controls 'driving' the ship. But as a passenger, he was as bad as a healthy patient in hospital. He had a lot on his mind and now he was having second thoughts and wasn't completely convinced going to Earth was the right way to tackle the brief -- he could ill-afford to waste his time with such a short deadline. But he always believed in doing a 'store-check' at the start of every job. Touching and feeling the product, looking at it through eyes that had seen things no other person alive had seen, and applying his built in crap-detector. Anyway, he always preferred to get out in the middle of a marketing problem, get his hands dirty on it and know what he was working with first-hand. Sitting at a desk billions of kilometres away, trying to imagine the situation or the product, was no substitute for experiencing the real thing face to face.

Besides, there was no way off the ship now.

He felt he'd already gone as far as his mind could go on the subject in the luxury of this travelling limbo, but he hated the idea of going under in case he missed something on the voyage. The colourful picture patterns of deep space always fascinated him. Every time his feet left the ground it was as exciting for him as his very first flight on a noisy two engine turbo-prop from Des Moines to Chicago in the 1960s. (He'd kept the sugar packets and napkins as a souvenir to show his Mom). But now even a magnificently swirling nebulae, a multi-ringed planet and the sight of a rare comet began to lose their lustre and magic in the grip of mind-numbing boredom.

Half-conscious, lethargic and space-doped, his eyes widened when he noticed a radio receiver built into a small ornamental four-armed sort of helmeted ape-man sitting on a coffee table in front of him - a tasteless waste of the potter's art from Praxis II. Leaning forward in his all too comfy body lounger, he grasped the ape-man sculpture by the neck and picked it up. At least he'd be able to receive the odd local radio station during the next sub-jump sector.

Why couldn't the long jumps be as easy as local telebooth jumps? Why did people still actually have to go aboard a vessel and be carried bodily from A to B? On the planets and platforms, the telecommunications people had become exactly that and were capable of sending *people* rather than just messages through their network.

Step into a telebooth, punch the area code of the place you're going, close your eyes against the momentary flash and step out the other side of the telebooth into your destination. The telebooth never went anywhere, but you did. It seemed to Jackson that the same Star Trek type physics and mechanics could be applied to hyperspace. It would cost a lot less time and energy. And energy, he so recently had learned, was not as plentiful as everyone thought.

Or was it just another myth starting to be circulated by the industrial giants? Time and again, since the advent of the early industrial ages, the people in power led the consuming masses step by step to the next expensive stage of technology. Perhaps they had actually been able to bribe Central Thought-- or at least to feed it with misleading information about energy reserves and entropy. It would certainly drive the price of energy space-high. Perhaps that's what this was all about and nothing more. Much of the wealth of the greatest and most powerful industrialists had been gathered from energy-related companies. Planned obsolescence, energy crises, fuel shortages, all of these phenomena were hyped and orchestrated by the 'pirates' of their times.

Jackson recalled that when it was widely reported that fossil fuels were running out in Quadrant Two prices soared and profits multiplied for a hundred years. It was only when the need for fossil fuels was displaced altogether by new technology that it came to light that there were still massive reserves still untouched on several planets in the Quadrant. The fossil fuel companies, who had ripped off thirty generations with their high prices, started leasing and renting suns for solar energy. Not even sun light was free anymore.

The 'pirates' developed all kinds of conversion apparatus that they sold and hired out and made more fortunes. Whatever the next step in technology, the 'pirates' had the corner on the existing level and the next levels as well. They successfully steered civilisation from planet to planet, galaxy to galaxy, until all the Inner Planets were exploited and the Outer Planets were not economical to develop.

And so the power of the Fifty Thousand grew and consolidated. They were always more clever than governments could ever be. Political leaders, placed in power by the 'pirates', were thus entrusted to maintain stability and preserve the profit centres. Their names were never publicised. This was very old money. It did not seek fame but stability and security for their lifestyle. But now their future, like everyone else's was jeopardised by Entropy and the basic common laws of Nature. Of course the effects were barely noticeable, nobody living now expected to be alive to suffer the consequences of using too much energy. But with the advertising brief in his hands, Jackson was forced to think about it as if it were as real as today. The problem posed by Madame Prime, the Quadrant Director of Advertising and Marketing, was causing him some painful introspection.

After all, he had made a living out of selling. It was more than a living; it was his total way of life. Showing growth every year, increasing profit, owning beautiful things -- all this mattered to him, very much indeed. If all human endeavours including his own were just going to end up as ash, what was the point? Why bust his ass? Why should anybody try at all anymore? Probably because he didn't know any other way to live, he felt compelled to come up with a professional response in a professional way.

Some slight change in the background prompted Jackson to glance out the window. He noticed the ship was slowing down. No longer the swirls and blurs of hyperspeed, stars were beginning to settle into sharply focused objects. Good. Now he could try the radio. The scanner shouted a lot of static and shrill oscillations before it locked onto the first station.

"Hello out there all you space jockeys on the cargo shuttle, this here's the Space Ace puttin' down all the sounds to warp your mind through every mile of Space Ace Country - Sector A33. It's all mine and I got you all to myself on my little screen! A great big hello to Pan Galaxy Flight 217. Right on time fellers. Most of you folk aboard are probably zonked out gettin some z's, but you won't be when I get finished blasting a zillion watts of sonic power your way!

"So get set, hold yer breath and cover yer ears, coz the Voice of the Void, Star Radio Colossal, is blasting out of Uranus with the new hit single 'Browned Off'! Hit it Clyde!"

Jackson punched the scanner before Clyde collided with him. Instead, he ran smack into the middle of another Outworld radio outlaw.

"Kooeee! I'm Kash Kard, the Fantom of the Grand Old Opprie, bringin' you the music that made the west of the Quadrant great. You re listenin' to the Voice of Beyond! Radio West is Best! Now here's a re-quest from that convoy of protein pullers waitin' fer its load over Laredo..."

Then something totally unexpected happened. She was tall, willowy, blonde and leggy. Jackson watched her cross her legs as she sank into a float sofa opposite him. He tried to punch the scanner 'off' but missed. At least he avoided the protein puller's request.

"And now here's a commercial - yeah, how 'bout that? I'm warning you, the next thing you're gonna hear is a commercial - for the best little eat 'n' run platform in the galaxy - the Hurry Down Beam Me Up and Keep on Fission Cafe." Jackson wished he knew which galaxy they were in so he could avoid eating there. It was radio ga-ga and radio goo-goo spewing out the primitive style ad message but Jackson was trying so hard to look up the blonde's skirt he didn't really hear it. [Sometimes a radio writer has no hope of beating the visual competition.] The blonde met his interested gaze with a smile, and then raised a screen to watch a magazine. It reminded Jackson that there was nothing more intrusive than television - unless, yes, he could feel it now, coming from the huge purple world they were passing now - an Impulse Beam.

The Impulse hit him that it was time to eat. It made him feel animal, less human, less in control. Like some four-footed protein beast, shock-programmed to eat on command. It was overriding every other urge in his body.

He'd used impulse beams himself on occasion a creative tool and had frequently recommended their use to most of his clients over the years. One of the most successful applications of the medium was used for advertising confections. Take a Bull Bar - if you were hit with an impulse for a Bull Bar, you'd instantly salivate. Nothing could control or satisfy your hunger except a Bull Bar, even if you'd just finished a twelve course Chinese dinner. Of course, the impulse beams provoked millions of letters of protest from as many consumer groups. And finally, under pressure, the government was forced to ban impulse beams for the entire category of confectionery products.

Then the Hi-techs found a way around it with second generation technology. They took their new type of beam off the shelf the day the original beam became illegal. Instead of one beam carrying the impulse, say, for a Bull Bar as packaged, you were hit with a family of related beams. So for a Bull Bar you got separate beams for glucose, caramel, nuts, nougat, chocolate and everything else that goes into a Bull Bar. Legally acceptable, and the same result: a craving for a Bull Bar. Or was it Bull Shit? Jackson couldn't remember.

The consumer groups complained again. This time even more vociferously. But their case was thrown out in 114467. There was no way of enforcing the restriction of the beams on commodity items. Within hours of the ruling, every major advertiser in the inhabited universe had thrown their megabucks into the newly-approved medium. Space was as cluttered as a Friday night newspaper and, the advertisers were back to square one again. With impulses for every chemical and taste formula known to man filling civilised space and cramming into your head, you couldn't tell a Bull Bar from a fish head curry. But that was centuries ago, and the advertising industry had successfully restricted itself in the use of the medium so that impulse beams were becoming practical again in less populated areas.

Of course, there were still justifiable complaints and there always would be. People who were allergic to eggs couldn't cope with a craving for them. People who didn't smoke, pop, or inject didn't understand the impulse for nicotine. And health fanatics couldn't bear the thought of all those Bull Bars! All this Jackson filtered and considered again, wondering if or how impulse beams could be applied to the brief that now threatened Earth.

Then, unexpectedly, his thoughts were delightfully interrupted again by the well-designed blonde.

"Are you going to the Sol System too?" The willowy woman jolted him into a new impulse.

It took him a little too long to answer. "Yes. Yes, I am."

"I'm headed to Saturn - there's a reunion of my level three school there. Which planet are you going to?"

When she didn't pause to hear a reply, Jackson figured she just wanted someone to talk to and didn't really care if he was listening or not. But who could blame her? There were only a handful of people awake in the whole damned ship, and she was probably going as stir-crazy as he was.

"Haven't seen my class-mates for macro years. I wonder how much they've all changed."

"I haven't any idea," Jackson said. And got a giggle out of her. He considered asking her what she'd studied in level three, but he knew she'd tell him sooner or later anyway.

"I just finished a book about the Fourth Reich of the Civilisations of Titan. That's Saturn's biggest moon, you know!"

"No, actually I didn't," he had to admit. And thought that he should have known it. He *should* know everything about the Sol System if he was going to be successful on his pitch.

He started to take a new interest in the young woman. He hadn't expected to learn anything from her chatter. But, well, it pays to listen - in advertising you never know where the next good idea will come from. Besides, she had exceptionally nice legs, possibly a little thick above the ankle, but the thighs held a very desirable shape right to the top. And the way she was sitting he could see right to the top. He imagined one thigh pressed against each of his ears - as he listened intently to what she had to say. "And what Reich is in power on Titan now?"

"The transport authority, I guess," she laughed. "Titan is now used entirely as a hyperspace-port for Saturn. People to-ing and fro-ing in and out of the Sol System use Titan as the platform for the jump to the Sol space-gate.

He noticed her eyes were blue-green. Little wrinkles spoked away from the corners of them. Her nose was a little too long and she smelled unpleasantly of cig-smoke. But she dressed very smartly--perhaps too expensively for someone of her class-- usually the sign of an executive secretary.

"I shouldn't have laughed; I forget that most people have never heard of Saturn, let alone Titan. But it is there on your ticket if you're interested."

Jackson warmed to her a little more. You can't always judge a blonde by the colour of her hair, he thought. He decided to risk entering cliché country by asking what she did.

"I work for a big mining corporation. My boss is the principal director of the diamond division." Jackson realised the glass on her finger was real.

"I'm his personal assistant."

That could cover a considerable multitude of sins and indulgences. "So, you help him in executive decisions?"

"Yes, I write all his letters, and make all his appointments."

"That sounds very challenging." Was he sounding sincere enough?

"It's very demanding. Anyway, what brings *you* to the Sol System, if you don't mind my asking?"

"I try never to talk about work when I'm not working," Jackson answered, thinking it might be fun to make him sound mysterious.

"Then it's a work trip not a holiday."

"I'm afraid that's right."

93

"I guess no one ever goes to the Sol System for a holiday."

"Don't they? Why not?"

"Well, practically no one. What's there to see, or do for that matter?"

"You've got a point. I never heard of anyone going there on holiday either."

"I mean the Sol System is the most *boring* place. Nearly as bad as this ship! The people who live on most of the planets in the system come from generations of mining families who became generations of warehouse keepers who have become the fiftieth generation of transit authority workers."

"Fascinating. But you said 'most' of the planets...?" Jackson didn't have to form the question completely.

"There's one called Earth that's never been properly mined. Legend says the planet surface looks pretty much like it did eighty or ninety centuries ago."

"Well that certainly sounds worth seeing!"

"Yeah, but it's a galactic backwater. Nothing ever happens on Earth. Let me think - I think it's the third planet from the sun, about 149 million kilometres out. It has one moon, Nixon, named after the leader of the people who reached it first -- I learned that in the second chapter of "How Green Was My Planet" and it has a population of just over a hundred million" she said proudly.

"On Earth?"

"No, on Nixon."

"What about Earth?"

"A few million, I suppose, just enough to keep the place going. They keep the Library, you know."

"Sorry, caught me out again."

"The Library of the Tree of Humankind. Of course, the World Park Service employs millions of Nixonites to keep the Earth clean and well-preserved."

"This 'Library'. It sounds like it's something out of a legend too."

"Yeah, s'pose so. In a way it is. The Earthlings and the Nixonites take it pretty seriously."

"You wouldn't like to tell me more about the legend, would you? Earth is starting to sound more intriguing."

"Do you *really* want to know?"

"If you have the time, I'd like to listen." Jackson was onto a live one here.

"I'll tell you about the legend first. The LEGEND, in capital letters, is a local story - at least, I haven't heard it outside the Sol System. The important bit is that they believe humankind originated there. On Earth."

He burst out laughing. "Isn't that the silliest goddam legend you ever heard?!" Fingers crossed he hoped she believed he didn't believe.

"You're laughing."

"Uh-Huh. And the next thing you're going to tell me is that every last human being in the Universe sprang from some guy named Adam and his wife, a woman named Eve, on the planet Earth!" He exaggerated the laughter a little further.

"Where did you hear about all this?" She was not amused.

"A comic book I think, years ago. Years ago. And where did you hear it?"

"I'm doing a night course in Archaeology," her tone was very serious "I came across the reference in several background studies on the ancient civilisations of the five other planets of the Sol System, Maras, Jupitron, Saturn, Neptonis and Vega. The other planets in the system were never settled. The legend doesn't seem to be a living part of the culture anymore. Except on Earth and Nixon, of course."

"And what do you think? Do you believe it? It's pretty spooky!"

"Sure. It sounds a bit goofy, but why not? People didn't come from thin air did they? We had to have a beginning somewhere. There is no other theory for the origin of our species that makes any more sense. Claims by other

95

planets to be the proto-home of human-kind are no more ridiculous than Earth s claim."

"That's certainly true enough. So what does the Library have to do with it?" Jackson queried.

"The Library has documented the human family tree of every person ever born on the planet Earth."

"Who'd want to know? And who'd give a damn anyway?" Jackson erupted.

"Well, originally the Library started as a databank for the taxation system. Have you heard of taxation?"

"Yes. It must have been terrible to have to pay money to the government out of your wages."

"Fortunately the Taxation Wars put an end to that. I'll bet you didn't know the first battle was fought by the miners on good old Titan to overthrow the First Reich!"

"Got me there", Jackson again conceded.

"And I bet you were thinking I was just a dumb blonde. Anyway, to cut what must obviously be a long story, the databank grew, the conservationists dominated Earth-Nixon politics, Earth was saved, and in many areas restored to preserve ancient treasures, and the databank was redirected. Over the tens of thousands of years the archaeologists have dug up everything in sight, except the polar ice caps of course, tracing everybody. New techniques in micro-archaeology enabled them to build accurate family trees right back to prehistoric times, from the most obscure relics. The old phrase 'ashes to ashes' gained a new meaning. From ashes, they could always find a bit of DNA. Eventually they'd identify the individual and properly position him or her onto the macro tree."

"And what does this Library with its ingeniously devised tree have to say about the legendary Adam and Eve characters?"

"Hey, I've told you all I know, and I've even guessed at some of that. Why don't you go to Earth and see for yourself. What are you going to the System for, anyway?

You never did say, although I gather from what you said before it's got to do with your work, whatever that is."

"You wouldn't believe it if I told you."

"Did you believe I was going to a class reunion?"

"Of course I did. Aren't you?"

"Yes. So I have no reason not to believe your reason to be here."

"Why don't we go to the Laser Lounge, have a drink and maybe I'll tell you something about it."

"What do you mean, 'maybe'?"

"We'll see, that's all."

"Trying to get me drunk, are you?"

"I'd never try that. I'm not that kind of guy."

"Why not? Okay, then if I have to get *you* drunk to tell me why you're going to the Sol System, the first round is on me!"

She gave him a wink, tossed her long blonde hair, and led the way between the float sofas to the lifts. They left the container at the 17th level down. Jackson kept his distance from her like a gentleman should, but he found her more delicious all the time. The doors ahead of them disappeared. They had arrived in the Laser Lounge. As far as he was concerned, it was the only exciting, entertaining part of the whole ship complex.

The theme of the bar was spacewalking. As they stepped into the bar area itself, the floor vanished from beneath their feet. It was as if they had walked straight off the ship into deep space - without a lifesuit! Starlight sparkled at varying distances in every direction. The illusion was perfect. If you wanted to go up, you could walk up - or down, if you pleased. But there were no stairs. No visible means of support. You could feel nothing solid under your steps, yet you were still safely inside the ship.

Cocktail glasses appeared in their hands. But none of this was surprising to Jackson or his companion. In many ways, it was just another bar. They spoke to an unseen robo-waiter.

"I'll have a Saurian Sailer." A flash of light struck the glass in her hand and it filled with the
frothy delight she had asked for.
Jackson ordered a malted brew called a Valkyrie, a wild tonic he had first tried on a visit to Vishnu.
"Come on now," she coaxed. "I don't have to do all the talking, do I?" She really had a way of growing directly into his confidence.
"I'm a Creator," he said, somewhat abruptly as he looked straight into her eyes. Lovely bedroom eyes they were too.
"A real live Creator!' She was incredulous with delight. "I actually am impressed. I figured you maybe for a journalist, maybe even a songwriter, but a Creator. Wow! But who's gonna believe me when I tell 'em?"
Jackson felt well in control now. "For better or worse, it's true. I'm a Creator."
"Oh no, I think it's marvellous. The people on the Outer Planets couldn't live without The Creations. I mean all those poor miners and farmers on worlds with no cities to enjoy no culture except what they can keep in their barracks or bungalows. But you've given them The Creations, and the chance to live out their fantasies.
"Tell me, did you create the Gladiator Arena? It must be the goriest personal screen-experience of all time - I absolutely love it!" She was squealing with excitement.
"No, a Toymech colleague of mine, Manfred. He dreamed that one up."
"Oh I do hope you created something I know. Have you?"
"Do you know of the Wuzy Doll Series?"
"My god! You didn't create the Wuzy Doll, did you?"
"I spent six years on the concept, positioning, design and consumer testing in secret before I even dared to make my preliminary presentation to the Creative Review Board."
"It was an overnight success! I remember everybody rushed out to buy them, including me."

98

"Hardly. Not at first anyway. The Chairman didn't like it. Didn't have a good reason, either. Said it was just a toy - and nobody played with dolls any more. So I left Toymech and scraped up a loan to make the first few thousand Wuzy units on my own."

"How do you dream up something like that? I mean, you made something out of nothing. I imagine that's why they call you a Creator, isn't it?"

"That's a bit over-simplified, and a touch too glorified. Creating isn't as miraculous as making something out of nothing. Creating something begins with an idea. The idea is all important. And the idea always comes *from* something or, somewhere. So it's a synthesis. Putting a piece of information together with a feeling and matching opportunities - that's how I come up with things.

Jackson knew that since the days of Archimedes, creativity had enjoyed the shine of the divine. That there was something mystical about it, something revered by those who didn't have 'It'. As he knew form his own first-hand experience, you had to be different – that to have a true cutting edge you needed a disciplined eye and a wild mind'. But how wild and how disciplined? It depended on the circumstances. A big idea is always a ridiculously obvious idea – it's just that no else has exploited it. It's like a huge money note lying on the floor of a crowded bar. It's there just waiting to be picked up.'

The blonde was completely mesmerised by all this. "Don't tell me there isn't any magic in what you do. I know about Wuzy Dolls, and it is a magical experience, every time."

"I'm lucky I have it. Fortunately creativity can flourish in spite of neglect and abuse. Creativity is a product of our brains and sense-abilities, and not really a Mystery. After all, apes are creative too! Even Plato recognised that creativity is nurtured by honouring it within the culture. 'What is honoured in a country will be cultivated there.' "

"Plato?"

"A great thinker from long ago and far away. The magic, as always with magic, is an illusion. It is intangible - and yet I know what you mean - it is unmistakably there. That's the result of Art in any form. Somehow the whole is greater than the sum of its parts. When you get the right combination of elements and everything is working for you and you get that little bit extra, yeah - I guess you can call it magic!"

The willowy blonde who studied archaeology in spare evenings, sipped her Saurian Sailer and transformed into a star-struck little girl. "So tell me how you came up with Wuzy! I'm dying to know!"

"You'll have to buy me another drink before I divulge my inner secrets!"

"Another drink or two and I'll be a push-over. How do I know you're not just some class Z journalist riding this space bucket on an eternal ticket to nowhere, preying on innocent young women?" Her eyes twinkled as she toyed with him.

"Who's the innocent one?"

"Well, at least I'm young, young-ish!"

"I am what I say. I have an unfortunate habit of telling the truth to strangers, and believing everything they say - until proven wrong, I'm as gullible as they come."

"And you tell lies to people you know?" She teased.

"When it suits." He confessed.

"I think you're telling the truth." She snapped her fingers and their glasses refilled. "I've always dreamed of making love with a Creator."

"You have?" Mason was shocked. He was getting in deeper than he was ready for. "And I have always wanted to create with a lover."

"I'll bet you say that to every doll named Wuzy, you old smoothie, you."

"Don't tell me your name is Wuzy!" So far he didn't know what here name was.

"No, my name is Amanda." She giggled slightly as she said her own name.

"Amanda is a, a, uh very suitable name."

It did suit her too. Perhaps even more so when she was younger. She was cute in a kind of outer world way, and Amanda was definitely a cute name. It was appropriate that secretaries be called Amanda. The space between them disappeared as he pressed close to her and kissed her lightly on the lips.

"Amanda. I'm glad I met you."

Face-off

"**M**y, you are romantic! Most men don't have any time for preliminaries like this anymore! Mind you, that's the trouble with men; they're either romantics or animals. If it's not soft light and dinner, it's 'brace yourself, honey I'm... well, you know'. I prefer things to be erotic but frankly, I don't expect men to be up to it."

"What am I supposed to say to that?!" Mason wondered out loud. "Look, if you want a debate, I'm game, but I hardly know you, and I warn you my tongue is acidic. I don't suffer fools."

"And you have a big chip on your shoulder too. All I said was most men aren't romantic. But if you're going to be an asshole about it you can piss off!"

"Fine. You know it really doesn't matter to me whether you think I'm romantic, erotic, animalistic, or even interesting. You have a delicious looking body and you can talk reasonably intelligently, but I don't need the hassle. We're the only two people awake in this whole goddam hull, but if you would prefer to argue, go to the computer and wake somebody else up!"

"Somehow I expected that."

Maybe it was because he stood up to her, maybe she enjoyed abuse. It certainly wasn't because he made any sense, but for whatever the reason, she took his hand and they made a kind of peace.

They sat in a cluster of bright blue stars as he told her about the creation of the original Wuzy Doll - the first of all the product groups immortalised in marketing history simply as The Creations.

She listened attentively, responding with animated interest as Mason Jackson told his story as no-one but the genuine Creator of the Wuzy Doll could have told it.

"Toymech had been in the centre of the games industry for only about five centuries before I joined them as a games tester.

"What did you do before that, Mason?"

"That *is* a long story, which I'll save until it seems we've run out of absolutely everything else to talk about. Anyway, the challenge to come up with a new game at Toymech was greater than at any time in their corporate history - the public demand for something really new created enormous pressure on the top management at -- and they passed the heat onto the creative teams.

"They were hiring and firing non-stop. The demand to perform cracked and crumbled some of the biggest egos in the galaxy. If anybody could give them something new and fresh and different success was guaranteed and billions could be made on a daily basis. The demand for realism was acute too. To create new, exciting virtual reality scenarios. Toymech management seemed to go through a phase when they had an obsession for complete environments where you could visit any period of history and be any kind of hero you fancied -- play any sport, fight any battle, win any contest you could imagine for any stakes you cared to play...

"Well, it finally hit me one day as I was testing a Naval War game depicting an actual set piece battle with historic fleets of the 35th century, that the emphasis on realism had gone too far. And that all the games had the same approach, with practically the same theme to them. You might even say that people were all playing exactly the same game-- only the setting changed. Every game was a test. Every player was trying to win something and to beat someone or some *thing*.

Equally important, I suddenly recognised that with all this realism, there was no room for genuine imagination. That in the quest for fantasy adventures, the toy makers had actually missed the opportunity for real fantasy! The kind of amazing fantasy you can only achieve, and only ever enjoy if you are forced to use your *own* imagination!

So I worked in a new direction - aimed at putting Imagination back in the core of the game experience."

"How do you mean?" Amanda asked, obviously puzzled. Up until now, she had been nodding with understanding.

"Take an ordinary ball game. You're a spectator. You're there, and that part is real. But more important to your psyche is the opportunity to see the good plays, the great plays, the plays the heroes of the game make. Every game has its heroes. Every spectator has his heroes. And as a spectator you can share the same elation of winning as your heroes do. And yet, because you're a spectator and not on the playing field, you don't risk yourself -- understand me? You don't actually put *yourself* on the line the same way the real player does.

"So what I set out to create was a focus for the masses of spectators that populate everyday life throughout the Universe. And really, when you think about, we're all spectators of a sort.

"You mean like the poor sods on the agricultural planets and those green faced miners living five miles under Pittsboro."

"Exactly. They could never be heroes in the glossy, glamorous sense. They must have vicarious experience to enjoy any sort of triumph beyond the satisfaction of their mere survival. Mind you that's quite an achievement in itself in some extreme places. Anyway all I had to do was offer these people a hero they could call their own. Someone who was personally and uniquely their friend and confidante as well.

"But importantly, for the concept to be a success in marketing terms, that is, if it was going to make money, the product had to be easy to take home; accessibility was essential to the concept. A doll was the logical choice because of its human form-- people could relate to that form easily, talk to it and enjoy any experience with it that their imagination was capable of. It had to so simple that anybody could enjoy their relationship with the doll with a minimum of effort.

Trance Technology gave me the breakthrough I needed. All you have to do is stare at the doll, turn on the tape to start the trance and you're off the planet and away with the fairies... doing whatever it is you enjoy doing with your best friend -- in the form of Wuzy."

"You make it sound so simple, Mason."

"In that case, maybe I should try explaining it again. Do you have a Wuzy Doll of your own, Amanda?"

"Of course. Everybody has a Wuzy Doll."

"What do you do with it?"

"I'm not about to tell you! Or anyone else. You should know better than anyone that nobody *ever* tells what they do with their own private Wuzy Doll!"

"I disagree. Remember I have all the consumer research on the subject - the latest kick with Wuzy is to talk to your friends about your sexual encounters with Wuzy - believe me, comparing notes is the best new development yet for the fuller enjoyment of Wuzy social dynamics! In fact it could lead to a whole new age of interaction and social communion. Imagine how much nicer the Universe would be to live in if departments and companies would stop making war on each other and sit down and have a good old fashioned heart to heart once in a while. Wuzy could potentially bring everyone together and make it happen you know."

"Now you really are fantasizing!"

"So tell me, Amanda, do you play with your Wuzy or pretend to *be* her? You can live out every fantasy that has ever entered your head, experience it to the full and no-one need ever know - you can remain completely safe, physically and mentally, or you can compare notes and put a little danger into the experience."

"Forget it Mason, you're a weirdo. You already said we hardly know each other. Do you really expect me to go blabbing my innermost secrets with a guy I just met? I mean, sex is one thing, communication is another. Anyway, Mason, what do you do with *your* Wuzy? Assuming you have at least one of the billions you've manufactured!"

"Right. OK. Well, I have one of each model. She wasn't so hot in the very first series. There were subtleties in the face that had to be ironed out. We gave her a nose-job for a start...

But I can safely say that consumer research has long since perfected her."

"I'll bet your 'research' is diabolical!"

"We introduced the prototypes to a typical Outer Planet. One of the grazing stations for the wildebeest herds in Sector Nine. The suicide rate amongst the shepherds was astronomical. Even with all the vidi-screen-games and screen-books and mags they could get their hands on, life was so boring they couldn't face another wildebeest. The only way off the planet was a slit throat just like the wildebeests got."

"What ever happened to good old sex?"

"The wildebeests didn't like the shepherds anymore than the shepherds liked the wildebeests."

"Ooh, you're the beast! You can be really 'off'. That's horrid."

He went on as if he'd never dropped the clanger. "The challenge was to see if the Wuzy Doll could somehow get these bored, disheartened people excited about life and watching the wildebeests again. In the end, I'm pleased to say, the Wuzy Doll made all the difference. A shepherd would come home after a hard day on the turf counting wildebeest; have his dinner of crustaceans..."

"Sounds like they eat better than I do!"

"A small consolation. I mean, if they had to eat steaks at night after herding the goddam things around all day, they really would go nuts. Anyway, after dinner, out came the Wuzy Doll. Placed on top of the coffee table, the whole family could sit around and stare at it. Flick the programme on, click into the trance, and hey presto Wuzy makes it all better for you. All the frustrations dissolve."

Amanda opened up a little more then, "All I can tell you is that I can't get along without my Wuzy sometimes. And for me at least, talking about what Wuzy does for me would jeopardise the unique and special relationship I have with her. Our trust would dissolve if I talked. It would be undermined, distorted and changed forever. I couldn't look her in the eyes again if I blabbed to you about what we do.

"Honestly, Wuzy is the one person in my whole life I can turn to. When I switch her on, she is whatever I make her. Whatever I want her to be."

"Yes. I know what you mean. Everyone's Wuzy is different for him than for anyone else. It's a very special and very sovereign relationship."

Amanda gave him a little squeeze on the arm. "Let's not talk about Wuzy any more, okay?"

"Okay. Let's go see what we can find to eat. I'm starved."

Working Under The Covers

None of the facilities inside the vast liner were very busy. Most of the passengers were still sleeping.

"Let's grab something quick in the self-service bar," Amanda suggested.

It was completely help-yourself. Amanda peeled some fruit with her own two hands. It was grown aboard the ship. Meanwhile Mason sampled some exotic wafers vended from their table.

"You still haven't told me what a Creator is doing way out here on his way to Sol."

"Creating, of course. Or rather doing some preliminary work in that direction." Jackson didn't think it would hurt to tell her that much. How could she possibly affect something he hadn't even really worked out yet?

"Hmmm, creating games way out here? Or something completely different?" she probed, playing mock detective.

"I'd rather not discuss it, but I can tell you that it's not about a game." Mason wished he hadn't said that. Later he would call it a premonition. But the fact was he'd never really learned to keep secrets. Invariably he ran off at the mouth with total strangers, especially female strangers.

Amanda saw through his charming smile and knew he was being serious again. They finished their meal and sat back with fresh drinks. Jackson had a hunch that Amanda wasn't satisfied with his answers and she wanted to know more about what he was up to. He put it down to harmless curiosity. After all, he was blessed with an abundance of the same trait. So it wasn't surprising that he wanted to know why she wanted to know.

"Why would you want to go to Sol?" She finally broke the silence. "It must be one of the ten most boring places in the Quadrant - especially for a Creator! Unless you're into wildebeests."

Mason accidentally slurped ice against the side of his glass and it made an embarrassing noise. "'Scuse me."

"I'll bet somebody is sending you there. You wouldn't go on your own notion." She was pushing for all she was worth.

Jackson still responded by not responding.

"Searching for your roots, maybe? Knew about the Tree of Humankind all along, perhaps?" She finished her drink and put the glass down hard, registering her frustration. The table gulped up the glass and fed it into a clean-machine.

"Hey, this is boring! I do all the talking! All you do is sit there and stare out the ports into space!"

Jackson was doing his best to keep tight-lipped, but he was never going to be able to keep the secret. He might even have told Judy all about it had she been at the office when she was supposed to be.

"Okay, don't tell me if you don't want to. I mean, it must be important - so maybe I don't need to know about it. I'm sorry. I won't bug you about it anymore."

It was too much for him. He couldn't keep it in, no way. Telling Amanda about a tiny corner of the mission wouldn't hurt anything. How could a mining company secretary jeopardise either the advertising plans or Anti-Entropy research?

"Look, I'd tell you if I could. In fact, I don't see any harm in telling you a tiny bit about it actually - I think you'd find it exceptionally interesting. But, well, Central Thought advised me not to talk about it with anyone other than selected government officials."

"Central Thought? Of all people. That does sound exciting!"

She'd believe anything he told her from here on in. But just to test the water he asked, "Not ready to go back to sleep for another week are you?"

"How could I? This is really exciting!"

His body stiffened with delight as his imagination painted a passionate portrait of an inter-stellar encounter with the willowy blonde. But he didn't want her to think he was over-anxious about getting her into his bed or hers. After all, she apparently had the silly notion that he was some sort of a romantic gentleman! And she already warned him she hated the animalistic approach.

"Let's go skiing," he suggested unexpectedly.

"What? Oh. Uh. Sure. Okay. Where?"

"I thought the ski field would be good place to start!" he chuckled.

"I didn't know they had one!"

"Yes. It's one of the reasons I booked passage on this ship. It's a far more enjoyable way to pass away the light years than sleeping. They don't have a very big range of mountains - it's only a Mark Three Ski Field."

"Fantastic! I haven't been skiing in a moon's age!"

The ski field was a three-dimensional projected marvel, affecting the same convincing virtual reality illusion as the space walk in the Laser Bar. In reality, the ski-field occupied a mere 20 metres by 30 metres by 50 metres inside the vast ship. But you could press a button and programme the area to simulate any one of twenty-five famous mountains from the 15,000 metre peaks of the huge Ceti system planets, to cloud-soft novice runs kids were often given for their birthdays.

Of course, in the tri-di projections, the skiers move very little, but the mountains can move up to 200 kilometres an hour beneath your feet. The feeling is total exhilaration. The runs can be as tough as you want them to be and as strenuous as your own style and proficiency of skiing.

Two hours later, Mason and Amanda checked their skis and boots back into the ridiculous but courteous little alpine reception robot dressed head to toe in Tyrolean costume at the ski desk, and then headed for the sauna rooms.

"Shall we undress together or separately?"

110

"Don't mind," Jackson said, not believing his luck. "Wherever you undress I will be grateful."

Amanda winked, and blew him a kiss. "Just give me a minute then." She slipped into a private cubicle and sent a short message.

TOP SECRET

Memorandum to T R Malone
Chief of General Industries Research Services
From: Field Operative 7X-14
Re: The Jolly Roger
Have made contact with subject aboard Pan Gal 217.
Confirm subject working under contract to Government Advertising with brief from CT.
My cover expires on Titan. Subject presumed to be proceeding to Earth via Nixon. Standing by to resume cover on return Pan Gal.

Moonstruck

The translation to the Earth System Gate near Nixon took several minutes from the Trans Port on Titan. Mason Jackson and Amanda Darling had parted quietly but fondly, promising to get together again before she had to leave the system to join her night class for a weekend field trip on a 'dig' in the Pleiades. He promised to call her - and with a little luck, maybe they could take the same flight out - who could know where things might go from there. Nowhere of course but it was fun pretending.

Mason stood at a window screen. There was nothing to see during the jump past Jupitron, Maras and the Icarian asteroid belt - the starliner's course was plotted to avoid dangerous large bodies of rock and invisible radiation pockets anyway. But he was looking forward to the first glimpse of ancient Earth since 2006 and the crater-pocked surface of the Moon. He wondered what the rambling old space architecture that now covered the Moon, according to Amanda's description, would actually look like.

As the ship slowed down, blackness became a blur of soft light. The blur sorted itself into myriad specks then pixilated into a dazzling shape. And suddenly a medium-sized moon filled his view. The moonscape surprised him. Not the dusty craters he knew through binoculars from neither his childhood, nor the tidy terra-formed lushness the Quadrant had provided for habitation in most places, but a pre-Empire low-tech sprawl of sheet metal and rivets, continuously covering the surface. Nothing Amanda said had prepared him for this scene. Not a square inch of open ground was to be seen. Not a crater. Not a scaric of dusty surface.

These hideous low-tech huts were appalling to look at – though Amanda's night class might have appreciated them as primitive relics of a barbarian age of architecture vomited onto the moon's surface. The structures were pathetic in comparison to the glossy art-form environments of the Capitol. The great graphics of space traffic systems, signs and arrows a hundred kilometres across, testified to earlier eons of local space travel. A few garden domes spotted around the equator provided a belt of green oases among the grey, corroded mega blocks of inhabited metal. A huge crystal billboard caught the refracted light of the local sun and flashed a prismatic message: "Eat at Joe's!"

What did they eat? The same old greasy hamburgers? And who the hell was Joe? A shoe manufacturer had put up a hoarding with one rather clever but clearly plagiarized of writing that Mason need not jot into his memory for future use: 'One small step for man...' Docking indicator lights flashed on inside every compartment and corridor. A chorus of descending musical voices counted down in accompaniment to the approaching shuttle ships. 'Three-Two-One. Ta-da!'

The long space journey was over. He was now only a quarter of a million miles from Earth. The ship's trajectory had thus far kept him from seeing the planet. Customs inspections and other entry processing had been finalised back on Titan, but Earth-Nixon apparently felt the need to do it their own way. A Customs Ship coasted up alongside the ship. Announcements came over the speakers in a sing-song voice that Jackson loathed. "Nice to have had you aboard for the journey..." and all that usual crap about hoping to see you on your return flight. At least no one said, 'have a nice day.' How do you make friends with a robot anyway?

Most of the nearly three thousand sleepers were still drowsy, even though they'd been firmly wakened for the descent to Titan Trans Port ages ago. They staggered around trying to find their legs and the way to the toilets. A really disgusting, foul smelling horde of humanity – Mason judged this lot would have slept through anything.

A man and woman in dark green uniforms came through the corridors, looking into each compartment. "Sorry to inconvenience you, sir, but ships of this size are obviously not allowed into Earth's delicate atmosphere. A local tour-craft will take you from here. Where on Earth would you like to go?"

"What's the capital city?" a woman asked, ashamed she didn't already know.

"Earth has no capitol as such, but New York is the official port of entry for out-system visitors."

"That'll do just fine."

"Me, too." Jackson piped up.

"I'll ensure you get there at the best possible time."

"Thank you." How nice to deal with real live people for a change.

The officer handed Jackson a small brightly enamelled chip. Red and white stripes on it and a blue corner with rows of tiny white stars." Just hang on to that and you can't go wrong. It's like having a VIP first class ticket. All your necessary details have now been transferred into the chip in your New York travel card."

Jackson wondered just what 'necessary details' entailed, and why the card looked so much like an ancient American flag, but didn't get the chance to ask.

"Please follow Officer Francis to your new seat. Your luggage pod is being transferred now."

Jackson had only the one small bag with him, so the line about the pod was obviously part of a standard spiel.

Another window seat. Another take off. Another surprise.

An Official Visit

"**M**iss Francis, why are we going back to the Moon?"

"I'll be with you in a moment, sir." And she was. "It's part of your Stars and Stripes Travel Package, Mr. Jackson. A trip to the Nixon is built into your ticket with Pan Galaxy," she carried on with the script, "You'll see where man first set foot on Nixon over a hundred

centuries ago, then..."

"Some other time, maybe. I'm ticketed for New York, though I sincerely doubt I'm going to get there today at this rate." Jackson made a point of looking at his timekeeper. A quaint little habit he had retained for several thousand years.

"Passengers for New York always arrive there at 0900. As you can see, the local time is already 2100, but don't worry, a comfortable room on Nixon is waiting for you, so you'll arrive nice and fresh in the morning." Somehow she held a smile through every word, even 'worry'.

"Why must I arrive at 0900? What's wrong with landing at night? Is someone afraid of the dark?

"Don't you believe in New York, sir?" She looked perplexed.

"What kind of question is that? What's to believe? I just want to have a quiet look around Earth, that's all!"

"Then you do *believe* in Earth?"

"I believe in myself. That's always been enough." Jackson was getting to the end of his tether. All this way, and a travel officer wanted to discuss philosophy.

"May I see your travel card, sir?"

"If you must."

She looked at it for only a moment. Flashed the smile again and handed the red, white and blue card back to him. "Don't worry, you'll love New York, and you'll love it on Nixon too!"

"Thanks for the hard sell, Officer Francis. I haven't seen Earth yet, but Nixon looks like a heap of absolute junk and an archaeologist's paradise."

"Do you sleep better alone or with company?" Miss Francis said casually. He hoped he heard her correctly. Pan Galaxy certainly seemed to understand the nuances of successful customer relations. Recognition, that's the big one. In fact, now that was noticing the little things, he could see Miss Francis was really quite attractive if you took off the plain green uniform. Which is exactly what he hoped to do before he left Nixon. But before Jackson could answer, Miss Francis added, "I can't get to sleep without an injection, I'm afraid." She sounded decidedly helpless. Mason took the bait.

"You have my room number, and as luck would have it, I am a part-time masseur," Jackson replied, with pride and mock authority. Twenty minutes later, he had checked into his room, lost in the labyrinth of the Neil Armstrong Hotel. Officer Francis had joked about there being fifty Armstrong Hotels on Nixon, at least".

He freshened up, changed into a comfortable lightweight cas-suit, tie-less of course, and picked up his card to leave just as the door announced a caller. It was Officer Francis. And she had changed into something casual as well. The little green uniform had given way to something that looked like thermal armour, but apparently was all the rage here on Nixon, judging by the fashion posters in the hotel corridors.

"Am I too early, Mr Jackson?" she said teasingly.

"No, I like punctuality. Shall we eat here or have you arranged a table somewhere on my Pan Galaxy Clout Class package deal?

"Room service will be here with an a la carte table in a moment. We can order from it and relax in privacy here... unless you'd like to go out?"

116

"I like your idea better. This is one great Travel Service you have here. I didn't know Pan Galaxy were so thorough. Why don't they promote it?"

They sat facing each other on two tiny float cushions.

"It's a local Nixon extra. It helps to make up for the lack of amenities on our somewhat ramshackle satellite. As far as promoting it goes, I don't know, perhaps they should, perhaps they shouldn't. We rely on word-of-mouth mostly."

A table set elegantly for two appeared at the door. Jackson invited it to come in and take up a position between them. Menus appeared on the eating panels, set into the top of the table. The words and pictures of the dishes were projected from underneath.

"Your travelcard said you're a Creator. I've always wanted to meet a Creator."

Mason smiled confidently, scarcely believing his luck might be in again. "What else does it say about me?"

"It says you're single, a lot older than me, and from the centre of the Universe."

"I'm even older than I look. The age, what does it say? 250 or so? That really only covers my second life."

"That's a new line. But I might have expected a fresh approach from a Creator."

He acknowledged her delight with a smile, "And do you have a card so I can read all about *you*?"

"No need. You're under no obligation. I don't expect to see you again, but in case we do meet, perhaps on your return trip, my name is Alexx, Officer Alexx Francis. I'm 117. I was born on the artificial world of Roton and I'm also single."

"So when did you come here? How did you get this job?"

"The usual way. About three years ago, I sat for the civil service exams on Roton and Giro, took the standard battery of aptitude tests, applied for a life of travel, and the next day I was offered this job - I can stay as long as I like. Getting a transfer is no problem either."

"You like it here, then, do you?""Yes, very much. There's something about seeing Earth everyday that I can't quite explain... anyway, I love the work." She looked straight into his eyes and winked slowly. Jackson wasn't sure if it was sexy or just cheap and he didn't care.

"I suppose you meet a lot of men..." her eyes dropped to the menu. He wondered if he had said something wrong. "Sorry, I guess I talk too much. What can you tell me about Earth?" He busied himself with the selection panel, ordering grilled proteins and sautéed carbos, and goblets of Earth wine.

"I can tell you word for word everything that's written in the in-flight brochure and various segments of the Lonely Galaxy's Guide to the Sol System as it pertains to general descriptions of the major land masses and ancient capitals, landmarks, etcetera, on the planet's surface. Beyond that, depending on the length of your stay, I suggest you talk personally with some real live Earthlings. Though I dare say that, in the true sense, there are very few real Earthlings."

"Presumably that depends on your definition of an Earthling?"

"Exactly. You see, almost all the Earthlings now live here on Nixon."

"Yes, I've heard that. So who lives on Earth?!"

"Mostly maintenance men, a few protected races of savages in 'life science' museums and of course, tourist industry support staff."

"Tourist industry? I thought nobody ever went to Earth any more. Unless you mean the daily commuting I heard about from a fellow passenger on 217."

"Yes. That's what I meant. Millions go every day."

"But..."

"But they come from the moon, Nixon."

"You mean Earthlings who now live on Nixon are constantly running up and down playing tourists on

Earth? They must be loony! Absolute screaming bonkers!"

"No. Just in love with Earth."

"Why don't they just move down there? It doesn't make sense. Here they are, cramped onto Nixon with not an inch to spare, when there's an entire planet down there - it looks beautiful to me-- why don't they live there?"

"You've more or less answered your own question. The moon is inhabited by nearly 100 million Earthlings. Before the era of the Great Lift Offs, Earth was a lush green planet with a highly competitive variety of flourishing civilisations. But as the planet inevitably became crowded, conflicts evolved into wars, industrialism ran rampant and the planet seemed doomed to self-destruction. It's all in your programme notes."

Jackson listened intently, knowingly.

"The Great Lift Offs were large scale migrations off the planet to colonise..."

It was a familiar pattern Jackson had encountered throughout his travels in each of the Quadrants, and a phenomenon well documented in The Histories kept by Central Thought. People with a common interest would form a company large enough to build or buy a great ship or fleet of ships and embark to start a fresh life away from their enemies.

"So who are the Nixonites? And what are they like?" he asked.

"The last true friends of the Earth. A community who now dedicate their lives and their civilisation to looking after the treasures of Earth."

"So why don't they live down there, closer to their work?"

"Because theirs is a labour of love. That probably sounds corny, but it's true. Maybe they don't want to mess the place up again."

Mason and Alexx sliced into thick juicy protein mats that still sizzled on the dining panels. Impressive cuisine, he thought as he tucked in. The hot steamy carbos released mouth-watering aromas that would be difficult for all but the most advanced Impulse Beam makers to duplicate with any authenticity.

"These people do not want to desecrate their home planet ever again. It's taken them thousands and thousands of years to get Earth's environment back to being virtually pollution-free."

"Seems like they keep it as a kind of shrine of remembrance. I can't wait to see it. Maybe the rest of the Quadrant should follow their example and clean up their act as well." Jackson asked the table for another glass of wine. "And yet, the same people who cleaned up their planet do not seem to have the same respect for the moon, the, uh, Nixon. They seem happy to live up here in rusting metal boxes, kilometres deep, in relative squalor. Extraordinary."

"Eighty kilometres deep at the equator, a little less at the poles -- measured from the top floor apartments to the paved surface. From the programme notes, word for word."

"A steel ant hill," Jackson joked, and then thought, "It's not human, is it? After all, this is the way they live on a day to day basis. The cold steel is their reality. Down there on Earth -- the gardens, the farms, and the wildernesses -- isn't that their *fantasy?*

"Nixon is the biggest slum in the Quadrant. I agree with you there, Mason. I think it's disgusting!"

Jackson wiped the corners of his lips and poured some more wine for her.

Miss Francis continued "With their beloved planet Earth preserved as a vast culture garden a short space hop away, they really have all they want."

"There are planets larger and more beautiful than Earth, I assure you."

"I agree, but not to an Earthling."

Jackson knew there was no rational answer to satisfy such an emotionally based argument.

Earthfall

Mason Jackson awoke abruptly, breathing heavily. Officer Francis was gone."Damn! Dreams like that are enough to make a guy go blind. Where the hell are my pants? What the hell time is it? And where is Alexx? My wallet! Good, still there. Crazy damned night. What did she want from me, anyway?"

After a short sharp drink of nutrient breakfast, an irradiation dry-cleaning of his birthday suit, and a flash session with his laser razor, Jackson made his way to the Earth shuttle station. His red, white and blue card gave him access to the queues for New York. A few minutes after that, he relaxed in a body chair with a view of Nixon shrinking away to a large dull grey disc. Ahead, but as yet out of sight, Earth, his ultimate destination, was at last within reach.

The digital readout on the back of the seat in front of him was counting down the kilometres to landing... 57,000... 53,000. The ship turned. Jackson peered yet again into a black void. The leading edge of a great arc of bright white light started on the left side of his viewport and spread across to the right, revealing a tremendous globe enrobed in reflected light.

Earth was an astounding swirl of blue and white. Clouds and oceans, interrupted with continental splotches of green and brown. Spiral storms marched across the hazy surface. Jackson stared. He had forgotten how a planet with its own weather systems looked. It was most unnatural and not a little unnerving to remember that this had been home throughout his first short and painful life. Pangs of sadness stirred within him for those he had left behind a hundred thousand years ago. If he had time, he'd look them up in the Library of the Tree of Humankind-- if there was anything to see. Was he on it himself? How did

121

they treat Resurrectees on Earth these days? He'd soon find out.

Earth grew larger by the second as the shuttle settled closer towards a green coastline washed by a great blue ocean. He peered and squinted, hoping to see signs of life -- man-made objects that might mark the progress of Earth's history. He fully expected the ancient cosmo-plex constructions of Nixon to have been dwarfed by the engineers of Earth. But there were no mega-structures to be seen from this altitude; only the straight lines and geometric curves of transport routes outlined a human presence below.

35,000...31,000. A patch of grey began to grow on the green coastline. He stared. A city? Yes, a great ancient city. Once it had spread in his first life time four hundred miles along the north-east coast of the North American continent. From Boston to Baltimore and south into Virginia it was one of Earth's first industrial-age megalopolis if there was such a word. Jackson felt a new twinge in his stomach as his eyes recognised the location where the Hudson meets the Atlantic near Long Island. This is where he had died. This was where his cryonic capsule had been warehoused for millennia. It was all coming back to him.

A sharp chill started at the base of his spine and rapidly sprang upwards, stopping briefly to cause more knotting in his stomach. Jackson found tears in his eyes as his face contorted with the memories of forgotten faces of people he had loved and those who had loved him. And he began to sob with pain. The homecoming pain of a man gone too long, gone far too far.

New York, New York

Mason stood on the observation tower platform of the Northern Hemisphere Bank Building trying to take it all in. Residing now as he did at the centre of the Quadrant, he'd seen bigger cities by far, but it wasn't everyday you stood on the 471st level in the *open air*. Besides, this and most of the other buildings in the skyline were not in his memory. The beacon of the signal tower soared another 100 metres above him, making the building a full 1800 metres in height. The ancient Earthling obsession with skyscrapers was in his blood. New York was still exciting to him. But skyscrapers were certainly not unique to Earth. Other planets expressed themselves and competed too for the title of tallest or longest or whatever. On Arcadia, skyscrapers were monuments to self-greatness - the tallest on Arcadia being some 30 kilometres in a single spire. Indeed, each Arcadian city was housed and sculptured into such structures. From space, the small planet bristled with so many great spikes that it resembled a steel porcupine.

Here on Earth, the scale was different, but in some respects more impressive. An archaic note from his first life rose from forgotten brain cells – in 1980, there were 235,000 building 10 storeys or more on this island of Manhattan. Today, as he visited, on this little island between the East River and the Hudson, the programme notes stated there were half a million buildings of a hundred levels or more. In some ways it was a waste. Why not build a single cost-efficient structure like the Arcadians did?

Of course, in some ways the Earthling slum on Nixon was even more impressive than the Arcadian spires. On Nixon, virtually the entire surface had been built outward to a height of 80 kilometres. They had not all been built at once. Indeed, there was some concern recently that the older buildings on the bottom might one day give way to the oppressive weight from above and bring the whole amazing labyrinth crashing down onto itself! Of course, the 1/6 gravity on Nixon helped substantially in lightening the load and keeping the building aloft.

Looking down, and up and everywhere from this astounding vantage point, Jackson found it hard to believe that nobody lived in New York. It looked so busy. The traffic in the sky and just above the ground was buzzed and bustled as intensely as any place in the Quadrant.

"Have you seen The Subway? I hear it's the engineering marvel of the planet!" A total stranger, a bearded man in a grey cas-suit and smart grey boots was looking at him.

"No, not recently. What's so special about it, anyway?"

"Apparently, now this is going back several millennia, New York had a major underground transport system. That's nothing to get excited about, but it's so quaint and full of paintings. Primitive, of course, but quite fascinating as an art form. It was all done by the pre-schizoid master, Graffiti. Have you heard of him?"

"Hasn't everyone?" Mason just smiled.

"Like to have a look with me?"

"I don't know if I'll have time, really. I have to be back at the station in another two hours. Thanks anyway."

"Plenty of time!" the stranger pressed.

"I'm afraid I have a great many other things I want to see as well." Jackson was trying to walk away.

"Oh well, you can always see the Subway next trip. Have a nice day."

Jackson looked out across the city. Standing atop the tallest building was something like looking down from a low-level satellite reconnoitring a new civilisation. For a moment he

wondered if this planet really was the birthplace of Man and The Mother Planet of the human race. Was this really where it all began? Not New York of course, but right here on Earth? In Africa? Or the Nile Valley? Tigris-Euphrates? Harappa? Did Earth still keep the answers secret?

"Come on! We have to go to the petroleum museum. Father said we *must!*" A girl, probably not more than 11 or 12, was pulling her big brother's arm. He obviously wasn't interested in seeing the petroleum museum at all, no matter what was in it.

There were tourists everywhere. All ages, shapes and sizes. All in fact, Nixonites. Jackson's mind wandered back to the hotel room on Nixon the night before. Was it all true - what Alexx had said about no-one living on Earth? That it was just a place for Earthling tourists. Or was there more? The visits seemed more like pilgrimages. And why was the Library here in this place and not at the centre of the Quadrant matrix, a division of Central Thought?

Then it suddenly occurred to him that Alexx's knowledge of Earth didn't quite tally with what Amanda had told him. Odd? Perhaps not. Amanda had been out of the Sol System for a long time while Alexx, working here as she did, ought to know the inside story. It was perfectly natural for two people from different parts of the Quadrant to have different knowledge and views about a place so extremely remote and unpublicised as Earth.

He stared out across the view until a sign caught his eye on the top of a very old building about 300 stories down. He needed a better view but he was sure he knew that sign. Not the building - it was too new for him to know - but there was something familiar, very familiar about the sign. Jackson hired a viewing frame at the souvenir counter and walked to the edge of the deck. Looking through the frame, he lined up the centre dot with the sign and activated the viewer. Instantly he could see the sign as close up as he liked.

There was a graphic design depicting two human hands protectively cupping a small spot of light -- the spark of

Life. Beneath the symbol was the sans serif logo-type of the New York Metropolitan Death Insurance Company. Again, as severely as before, Jackson was uncontrollably gripped with a sickening pain in the top of his stomach. The pain of knowing the unknown, wrestling with the long-forgotten and remembering it as if it had happened this morning. He had died, was frozen and arose again from the dead.

As the subway train pulled away from Times Square station, a man unconsciously stroked his beard as he marvelled over the colourful panels painted by Graffiti. He spoke quietly into a tiny microphone.

"Memorandum to T. R. Malone from Field Operative 6F-71, Re: Jolly Roger. Have made contact with subject on planet Earth, System Sol, City of New York. Continuing surveillance..."

Lexington Avenue

Jackson stood across the street from the copper-glass reflections of the New York Metropolitan Death Insurance Company. He stared up at the cupped hands graphic, and then let his eyes fall to the entrance at street level. A twenty-third century replicar that might have passed for a VW wheezed past in front of him. Jackson instinctively coughed, but to his astonishment the car left no exhaust.

He reached the entrance of the building and put his hand on the door bar. It didn't move, but it spoke to him in a civilised manner, "I'm afraid the building is closed today."

"Sorry to disturb you. I'm a visitor." Jackson said.

"Everyone is a visitor these days." the door responded.

"Yes, I know, but I first came to this door in the year 2005."

"I'm sorry; my records do not go back that far."

"I only wanted to have a quiet look around."

"I'm afraid the building is closed today."

"So you said. Perhaps I should come back tomorrow."

"Everyone should come back to New York tomorrow. But the building is closed every day. I can only open the door for maintenance engineers and only then on the thirteenth Tuesday of odd numbered years."

"And this year is?"

"This is an even numbered year."

"Somehow I knew you'd say that."

"Have a nice day and thank you for visiting New York."

Jackson sauntered over to a water sculpture and sat down close enough to feel the spray on his heated forehead. His face yellowed in the glow of the copper coated cladding of the nearby building. He didn't feel particularly well. His stomach really hurt. Passersby noted with curiosity how he held his wrist close up to his face. Light blue veins stood out a little in the soft flesh below Jackson's palms. He stared in awe, watching the steady pulsing of the blood flowing within. He could feel it rushing when he pressed his fingers to the skin. Then he put his wrist up to his ears to see if he could hear the rush. A patrol craft came to a stop about five metres above his head - just to watch the strange antics of the eccentric tourist-- then scurried off.

Through dissociative thought training and a regimen of mental dieting Jackson had put Earth and the 20th century completely out of his mind but it had taken one hundred and seventy years of trying. Now the effort was all undone. Sitting here in front of the Death Insurance Building, a torrent of memories came back to tease him, like an alcoholic torturing himself by holding a glass of wine to his lips--smelling the bouquet, but daring not to drink.

So much had happened. He had restarted his marketing communications career with the help of Central Thought and had found new professional fulfilment among the stars. As far as commercial writing and creative marketing was concerned, he was as much at home in the 121st century as in the Twentieth. But now, the 20th century was rushing back at him, ripping at his guts and cornering his conscience. He had suppressed the past, hidden it, and buried it so deep he had thought it gone forever. Not so, and now he had to confront it head on or lose his sanity.

A new realisation was dawning on him: He'd won his gamble to have a second life and in some ways his second life was even better than his first life. But now he was being made to pay for his flesh.

"There's no such thing as a free lunch, "he reminded himself." It's the law of cause and effect. Yin and Yang. Harmony and contrast. Give and take back."

He'd always felt indebted to Dr. Kowalski and her Resurrection Team but now he wasn't so sure. Why did the government provide the funds for *his* Resurrection? He'd never been famous. In the Mississippi of life, he had been but a single atom of H2 0. Maybe the Pirates had taken over the Resurrection Programme and turned him into a sleeper agent for a sinister plot, placing an electronic minder in his brain like they did in 20th Century sci-fi films. He might even now be totally under their control, and as soon as he strayed from approved thought, they'd stun him into obeisance. Ridiculous. He was fantasizing. They wouldn't even accept his money when he offered to pay them for the resurrection service -- and the gods knew he had countless money accrued from his savings over the millennia.

At first he didn't notice the maintenance man standing next to him, trying to tell him the curfew was only a few minutes from now. Jackson stared trance-like into the reflective glass on the NYMDI building. In his mind he saw again the friends and colleagues he'd left behind in Melbourne with no explanation in 2005. He assumed they'd think he'd gone off and committed suicide because of his terminal illness. Those he had included in his will had quite a battle in the courts to get the insurance money. With no body, there was no proof of death. The circumstances pointed to suicide and threatened to negate any claims on collecting legacies from the insurance policy. Eventually after years of wrangling and delays, the money came through to his beneficiaries. Suicide could not be proven either.

If only they had known what he had done. Had achieved. No! He'd achieved nothing. He'd only taken a gamble and won. Any drunk or drug addict without a brain could have done the same. Jackson was still entranced in memories and self-pity when a night patrol picked him up, checked his red, white and blue travel card and delivered him to the spaceport for the last flight to Nixon.

Alexx

Hours later when Mason awoke in bed in his room in the Neil Armstrong Hotel. He was surprised to find he wasn t alone.

"Are you hungry?"

"Alexx? What are you doing here?

"I hope you don't mind that I dropped in on you like this. Some maintenance men on Lexington Avenue in New York reported to our office they had found you somewhat non-compus. I thought you might need a

friend as well as a nurse."

"It's very kind of you, Alexx. God, I'm sorry for all this. All the trouble. I don't know how to make it up to you."

"Think nothing of it. What happened down there anyway? The hotel doctor had a look at you and said physically you were a hundred per cent. In fact, he rather admired the job somebody did on your lungs."

"They're not mine."

"What's not yours?"

"The lungs. That's the problem. I don't deserve to have them."

"Don't be ridiculous! That's an absurd, and frankly old-fashioned attitude I haven't heard for ages. Nobody's walking around with everything they started out with! What's

gotten into you? How do you think we live hundreds of years? Surgery, transplants, technology makes it all possible."

"I suppose so" Jackson glumly responded.

"Hey, where's the super-confident Man-about-the-Universe who thinks he's C.T.'s gift to women? Where's the sexy silver-haired fox on the flight from Titan?"

"I - I don't know. There really isn't anything to be confident about, when I really think about it. It's all just a sham."

Alexx sat on the edge of the bed. "Come on, everybody's plastic and pretence, in varying degrees. So tell me what happened down there. I want to know. Maybe I can help. Besides, I prefer the other Mason Jackson, not this one."

"I *remembered*. That's all. Remembered pieces of my past that I would not like to discuss. So can we just leave it at that?"

"You look terrible, you know. I had quite a time convincing the Psyches not to keep you under observation for a few days. I said I knew you and I would be responsible for you. So buck up!"

"I'm sorry, Alexx, I really am, but I can't discuss it, please try and understand."

"I am trying. But you really are being impossible!"

"Calm down, please. It's my problem, not yours. I have to live with it, not you. I have to come to terms with it and no one else."

"You sound almost suicidal! Damn!" She looked at the ceiling in utter frustration, "What the hell am I doing here anyway. I was only trying to be your friend."

"The easiest way out is the door."

"Are you asking me to leave?"

"Of course not. I'm just asking you not to get too close."

"You know you'd be a lot better at making love if you really did get close to someone, anyone. The problem is that men have a brain and a penis, but only enough blood circulating to operate one at a time."

"Thanks for the ball-breaking compassion."

"You're one of these aloof bastards who never really puts himself on the line for anyone but himself! Oh, you like to claim you get close to people sometimes, that you're a great communicator and all that crap, but you always hold something back - always hold onto something that you'll never let anybody else get near."

"Alright. If you must know, it's just that I'm afraid of *losing* myself. Well maybe that's a little inaccurate. It's easy for women; they only have to fake orgasms. Guys like me have to fake entire relationships."

"Good! OK. Interesting. I'm not sure I understand you completely yet, but we're making a start here. You want me to feel sorry for you, I don't. Let's re-focus on 'losing yourself'. OK? I think there's hope for you yet. But I wonder if the frightening part is that if you didn't hold anything back you might actually *find* yourself."

"Why me? Why are you talking like this to me, Alexx? What do you care? We just met.

What the hell do you really care?"

"Something else happened to you down there on Earth, didn't it? What was it? What did you

remember when you were down on the surface – remember from your dim past? Tell me and maybe we can work from there."

"I told you I remembered. I mean really remembered all kinds of details. It was extremely unsettling. I was born there. And I died there. Right there on Lexington Avenue in the centre of New York City."

"You! Born on Earth? When?"

"In 1945. At the end of a great war."

"That's over a hundred -- of course! You're a Resurrectee! That explains the lungs and the archaic attitude that you don't deserve them."

"So now you know I'm a freak."

"Will you stop feeling pity for yourself? You're a lucky fellow. Practically unique, but not a freak. What a marvellous opportunity you've had! You know there are only fifteen or twenty thousand of you people in the whole Universe?"

"The Resurrection Club lists fewer than six thousand members now, actually."

"First you're a Creator, now on top of that you're a Resurrectee? Fantastic! You're quite the cool dude. You have simply got to tell me all you can about ancient Earth. I'm dying to know!"

Jackson still sulked. "Lovely choice of words, Alexx."

"Listen, why are you acting so silly about all this?" She was starting to get bored with his melodramatic behaviour.

"I had suppressed these memories so hard and so long I had forgotten most of it. I mean, blocking it all out made adapting to my new life a lot easier. Look, Alexx, I didn't book my ticket here for old times' sake. It was just another destination on another job. It wasn't until I was in New York that the recognition of the past swelled up inside and overwhelmed me."

"Right there on Lexington Avenue?"

"In front of the Insurance building. It was the same company, the same address I bought the Death Insurance policy from in 2005. I died at that address on Lexington Avenue a few months later... early in 2006. Today was like walking into a graveyard and seeing your own headstone. I wanted so much to live. I was willing to try anything. But I kept my resurrection plans secret from my friends -- everyone who knew me in fact.

"You didn't tell them?"

"They never knew. What did they need to know for? Besides, it added mystique to the memory of me."

"Does this story get any shallower or can I still paddle out?"

"Oh, they were well looked after - my investments, my insurance policies... but they never knew I had made arrangements for my life after death."

"I guess it was a pretty big risk in those days though I find it impossible to imagine how dreadfully primitive life must have been in the 21st century."

"It literally pains me to remember all this. Everyone's life was so short. My mother and father, my friends. I feel I've cheated them somehow. Betrayed them. I've lived several of their lifetimes already -- I've had enormous opportunity to get things right, to get my life right and they only had one crack at it..."

"Don't be absurd! You made your own chance! Death is the only one who's been cheated. Look at me! In some ways I'm much older than you are! I don't want to die, nobody does. Snap yourself out of it, Mason Jackson!"

Alexx called up a hot cup of stimulant for him, brought it to the bedside, and propped up his pillows.

"Thanks, Alexx. I didn't know if I could talk to you in such ways or not."

"It takes time to get to know people, Mason. Even with life lasting up to 2000 years, sometimes it's too much trouble to spend a few extra minutes. Well, I've done my good deed for the day. I'm going home to grab what's left of the night."Goodnight, sweet Alexx. You have been my friend when I needed one most."

"Goodnight, Mason." Alexx hesitated at the door, looked back to the bed and added, "You should look up your family in the Library. It might set your mind to rest to find out what happened to them."

Tall Corn

The next day, Jackson joined the millions of day-trippers down to Earth again. And for the first time in his second life he appreciated the meaning of the ancient phrase 'coming down to Earth'. It meant coming down to all the old values.

Coming into land was coming home again. It didn't matter that practically everything he saw was different from the way it was in the 20th century. The land was the same. Only the objects upon it had been altered. And even then, a surprisingly large amount of the 20th century had been preserved as working exhibits. It was all part of the Library of the Tree of Humankind.

Today he had decided to go to Iowa. Back to where he was born. As he left the arrival platform at Humanity Spaceport and headed for Grand Central Station, he saw an ancient plastic back-lit sign that triggered a more recent memory - The Subway. He wondered if the guy with the beard enjoyed the graffiti. The last time he'd been down there was in September of 1964. He and a college buddy had taken a Greyhound bus from Mason City in North Iowa to see the great World's Fair here in New York; well actually it was Flushing Meadows.

Now it seemed the subway had become a sort of history buff's paradise - a unique encounter with early New York. Mason bounced down the steep stairs into the station. Not the rushing crush of purposeful people racing to catch a train in the days he remembered but calm orderly groups patiently waiting a few seconds on gleaming self-cleaning sterilized platforms. Jackson stared fascinated at the walls of the station. The ceramic tiles that graced them might once have been found in the best bathrooms in the country.

But New York had found its own special use for them. Countless messages, murals, pleas, slogans, threats, phone numbers and advertisements were painted, scribbled, scrawled, carved, chipped and plastered over every square centimetre to heights that only a pole vault champion might reach. And to think that people now attributed them to a single 'artist' named Graffiti! But to Jackson it certainly didn't represent any sort of New York Italian Renaissance in the least. Graffiti was the old familiar 'the scrawl of the wild'. Jackson read the walls and discovered real wit all over the place.

'God is an American
'No. He's Puerto Rican'
'You're both wrong. He's a woman'

'Bob loves Bill, 3167'
'The Creeper was here, 2334'
'Nuke the Rich'
'Freeze. Wait. Regenerate! 2991'

'Down with Evolutionist propaganda!'

'He's gone. He's not here now. He's in the hills. But he'll
be back when we need him'

Who in the world was 'he'? The hero that people always hoped would emerge to sort out problems in times of disaster, frustration or consternation. It was just an expression of Hope. It seemed the whole gamut of social history on Earth from the 19th Century to the time of the great leap to Nixon was all there to read and work out if you had the time. Jackson did not.

Getting to Iowa was as easy as walking through the appropriately marked tele-gate at Grand Central Station. The tele-booth said Iowa over the door and Iowa it was when he stepped out the other side. Right in the middle of a farmyard, 500 kilometres beyond the black stone obelisk that marked where Chicago had once been.

The farm was typically laid out with a white-painted timber frame 19th century American Gothic farmhouse. A big red barn, three huge grain silos, 240 acres of corn and rows of pig shelters. It was very similar to one his Uncle Eugene had managed just after World War II. The farmer and his family ware dressed in clothes typical of a much later period than Jackson had experienced in his childhood. Like the day-trippers, the farmer lived on Nixon. Because he worked here, though, he had a priority transport card and commuting took practically no time at all.

The smell of new mown hay had Jackson sneezing in no time. The pig sty had him holding his nose to reduce the likelihood of throwing up. And the dust in the barn watered his eyes. Still, he went walking through the tall rows of corn, the black Iowa earth sinking softly under his borrowed boots. This was just the kind of communicative experience he was looking for.

Could he convince the trillions who lived on the other worlds that such a first had real life experience was worth saving? Not merely replicating somewhere else? It was a solid relevant thought. His creative mind was on to something. Yes. Perhaps if he could collect a series of such experiences from Earth and translate them into impulses for the Beam ... then he had the kernel of a marketable idea.

Leaning against the out-sized tyre of a replica tractor, a communication strategy began to take shape in his mind. For Jackson a carefully structured strategy was a necessary discipline to creativity. It always began with establishing his objectives, then working out the method. The details of the actual execution of the Idea were the last little pieces to fall into place.

He had always worked in this way and he was certain it was a major reason for his success. Most creative people, he knew, came up with a technique or an executional idea first, and worked back to construct a concept and rationale

137

to suit. Jackson considered such an approach to be 'cutting corners at the expense of the fabric'.

He preferred to think of his audience in communication as a friend he was writing a letter to, not just a mass of faces in a million places. Because his objective was to persuade his audience, he naturally expected to achieve a certain response to his message. As he walked the rows of tall Iowa corn, his shoulders slapping the long flappy leaves, he drafted his first battle plans. As a result of seeing whatever screen-messages or receiving any formulated impulse he might concoct, he wanted his audience to know, think, feel and believe certain things about Earth.

First: He wanted everyone he could reach to Know that Earth is the home planet of the genus Homo sapiens, the starting point of the human race.

Second: He wanted everyone to Think that Earth was in danger of being needlessly destroyed.

Third: He wanted everyone to Feel a sense of belonging (as he did) to Earth - as the Mother of Mankind. If everyone felt kinship as a child to its mother, then all of Mankind would rally to protect their mother.

And finally he wanted everyone to Believe that Earth was worth the price of salvation.

But what if Earth was *not* the home planet of the genus Homo sapiens? In his own time on Earth there had been much conjecture about the possibility of UFOs -- and science fiction literature often put forward the theory that Earth was colonised by people escaping holocausts on other planets. If that were true, then Earth was no more worth saving than any of the other millions of inhabited worlds. Of course there was always a case for saving the Library. Hmmm. Moving it or recreating it literally meant moving or recreating the whole planet Earth!

Earth was as much home for himself as for the millions on Nixon, but for the common benefit of the entire inhabited Universe, the Leadership would still be justified in confiscating the planet for any use they required. He had to find out the truth, or as much of it as he could ascertain. He could go to the Library and wade through the volumes, but it hardly seemed logical that the Library would point to *alien* origins. Perhaps there was someone he could ask? Yes, he could put in an emergency call to Madame Prime and ask the direct question. He needed to think about that for awhile before he did it.

Mason wondered where exactly in Iowa he was. He hurried back to the barn and found a location map at the tourist desk. The grid showed he was just north of Kanawha in the north central part of the state. That's where Uncle Eugene's farm had been! He thought the house seemed familiar. But it was probably just wishful thinking.

He checked the grid for Rockwell, Iowa, where he was born in 1945. But the local Iowa tele-grid didn't allow travel access to Rockwell from here. For a moment he considered going there, but decided against it. He didn't really feel much like making the effort of hiring ground transport to get there. Anyway, he'd only been born there: it was never his home. But Mason City, in the county of Cerro Gordo about 10 kilometres north of Rockwell did have special meanings for him. It was home for much of his schooling in the late 1950s and early 1960s. His parents spent most of their lives in a comfortable house on the southern outskirts of the town for three decades of the last half of the Twentieth century.

By now, Mason City could be anything. It might not exist. It had hardly been worth preserving. Jackson checked the guide screen and saw that the site of Mason City had been turned into a life museum for the cement industry. The whole town had been swallowed up by a great expansion of the Portland cement diggings on its northern edge, sometime in the 26th century. It was now one of the biggest man-made holes on the planet. Without terra forming techniques (which Earthlings were opposed to), the site was simply not worth the effort to restore to farmland or the original prairie. Besides, the cement museum was unique on the planet.

Jackson wondered what had become of his parent's home. Loaded onto a truck and towed away for cheap housing somewhere else, he imagined. Or maybe fallen over the precipice into the cement abyss. Leaving the neat red barn with its tidy white trim, Jackson

took a last slow look around at the white clapboard farmhouse and the other outbuildings, then headed for the tele-gate to New York. He thought about contacting Judy at the office. And what was Alexx up to tonight? Would she be available? He also decided he needed to contact Madame Prime as soon as possible. After that, he'd check things out at the Library.

Phone Call

That night on Nixon, Jackson had little appetite. The Library had been so crowded, he'd been advised to come back another day - early. He skipped dinner in New York in favour of an early return to Nixon for a solid work session on his ad-plan. After munching a chocolate bar for supper, Jackson walked to the inter-galactic communications suite in the Neil Armstrong Hotel and secured himself into a private booth with a private line to the Centre of the Universe.

He slid his identicard into the transmitter. He started to punch the code for the office, but on a hunch, re-punched for Catherine Prime instead. He was lucky. Or perhaps his Resurrectee status cut through the system. He asked for visual and audio direct communication.

The screen flickered into life and settled down, almost immediately presenting him with a view of the energy room where he had first met the Director. Now it was empty. The screen flickered again and this time the picture that emerged was a lounge room set in a small forest clearing by a sparkling waterfall. He recognised the Director as she walked towards the screen.

"Mason Jackson?"

"Hello, Director. I hope I haven't disturbed you."

"You wouldn't be seeing me now if you had. What progress have you made? The signal says you're calling from Earth."

"From its moon, Nixon, actually. The shape of the project is forming in my mind. I am sure I'll give you a unique and exciting solution to your brief..."

"We are pleased to hear it, though I did expect as much from you. We appreciate your effort. Now, what can I help you with?"

"A simple question."

"They are always simple. Proceed."

Without the slightest hesitation Jackson asked "Is Earth the original home of the genus 'homo sapiens'?"

"Why don't you ask Central Thought, Mason? I'm sure that's not classified material."

"I preferred to ask you."

"In that case the official answer is 'no'."

"I thought that might be the case. The official answer, that is. Then where did Man come from, according to Central Thought?"

"Planet Alpha One-A."

Jackson responded with a lower tone and a wry smile. "Makes sense. Too much sense. Numeric logic that's all. Typical of C.T. It's trying to cover something up. Where is Alpha One-A, Madame Prime?"

"Its location has never been identified."

"You mean *revealed.*"

"I mean what I said."

"For argument's sake, couldn't Earth and planet Alpha One-A be one and the same?"

"I refuse to have an argument."

Jackson could see her annoyance. She could have terminated the call but she didn't. "I cannot see the point of your enquiry. In the early stages of developing humanoid life on each planet, indeed for many centuries after colonisation, a sense of loyalty to the home planet is very strong. It almost always manifests itself as a belief that the home planet is the Mother of the human race until of course the larger fraternity of planets lets them in on the little secret of their *colonial* origins.

"Sometimes though, a planet's population will hold onto their belief long after they know the truth -- but the mythology always disappears eventually. And each adolescent civilisation takes its place as an adult in the larger community of intelligent life."

"As it becomes aware of the whole, the part loses significance?"

142

"That's one way to interpret it, Mason, according to the observations published by Central Thought, yes."

Jackson looked intently into the little view screen, trying to pry into Madame Prime's eyes for hidden clues. For a moment he wondered who she slept with. Then he remembered how important this call was and he snapped back to alertness and propriety. But not before she felt the weight of his peculiar gaze.

"I think the only reason you chose me was because I was resurrected from ancient Earth."

"Mr. Jackson we chose you because of your well balanced whole-brain approach to creative problem solving. We did not expect you to have an ego that needs constant massaging."

Mason winced visibly.

"Central Thought chose you because it was logical that you would be capable of understanding the problem from the inside out. You are a respected Creator. The choice was, therefore, not surprising, and it has gone entirely unquestioned in my Department."

Jackson reconsidered his position, wisely deciding that even having fantasies about this woman was too dangerous. So he played it straight. "If any other planet had been short-listed for incineration, I would not have been chosen."

"That is difficult to say. Doubtless you would have been short-listed almost certainly, regardless.

"My intuition still suggests C.T. is trying to cover something up. Consider Alpha One-A. That's such a logical alpha-numeric designation it's preposterous! Again I wonder what C.T is protecting. Or whom?

"Choose your words carefully, Mr. Jackson. As yet, there is no law covering treasonous statements against a computer, but the day may come..."

Jackson managed a smile in the face of this warning, hoping to diminish the force of his accusation. He moved onto safer ground. "As a Creator, I have to determine the strongest statement or claim I can make about whatever it is I'm selling. Here, I smell a strong story based on the belief that Earth is the mother planet of the human race. I simply wanted to check out the facts. I have to be accurate. I'm sure you understand the ethics of my point of view, Madame."

The Director, Catherine Prime, continued her hard line, "May I remind you that we asked you to convince people that Earth should be *destroyed* for the common good, not saved."

"The strongest thing that can be said, Director, is not always positive, it may be a negative. I must be sure that Earth is *not* the Mother Planet, not Alpha One-A, before I myself can be persuaded it should be destroyed, let alone asking me to convince anyone else of that. And at the moment I believe quite the opposite. It makes complete sense to me that Earth is the Mother Planet of the human race. And therefore I cannot work to the brief until I am convinced otherwise."

"Then you are resigning the commission?"

"No, Director, not unless you wish to fire me. All I am saying is that I must have the Truth. I cannot work on a false premise. If I find proof here -- in the Library of the Tree of

Humankind, or anywhere else -- that Earth is the Mother planet, then I will share the evidence with you. And if you and your superiors in the Government still feel that Earth should be destroyed, *and then* you must fire me."

"And if Alpha One-A cannot be refuted?"

"Then Earth has no special meaning, no extra value, its living museums will have no more significance to me than a closet full of irrelevant rubbish and I will be happy to complete the project to your satisfaction in as short a time as possible... unless of course you have plans to destroy Alpha One-A as well...

"You don't let up, do you?"

"You think I'm just being a 20th century human, full of the flaw of the Mother complex. That's all you can see isn't it? A man one hundred thousand years past his sell-by date." He wasn't sure she would understand his archaic reference, but he let it ride.

"Your meaning is clear enough. It is irrelevant what I think about you. You have been chosen and that's that."

"I'll be in touch after I've visited the Library." He spoke to a blank screen. She had terminated the call.

Root of the Problem

Jackson walked freely with the crowd through the entrance to the Library of the Tree of Humankind. He decided to take the Introductory Tour to orient himself better with the general span of history. A tour leader stood by a white circle on the floor. When he blew a whistle, anyone wanting to go with him stood on the circle too. When it was full, the group was closed.

He chose a guide named Arnold who looked intelligent, although that was never proof of anything as he well knew. As Arnold polished his name badge and then his whistle, Mason walked to the edge of the circle, ready to step in. So were forty school children aged about eight.

The whistle blew and Mason stepped in. They were off! The circle lifted above the floor and across the hall. As the disc approached a mirror, an abyss opened beneath it. Arnold manoeuvred the disc down a great glassy walled shaft bathed in shifting light. It reminded Jackson of the hall of plasma walls in the briefing session with the Advertising Director, Madame Catherine Prime.

Arnold began the tour with his standard speech. "Welcome to the Library of the Tree of Humankind. On this programme I will take you down to the bottom of the Tree itself to see how Mankind began. Then we will rise up through the branches of the Tree to get an idea of how humanity has grown and spread its branches throughout the galaxies and the four Quadrants of the Universe."

The disc floated out of the tube and they found themselves in an enormous open space.

"You are now several kilometres beneath the streets of New York at the base of the great Tree. Beneath us even further, as you can see through the transparent floor, are the roots of humanity. These roots tell the story of biological evolution from the first living cells to the first land-living animals, the amphibians, the reptiles, into the mammals and finally our simian ancestors who first lived in trees, developed the first societies, and learned to use tools.

As the presenter continued his story, animated graphics appeared in the air among the crowd. Jackson was soaking up the information as fast as it appeared. A bar graph with a parade of hominid characters performing basic walking, sitting and jumping movements brought the whole thing to life. Beginning with an Australopithecus amenensis walking on all fours then abruptly standing upright, the graphic showed the time to be about 4.2 million BC. Jackson wondered if BC still meant Before Christ. He saved the question for later.

Australopithecus africanus, Arnold explained, appeared around 3 million BC and was the oldest direct ancestor of modern humans. Then there was Homo habilis, once thought to be an evolution of africanus, but proved to be an evolutionary dead end in 2007. So it was Homo erectus who ultimately gave rise to Homo sapiens. "Homo erectus appeared in sub-Saharan Africa about 1.1 million BC and spread through most of the world. Homo sapiens, anatomically the same as us, appeared around 100,000 BC.

In the Library of the Tree of Humankind, you will also meet the Neanderthals who lived about 370,000 years ago and disappeared as recently as 26,000 BC. As you go through the earliest time of life on our planet, there was generally more than one species of hominin living at any one time. Indeed, erectus and habilis co-existed for hundreds of thousands of years. Yet, as you very well know, today Homo is represented by only a single successful species: us."

Arnold delivered his spiel with the relaxed confidence of someone who enjoyed the job and did it almost every day. "The roots lead up to the trunk of the Tree. Several thousand years of painstaking exploration, cataloguing and analysis -- still going on of course -- have given us the first true human beings on the Tree. As these earliest creatures are believed to have lived about 3.8 million years ago, you can understand there are no records of how these men and women referred to each other. So the Library has given them names to help personalise them.

"Excuse me," Jackson boldly interrupted, "I thought the origins of the human race on this planet went back only about 1.95 millions of years, not 3 million."

The school children giggled behind his back. They couldn't believe the funny old guy's questions.

"I'm afraid, sir that your information is about a hundred thousand years out of date. By the end of the 20th C, if my own photographic memory serves me well, man-like creatures were unearthed in a place called Tanzania. In Africa, of course. Their remains were carbon-dated to already be 2.1 million old at that time. Later discoveries and far more accurate DNA cataloguing and a host of other dating technology now establishes our ancient ancestry to a proven prehistory."

Arnold resumed his set-piece introduction. "The creatures we have named are the only ones we have actually found. It is a mere handful -- obviously hundreds of thousands, and probably millions of their ancestors can never be exhumed from beneath glaciers, lava flows and sea beds."

"Through careful and precise dating techniques, we were able to distinguish thousands of these proto-people and follow their family lines to the present day. That's what the Tree is all about. And that is why it is so enormous. Each time we unearth another new individual, he must be included on the Tree. The new name and any vital statistics available are programmed into this living record, which grows another leaf or another twig or another branch as necessary, to keep the story straight."

Jackson gaped with disbelief at the enormity of the statistical claim Arnold was making. The physical scale of the project was almost beyond his comprehension.

"Anything we know about anyone who ever lived is catalogued in our great filing system. Naturally, many entries are exceedingly small. However, some of our prominent ancestors, such as Nebuchadnezzar, Newton, Napoleon, Stalin, Tung, Chandra, Antron, Kez, Purkin, Dorman and the like, have enormous volumes on record."

Jackson started to wonder what the record said about him as the disc floated evenly and gently amongst the great branches near the main trunk of the mammoth tree.

"We're coming up now to the first self-recorded individuals. And these have fairly wide-spread origins. The Middle East, Southern China, Northwest India and the Iberian peninsula were home to the first writers, painters and carvers of names and identity symbols."

Jackson was still trying to take it all in. Already the Tree was literally growing out of sight to each side. And the disc had risen to a level approximating to the time of 8000 B.C. Next to him, two kids started scuffling.

"Shhh. Break it up you two little monkeys, I'm trying to listen" Mason whispered. "You guys oughta be listening to this too."

"Who you callin' a monkey, mister? Go climb a tree; I already know all this stuff!"

"Sure you do."

"This Library shit is boring. We're just along for the ride on the disc."

"I'll bet your teacher is going to ask you questions about it later."

"Let him! I've already memorised the contents of the entire Tree."

"How? I mean how in the hell could you memorize all this? "

"What an old fogey, hey, Brad?"

"Here, mister, you musta missed the free handout. Take mine. I don't need it now. It's all a load of dross anyway."

"Shit, Ralph, how come I always get the weirdo standing next to me. What's the big deal about memorising a few

149

hundred headings? You'd think he'd never heard of holistic learning!"

Jackson took the printed sheet and saw that it did indeed list the entire outline and format of the Tree. As well as some astounding statistics, the Tree, according to the Tour blurb, was 17 kilometres high by 13 kilometres in diameter, and still growing. The oldest individual on the Tree was a hairy proto-African, denoted AF-000000001 who died about 2,997,000 B.C. and was found in the Great Rift Valley in 5163 A.D.

Jackson started to scan the sheet, but his eyes kept stopping as he tried to imagine the events surrounding each major heading.

1990's: The Brush Fire Wars. Bosnia, Iraq, Lebanon, Afghanistan.

Well he knew about that first hand. He had seen for himself the collapse of the Soviet Union, the rise of India and China and the threat of Iran.

2070's: Continental Political Alignments. The Twelve Disciples: the CIS, Great China, IndonAsia, South Africa, North Africa, United States of Europe, North America, South America, Australasia, Scanditannia, Great India and the Pan Islamic Alliance.

Jackson envisioned a world nearly united. Twelve great tribes of the world, something like the old EEC multiplied globally with just twelve partners. He noted wryly that Canada and Mexico had finally been absorbed by the sesame seed buns of American economics, China re-achieved its ancient greatness, India struggled with too much democracy and too many religions, but the power of money finally catapulted it to global greatness and in the following century it surpassed China. Britain aligning with Scandinavia in their last act of belligerence toward the French and Germans, the Soviet Union re-emerged as

150

a Russian Confederation and the Islamic world
fundamentally isolating itself. Fascinated by the list of
techno-exploration benchmarks re avidly read on.

2088 The Solar Age begins.
Manned colonies on Mars. Manned orbiter goes to
Jupiter.
Major break-throughs in Bionics.'
Amused, Jackson's memories sifted back through the
halcyon days of 1970's network TV. Lee Majors, The Six
Million Dollar Man with the bionic dick. Or were they
referring to John Major the one time U.K. politician? No.
Never.

2155:The Utopia Expedition.
Major break-throughs in Cryonics.
'Hmm, only a century after I froze my ass for the
future...so whatever happened to Utopia? Is this supposed
to be it?'

3098: Gannymede Manned Voyager.

Faster and faster, he scanned ahead trying to cover a
hundred thousand years in a few minutes whilst keeping
his ears tuned to Arnold's tour talk.

5010: Utopia Colony departs.
'So much for Utopia...'
Major break-throughs in DNA research.
'I wonder how they'd go for a holographic series called
Helix the Cat?'

8033: Nixon accepted as the 13th Disciple. Mars wars.
'Take that Cadbury! Zap! Pow! Biff! Bang! You're dead,
Rowntree!'
The Cloning Laws.

13147: Antron returns from Utopia.

"It really wasn't what it was cracked up to be."
Titan Colony.

17160's: The Great Lifts Off begin: New Chicago.
Asteroid settlements.

23189: The Samurai Expedition.
Earth II in orbit around sun.

24000: The Chinese Solution: New China Lift Off.
Earth III in orbit around sun.

34011: The Indian Solution: New India Lift Off.
"Christ, this is getting monotonous."
Earth IV in orbit around sun.

40027: The departure of the Free Space Greenies.
"That's perfect."

43055: Out-Farms established.

44107: The African solution: New Africa Lift Off.

48136: Free Socialists Lift off.
"It certainly took them long enough to decide."

49908: New Ice Age on Earth commences.

54200: Departure of the Free Catholic Mission.
"No wonder the population of the planet still fits on
Nixon. At least there aren't any chinks, blacks, greens,
pinkos, Catholics or weirdoes left around the place.
Except me, I suppose."

57000's: Era of the Cargo Cults and Merchandise
Worship.
"A recent re-establishment of religion? Sounds
interesting. I didn't know about this."

152

Earth Ice Age ends.

62000's: First Extra-Galactic Colonies.

65300's: Chivas founds first Galactic Empire.
'Not Chivas the Regal?"
Chivas founds Central Thought.
The Golden Age of Chivas.
"Twelve years old and aged in oak no doubt."

65600's: Earth to Nixon Exodus.

76200's: Age of the Quadrants begins.
Earth assigned to Q-4.
Intergalactic expansion increases at geometric rate.
Death of Chivas.

76800's: Break-through in solar power increase: suns seeded to burn faster.
"Is there nothing new under the sun? So it's a very old problem after all. Surely C.T. has seen this coming, the Leadership has seen it coming and typically nothing has really been done about it. "

77300's: First Leadership Triumvirate.
Government seated at centre of known Universe.

80000's: Age of Wisdom under Central Thought.

84700's: Library supervises planet-wide restoration of heritage sites.

90005: Universal census. Economic expedition surveys limits of known universe.

91124: Recycling technology given Priority B status by Central Thought.

91236: Earth sends Recycling Exhibition from Antiquities Foundation to All-Quadrant Conference.

92640: Earth Heritage site restoration complete. Wilderness areas re-established on Earth.

93200's: Earth installs P.C.C. (Permanent Climate Control)

94781: Archaeologists discover ancient civilisation on Alpha One-A.

"Ah hah. I wonder if this is for real? Why did it take so long to discover it given that such a huge proportion of the universe had been probed and nothing else apparently had been found?"

95050's: Era of Universal Expansion comes to natural end. Manifest Destiny is achieved.

96000: Central Thought declares start of the Age of Introspection.

"Come on, mister!" a boy's voice called. And Jackson looked around puzzled. He was standing all alone in the middle of the circle on the floor. The flight up the Tree was over. The disc was down on the floor again and Jackson was in a daze by the scale of it all. The boy and his classmates disappeared into a corridor. Jackson struggled to make his next move, not really knowing which way to go or what to do next. Instinctively, he began to walk, and then regaining his wits, he found the route down to the Roots of the Tree.

The Tree of Life had become a tree of Knowledge – offering a new perspective of the Universe. CT had programmed Jackson's memory during the resurrection process with CT's view of history, politics, economics, sociology and science. He had always relied on the update provided by Central Thought - until now there had been no reason to challenge it. But, here was a new way of looking at things, and it was exciting. The Universe had to be told about the Library. The Tree offered The Truth from a different perspective. People must be allowed to make up their own mind whether Earth or any other habitable plant should be destroyed.

Jackson had not found CT's depiction of events strange in the least at the time or since. Neither would anyone else. Gulfs of time always caused confusion and made accuracy virtually impossible. Corroboration of events several thousand years previously was impossible too. That's what made History interesting. Viewing events with hindsight was always different from first person or eye-witness experience.

And now, here he was in the Library. But was it anymore objective that CT? Was it really possible even with all this data for anyone to prove or disprove that the human race had been born, or more accurately, *originated* on earth? Perhaps Earthlings insisted their version of the origin of the Species was the only correct version and had gone to infinite lengths to be seen to substantiate it because it was Earth's only reason for being. And if it were indeed the Truth, then Earthlings were right. If it proved to be a lie, a fraud, whatever you want to call it, then the bonfire awaited.

Jackson found a lift going down. He missed it and waited for another. "Are they telling the truth here or feather-bedding local mythology?" He said it aloud and drew several stares. He remembered the Cold War of the mid 20th Century. Radio Free Europe was barfing out as much propaganda as Tass. On the American side, Time and Newsweek, even the National Geographic was full of stars and stripes bullshit. Who could you believe in those days? Who could he believe now? Perhaps a third party.

The BBC, though in his opinion socially corrupt, had always seemed to be the impartial voice of the West. But they were located *in* the West and Britain provided the institutions of a modern functioning democracy like freedom of speech and accountability that the East didn't have. Britain in fact had been paranoid about Russian expansion since the days of Catherine the Great, and was terrified the Russians would be a world threat as soon as they acquired a warm water port and gateway to the world's oceans. Catherine the Great, Catherine Prime, he thought. What was her hidden agenda? Or was she just following orders? Who's order then? CT? Was it that simple?

Another relevant 20th Century thought struck Jackson as the lift car reached the base level of the Library. 'Could the human race have been born on more than one planet? Either in different times or at the same time?' If that were so, it would be the strongest implication yet of the existence of a divine being.

"Christ! What am I saying!? God is only for people who don't believe fully in themselves!" Jackson found himself talking aloud again. Several people were staring at him, some children were pointing. A little girl asked her Mother what 'Christ' meant.

"It's an expletive I believe, Scarlett, like 'shit'. But it sounds more polite, so I think it's alright for you to use it."

"Christ. Christ. Christ! Yes, I like the sound of it Mummy."

Jackson pulled the souvenir guide sheet from his pocket, racing down the ages, looking for something that was crawling out of his subconscious memory.

"That could be it. The Ganymede Manned Voyager, 3098." Jackson slapped his tourcard into the nearest Library viewer along the wall, punched the code for the year 3098 and gave his verbal instructions to the electronic Librarian. "Ganymede Manned Voyager - destination co-ordinates, if you please."

The response appeared instantaneously on the display screen.

"485-54-0255."

The numbers were just numbers, they meant nothing to him. But they did mean something to the Library. Of course! Those were the original pre-Quadrant co-ordinates with Earth as the centre of the Universe - which to all intents and purposes it was - back in 3098.

"Extrapolate. 485-54-0255 to new co-ordinates ex 0-0-0, Central Thought Data Base."

This time the machine clicked silently inside itself and answered, 0928-751-3244. Then it flashed a simple and somewhat embarrassing statement: "Why didn't you ask for the modern name for Ganymede?"

In any event, Jackson had the answer he'd hoped for. Ganymede Manned Voyager had gone to Alpha One-A.

Of course, Jackson as yet had no idea what the Manned Voyager found on Ganymede/Alpha, but he was playing his hunch that it was not inhabited by humanity prior to 3098, and the relics of an ancient civilisation found there in 94781 were icons or relics brought there by the Ganymede Expedition *from Earth*.

Using a view-frame, he was able to dig into the Root model as far back as he liked. He remembered the disc trip guide talking about proto humans in pre-history and that's what fascinated him most. But as he scanned the millions of classification tags of nameless pre-humans and proto humans, he hit a barrier he couldn't find his way through or around.

Several minutes passed before Jackson identified the problem properly. He just didn't know what he was looking for. Whatever it was must be right in front of him -- he felt sure he'd know it when he saw it. The millions of numbers, tags, root endings and beginnings - they meant something beyond what he could as yet see.

He stared through the view-frame for nearly a minute, his eyes fixed at the bottom of the great Root system. He increased magnification until he could see the very lowest root-tuber. Then Jackson fixed on the identity point and keyed into his Librarian.

"Identity, please."

'AF-000000001. Female proto human, simian biped mammal. Inhabited Great Rift Valley, African continent Minus 197071 to 197045 plus or minus 2 Uni-years.'

There were no lower, earlier roots. No lower identity numbers. She was the beginning. This hairy African half man, half ape, was the Mother of Mankind. It was there in front of him. Jackson was stymied. There still has to be more to it than that, he thought.

Jackson stared at the base point for several seconds more before impulsively twisting the magnification another notch. It was a fateful moment. The root follicle, itself a scant 3 or 4 millimetres in length on the model, pointed down into an empty void. It reached up and formed a junction with another node, presumably -and logically - AF-000000002, a hairy ape-man and henceforth the father of the human race. But at the exact junction of the two prime nodes, Jackson saw something else. Not quite a node, not much more than a bump on the root. But a definite 'something'. Was it a fault in the manufacture of the model?

He excitedly increased magnification. The bump now appeared more than just a bump. It had a proper welded junction to the other two prime nodes. Jackson fixed the viewer on this new target. "Identify!"

Words flashed in reply on the display screen. 'Identity unknown. Unknown origin. Unknown link.'

Jackson shook his head. "Shit! A hundred thousand years of science and technology and the Missing Link is still missing!"

He got up to leave. So excited he was sweating everywhere. Then, glancing down to turn off his terminal, he saw that the Librarian had displayed an additional item of information on the unknown node.

'Discovered Ross Coast, Antarctic continent 3089.' Nine years before the departure of the Ganymede Expedition.

Jackson frantically keyed for additional references. "For further reading, visit the Public Reference Library in the next building, thank you."

Jackson replaced the view-frame and hurriedly left the building and went next door. The tiny bump on the root was erupting into the proverbial mountain in his mind. In the References, Jackson made a list of sources on the archaeology and palaeontology of Antarctica. And as he worked, he remembered a strange map of a super continent called Gondwaland. He had first come across it in high school geology. Gondwaland was central to the Tectonic Plate theory of continental drift.

At one time, so the Gondwaland Theory proposed, all the continents on Earth were joined into one vast land mass called Gondwaland. As pieces broke off and drifted away, so they became the shapes still recognised as Africa, Europe, the Americas, Australia and Asia. The piece that was left behind, the remnant of Gondwaland, drifted south and was to become known as Antarctica. There was plenty fossil evidence to prove that many animals in the Americas had originated in Asia when the Bering Straits were bridged by land during the Ice Ages. Was it not possible, therefore, that many of the animals of Africa and Europe had their origins in Antarctica, when those lands were still connected?

"Even if by only a few feet of land, or a measly sand bar, it was certainly possible," Jackson thought. "Were there more ape fossils in Antarctica? Was the Missing Link solution to be found in Gondwaland?"

In the corner of the men's lavatory on level 42, a boy named Brad spoke into a tiny transparent microphone that fit precisely on the end of his thumb on his left hand. It looked exactly like a thumb nail. "...subject has found something visually unusual at root of tree and is now examining records in reference library..."

159

Lunacy

Four days later, Jackson had given up on his theory. There was nothing to support this idea. Nothing even pointing to the possibility had as yet been discovered in Antarctica. Nor was there likely to be -- at least not until the ice cap was removed or an improved method found to probe it in the precise detail a trained palaeontologist would need.

Obviously none of that was now ever likely to happen. The Permanent Climate Control System had been installed in the 93200's, relatively recently, ensuring preservation of the ice cap, as well as every other climate on Earth. And, as much as he could see from his investigations, it was nearly 15,000 years since anyone had mounted a scientific expedition in either of the Polar Regions.

And that realisation impacted Jackson nearly as strongly as the tiny bump on the root model! For it lifted the curtain of secrecy over the entire Earth-Nixon system that had bothered him from the beginning: Why had this become a *closed* society? Why didn't Earth-Nixon bother to participate in the commercial style of life common to the rest of the Quadrant? Why did Earthlings preserve their planet as no other had been?

There were two possibilities that Jackson could think of. One was that CT, a highly sophisticated machine, but a machine none the less, wanted to run the entire Universe as a machine, as part of itself much as the pre-Stalinist technocrats of the old Soviet Union had wanted to do when they put their first 5-year programme together in 1927 for turning Russia into an industrialised society overnight. The Plan almost worked. If Stalin and greed and paranoia hadn't interfered maybe it would have. But industrial engineering and social engineering had become tightly enmeshed with each other and for a while it

160

seemed it might prove successful. Perhaps that was what CT was up to. After all, planning and logic were entirely in its make-up. It came naturally to it as a machine. But the Soviets got it wrong partly because the Plan became everything. The Plan was the Plan. And as had been the case so often in human history, absolute power corrupts absolutely. Transparency and accountability were sidelined in favour of the lifestyle of the leaders. Touted objectives were obscured and lost. Could CT conceivably get it right where the Soviets had failed?

Perhaps Ganymede was an experiment in social engineering. Perhaps that's why CT was planning to glorify Alpha-One-A. To consolidate its power base, CT might be manipulating the government and the economy to re-write historical records in favour of the way it wants to do things. But, aahh! Isn't this sounding like something the Pirates were good at? Of course! The Pirates were behind all this. They put people in power to maintain their own power.

The more Jackson thought about it, the more he felt sure that must be the answer. And then there was the resurgence of religion. The Cargo and Merchandise Cults. And, Christ -- whatever happened to Christ? Or Buddha or Mohammed? Getting rid of Earth would get rid of a lot of tangible evidence and heritage for all of those belief structures. In all the industrialised, commercialised, hyper-technical Universe, the Expansionists prevailed. But not on Earth. Earth had dug up its past and dwelt within it.

He checked his notes for other possibilities. One explanation was the civil "Future Economic Wars" fought on Earth in the 2080's which saw the Expansionists win as surely as they must; for only they had the power and force of destruction that the druids of Industrialism could hold.

The Ecologists had fought for an end to the Industrial Age. And for a new age in which the majority of people would no longer be shackled in their human development

161

by the phenomenon of jobs, and no longer be stigmatised by the fear and reality of unemployment. Though the Ecologists had lost, they were merely dominated, not eliminated. The wars were civil. Thermo-nuclear weapons were not used, just millions of riot force police. And by the end of the 23rd century, the Ecologists, like countless waves of pilgrims in earlier history, mounted their own expedition to find a new home and make a new Utopia. That was in 3248. And their expedition was the first to leave the Sol System. Or so they thought. Fifty years earlier, an Expansionist manned probe force had been secretly sent on the Ganymede expedition. The Pirates had more than a fifty year head start.

A hundred years later, a transmission was received from the expedition that the paradise planet had been found; the road was paved for those that followed. The Universe was there to be taken, to be exploited for profit just as Earth had been in the beginning. Paradise had been regained.

Jackson was enthralled as he read through the news reports from those times describing the immense social and political power of the governments. It was the end of unemployment. The end of most of the symptoms of social strife. Everyone who chose to work could work; it was a time for nothing but positive thinking and positive action.

As political control fell away from earth, migrations continued, culminating in the Great Lift Offs to greener pastures. Of course, the irony of it was, the fewer pressures there were on Earth's resources, the more Utopian the environment became at home!

Jackson had not seen Alexx for five days. As he fell into his sleep mat, he wondered what she was up to and whether she would contact him again. It was only then that he realised that he had no contact number for her whatsoever. He might go down to the spaceport tomorrow and see if he could locate her. But for now, it was sleep he needed. He managed to set breakfast for 0700 before closing his eyes. Full of satisfaction, he dozed off. Planet-saving was hard work, but small beer compared with convincing the entire industrialised Universe to change their ways!

- - -

It was a dream he had not had since childhood. And one that always disturbed him when he awoke. He was dressed in a long nightshirt and standing in front of his childhood home in Connecticut. It was a white stucco cement house, two storeys, with a white rail fence all round and sited by a small lake. A boy stood in front of his house, a crowd gathered. Cars, buses and trucks stopped and spilled their passengers into pressing rows along the white rail fence. They were looking at the boy. Cut to boy's perspective. He looks down at his bare toes sticking out from underneath his night shirt. He stands up on his toes. Then he puts his arms out stiffly at his sides, level with the top of his shoulders. Spreading his palms, he gently pushes down upon the air with his hands. He extends his toes to their limit -- and he is floating on the air! Two inches. Four. A foot off the ground. Women faint. Children point. A man takes a photo. People fall to their knees in prayer as the boy lifts to the height of the roof, sails silently above the chimney and floats directly over the crowd, looking straight down into their gaping mouths.

- - -

Mason emerged from sleep like a slug with a hangover. It was 11.05 pm. He stretched and yawned and fell back on the bed, touching a control that slid the ceiling back so he could view the stars through a porthole. Such a powerful dream. It shook his very fibre to the roots. What could have caused it? The outstretched arms, the standing on tip

163

toe, the visual content of it all was somehow uncomfortably familiar. Yes! He recalled a possible source and cause. In 1984 on a visit to Wells Cathedral in the West Country of England, he had seen something very like it. Hung on a wall was a sculpture of a man in exactly the same suspended pose as the boy had been in his dream. The figure was exquisitely carved in a light coloured wood in 1973. It depicted Christ in the pose of crucifixion but *without* the cross. Unusual, intriguing, he had never forgotten it.

The carved figure was also draped in a gown rather like a nightshirt. He held his arms out level with the top of his shoulders. His legs were firmly together, the feet *en pointe*. The whole sculpture was several feet off the ground, its eyes seemingly staring at every visitor. The idea that the boy, the young Mason in fact, had taken a crucifixion posture during his dreams of flying was fascinating and perplexing. What did it mean?

Then he switched his mind to the Expansionists. He remembered the green revolutions and confrontations he had witnessed in the 1970's, 80's and 90's. His Earth had been forced to face two opposing choices for the future of the planet. One, HE or Hypertechnic Expansion and the unbridled continuation of the Industrial era, or, Two, SHE -- a Sane Human Ecology based on self support with much greater individual leisure time and greater working hour flexibility. Now, a hundred centuries later, it seemed the SHE-ites had won. On Earth, and only on Earth.

Even now it seemed they only had it half-right. Though they were conserving and preserving the environment on Earth, the Nixon was an abominable place to live by comparison. Man's ability to live with Nature was still, it seemed to Jackson, somewhat out of balance here.

Hundreds of thousands of years earlier, in Man's pre-history on the planet Earth, Homo sapiens perhaps had held the Light so to speak, but as they developed tools and learned to change their environment to suit themselves, so the Light gradually became extinguished. Could it ever be rekindled? Or was it Mankind's destiny always to use, to consume, until everything was gone and the Universe was empty?

As Jackson lay on the bed, his arms outstretched, the image of himself as a boy in a crucifixion pose disturbed him once more. But he had *flown*. In the dream he had risen above all. The ability to float free and fly was thrilling. He closed his eyes and hoped the dream would come again. True happiness is when you are in your dreams awake, he reminded himself. He wanted true happiness and he wanted to live the dream, *this* dream.

At 0700, the smell of crispy bacon awakened Mason Jackson. He quaked once more with the weight of the ancient dream, prompting him to decide to do one more thing on Earth before saying good-bye to Alexx and jumping back to the Centre of the Universe.

Unholy Land

The Hostess at the Nixon Eastern Hemisphere Travel Centre greeted him at the entrance to the telegate. "The Middle East? May I see your travelcard, sir?"

Jackson handed over his red, white and blue travelcard. As she looked at his card he studied her silky black hair, her high noble cheekbones. She looked up and said, "Fine, Mr. Jackson. You'll need this sunscreen, and this spray to refrigerate your clothes. It's hot, dry and sunny where you're going. Here's a local map of the Middle East too, but as long as you stay out of the designated Wilderness areas, you'll have an easy time of it. Oh, did I tell you your entry point is Jerusalem?"

"Thanks very much. Just one thing. Is it possible to get around in a replicar in that part of the world?"

"Of course. I'm sure you can. They're not very popular for reasons you'll soon discover, but if you like..." She bent under the counter for a moment and came up with a leaflet. "Did you want to try something really ancient and primitive?"

"Yes, sure. Why not. Anything from the 20th century?"

"Only one. Something called a Land Rover. The replicar is hydrogen powered of course, but I believe the originals derived their motion from a liquid fuel called petroleum or some such which used to be found in great abundance beneath the sands all over the Middle East. I can't imagine how it worked."

"I presume the Land Rover will have an operator's manual. It's been a long time -- I mean, it can't be too hard to handle, can it?"

"If you can't drive it, talk to it. All our replicars obey voice commands. Or program the auto-pilot to take you on one of the pre-programmed tourist routes."

"Thanks!" Jackson smiled excitedly as he turned towards the Middle East telegate. In one step, he passed into a brilliant but not blinding white light. He knew he was in a booth of some kind, but he could not see the walls. He felt substance under his feet again and that was all. He lifted the weight from one foot and stepped forward, left the light, and came out on the other side. In Jerusalem.

There were tourists everywhere. He wondered how Jerusalem had sustained such a high level of interest among the peoples of Earth for so long. To say that it had the charm of an ancient city was almost meaningless. Jerusalem was already ancient in Jackson's first lifetime. Yet this was his first visit. In the 20th century, Jackson had been an agnostic, feeling little interest in visiting religious centres or monuments. More of a disciple of Richard Dawkins than Jesus Christ or Gautama Buddha or anyone else.

In 1995, if you'd asked him he would have said that Jerusalem was a great place to visit if you were either Jewish or religiously Christian. And he was neither. Now that he was here, he could not deny that the place had an intangible magic, an aura and fascination about it.

The telebooth exit was in the Old City. Street signs placed him on the Via Dolorosa where it intersected Bet Ha-bad. From photos he recognised the Church of the Holy Sepulchre nearby. But Jackson was not here to go to church. In fact, he didn't really know why he was here. He hadn't suddenly become religious. If anything, he thought it must be the effect of the levitation dream...but he knew he was here because of a feeling... the same burning excitement he had felt when he first thought of the notion of a human Missing Link being found under the south polar ice cap here on Earth.

Something was happening to him. He could feel it, *sense* it. He was being drawn into something. There was a reason for everything he just didn't know what it was yet. He himself had always been a consumer, an Expansionist.

Now he was questioning it comprehensively. Earth was doing something to him. Not that he was taken to believing in dreams of that sort. He certainly wasn't. Jerusalem was merely the convenient Tele-gateway to the region. He had the whole Middle East to wander through if he felt like it. And now a nice long walk would help sort out his thoughts.

His mind was stretched to its limits trying to work out the puzzles of the last five days. The unexplained node on the basal tip of the roots of the Tree -- and the uncorroborated story of human origins on Alpha One-A being perpetrated by Central Thought. Here in the Middle East perhaps he could somehow find a new approach, or at least a fresh inspiration.

Human civilisation on Earth may well have had its roots in this region. It had always been an area of intense activity, a crossroads for people in conflict over trade routes, religion and other ideologies. He might never be this way again. He'd missed it in his first life; now he was already glad he had come. As Jackson wandered the streets with the great crowds of other day trippers from Nixon, his humanity was further touched by the immense antiquity of the buildings and the lack of any attempt to replace them with synthidium and transpex.

It was oppressively hot. He was not used to being touched by so many people. It was a crush. Great numbers of tourists squeezed panting through narrow lanes. The crowd closed in on him. He wouldn't be able to take this much longer and knew he'd have to get out to some wide open space pretty soon - or fight his way back to the telegate and step back through, anything to get out of the crush! Oooff! He was pushed nearly to the ground by some inconsiderate sod with the bodily strength and rough manners of a Spaceball player.

Jackson turned to see who the pushy bastard was, and was astonished to see a dark-skinned Bedouin tribesman in a striped robe and wearing a plain white kayefah on his head. He was even more astonished when the Bedouin took one step into the crowd and absolutely disappeared, leaving Jackson stuttering abuses to no effect. He had half a mind to follow the man and give him a short sharp lesson in public behaviour as well as some good old fashioned 20th century abuse, but the sheer weight of the crowd made it impossible to chase anyone. Then, a flash of striped colour caught his eye and, looking up, Jackson saw what appeared to be the same Bedouin perched on top of a wall about fifty metres ahead.

How could he move that far so fast? Of course, there were probably thousands of people dressed like that in Jerusalem. But as he looked around, Jackson was eerily aware that no-one was. Every one of the hundreds of people in sight was dressed in the bodyskins and cas-suits common to Nixon and, as far as that went, virtually all of the out-fashion fringe worlds.

Maybe it was the heat. The glare of the sun giving him a headache. Eyes and imagination playing tricks. Like a horde of lemmings heading for the cliffs, the crowd carried Jackson along the wall beneath the spot where the Bedouin, real or imagined, still stood. Jackson kept his eyes fixed on the stranger and tried to hold his ground against the crowd as he looked up at him.

The Bedouin looked down with the most piercing eyes Jackson had ever seen. And then, as he stood there atop the wall, the Bedouin fellow seemed to rise up on his toes. Higher still he rose on them, and when Jackson could see that there was no way he could extend his feet any further, the Bedouin lifted off the ground about an inch. Jackson would swear he could see space between the Bedouin's feet and the top of the wall! How did he do that? Raising and stretching his arms out to his sides, the Bedouin then brought his hands slowly down about eighteen inches. And as he did so, his body floated up about the same distance. The action was like a great bird stretching his wings and lifting off in ultra slow-motion from the immense power of a single downward swoop of the arms! "My dream! My God! It's like my *dream*! Look! Look!" He was pointing at the Bedouin, but nobody paid him any attention. The crowd shunned him and gave him space as they hurried to get past him, away from this strange stranger.

Jackson had read about the strange supposed powers of Sufis and other mystics down through the ages. He suspected this was like a rope-trick rather than a real demonstration of supernatural powers. Still, without an anti-grav device, the levitation trick was awesome.

"Look! Did you see that?!" Jackson grabbed the arm of a man next to him. He pointed to the hovering Bedouin. The tourist looked up and apparently saw nothing.

Jackson looked into the tourist's face. The man sneered at him and shook his arm free of his frantic grasp. Jackson looked back at the Bedouin. He was gone. Vanished into the proverbial thin air. Jackson gushed with sweat. He had to have some space and a quiet place to think. What was going on here anyway? Was it just him? Was it a hallucination? Did other people see it too and merely pretended they didn't?

He could just make out the wooden corner of a great gate leading out of the Old City. Lions Gate was dead ahead. And leading away to the east was the Derekh Yeriho, the Jericho Road.

Jackson made for the tourist office symbol just beyond the Lions Gate. Much relieved, he went in and sat down in the cool controlled air. A few minutes later he left with the keys to a replicar, the old Land Rover. Once inside he could close the doors and think things through.

As soon as he sat in the operator's seat, Jackson was grimly reminded how inept he had always been with mechanical things. 123rd century technology left little for anyone to do physically as far as operating any device. But this was a replica of 20th century mechanical charm.

170

And at school, Jackson had consistently scored the lowest possible results in the mechanical sections of aptitude tests. The evaluations said he just didn't have the right brain patterns for working out mechanical problems. Little wonder the Land Rover was proving to be virtually unsolvable. He simply could not work out how to keep the engine running and the vehicle moving ahead at the same time.

"Shit!"

"I am not programmed with that ability" the Land Rover replied.

"How the hell do you start u p? Isn't there supposed to be a key?"

"Just ask me to 'go' and I will do the rest."

"OK, then, let's go!"

At least he could *pretend* he was Indiana Jones navigating crude dusty roads with nothing but a few gauges and a road map!

Caveman

T he seat smelt of old leather -- it was an oddity he faintly remembered and sentimentally enjoyed from his first life. People on other planets could experience the same sensation by checking out a smell chip from their local library. Technology had replaced leather almost everywhere with synthetics, much the same way it had replaced real food with artificial flavourings, sweeteners, bonding agents, emulsifiers, preservatives, and energy additives. It was a matter of evolution. Commercial evolution. But on Earth, leather at least, could still be found in abundance as could the animals that supplied it.

To Jackson's ultimate horror, it appeared that the replica Land Rover had no automatic directional system except straight forward or straight back. It took a moment to work out that he would actually have to steer the thing himself. He hadn't driven a car for a hundred thousand years or so but he reckoned it was like riding a bicycle; once you've done it you can always do it again. The huge black wheel in front of him could be turned to change the direction of the front wheels. This was either going to be great fun or a disaster of embarrassing proportions. "I wonder what Judy would think of you?" he said to the vehicle.

"I am not programmed to respond to hypothetical questions."

The Land Rover was beginning to cause him to feel more ridiculous than he already did, just steering rather than full-on driving. Machines almost always had a knack of making Mason feel inadequate.

"A little faster, please," and he was away, through the Lion Gate and down the road towards Jericho.

The desert sun beat down on the vehicle, streaming in through the windows magnifying the rays and building up heat so quickly the cooling unit could barely cope. The thermometer gauge showed 52C – outside the window in the full sun. Jackson realised it was a helluva way to finally get warm and fully thawed for the first time since his cryonic resurrection.

As he looked around at the changing landscape, he was glad he'd made the effort to visit this part of the world. The vehicle's speed increased at a rate directly proportionate to the increase in the bangs, bumps, jolts and rattles of the road. He slowed down to regain stability, but the replicar still jarred his skull on the ceiling. He stopped in a parking lot overlooking Jerusalem. The Middle East had seen more fighting than any other region on the planet. The crossroads of early civilisations, philosophies, religions - Jerusalem had been levelled by the Romans in AD 70 to put down a revolt and punish the Jews. Wars had long been commonplace as invaders came and went every generation. And so wars continued as a way of life for across the Holy Land and the entire Middle East for the next 3000 years. An eye for an eye, a tooth for a tooth, a son for a son. Both sides as bad as each other, killing each other like a perpetual human harvest. It was disgusting.

The surrounding countryside was more of a desert than it was at any time during the Roman oppression. A legacy of nuclear conflicts in the 21st century, radioactive ground did not support agriculture. And though there was no radiation danger to people travelling across the area now, the museum officials decided to leave the desert the way it was to give a more accurate impression of the wilderness faced by the biblical characters immortalised in the Gideon adventures.

Mason's eyes found a gadget he could understand, "Hey! A radio!" Mason's memory tripped back over the centuries to hot summer nights of 'scoopin' the loop' in a 1956 two-tone blue Ford V8, singing along to the radio, hanging his arm out the window, sitting as tall as he possibly could behind the wheel and hoping to attract the attention of the girls. The loop was a stretch of US Highway 69 that ran north to south through Mason City, Iowa. It was called Federal Avenue. In the 1960s it boasted 24 of the 28 stop lights between Minneapolis and Des Moines. The loop started at The Hop Drive Inn on South Federal and turned around at Hasse's Drive-In on North Federal. Any night of the week from about 8 o'clock onwards, it was a slowly cruising traffic jam moving from a Coke and French Fries to a hot fudge sundae and back again.

Secretly hoping that he'd tune in to The Great Pretender, Teen Angel or Run Around Sue, Mason flicked the radio into life. He couldn't believe his luck. The replicar designers hadn't missed a trick. The radio blared a programme from a typical Sunday morning Bible-belt broadcast from the mid-20th century.

"Friend, when was the last time you let Jesus into your life? Was it this morning? Before or after breakfast? Was it yesterday, or last week? Last month, last year, or haven't you ever let Him into your heart? Friend, hear the Voice of God, the program that's more than entertaining, it's vital to saving your soul. In a moment, I'll be telling you how, at a very low monthly cost, you can save enough of your soul to practically guarantee entry through the Pearly Gates..."

Mason chuckled as he tried to change the channel, but no matter how far he turned the dial, the program wouldn't go away.

"This month God is making a special deal. Send your prayers with an S.A.E. and for just 5 credits per word, He promises they will be answered. If not in writing, then certainly with His Heart. Act now. With Faith, Contrition or any other Act you choose, God's Chosen People will send you absolutely free --"

Click.

"Thank God I found the button to turn the damned off!"

Jackson put the Land Rover replicar into first gear and once more headed out on the Jericho Road. Jerusalem disappeared from view behind a ridge. Ahead lay bleak barren desert, strewn with rocks, brittle and thorny vegetation and searing hot sand filling all the spaces in between. Harshness surrounded him, but he was free of the hustling tourist centre and could finally give his mind a chance to work out what the hell it was he had seen back there with that floating Bedouin act. Was he having day-dreams now? Was it a nightmare? He knew what he saw, didn't he?

The Jericho road ran fairly straight for about 5 kilometres. There was no other ground vehicle traffic so he could enjoy the drive and look out the windows. He flipped the toggle for the auto over-ride and let the computer do the driving - at a restful 20 kilometres per hour. At this rate he was no longer bouncing his brains into a bloody pulp on the ceiling - just gliding along quite comfortably.

That's when the rock moved. It was on his right. Instinctively, Jackson grabbed the wheel and took over the driving from the computer. He left the road, jolting over the stony terrain towards the moving, shimmering rock. It looked to be several hundred yards away. Heat rising from the hot sand wriggled the mountain backdrop, rippling the suspect rock like a reflection in a slowly flowing stream.

But then the rock stood up. Jackson wasn't sure what he saw, but he drove on, still heading straight for whatever it was. His eyes were fixed on the lumpy black boulder as it lengthened and thinned into a small pole, then broke into a dotted line as the shimmering heat and desert glare played more tricks with the shape. The pole added a leg for support before Jackson now knew his quarry was a man. It was the Bedouin. The floating man from the market street. Jackson's heart leapt dangerously into his throat.

175

The Land Rover struggled as it left rocky soil and sank steadily into soft sand. Jackson gave the command to engage the four wheel drive and the replicar churned sand in every direction, grabbing the steepening slope and hanging on. The tyres also hardened and softened automatically to keep traction across the sinking sand or bare rock.

The rock-pole-man stood firm. A shroud draped his head and shoulders, curtaining off the body and concealing the arms. But a thumb stuck out of the folds. It was as if the Bedouin seemed to be hitching a ride! The Land Rover reached the hitch-hiker and stopped. Jackson met steel blue eyes through the relative safety of the driver-seat window. The Bedouin spoke. And it wasn't in Yiddish or Swahili, but in good old USE. Universal Standard English.

"Can you give me a ride?" The Bedouin whined in a brash, distinctively American accent. The wind whistled up a small column of sand spinning it upwards about twelve feet before spreading it out on the ground behind his robes.

Instinctively Jackson rolled the window down. Despite the obnoxious twang, there was a tone to the Bedouin's voice that he trusted. And though he would later admit that he was shit-scared at what might happen, Jackson made no attempt to drive away from the situation. Perhaps it was his insatiable curiosity rather than the power of the Bedouin's forceful stare that held him transfixed.

"Who are you? What do you want?"

"A ride, cloth ears. It's friggin' hot out here!"

Jackson was wary. There was more to this primitively dressed man than met the eye. The unexpected accent had put Jackson on guard. He wasn't about to be robbed, ripped off, hi-jacked or made the fool by a conjurer dressed in dust rags. The Bedouin's eyes sparkled with intelligence and cunning as he smiled through window at him. Jackson wasn't quite sure if he wasn't being laughed at.

"I'm not laughing. Only lightly amused that you ask such predictable questions!" This time the accent was Quadrant English, with a suggestion of Proton 3.

Jackson certainly found the Bedouin unpredictable.

"If you're looking for the Ten Commandments, they're over that way!" The man in the bed sheet teased pointing toward some low hills further to the east.

"And I suppose Cecil B. De Mille is directing it," Jackson rejoined. Then added apologetically, "Sorry. Unfair. You wouldn't have any idea what I was talking about."

"Cecil B. De Mille was a 20th century American film director and producer, well known for the epic scale of his productions." The accent was Earthling again, but otherwise vague. Perhaps South African, perhaps Kiwi.

Jackson was surprised again to say the least. The more the Bedouin spoke, the more he broke all the rules that Jackson had carefully pre-conceived for Bedouins.

"Tell me if it's none of my business, but are you a Bedouin or a Berber, or maybe from one of the lost tribes of Israel?"

"I'm not a Bedouin at all. I just dressed this way to attract your attention."

"But you didn't attract anyone *else's* attention by dressing like that."

"You have more imagination than the others. I was - I am - communicating purely with your imagination."

"You mean I'm just dreaming all this?"

"No, not at all. It's telepathic. But everyone's telepathic key is different. The telepathic key to the essence of 'Jackson' is through your imagination.

"The 'Essence of Jackson', I like the sound of it."

"Which is why no-one else saw me in the Old City streets."

"And that's why you knocked me down too?!" Jackson recalled, a bit pissed off.

"Rather rough for an introduction, I admit, but I wanted you to follow me." The Bedouin had settled into a well-articulated West London Earthling accent that his key told him was more pleasant to Jackson's ear.

"Why?"

"In due course."

"So you're not really a Bedouin. What are you? A contestant for Film Buff of the Year? You say you are communicating with me through my imagination. Great. My mind has finally packed up and gone on vacation. You're just a figment of my imagination. Yet I swear I can see you as clear as day. I *know* you're standing right there on the ground in front of me. Or at least I think I know it."

"Am I? You thought I was a rock a few minutes ago!"

"The sand is swirling around your feet and robes just as it is around the wheels of this ridiculous replicar I'm sitting in."

"If you say so."

"You *are* talking to me loud and clear."

"I already explained that."

"A holo projection? A new kind of impulse beam that suggests people instead of products?"

"Do I look like a holo? You know holos better than most people; after all, you programme and produce them for interstellar media."

"How do you know all that?" Jackson didn't like the answers he was getting. They were distinctly un-Bedouin like, if there was such a thing. "Are you from Central Thought? Or the Quadrant Police? Or maybe the Spanish Inquisition was resurrected too! Don't tell me you didn't get the cheque I sent you for the parking tickets in Yukay."

"No. None of the above."

"Okay. I've flipped. Nutted. Gazorked. I'm completely crazy, right? None of this is happening. It's all in my imagination. It's all in my mind and I..."

178

"True. Your imagination is helping things enormously. But let me assure you, you are not gazorking, flipping or nutting."

"I really don't find you very re-assuring. In fact, you're doing a lousy job for someone with such a forceful follow-me-anywhere gaze. You're not convincing me I'm in good hands here."

"I'd like to make a suggestion," the UnBedouin interjected. "Why don't you spray on an extra coating of coolant, bring your bag and come to my cave. You'll be a lot more comfortable there."

"No thanks. I'd rather stay in the Land Rover, thank you very much. I don't like caves. Bad things happen in caves."

"If you stay in the Land Rover, you'll be buried in it. The sand is already over the axles and you don't even have a shovel."

The UnBedouin opened the driver's door and Jackson cautiously sank his feet into the soft blisteringly hot sand. The axles were indeed buried. He had little choice but to follow the shrouded figure. At least he seemed to know where he was going. 'Why am I following this man into the desert?' he thought, 'I don't even know his name! '-- "Hey, what's your name, anyway?"

He was ignored. As they walked, Jackson found it somewhat unnerving that the UnBedouin left no footsteps. "Pardon my curiosity, but you're not leaving any footsteps."

"I'm light on my feet" the UnBedouin yelled back, attempting to explain away his unfootsteps. 'And how many times do I have to remind you that I am a product of your imagination? Albeit a very real product. If you want me to leave footsteps in the sand, just imagine that I do and you will see them."

"This isn't happening."

"Oh yes it is."

"How do you know who I am?"

179

"We are in telepathic communication. I know a great deal about what is in your mind, at least just below the surface. But I would not delve deeper without your permission."

"Listen, you may call it communication but I call it invasion! You're probably going to take over my body next! Communication is by definition a two-way process, and I'm getting bugger-all out of you."

"Ah, but you will. This is a new experience for you. Start gently. Ease into it. My mind will connect more and more links with yours as we go. A trickle will become a stream. But if I give you a deluge now, your mind will be drowned and not comprehend. To use an ancient idiom coined on this planet, you will be incapable of seeing the forest for the trees."

What the spooky stranger said made some sense, so Jackson didn't push his argument further. He still wanted a lot more answers but his questions took a new turn as the air was rocked with the sound of an explosion "What the Hell?!"

"Your Land Rover, I m afraid it somewhat over-heated."

"You blew it up didn't you! Where are you taking me? I've been hi-jacked or kidnapped or whatever they do to you in the Middle East! This place will never change. I'm not going to get out of this alive am I? I'm a hostage for whatever extremist front you work for. Martyrdom is not why I came here!"

"Hold on. Calm down. You can turn around and go back whenever you wish. I'm not holding you. But you really must trust me on this; you'll die out here alone if you turn around now."

"It's some sort of plot isn't it? You're a resurrected Palestinian kidnapper aren't you?"

A column of black acrid smoke rose higher from the ruins of the Land Rover. It hadn't just overheated, it had been detonated. The question was – was it a self-destruct programme or something else?

The Bedouin spoke from thin air, "That was undoubtedly a bomb. And that is not good news. You would have been killed if you had stayed in the replicar. But -- you were with me and you were not killed. Thank your god you are still alive. Thank your god you are with me."

"I could have been killed. Why me? Who'd want to kill a harmless goddam Creator for chrissake?"

Jackson quaked with fear as he looked back at the pall of rising smoke and the widely scattered bits and pieces. Was it really a bomb? "Yes, you're right. I'm sorry. Maybe you did save my life, I don't know. You knew there was a bomb in the car, didn't you?"

"No. But it seems logical there would be one."

"Why? Why me? I'm just a Creator, for chrissake. I don't kill people. I don't hurt anyone."

"Perhaps you insulted someone who does these kinds of things."

"The Expansionists?"

"You called them Pirates if I'm not mistaken."

"But nobody even issued a writ against me, and now a bomb?"

"Would you really expect them to issue a writ?"

"No. I suppose not... maybe I'd better lie low for a while. You mentioned a cave." It seemed like a good idea to get out of sight.

"Of course. It's not far."

The Bedouins form appeared a few steps in front of Jackson. He moved away toward the hills, motioning Mason to follow. As they walked, they talked. Jackson resumed his barrage of questions, "But where did you come from? Who are you? What interest do you have in me? Why do you know so much about me and what I do? What's in it for you to rescue or protect me? Do you want money?"

"I have no need of money."

"Why me? Why here? Why today? There was a huge crowd. Out of all the thousands of people thronging the streets of Jerusalem every day, why me?"

"They are all the same. You are different. I can survey thousands of minds at a time. I can mentally chart certain patterns in cranial activity. Your chart was immediately different. I can draw it for you sometime if you like. What you and I refer to as 'imagination' makes a very beautiful pattern on a brain wave chart. I had not encountered anyone like you for hundreds of thousands of years."

Jackson became aware of something touching his skull, on the inside. It was like someone gentling massaging his scalp but it was deeper, he could feel the outlines of the convolutions of his own brain being revealed to him. It was exciting.

"I am a Creator." Jackson stated proudly before all the words of the UnBedouin had sunk in. "Hundreds of thousands of years?"

"Many. But, as you say, you are a creator and that explains much."

"It does? Yeah, I suppose it does. In fact, I'm here to think about an advertising campaign I'm developing for the, uh...!" Jackson stopped himself from saying it then knew the Bedouin was completing the sentence for him.

"...for the Director of Marketing and Advertising of Quadrant Four."

"In truth, I have little use for advertising, I'm afraid."

"That's what everybody says. Especially women at cocktail parties. They're always moaning that advertising is sexist. I say, 'Look, of course there are exceptions, you can never completely eliminate bad taste, but the truth is, hundreds of thousands of advertisers simply do not spend billions and gazillions of credits to insult the people they are trying so hard to impress. It's not good business is it? Campaigns are always researched with groups of people they are actually aimed at well before they ever run. So the masses get the kind of advertising they like and understand. I mean, there are literally dozens of filter processes that make ... I'm sorry, I get passionate about some things..."

"I don't see why, but if you get a thrill out of it carry on, it's a relatively harmless occupation. You said so yourself."

"Look, oh great-and-wise-robed-one, whatever your name is -- have you ever bought anything off the shelf or ordered anything through your screen, anything at all that wasn't advertised? Advertising is necessary! Vital, damn it! Thank your lucky stars for it!"

"I admit that advertising has had its place in the history of Universal economics and is an integral part of the cultural base on many planets, and that it has made a remarkable impact as an art form."

"...and the dissemination of vital consumer information so people have some rational or emotional reason for making their choice -- don't forget that, and it provides challenging jobs too..." Jackson got his two cents worth in.

"And there is much you can tell about a society or an individual by looking at the advertising and promotional Art it has produced."

"...now you're talking..."

"But my talking to you has nothing to do with advertising."

"Oh?"

Jackson could no longer see the Jericho Road or the replicar as they climbed between great rocks around the hillside. As they turned a sharp cleft and entered a narrow ravine, there was a large warning sign. 'Designated Wilderness Area. No Entry Without Prior Authorisation'.

"Ah, what the Hell," Jackson muttered as they walked into no-man's land, "It's probably a minefield too."

"You're not from an enemy ad agency, are you?" Jackson asked.

"Do I look like an ad-man dressed in this Bedouin suit bag?"

"Could be. Stranger things have happened. In fact, you remind me of an art director I worked with once. Always wearing weird get-ups. Jeff Frye his name was. Don't know what he thought he was - used to come in wearing outrageous capes like a comic book hero. I ran into him once at a cocktail party given by a model agency and he was wearing a snakeskin suit. Snakeskin from top to bottom and cut with wide flairs on the trousers and wide lapels on his weedy shoulders. Those were the days. Give me the future any time. He was a snake in the grass and a real turkey at the same time."

"Fascinating, I suppose. But tell me, why do you think of other ad agencies as enemies?" the robed man probed.

"Because they are. They'd do anything to get my business. The general public has little idea of the savagery and ruthlessness and even cold-blooded murder that occurs beneath the glamorous surface of advertising. Little companies like mine use friends to get things in and out the back door of places. Bigger agencies use thugs and petty cash to get things done. On Selangor, the Robinson Company is well known for beating up clients who don't fall into line with the Creative Director's rationalisations."

"They must attract some unusual clients."

"Mostly rubber and leather goods." Jackson chuckled. "Where's this cave of yours? I have to get out of this sun, and if I was a soft target in the Land Rover I'm a sitting duck now. It's not far now I hope."

"Sorry. I forgot how long it takes to walk anywhere. I'm used to flying everywhere. Only sixty metres to go. I hope the trek hasn't been too unpleasant" the Bedouin pointed to a dark cleft beneath a ledge just ahead.

"I suppose I've bored you stiff about advertising."

"Yes, actually, you did. But at least you got some valuable practice in telepathy."

At the sight of the cave, Jackson felt weaker and rather more vulnerable. Anything could be lurking in that cave and he was unarmed. Totally alert to the danger, everything assumed a crystal clear dimension of reality instead of the dream-like unreality he had thus far experienced in the presence of the stranger. It didn't make sense that all this was the product of his imagination. Even if the Bedouin character was feeding his mind right down the line.

When the Bedouin had told him he was using telepathy and that he wasn't really there, Jackson imagined that maybe the guy was an alien. In his first life, beings from outer space were popular subjects of fiction. Now, human beings were the ones from outer space - and in all the millennia that man had explored and commercialised the Universe, never once had they encountered a superior intelligence, but Jackson often wondered if there had been a massive cover-up and that 'aliens walk among us' on a daily basis just waiting for the signal to take over. Oh, there had been many unusual plants and new forms and types of creatures, but nothing even approaching the complexity of man himself, neither biologically nor mentally.

So what was Jackson encountering now? A sophisticated new mind probe developed by a big advertising or marketing agency? Perhaps that was the most plausible explanation. 'Best to keep jabbering about people from his past and case histories - eventually whoever is watching will get bored with me,' he instructed himself. 'And this nonsense about reading my mind ... hell, if this character in the bed sheet can do all that, he'd already know what I'm doing on Earth - he'd have what he's after and be gone."

The cleft deepened into a cave. A worryingly dark one at that.

"I think I'm in deep shit."

"Did you say something Mason?"

185

"What about some light in here?" Jackson suggested.

"I don't need it for myself, but as you are my guest, 'let there be light'."

And there was light!

It seemed to come from the air itself. There was no apparent source for it. No tubes, panels, globes, bulbs, switches, cords, lines, points or plugs. It was an even light, soft and clear at the same time, rather like a radiation shower machine coming from all sides at once.

"Welcome to my lifepoint." The Bedouin crouched and crossed his legs, sitting on the sandy floor.

"Great. Nice touch. 'Lifepoint'. I like it. Original. So for the umpteenth time, what's your name? What are you called?"

"I am called Atos by all who know me."

"Atos? Are you serious? Shah, or David or Saddam might fit the image of the dusty cape a bit better."

"Mason, if you don't mind, I'm not really interested. I happen to think that Atos is an ideal identity tag for me. Oh, please excuse me for a moment; I have to answer a private call. I hope you don't mind."

"Not at all, go right ahead."

Jackson was hardly prepared for Atos, to disappear. Jackson had perpetrated countless illusions and contrivances himself in the name of advertising and selling products. But this was supposed to be real life! One moment Atos was sitting next to him on the floor, then zap! Poof! Gone! Not even a cloud of smoke to screen the departure. And talk about dark!

"I knew I shouldn't come into this cave" he spoke aloud to himself and the walls. "Okay. Time to wake up. End of dream. Let's snap our fingers and get back to reality. Wakey-wakey! Time to get out of bed and go to work."

The cave remained black for a moment, and then Atos was back, filling the space with light once more.

"I apologise for having to leave you. I assure you it was urgent."

"But you're not really here anyway," Jackson reminded him.

"I am and I'm not. I'm not here in the same physical sense as you are. And, nonetheless, my *being,* my essence is certainly here with you. Otherwise it would be somewhere else. Just now, someone really needed me ..."

"Hell, I thought you went out to the toilet..."

"I do not have such needs. As I was saying, I was required elsewhere. And I cannot be in two places at the same time."

"You could always do a hologram to stand in for you."

"If I ever do, you've got the business."

The two men looked intently at each other. Smiles melted into anxiety about what was going to happen next.

"What was that crack about 'hundreds of thousands of years' a few minutes ago, Atos? You have lived hundreds of thousands of years? You expect me to believe that"

"Essence of Jackson, all will be revealed to you in good time. Before I begin, let me outline the scenario: First, the person I went to see just now told me about your visit to the Library. *All* about it.

"Second, I and others like me have survived for hundreds of thousands of years. There is little about humankind we do not know.

"Third, since you were a small boy you have known in your innermost self that you have a special kind of imagination. You have often wondered about the meaning of it, and never understood the mechanics of it - but let me assure you - if it were not for the sheer force and power of your imagination, you would not be here with me now.

"Fourth...."

"I know I'm a dreamer, Atos, but do you mind if we start by clearing up a few much more elementary questions? Like whether or not you're even real!"

"I assure you I am real."

"Then may I touch you?"

"As you wish."

187

Jackson extended his right arm towards Atos's left. He carefully stretched and pointed his forefinger towards the outstretched forefinger of the Bedouin. Together they looked like a detail from da Finci's famous family portrait of The Extraterrestrials. At the last moment, Jackson hesitated as if expecting a bolt of lightning to flash between their fingertips like God and his Creation.

Closer and closer he moved his finger. Nothing. He could swear he was touching Atos's finger. Finally, Jackson flicked his finger in desperation. And saw it spring through Atos's hand. There was no sensation of the other man's flesh. For indeed there was none.

"You're a goddam ghost!" Jackson shrieked, pulling back his hand.

"I am an illusion," Atos stated matter-of-factly.

"A real illusion. Best damned holo I ever saw!"

"Not a holo."

"Please! I must see you as you really are. That is unless you turn into a hidecus monster, I mean I don't want you to scare the crap out of me. So don't do it if you're going to turn into a slimy faced gorgon or something. OK?"

"As you wish."

"You said that before."

Atos responded by shrinking to about half his size. And then he started to grow. A soft warm glow at first, then pink, then quite red. Then, suddenly he incandesced. White hot! All this took about 30 seconds.

"I'm doing this slowly so you can see it better," Atos' voice came from the hot white shape. Then the burning Bedouin condensed to a fine bright single spot of light about the size of a sesame seed.

Jackson laughed with obvious relief. "I thought you were going to turn into a gorgon with poisonous fangs but you're no more frightening than Tinker Bell!"

"A child of the Universe," the light spot spoke.

"Did you get that one out of Asimov or Clarke?"

"Where do you think they got it?"

"Sounds like we're moving towards the old god-is-a-spaceman routine."

"Something like that. Your religious fanatics always explain the unexplained with statements like 'The Lord moves in mysterious ways'. And haven't you heard the countless tales of the skies being streaked by mysterious lights over the millennia?" The light spot spoke with authority on this matter.

"Yeah, meteors."

"Philosophers and other great thinkers have long talked about Enlightenment. The Greeks had a word for everything - they referred to the Muse of this and that for inspiration. Plato, Aristotle, Abelard, Newton, Einstein, Brandor, Chivas, they all had their moments of insight, their moments of contact with their Muse.

"And Aristotle called creativity the Shine of the Divine.

"I and others of my kind, Mason, are the Light and the Way. We are The Muse, the inspiration, the spirits, the strange lights in the sky that have followed men wherever they travelled."

"And I suppose you always were, and always will be," Jackson quipped sarcastically.

"No, like you, we are an evolved race. As mortal as you are. Now try to grasp, 'as you are I was, as I am you could be'."

"My old man always used that line whenever I was being a wise-ass teenager. But he said it with a slight difference: 'as you are I was. As I am you *will* be'."

"Will or could, it's still your choice, Mason."

"Listen, Atos, I don't mean to be rude, but your light is hurting my eyes a bit, I mean, to look you in the face is a bit uncomfortable -- er, that's not quite what I meant, sorry."

"I know what you mean. Would you prefer me to go back to my Bedouin form?

"No, not at all. I like you the way you are. You're rather cute this way, you know, just floating around the cave like that. I don't feel at all threatened when you're in this state of enlightenment."

"Let me try a softer approach." Atos dimmed his aura. "Is that better?"

"Yes, much. Thanks. Now, about these hundreds of thousands of years you say you've been around for, who am I to say that isn't the truth? I mean how would I know? But..."

"You want some proof, right?"

"How would I be able to judge the validity of your proof? I wouldn't. But it might at least be entertaining to let you try. Perhaps you might like to begin by corroborating the Tree of Humankind? So what have you got to say about that, Atos?"

"What would you like to know?"

"Well, for starters, how accurate is it?"

"As far as it goes, very accurate."

"What do you mean, *as far as it goes*? In breadth or depth or accuracy?"

"Mason, I would like to tell you about human Evolution. I think you might like this story... "

Jackson leaned forward eagerly.

"You believe that mankind first developed on Earth, don't you?"

"Yes, I think I do."

"And that proto-men evolved from specialising apes?"

"All creatures specialise, Atos."

"Then from certain, specifically organised specialised apes."

"A specific, certain special ape - the Missing Link, is that what you're getting at, Atos?"

"That's the general drift."

"And does that have anything to do with continental drift? Tectonic plates and all that?"

"Yes and the creature that almost eluded you on roots of the Tree."

"You mean, the one I think was indicated but wasn't put on the base root properly?"

"You were very alert to find that tiny bump on the root model - it was hidden as well as it could be by the Expansionist technician who moulded that part of the Tree."

"Then there was something to hide."

"More than you could have guessed, though you were on the right track. But the bump was only a theoretical indicator; the Expansionists have yet to find tangible evidence of the true course of human evolution."

"I'm all yours, Atos. Keep going."

But the light spot hesitated, so Mason leapt in. "How about the Missing Link buried under a mile of ice at the South Pole?"

"Much more."

"Space-nuts! Then I'll go for an entire primitive civilisation under the ice – you must mean there's a civilisation so old that it proves beyond doubt that mankind evolved on Mother Earth alone! Do I win the prize?"

"Age is not necessarily proof of Origin, Jackson."

"Yeah, but just for instance, how old are we talking about here?"

"In the twentieth century, it was calculated that the Big Bang had occurred 13,000 million years prior. In fact, the correct answer was about 17,000 million. Your contemporaries also placed the origin of this solar system back 4,600 million years. The correct answer was 4,990 million. Your scientists dated dinosaurs in the period 235 to 65 million years. Quite correctly. The rocks told the truth there.

"And Australopithecus about 2 million years," Jackson confidently added.

"Give the monkey credit for evolving into man another 2.2 million years earlier. Of course, none of your scientists could have known. They could only work from

191

sites they found. Not the ones they didn't find. Deep beneath the Antarctic ice mantle, the real origins of the species are still to be found. But my people, The Freea, took a higher path of evolution than that found at Olduvai and other African digs."

"Fascinating. Then you are from Earth too. Your people, the Freea, you call them? Also evolved on Earth?"

"Yes."

"I must be dreaming this."

"We both are, in a way, do you not remember?"

"Aside from the telepathic communication tapping the tendrils of my imagination... Tell me about your people, the Freea. And what do you mean about a higher path of evolution?"

"Do not doubt the higher path, Mason. Have you ever seen anyone else do what I have done today?

"You're a master illusionist, no doubt about that."

"The communication is real. You are not dreaming, you are fully aware, and afterward, you will have complete recollection. I am tapped into your imagination because it is an open channel, but you are not asleep."

"Okay. I hope you're right."

"Expansionist scientists were quite correct in believing that there were two great exoduses out of Africa. The first being initiated by Homo erectus about 2,000,000 BC, and remember there were also Neanderthals that flourished in Eurasia about 250,000 BC. The second exodus, of modern Africans took place about 100,000 BC. The modern Africans gradually displaced the peoples of the first exodus so successfully that by around 30,000 BC, the Neanderthals had disappeared. True modern man, rather like you, emerged as recently as 35,000 B.C. "

"Yes, yes, go on!"

"Well, my ancestors didn't. We emerged a few million years earlier."

"And where was that? In Africa too?"

"Yes and no."

"Are you of human origin or not, Atos?" Jackson found it difficult to grasp the concept of a human light bulb.

"We evolved just like you did."

"Either you're human or you're not."

"If you mean, did both the Freea and Homo sapiens arise from the apes, then the answer is yes. But not the same apes and our evolution took place eons earlier, at a time when Africa was still connected to what you know as Antarctica. And long before the climate of Antarctica became polar cold and was buried under ice and snow. Freea-Man developed there. And a portion of them evolved mentally to a degree unsurpassed for its effectiveness and efficiency of thought."

"Well you said it would at least be an entertaining story, but even with my imagination, it stretches the realms of credibility to new dimensions."

"Shall I keep going? Are you with me? Good. Even as apes, the pre-Freea beings evolved telepathic powers beyond anything your species has yet experimented with. And after a million years of pursuing thought processes, we finally freed ourselves from the shackles of physical life and disability."

"How do you mean disability?" Jackson wanted to know. "Were you deformed?"

"I simply mean we freed ourselves from the need to have physical bodies. We no longer suffered the time consuming inefficient needs for shelter, warmth, or food that your version of the species does. And we also became free of the tedious cycle of life and death. We became as One with the Universe."

"You mean you became spirits?"

"The essential entity of our former physical state has been sublimated and purified to a minimum essential mass whilst retaining all the individual characteristics of the mind. We are essentially the same beings we were in proto-Africa, although we, our minds, have continued to develop."

193

"Then how come you appear to be so small?"

"I stress again, development does not equate with an increase in size. You should know that already. Ours is a convenient, efficient appearance and size. In short, it is the most practical possible form of being. And our mind is no longer limited by the size of a brain because it *no longer occupies one.*"

"Geesh!" Jackson was visibly stunned. If all this were true it was beyond belief because it was beyond not only his experience but the limits of his imagination. But there was his original line of questions that still needed some big answers."So what happened to the other apes, the other early men, my ancestors?"

"You have misunderstood. Your ancestors merely came *later*. From a later species of ape. You know their story pretty much already. The Tree represents it as far as it can. My species is superior because it has been evolving much longer than yours has. Yours may catch up in time, or at least reach the level my species is at now. But there was a time I would like to tell you about. A time of great suffering in our evolving society.

Just as all men are not created with equal abilities, so too there were differences amongst the Freea. Some adapted superior mental abilities to others. Altogether, about a quarter of the population eventually developed enough mental power to 'go over the top'. The majority, I'm afraid, were incapable of it. They were mentally inferior and pursued a different and essentially physically oriented existence culminating in a great civilisation founded to the south of Africa. And, as you have guessed, now buried under the ice of Antarctica. The evidence of their civilisation was largely wiped out by the succession of Ice Ages."

"Hold on, I love the story and you tell it so well," Mason said with genuine gratitude "But what for? Why me? Why tell me?"

"Because you wanted to know. Pure and simple. There are exceedingly few inquisitive souls. Few men of real imagination. I tell you because you wanted to hear, nothing more." The point of light continued to hover in the middle of the cave, its soft glow illuminating the grey stone. "My ancestors simply disappeared. Undoubtedly crushed and ground away so that no one would recognize them for being what they are."

"But what became of your branch of the Freea I'd like to know, if you have the time."

"All the time in the Universe, Mason. When we first escaped our bodies, we roamed the world at will. Then we explored the solar system and taught ourselves to reach the stars. All we had to do was learn to navigate in space. We have no need for life support systems. No need for mechanical contrivances or conveyances of any kind."

Jackson was again agog and could only shake his head in astonishment as Atos continued.

"Whereas your technically-oriented branch of mankind has concerned themselves with recreating your environment in transportable forms so you can take it with you wherever you go, we never restricted ourselves like that. We have travelled the Universe for all these eons. Apart from curiosity and sentimentalism there was never any need to go back to Earth. We watched over those we left behind until they died out then we simply moved on. Believe me; no amount of help on our part could save them. They were incapable of following through on our advice and instructions. And we were limited by a lack of physical abilities.

"You must understand that we Freea were never technology-oriented. We did not build much. We expressed ourselves through art and profound thought, not through *things*. When it became clear that men would have to leave their land to escape the ice, we thought of a ship. And we told them about it. We thought of how ships might be built, and we told them about it. But they had precious little understanding of the concept. And without our own bodies, we couldn't build the ships for them. They needed more time to develop their mental powers. And they ran out of time before the Ice Ages swept them away."

Jackson sat cross-legged listening intently. He wasn't used to sitting on the floor like this and his hips and knees ached like hell. Painfully he stood up, stretched and sat down, this time leaning against the wall with his legs stretched out before him. Atos continued his account, "You have no idea how frustrating it's been watching and waiting for your species to grow up, one small step at a time. But the physical changes have been fascinating nonetheless. Your species has developed beautiful bodies. We Freea were always more ape-like than you in the beginning. Then our legs and arms diminished and our heads enlarged -- but our minds grew faster than our brains. So you see, something had to give, didn't it? "

"Have we *never* pleased you?" Jackson wondered.

"The mechanical ages of your species have been the most interesting phenomena and also the most bewildering. Your species was highly inventive and entertaining, but it has been so frustrating pouring all your energies into physical thing. For example, you have wasted so much energy and mental effort to build and erect – structures to live in and work in, machines to do work, take you places and kill people with. When all along it was possible to be free of the need for shelter, free of the need to physical work, free of the necessity to make war, free of the need to get in or on anything to go from one place to another!"

"What do you mean? We have telebooths that take us considerable distances in an instant."

"True." Atos conceded that point, but no other.

"And if you ask me, we've made a very balanced progress. Your fore-fathers were incapable of engineering. We have great engineers, great artists and great thinkers. We can do it *all*."

196

"Great? You barely know the meaning of the word. "We have often tried to give the better thinkers among you a glimpse of the reality and simplicity of what is possible. And we are well balanced thinkers. As creative in engineering as we are practical in creativity. Take Descartes, one of your so-called great early philosophers. I myself planted in his mind an intuitive moment I was sure would come out right. But he got it wrong. 'I think, therefore I am!' he cried. Imagine it! He saw it as proof of his own existence, whereas I wanted him to grasp our basic principle of propulsion! You see, Mason, we need only *think* of a place and time in order to go there -- of course we have to will ourselves to actually move the distance, traverse the space and go in the right direction; but all those processes are almost instantaneous when you know how to do it."

Outside the cave cleft into the Israeli countryside, the light was fading. Soon, all good Earthlings would be boarding their shuttles back to the Nixon. But inside the cave, Jackson was still tightly locked into every word that Atos, the guiding light, could tell him.

"Atos, can I ask you something?"

"Yes, anything."

"Your story, incredible as it is, and I still don't really know whether to believe it or not, even though it sounds like a lovely theory, -- seems to me that you are concerned about the Expansionists as much as I am, and that we have something in common there. A common agenda for the future, perhaps."

"You didn't sound very concerned when you were going on and on about advertising and the tedious details of the thinking behind marketing communication."

"Yeah, OK, sorry for droning on like that. It's hard to turn your beliefs upside down and toss them out, especially when you haven't found a suitable alternative to replace them with yet."

"I understand, Mason. The Industrialists, the Expansionists, the Pirates as you have referred to them recently, are on my mind and every one of the Freea."

"What do you think about the government's programme of Anti-Entropy research?"

"It's all being manipulated by the Expansionists who know they've found another bottomless expenditure pit to profit from the government and the people. They're not finding anything in their research except ideas for manufacturing more new products - that they'll eventually brief people like you to launch onto the markets in the next century or two when the current stock of mechanical and technological toys and gadgets becomes obsolete or in some other way boring to the whims of the all-consuming human animal."

"Ha! You have a sharp commercial mind, Atos."

"I am known to certain academics of your kind as the Muse of Economics." Atos' night light glowed a little brighter.

"Eventually all this Universe of ours and yours will end. The fires of the infinite suns will become finite and fade to ash in a precisely calculated time. There will be no way of stopping it. No way open to let your inevitably redundant legions of Expansionist profiteers to run rampantly through resources. The well will run dry. Entropy will be the final great leveller."

The light continued to fill the cave and warm it, whilst outside, cold desert night fell heavily on the surrounding sand and stones.

"You said you were mortal, Atos. So how long will you live? Do you know? Will you survive this Universe? Outlast entropy? I mean if you have no need for life support systems, then perhaps you are completely self-supporting?"

"We don't really know how long it is possible to live. We are not indestructible. Some of the Freea have been killed by accident, getting caught by exploding stars -- such are the hazards of wandering the physical universe. But none of us has yet reached the apparent natural limit of life, nor do we know old age as a physical entity might. We Freea left our physical bodies, our humanoid forms, if you prefer, back on Earth. They are lying as fossils beneath the ice cap of Antarctica. As far as being self-supporting, I am not sure. Light attracts light. We like to illuminate dark spaces, but we like to be able to see suns. Only at the end of the Universe will suns not exist. We do not yet know whether we can exist without them"

Atos seemed to pause as if to catch his breath. It was quiet in the cave for several heartbeats. Then Jackson broke the silence."I am still curious about something else. When I first saw you in Jerusalem, you appeared on top of a wall, and then floated above it; that was exactly like a dream of mine."

"The floating dream? Ah, yes, I see it sitting there in the front of your brain ready to pop out at any time. I find it curious too. Curious in a homo sapiens descendant that is."

"Why?"

"Because it is exactly like the way we Freea first left our bodies."

Jackson was breathless with the excitement of the possibilities. "Please, you must tell me more! You must tell me about leaving your bodies. Was it like dying? Or being reborn? Or something else altogether?"

"The process of evolution normally takes a very long time. But we selected our own evolutionary 'difference' very early and supported our own mental development. We consciously assisted our own selection and specialisation. Our evolutionary path was, after a certain point, no longer left to accident. We designed and followed through on our own chosen evolutionary path – and fulfilment."

"How on Earth did you do that? You're losing me and I want to get this right. Go back to the beginning, your beginning. Tell me what happened!"

"As I said before Homo freea evolved from a different ape than Homo sapiens. But, as in your evolution, we recognised that some individuals were slightly more intelligent than others. In the beginning, it also helped if they were stronger too. But the innate intelligence of some individuals ensured that they out-witted less intelligent members of their groups -- they could motivate and manipulate them into doing things for them. What developed was the most primitive form of leadership and royalty.

"Over thousands of years, the royal apes became wiser and ever more cunning. Eventually, the class distinction had become so perfect that they recognised they had truly evolved into a superior species. Life was good for them because they didn't have to do anything they didn't want to do. And they thrived on thought and communication. Naturally, their intelligence continued to be the selective determinant that ensured their survival - the Royal Apes were the forefathers of the Freea. They had the brain power, reinforced with every generation, to expand their mental processes so far that they could eventually see a time when they could free the mind from its physical prison of the animal level ape-body."

Jackson stared with a new intensity at the glowing light of Atos. It seemed to him that the light point, no bigger than a sesame seed, vibrated, pulsed and twinkled as Atos talked. H4e, sounded like a male, but there was no way of knowing whether Atos was male or female. Of course it didn't matter really.

Atos carried on, "This era of thought and future promise occurred coincidentally with great cataclysms of the Earth's surface that left the royal enclaves virtually isolated, geographically speaking."

"An accident of Nature?"

200

"Hardly. The mental powers of the Royal Apes were such that they were in perfect harmony with the earth, the sky planets and all the plants and animals they knew. They foretold of the cataclysms and made their escapes. You would call it an intuitive hunch. But they *knew* it was coming and where. The inferior stupid apes who worked for them did not believe the prophecies and were nearly wiped out in the massive eruptions and earthquakes. As you have worked out for yourself, the royal apes escaped beyond the mountains and gathered for their great lift off. But several years passed before the Royals elected to become the Freea and be free of their bodies."

"Why was that? Why did they put it off?"

"Because they all wanted to make the jump together. They didn't want to create gods amongst their own kind. They knew the value of maintaining their cohesive community, and wanted it to stay together. It took an enormous amount of coordinated effort and great determination to fill all the minds of all the Freea to bursting point. I remember the tragedy of many of the Royals who died of old age before the lifting time was reached. So much the sadder, because they were among the first who were fully able and prepared to go."

"And *how* exactly did you go?"

"We gathered in a great and majestic valley. A paradise of fruit trees, streams and waterfalls, hibiscus and frangipani. There were nearly a million of us. There was no real ceremony about it. Each person wore whatever clothes he or she felt was appropriate. We marked the event with a final meal, a kind of last supper, except it was actually late in the morning as I recall.

"I recall it was a beautiful day, auspicious by its crisp blue sky punctuated with gathering white clouds that began building into a mountainous thunderhead. There was the greatest feeling of anticipation that you could ever experience. The food had been in preparation for many days. Nothing was spared; there was no point in saving anything. As you might expect, there was a great deal of promiscuity going on too. But the higher meaningfulness of the occasion prevented the morning from deteriorating into anything undignified.""I imagine most of you were too old for that kind of activity anyway!" Jackson said, somewhat amused by Atos's tactful description.

"You're never too old for it! But we had stopped having children about fifty years earlier. Anyone who had children did so in the knowledge that the young would be left behind because they wouldn't be mentally evolved enough for the Leap."

"But surely there were some children and they would see their parents go and know what was happening to them?"

"Yes, of course. They did. And it was a tragedy waiting to happen. Their parents continued to visit them as I am visiting with you now. But the children tended to have minds of their own, and rebelled, ultimately growing up in comparative ignorance, their minds unfulfilled with our degree of mental ability. Lost, abandoned, they turned to drugs and died insane in their earthly paradise. Like I said, it was a tragedy "

Atos paused briefly before continuing. As Jackson listened to Atos's description of the Great Lift Off, a tingle began at the base of his spine and moved upward to the base of his brain. He knew exactly what Atos was talking about.

"Linking our minds towards the sky, we held the hands of our fellows and loved ones. As the sun reached its zenith, we hushed our minds to silence. The whole valley heard us. We were in absolute harmony with the earth, the air and the sky. Not a bird twittered. Not a snake slithered. Not an insect crawled or buzzed, A million of us stood in unison, holding our arms outstretched and level with the top of our shoulders. Then we begin to chant a single syllable. A sound that echoed the birth of the Universe. A sound that reverberates across the galaxies even today. 'Ommmm!'

"We lifted our bodies to full height, standing on the extremity of our toes. 'Ommmm!'We hummed over and over as one. In a single downward sweep of the arms, we each lifted from the ground by a few inches. 'Ommmm!'

"We were free of the Earth! Free to float as high as we wished. But this much we had all done before. Together and individually."

Jackson felt an intense shiver shock through the full length of his spine. How could Atos' words have such an effect on him now, here in the cave?

"Then it was time to take the next and final step. This time, we repeated the action, but *all in the mind*, not actually vocalising it physically, but by visualisation. We strained together with total and absolute concentration: 'Ommmm!' We raised our arms. 'Ommmm!' We held the arms outstretched. 'Ommmm!' We brought them down with all our force! 'Ommmm!' The vibrations of a million minds chanting the same Universal syllable rippled through me, through all of us and we were released!

"In the final moment of bringing my mental arms down -- it was like being underwater and pushing up to the surface -- I shed my body. My mind, my whole essence, floated up through the top of my skull into free air, and free existence. I looked down with tremendous exhilaration upon my body standing immediately below me, my physical eyes were wide open and looking at up at my floating spirit. Then it crumpled. In a single moment, my body and a million others fell dead, crumpled and lifeless, empty of energy and spirit.

"It must have been horrific for the children!" Jackson said.

"Yes. Absolutely horrific. But there was no other way. It appeared to them that somehow we had all committed mass suicide. Bloodless, of course; but nonetheless all the bodies were lifeless. Then we rose far above the scene. Life was with us and in us and we smiled upon one another. We were free of our bodies! We, the free. The Freea.

"We could see ourselves and each other. But it was obvious the children could not see that we had evolved that it was only our bodies that were dead. They could hear us when we spoke to them trying to calm them. But it did not stop their hysteria and in fact it only added to their confusion. Finally we had no choice but to put them to sleep. Then we transported them away from the valley before the stench of our million dead bodies became overwhelming in the semi-tropical sun."

Jackson sat spellbound, mesmerised and drained by the vivid detail of the story. Eventually he stammered out another question. "Y-you were not in your light bulb form at first then?"

"No. We were simply ghosts of our former selves. Wispy, thin, white auras in our previous size and shape. The light form is a further form of our evolution. It is neater, tidier, and safer and does not alarm other life forms. It's basically a condensed form of the larger ghost, concentrated for more efficient thought and movement."

Suddenly the sound of a distant force thruster broke the spell of the narrative. Outside in the darkness, not far off, a patrol was out looking for Jackson.

"Don't worry, it's just the night sweepers," Atos said calmly.

"I was supposed to go back to Nixon with everybody else. I suppose I'd be in very big trouble if they find me here." Jackson said, somewhat jittery.

"One man, alone in a cave sheltering from the night because his replicar is buried in the sand? It's a strong enough alibi. I shouldn't worry. Of course, you're still free to go anytime you wish."

"No, I want to know more. But maybe you should douse your light so it doesn't attract their attention."

"I'm afraid they have heat seekers too; but if you don't want to be found, I will simply close the door and they won't see in." With that, the entrance to the cave was sealed by a great boulder.

"Looks like I'm completely at your mercy."
Atos ignored the comment, "I find this cave a bit dreary at night. Like to go for a moonlight swim?"
Mason grinned "Yeah, sure! Here in the desert?"
He didn't know where they came from, but three more lights appeared in a row next to Atos.

Freespace

Down at the Middle East Travel Centre in Jerusalem, all hell had broken loose. "485 dash 54 dash 0255 has not returned with his replicar, Mr. Laker."

"Well ask him why, Shelton."

"485 dash etcetera hasn't returned either."

"How do you know he didn't leave the car somewhere else and simply moon-beamed without telling us?"

"I've checked all the telebooth records, sir, and the visitor has not left the Middle East sector."

"Do a malfunctions check."

"Affirmative. That check is negative, sir."

"Then double check, Shelton."

"Double negative, sir. Systems report no malfunctions. Tele-booths and recording back-ups operating perfectly."

"Very well. Get Hardman." Hardman appeared on the screen.

"Hardman I may need your help. Damned Out-System visitor took a replicar and hasn't brought it back."

"Okay, sure. Who, where, what and when? If there's any funny business I'll find out how and why."

"Records show a 20th century Land Rover replicar booked by a Mr. Mason Jackson, 485 dash 54 dash 0255."

"That damned thing. Never could see the attraction in driving off a perfectly good road, myself. It's the only one in the pool and if it's lost, it's a blessing. So when did this Jackson fella go missing?"

"What you got on that, Shelton?"

"Sir, uh, Mr. Hardman, Lion Gate security records show the vehicle heading out on Derekh Yeriho about 14:30. We were only alerted when Jackson was not re-accounted for on any of the moon-beam shuttles at curfew time."

"There were scan reports of a small unscheduled sandstorm in the direction Jackson was heading, I'll sweep there first, Mr. Laker."

"If the vehicle broke down and he got caught in the freak sandstorm...shit, that sonofabitch better be alive or my ass is grass."

"If that's what happened, and we don't know yet, he probably stayed in the replicar to be safe."

"Get onto it right away for me, will you Sylvia?"

"Aye, sir. We've got a Night Sweep out in that sector now. They haven't reported anything one way or the other, but I'll talk to them and tell them what they're looking for. Leave it with me."

"I'm counting on you Sylvia. We've never lost a single goddam visitor in the whole region in my entire time as Middle East Centre Director. I'm sure as hell not gonna lose one now -- especially a moronic nobody from Out-System! The last thing any of us needs is a Quadrant Commission poking their over-sized noses around the Middle East."

Sylvia Hardman saluted smartly and dissolved from the screen.

"Let's get some coffee up here! We might have to stay awake tonight."

Corporal Shelton picked his nose and shuffled noisily. He brought the steaming coffee from the vending panel. "Pardon me for asking, sir"

"Then don't ask. Oh hell, what is it, Shelton?"

"Sir, hadn't we better report on this situation to Nixon Central?"

"Not yet. Let's give Sylvia's Sweepers a little time. Besides, Nixon knows the guy is missing because he didn't arrive back. I'd rather wait a little while and hope to come up with some positive news before I contact the 'higher ups'. When's the next routine Night Sweep check in?"

"Thirteen minutes, sir."

Laker sipped quietly, "What the hell did that alien bastard want to go into the freakin' desert for anyway? All on his own and in that weird old replicar? Beats me. We've got tours that take people everywhere, show them everything and explain the whole history. Who does he think he is? Moses?"

"Beg your pardon?"

"Moses! Moses! Moses! Take the tour sometime, Shelton."

"Holy Moses, what if the dumbo's gone into the Wilderness?"

"Moses in the Wilderness? I don't get what you mean..."

"I haven't the time to explain." The Centre Director watched all the surveillance screens as the status reports updated themselves. But it was still a little too early to expect anything from the Night Sweepers.

"Don't worry, sir, those sweepers are equipped with heat seekers so they'll find him even in the dark."

"Unless he's dead and cold."

He felt their minds surround him. Tendril fingers of mental contact flowed across Jackson's face, over his hands and wrapped around his shoulders. An undeniable double presence. Damned spooky it was too. Then each voice spoke from a separate light source.

"I am Dharman."

"I am Prem."

The voices of a man and a woman.

"How am I supposed to know which light belongs to which voice?" Mason wondered. "You all look the same."

It was Dharman who chose to answer, "You will learn to look into our essence and make associations. When

208

physical form is important, we can appear differently, as you saw when Atos chose to be a Bedouin."

Then Prem picked up the thought-line. "Speak to a name or to an essence and the essence will respond. Your own essence, your own inner Self will know."

"As long as you speak form the heart," Atos added, "you will be able to speak directly into an essence."

Mason squirmed slightly, uneasy at the prospect of spending the night in the cave with three light bulbs speaking a lot of semi-religious mumbo-jumbo, even if he did happen to understand what they were talking about. He felt a little too warm for comfort. It was claustrophobia. He wanted some fresh air. "Look, I don't mean to be rude or anything, but before you, uh, Dharman, and uh, Prem, arrived, Atos and I were going for a moonlight swim, weren't we, Atos?"

"That's right. We were."

"To tell you the truth, it's getting a bit warm for me in here with all these bright lights."

Dharman's light smiled, "A sense of humour is essential in troubled times."

"Any place you would especially like to go?" Prem asked.

"Any place cool. It's your territory. But don't forget visitors are not supposed to stay overnight on Earth. There could be patrols out looking for me, you know."

"They won't present any problems, but you'll have to change first."

"For swimming, oh yes, of course. But I didn't bring a suit. I don't mind swimming in my underwear -- I mean, if you don't mind."

"What Prem meant is that you will have to change *form*. Your physical body cannot live where we're going."

"Oh no you don't. You're not pulling that on me. I wasn't born yesterday. You guys are vampires, right?" Jackson made the sign of the cross with his forefingers and held it out toward the three lights.

"You must leave your body completely."

"I do it all the time, of course. Stay back!"

"Wouldn't you at least like to try to take on the form that we have?"

"What? A light bulb?"

"We are the Freea."

"We've been through that, Atos. I'm from an inferior species, remember?"

"We believe you have the potential to be one of us." Dharman said to his heart.

"Our species and yours can yet share a common destiny." Prem's words made an impact. Mason began to rethink the situation. A new destiny, a change in the future, it was very intriguing. Nearly a minute passed before the next words were spoken.

"I'm not sure I'm going to like this, even though I've dreamed of doing it since my youth."

"Ah, Mason, we knew you would see the light!"

"We will help you every step of the way."

"If it had not been for long years of intensive training, discipline and the grace of our teachers, I never would have made the jump myself," said Dharman.

A collective voice assured him, "I am with you."

"I'm still not totally sure about this..."

"Believe in yourself, Mason. You have within you the ability to be Free."

"I don't want to jump out of my skin unless I know I can get back in. All this stuff you're hitting me with. I mean it sounds great but I've still got a lot of living to do before I turn into a head lamp."

"Trust us. You will be fine." Prem's tones were more persuasive and reassuring than the others. Almost seductive.

Atos floated a little closer. "We promise you will be able to come back to your present state whenever you wish."

Mason nodded approval, and finally, acceptance, "OK then, let's go for it."

All three lights seemed to twinkle as Prem spoke again."The Universe dwells within you as you."

A change came over Jackson immediately. He felt a sudden surge of heat in his head, his heart and at the base of his spine. It was as though an ultimate truth had struck a chord. His spinal cord tingled. It was like a separate entity, a hot river that flowed up his back. Not unpleasant.

Moving higher and becoming brighter, the three lights flew in a ring around Mason's torso. With each pass the pace quickened. At first he tried to watch them, but it became impossible and he soon felt a little dizzy. Their orbit around him climbed higher and higher until it stabilised at eye-level. He imagined it was like being at the nucleus of an atom and watching the electrons whizzing around.

Then the lights spoke to him as one voice. "Do not try to look at us. This is not hypnosis. Look straight ahead." By now the lights had increased their speed so much they had become a continuous streak of light, a continuous glowing line against the dark stone walls of the cave.

"Hold your arms out to your sides" They told him.

Mason lifted his arms as he was told -- like wings. He dreamed his boyhood dream. He was finally going to fly. He recalled once again the dramatic crucifix at Wells Cathedral and he stood tall on the tips of his toes like a man newly nailed to a cross.

"Close your eyes." They instructed.

Mason could still see the streak of orbiting light through his closed eyelids.

"Empty your mind. Relax, but keep your back straight. Now, repeat the most ancient words in the Universe, 'Om nama shivayah'. All the sounds of the Universe are contained in these words, 'Om nama shivayah'.

Mason made the sounds of the Universal syllables, "Om nama shivayah."

"Repeat the words once on the in-breath and once as you breathe out. Say them silently to yourself."

The dream of flying over his boyhood home faded to black his mind seemed to be emptying itself out.

"As new thoughts come up, watch them but do not attach yourself to them. Empty your mind and go into the Void."

"Om nama shivayah." As Jackson synched the phrasing with the steady in-out of his breathing, fewer and fewer thoughts arose. More and more, his mind stared into a black emptiness. He was at the precipice, but friends stood safely with him.

"Concentrate on your breath. Feel it start deep. Feel it leave your throat. Feel it move across your tongue, drift over your lips. Feel it leave your body."

Mason felt himself falling forward into the Void. Then in the next moment there was nothing to fear as he surrendered himself into empty blackness.

"Feel your heart. Feel it fill. Feel it beat. Feel it push your blood through your body."

"Om nama shivayah." Mason felt the subtle pump in his quiet heart. He listened to his veins carrying the surge of blood. It echoed in the stillness of the cave.

"Feel the pulse. 'Om nama shivayah.' Your pulse is our pulse. It is the beat of the Universe. The Pulse of the Absolute. Know this to be true."

Mason was now aware of even the most infinitesimal micro-movement of every atom in his being and every electron in the cave and every meson in the Universe throbbing with the energy of the Absolute. Everything was alive with the pulse, and so it seemed, on the same wave-length of subtle vibration. He had never before perceived matter and energy as being of the same consistency. But it was. Is. He understood now. Everything is part of the whole. Everything is the Absolute. Even me. I am of the Absolute.

"The threshold is at hand. You must push through it or you will die. On our command, push up with your feet and down with your arms. Exert your inner power." The emphasis on the word power implied that speed of movement was not what was required.

The lights were still visible through his closed lids, ringing his head like a dazzling halo, but Jackson was no longer aware of them, he was in the Void. "Om nama shivayah, Ommmm"

"Now!"

It was as if Mason Jackson had lived all his life under water. For, as he pushed down with his arms and arched up on his toes, he felt the crown of his head break through a surface and into something void of weight. He slipped upward, shedding skin, flesh and skeleton as he rose above the heavy air into weightlessness.

"Ommmm."

A sweet smell filled his nostrils. Air that was fresher and livelier than any he had ever known. He recognised within it a fullness of frangipani, a hint of jasmine, glorious roses and orange blossoms and an alpine coolness.

"Open your eyes now, Mason. Open them."

Mason saw the three bright lights still orbiting around him. But now they were moving slow and could be seen separately, no longer a high-speed blur. There was more. As he looked at the lights, he could see beyond the glare and into faces. He knew them and was comforted by that knowledge. One was Atos, a young shiny faced man, handsome and curly haired, beaming with intense white light.

Dharman was the eldest of the three. He was grey and silver with rather sharp features possessed of quite the kindest eyes Mason had ever seen. His light was peculiar in not being white so much as it was blue.

And then there was Prem. An image that twinkled from girlishness to maturity in alternating moments. She was knowing, strong and assertive. Beautiful but not pretty. Attractive in a myriad of contradictions. Her eyes shone with immense energy.

Mason looked at himself and saw the face he always saw in the mirror, but now found it swathed in bright white light and contained in a shimmering sphere. He looked over his shoulder and saw the Nixon. And a thousand miles or more below him, Earth was a mesmerising swirl of blues, greens, whites and browns. So much beauty did little to prepare him for the ugly shock to follow. When Mason looked down he saw his own empty carcass staring up at himself. And he remembered sloughing off his body. "Am I dead? Is that my dead body down there in the cave?" He knew it was.

"No, you are not dead," said Atos, coming a little closer. "We only brought your Self up here. Your body is alive and well in a mindless deep sleep secure in the cave and out of reach from the night patrols or anyone else."

"But I distinctly remember that you said the Freea left *dead* bodies when you jumped off the planet."

"You are not dead," Dharman reassured him.

"Just because my body looks dead, why shouldn't I believe you? I feel terrific! More alive than ever! Before or after my cryonic resurrection. God, how many lives do I get, anyway? Surely I don't deserve this incredible experience. How can I thank you?"

"You have all of eternity ahead of you."

"I'm not sure I want quite that much time. Life is becoming, well, tiring. Besides, I can still go back to my body, right?"

"Yes, you may return to your former state of being any time you wish. Would you like to go now?"

"Not just yet. Let me enjoy this detached state for awhile. Hey, this is weird. I can say anything I want and my lips don't move."

"And you can travel at the speed of thought," Dharman added.

"Faster than light, then? Unbelievable. Is there anything I cannot do?"

214

"You are only limited by your imagination and the confines of this Universe."

"God, Dharman, you mean there are other Universes?"

"Perhaps, but we haven't found them or had any contact so it is still only a theory."

"With eternity on your hands, what do you do all day?"

"We travel a lot."

"We think."

"We monitor human development."

"That can't be much fun."

"It isn't."

They drifted as a tight little group out beyond Maras and mingled through the asteroid belt. Mason asking questions all the time. Gradually he became acutely aware of the enormity of the culture gap, or more accurately, species gap evidenced by his human interests as opposed to the Freea realm of experience.

"I really like food." Mason thought he heard Prem yawn. "And I appreciate a good woman and I enjoy sex. It's one of the best things money can buy. Theoretically of course."

"Such things have a place. Experience is important" Dharman muttered.

Mason was determined to see if he could get them excited about something, *anything* he had to say. He knew they were interested in his mind, so he began to build on that. He didn't want to be a boring guest a sentence longer, so he chose his next words carefully.

"Dharman, tell me of the great Truth."

"Ahh," the blue light of his face intensified, "because you seek the Truth it shall be revealed to you, thought I shall not be the Revealer. You are both the Seeker and the Revealer. You must learn to recognise that which is real from that which is unreal. This is called Discrimination."

"And are you real, Dharman?"

"I am as real as you are. I am That."

"Is That the Absolute?"

"It is."

"Then I am That. I felt its pulse and power in the cave."

"Yes. And you may be aware of it here and now, right in front of Saturn Gate.'

"Then what more can there be? If I am That. And That is the Absolute, what more is there to seek?"

"An insightful question! The difference between you and I, you and any of the Freea, is not one of species, but of fulfilment through surrender. You question the nature of Truth. We *know* it. You ask the value of seeking. We do not. You are going somewhere. We are already there."

"Do not be dismayed by Dharman's observations," Prem said caringly. "It is good to ask questions at first, but keep things in balance. It is not wise to over-intellectualise. Your questions will be answered in good time. You will no doubt answer them yourself. Now, it is time that I must go, Mason."

He didn't say anything, but it saddened him that she should be leaving so soon. Prem twinkled and moved away. Seconds later she had disappeared amongst the backdrop of stars. Then Mason felt something like a kiss land lightly on his cheek, and a gift-wrapped thought, like a secret letter, drifted into his mind. "Perhaps someday we can visit the most beautiful spot in the Universe together."

Mason was exuberant to say the least. "Atos, let's glide through the galaxy, sail the spaces, see it all!"

"Good! Very good! Dharman, thank you for your help, please pass on my regards to Rajesh."

"Good luck, Atos. Good luck, Mason. May you always honour the Universe that dwells within you as you." There was a tiny blue flash and Mason was left alone with Atos.

"I've always wanted to visit my star sign. Do you think we can go to Sagittarius? Or is it too far?"

"If you *think* you can go there, you can. So what will it be, Riga? Betelgeuse?"

"Betelgeuse," Mason said, without the slightest suggestion of a doubt.

"Do you study astrology, then, Mason?"

"Not now. But I did a little when I lived on 20th Century Earth. From there, the zodiac patterns made some sense. But the perspective is completely different from my new home on Omicron. Anyway, I only used to read my horoscope in the newspaper occasionally. Sometimes it was, shall I say, useful in chatting up women, to know something about star signs was the sign of a liberally minded male. Can you believe that? But why do you ask?"

"Just curious as to why you want to go there, that's all."

"The name just popped into my head. It's a place among the stars that I could spot easily when I was a child. And as for Betelgeuse, again, the name sounds like something silly and fun I guess. I mean, this is just a joy ride isn't it? And my business travels have taken me everywhere else I want to go."

"Of course. Relax and enjoy the stars. Hold onto my shoulder." Mason imagined grasping a shoulder, and just for a moment thought about Peter, Paul and Wendy flying off to Never-Never Land. Atos and Mason travelled far faster than light as they looped across the spiralling edge of the galaxy, Mason grinning all the way. Occasionally a freighter or a commuter shuttle sped across their path.

"Can they see us?" Mason asked.

"Not as you and I see each other, but I expect we are measured along with other microscopic bits of space junk, particle asteroids and such. We certainly wouldn't register as either a life form or sentient."

"I love it out here, Atos; it's great! I've always been the kind of traveller who asks for a window seat. Flying is a thrill every time, and this is the ultimate!"

"Yes, I agree. It probably *is* the ultimate."

"Am I doing alright then?"

"You're doing fine, just fine, Mason. You learn quickly. It takes real imagination to fly like this and this is only your first time out."

They flew on in silence for quite some time. Mason saw the stars as he had never seen them before. Incredible beauty, system after system. But here and there was a dying sun, a red dwarf going cooler each year, its life being sucked away by the siphons of Man's consuming ambitions for technical power and wealth. Each red dwarf surrounded by great fleets of transporters towing convoys of solar cells, each the size of a planet, each soaking up and storing valuable energy for commercial enterprise in tax-free zones near the centre of each Quadrant.

"Mason, what will you do when you go back?"

"Back to Earth? Or back to the Centre?"

"Whichever."

"I'm making it up as I go along. Yesterday I had it all figured that I'd spend a couple more days on Nixon sorting out the strategy on my current project, then catch a PanGal flight back to Omicron, then maybe see the Director of Advertising with my preliminary concept development, then spend two weeks hard at it pulling the presentation together, then put on the show, and after that, who knows?"

"As you said, that was yesterday."

"Now I'm seriously considering dropping out of all that and spending maybe a month or two with you and Dharman if he can spare the time. I'd like to find out if this light-bulb stuff is really for me. Now or later. If it is, maybe a lot of other people should know about it too."

"We hoped you might be thinking that way."

"Of course, I might decide not to go back at all. This is so beautiful I might decide to stay up here floating around forever."

"I'm afraid you'd soon be bored. If I may be somewhat impertinent, you're not quite ready for the higher life on a full time basis just yet. You would miss your food and your genitals too much."

"I guess you're right. And then there's the job, the unfinished projects, and all the people who depend on me."

"Perhaps someday all that will seem unimportant."

"Sometimes it already does seem very unimportant."

"Keep your goals, Mason, but keep your sense of balance too. For now it is sufficient that you are on the Path, and that you keep your imagination stimulated. The Freea have chosen you because of the highly developed power of your imagination. Do you understand the nature of your imagination?"

"Never thought about it, really. I suppose it is a special ability to see things in a different light."

"Excellent. But it is more. It's an ability to see deeply. Many people have some imagination. A few have developed it. You are expert in the skills of mass persuasion. You have a balanced mind that works within disciplines and reason as well as inspiration. And you are rather more ethical than most. Therefore it is our hope that you will reach the ultimate Truth with our help and carry this Truth back to the Centre of your civilisation, convincing all of your species that there is a better way to live than mindless consuming of all matter and energy. You see, Mason, your species is killing the Universe."

"Is that all? Wow! That really is the Big Picture. I thought the brief from Madame Prime was tough, but this is Cosmic. You want me to do nothing less than work a miracle with a capital 'M'. Do you remember what they did to Jesus Christ for working minor ones?"

"An unfortunate experiment."

"Christ was an experiment?!"

"Not unlike our project with you. He was imaginative, creative, persuasive, an excellent communicator. Perhaps we got the timing all wrong. It may have been too early. If it is any consolation, Jesus did achieve his own enlightenment and ultimately joined the Freea. So you see it can be done by a member of your species. The Jesus experiment certainly gave us a lot of hope for this current project."

"So was Jesus really resurrected? The Muslims say he wasn't that it was an illusion-- that you were meant to believe it happened but it never really did. Of course they also believe that Mary was never married to Joseph. That she was a single mother. And that the Christians changed all the stories to suit themselves." Jackson wondered if the Freea could clear up some old mysteries for him right then and there.

"They were both right. Mary clearly was a single mother and Joseph was a close friend who looked after her. The early Christian stories were in synch with the Koran, but they were edited out and deselected over the centuries as the Christians wished to elevate the role of women, and have a stronger overall appeal to family values. The debate still continues as you know. But Jesus' resurrection was actually his evolution as he become a Freea."

"So Jesus is still alive?"

"Sadly, no. He was hit by a rogue comet. Never had a chance."

Jackson's innate curiosity was still piqued, "But what of God? Did you find God in the heavens or perhaps at the centre of the Universe? The Christians of my Earth era were divided on the subject of space exploration with many thinking that man would ultimately find, and I mean actually locate, God out in the star systems; at the same time many Christian groups were against space exploration because they felt that it would prove that Heaven didn't exist as such and Paradise would have to be re-thought or re-invented."

Atos had observed people turning this question over for millennia, "And the third argument was simply that God is everywhere anyway, so you don't need to actually see God to believe in God. That his efforts are everywhere to be seen."

"So that means you have not yet found any proof for the existence of God."

"No," replied Atos, "but perhaps we can talk about it again sometime if you like. It is after all, a deep and interesting subject.

Jackson shared his next thoughts aloud, "I don't like being the subject of one of your experiments, and on the other hand, I really have nothing to lose and possibly a great deal to gain. Not that immortality appealed so much to my ego as it does to my stomach and genitals. I'm sure you realise I'll need a lot of help even if I do decide to take on the Universe with you."

"It's already been well taken into account, I assure you."

Rock and Roll

"**D**irector, this is Hardman. We've got something out here, you're looking for."
"What have you got, the missing replicar? The body?"
"We've got Jackson. Alive and looking healthy. I'm bringing him in straight away. And there's something strange I think you should know about, sir."
Don't joke with me, Sylvia. That's the last thing I need. Damned out-system day-tripper coming back from the dead. Look, I've had 'strange' up to my neck. Friday afternoon Jackson disappears on a normal holiday visit, the night sweepers find nothing, not even a heat trace; the day patrols find zip-nothing and I can only conclude death by misadventure. I report the death according to the book and now, Sunday morning you say he's alive. Now how in the hell am I going to find an explanation for him being alive and for not having found him for two days! Screwed my weekend totally."
"Well he's alive alright. Very alive."
"I filed a report that said he was dead and I'd prefer to wash my hands of this affair and leave it that way."
"So you want me to kill him?"
"Hell no, but you can help me with the paper work! We'll have to face an official enquiry as to how we lost a tourist from Friday to Sunday."
"Maybe Jackson has an explanation. He certainly doesn't look as though he's been through an ordeal."
"That's more than a little strange, but he might be a fitness fanatic or something."
"I hardly think so. You haven't met him, I have."
"Get a medical officer on him, in him, all over him. And he gets a personal escort back to Nixon; I don't want to take any chances on losing him again. How'd you manage to find him anyway?"

"One of our surveillance cameras picked him up, sir. They scan a pretty wide area. The moment a movement is detected, it does a crash-zoom on the object and records the action."

"You don't have to tell me how my own equipment works, Hardman."

"Yes, sir. Well, as soon as the zoom started, one of our sweepers got the signal and was routed to investigate. The team then spotted Jackson picking his way among boulders. He was walking in the general direction of the Jericho Road -- towards Jerusalem."

"OK, but what's the strange bit you were so eager to tell me about?"

"When we replayed the surveillance tape, we got quite a shock. The movement that triggered the camera was a huge rock rolling from right to left revealing the entrance to a cave."

"A tremor could do that."

"In the middle of the zoom-in, we saw a man pushing the rock aside with his bare hands. You'd have to be super-human to move a rock like that."

"Nonsense. Nobody would attempt heavy work like that without a Force Lever."

"Jackson didn't have one. He didn't have any tools at all, only a small day-bag of personal necessities. We checked the whole area and came up with nothing."

"Did you ask him about it?"

"Not yet. I didn't want him to know we saw him do it."

"Good. Keep him under very close watch. Consider yourself joined at the hip. Certain people may like to have a little chat with Mr. Jackson. Did he volunteer any explanations at all as to what happened to him?"

"Quite readily, sir. I'll play you the recording now. We followed the ops manual on this one to the letter, Mr. Laker. The manual recommends recordings of rescued tourists in case there are any legal repercussions later on."

"I know that, Hardman. I helped write the book. So play me the chip."

"Here goes."

"Mr. Jackson? Are you alright?"

"Yes, yes! I'm fine. Very glad to see you!"

"We've come to take you home."

"Thanks very much. I'm sorry about all this. I must have caused you a great deal of inconvenience, I didn't mean to."

"As long as you're safe, that's the main thing. You look well enough."

"I was driving on the Derekh Yeriho, you know, the Jericho Road. The hills seemed so beautiful. I decided to drive right up to them. I guess I shouldn't have left the paved road. The Land Rover was built for it, but the wind blew up a lot of sand and the replicar got bogged and I couldn't see very well."

"Why didn't you radio for help?"

"I didn't know I could. I'm not very mechanical. I didn't think of it. I thought the radio only played or received entertainment; I didn't know you could send anything on it. What a brilliant idea. A car radio that sends as well as receives."

"All our replicars have such radios. It's in the leaflet, loud and clear. It's on the visor, loud and clear. You get into trouble; you radio for help, loud and clear."

"Uh, sorry. I really felt stupid. But I honestly didn't notice any leaflets or stickers about the radio system in the replicar. Well, anyway, I figured I was only a few miles from where I left Jerusalem and when the sandstorm finished I could walk back if I had to. After a while, I tried digging the car out but I didn't get anywhere with that so I decided to climb up in the rocks to look for a vantage point. I climbed up alright but I couldn't see much when I got up there and I had a lot of trouble getting down. By then it was beginning to get dark. When I reached the Land Rover it was so well buried in the drifting sand that

I couldn't open the doors to get in. Even if I had, I might have been buried alive in it."
"Sounds like a lucky escape alright."
"Damned lucky, that's for sure. I had no choice then but to try to hole-up somewhere in the rocks."
"Hole-up? Unfamiliar term."
"It means get some shelter. Luckily I found a cave to spend the night in."
"Didn't you hear or see the Sweeps out looking for you? They covered this area on both sides of the Jericho Road with meticulous care."
"I'm not used to so much physical exertion. I went out like a light. Sound asleep in minutes. Dead to the world you might say. Never had a night's sleep like it. And now I feel fantastic!"
"But Mr. Jackson, you disappeared Friday afternoon. This is not Saturday, it's Sunday. You arose on the third day. What happened on Saturday?"
"I must have slept through it." End of recording.

"The lying sonofabitch. Hardman, I want you to scour that cave for fingerprints, glove prints, foot prints, breath gases. If he farted I want to know about it. Any signs of anything. You read me? I also want this man out of my region and off this planet a.s.a.p."
"Yes, sir! Immediately, sir! If not sooner, sir!"

Mistaken Identity

The Sweeper squaddies were glad to hear Jackson was in for a rough ride. Anybody who caused this much inconvenience should never get off too lightly. With some delight they put him aboard a garbage shuttle to Nixon. Jackson didn't seem to notice anything amiss. Besides, the flight only took a few minutes. Back on the metal moon, he left the shuttle port and took a taxi back to the Neil Armstrong Hotel without any fuss whatsoever. The machine-formed walls and fittings of his room were a welcome sight. He took a soothing shower, ray-cleaned his clothes and sat on his bed reading a note from Alexx: *"Mason, dear - Meet me in the alco-bar on the roof garden tonight at nine. Alexx."* The note was three days old.

"Damn, she'll think I stood her up!" He put the note aside just as another slip of paper started rolling out of the communicator on the wall. It was a surcharge from the replicar company for retrieving the Land Rover from the desert. He wondered how that could be. He and Atos saw the replica blow up! There wasn't anything left of it. But Jackson thought it better to keep his head down and his mouth shut in case the rental company decided to charge him for replacing the whole car. He read further and saw he was also being charged the one-way rate rather than the return rate. The rent-a-car company had managed to replicate 20th Century *service* too!

Jackson reckoned he still faced a further enquiry to be conducted by the Transport Police. He had a good idea of the kind of questions they would ask and as long as he answered them calmly and consistently he thought there wouldn't be any problems. Maybe then his name could be taken off the death list and he could get back to work.

He thought of trying to contact Alex in the hope that maybe she knew somebody who could cut the red tape, but when he punched her number, the monitor told him she was not on the Nixon. He tried to reach her at the transport terminal too and was told she had taken a transfer out of the system. Most peculiar he thought, but people in the travel business do travel, don't they. Anyway, she might get in touch with him.

That night the Police took him in for interrogation. Just routine they said when he greeted them at the door. At the station, the Police interrogator sat Jackson in an iso-room and interviewed him through the glass. Cameras recorded everything. The walls of the iso-room were filled with sensors for virtually every bodily function. Standard procedure for lie detection. The interrogator apologised for the style of the interview and the mass of equipment, "It's standard procedure for cases like this when someone has gone into a designated Wilderness area. It's for your own protection of course. In case you picked up any harmful radiation, or contracted any ancient viruses or the like. I'm sure you understand."

"Yes of course." He had intruded into the Wilderness. And there had been a nuclear war there long ago. "But you also wonder if I'm lying?"

"No of course not, but if you are, we'll know."

He told the same story about his disappearance that he had told to his rescuers – about the sand storm, the cave, and the long sleep. How in the world could he tell them about Atos, Dharman or Prem? How could he tell anyone? But tell he would, somehow. Some day, but not today.

After the interrogation, which lasted about twenty minutes, the police officer thanked Jackson for his kind cooperation. "We know where you're staying. Feel free to carry on normally. If we need to ask any further questions, we'll be in touch."

"Everything's alright then? Okay, I'll be off." Jackson left the iso-room, shook hands with the Police officer and departed.

Frank Laker emerged from a hidden door and approached the officer. "What do you think? Was he lying?"

"Definitely."

"About what?"

"Everything is essentially acceptable except for Saturday."

"What about Saturday? What did he do on Saturday?"

"He certainly didn't sleep through it. I don't know what he did. It's as if he was in the cave, but a part of him wasn't in the cave. I admit it sounds confusing, but that's really all I can tell you."

"Not asleep on Saturday, in the cave, but part of him not in the cave," Laker repeated. "Puzzling, inconclusive, devious."

"Anything else, Mr. Laker?"

"Get some specialists onto this, analyse all the iso-room data again; I'm not convinced we should let Jackson leave Nixon until we have some more answers. Mind you, a mere advertising man ought to be harmless enough."

"Maybe he's just a bit weird. Nothing criminal that I can detect."

"Perhaps. We'll see."

Back in his hotel room, Jackson was worn out with writing and thinking. He'd managed to block out Atos and the light bulb gang all afternoon so he could get on with his work. After about four hours of furious concentration he was wrung out. He really couldn't face being in this tiny room another minute. After a quick change of clothes and a fresh-up, he locked his door and headed off to explore the local delights and find some escape. Maybe he'd find that alco-bar Alexx had suggested as a rendezvous.

He took a lift to the roof garden. As far as the eye could see, the moonscape was totally built-over. The roof garden was at the same altitude as the top level of virtually every other structure, giving the impression that the roof line was the real surface of the Nixon. Very few towers spiked the space above this level, though here and there a few garden bubbles pimpled the flatness. Unseen between the separate buildings were black crevices that dropped sheer to the lowest levels, sometimes barely a hundred feet above the original lunar landscape.

Jackson sauntered dozily around the circumference of the bubble, enjoying rhododendrons growing in massive tubs. Long beds of tulips and daffodils basked in the daylight. It was spring now in the Northern Hemisphere of the planet below, and Nixonites kept their moon gardens in adherence to Earth's laws of Nature.

In fact, Jackson noted the conspicuous absence of plants from other worlds. He himself was especially fond of floating air plants. He had a large blue one on Omicron that floated tranquilly in the dining room. It was lighter than air and used its fairy petals as wings to push and pull itself from one part of the room to the other, or to turn itself slowly in the sun like a self-spit pig, then sailing up to seek the warmest part of the ceiling during the night.

About halfway around the bubble, Jackson followed the edge to the brink of an enormous canyon in the city structure. Alexx had told him it was fifty miles down to true surface level. He couldn't see that far, the other buildings huddled in too closely and the perspective of the parallel lines converging into infinity produced a simple black dot.

As he peered into the abyss the lights on hundreds of levels twinkled in the earthlight. The myriad glowing panels produced a kaleidoscope in freeze-frame. It was absolutely mesmerising. He shook his gaze away from its pull. Ahead of him, he discovered gaily coloured lights in the midst of the greenery. An intimate little alco-bar was neatly secluded behind a copse of potted Eugenia. Past that a tubular glass tunnel carried the garden walkway across the chasm to the next structure-plex. Chase was in two minds about which way to turn when a slim young woman came out of the tunnel and headed for the bar.

Jackson instinctively followed, he had the scent and he was eager for some recreational activity. After a pause to size up the situation, he decided to use the direct approach he'd learned so well in Australia. After all he would probably only be here for one more day at the most.

The young woman appeared to be alone. So for that matter did virtually everyone else at the alco-bar. That was good. She didn't seem to be fidgeting as though she was waiting to meet someone. And, he thought, she didn't look like a hooker. At least not any hooker he'd ever seen before.

"Well cut clothes," he thought."With a Rigellian designer influence. Might even be a fashion designer herself. Certainly not typical of Earthling apparel."

Jackson had built up an impression of current day Earthlings as being incredibly insular and parochial. Never ventured out much, save for the faithful commuting to Earth.

"Maybe she's a model." he thought. He concluded that her face somewhere between girlishness and the full bloom of womanhood. "Big eyes. Long brown hair that can't help curling itself." Jackson was getting carried away. The light spots were right. He still needed flex his stomach and his genitals. The Path could wait a little longer.

The bartender took the young woman's order as Mason casually took the seat next to his prey.

"Lovely place to have a drink" he said looking around but casting the line in her general direction. It was the bartender who caught it though. -

"What'll you have?"

"Make mine a... a Miner's Explosion." The impulse beam from over the bar hit Mason full in the face and compelled him to ask for it. The bartend served up the lady's drink before reaching for the automatically mixed Miner's Explosion.

"Could I pay for that? I really hate drinking alone."

"Thank you. That's very gentlemanly of you to offer" she said gracefully.

"My name's Mason. What shall I call you? And please don't say 'a cab'." The 20th century joke fell absolutely flat.

"I'm Jeannie, and I don't get the joke, but I don't like to drink by myself either."

The bartend put on a stainless steel glove before gingerly pushing the canister containing the Miner's Explosion in front of him.

"What's in it, anyway?"

"So you've never had one of these before?"

"Uh, no, I don't think I have" Jackson said with some innocence.

"Nothing to worry about unless you're allergic to something" the barman smiled.

"Cats. I'm deathly allergic to cats."

"I can honestly say I didn't put a single cat in that drink."

Everyone allowed themselves a giggle.

"But if you don't like it, I'll change it for you."

Jackson took a cautious gulp of the explosive mixture that billowed under pressure. The bartend watched for the reaction. Mason tried to hide what was happening. The Miner's Explosion was causing a fire down below. But somewhat lower than he cared to admit. He was getting a hard-on he couldn't control. Bending over slightly, and ever so subtly, he rested his forearm across his crotch hoping to hold his rampant member down flat.

Jeannie could see exactly what was happening. The bartend walked away chuckling.

"Your first one, huh?" she was beside herself trying not to laugh out loud and attract the attention of everyone in the place.

231

Jackson was suffering third degree burns of embarrassment. He felt as though everyone in the whole alco-bar was staring at him. God knows what would have happened if Jackson didn't have a sense of humour. The moment he started to laugh at his dilemma, the bulge limped in under control.

"Don't be embarrassed," Jeannie said. "It's only a drink. Go ahead, have another little sip."

Jackson didn't know if she was just kidding or not.

"Here let me have a sip with you."

"Does it have the same, uh, you know, effect on you too?"

"It did the first time, I can tell you! I nearly wet my pants in ecstasy. But I'm used to them now. The effect isn't dramatic, just tingly and warm."

Jackson was embarrassed again, hearing the nice young woman he'd only just met talking this way. He preferred his pick-ups to be aloof and at least to pretend to be innocent. Then she felt his embarrassment and changed the subject.

"Where are you from?"

"The Centre. Quadrant Four."

"So am I, originally. But I live at the centre of Quadrant Two now."

"So what are you doing here?"

"Trying to sell my latest range. I'm a fashion designer."

"I guessed as much. You're the only woman I've seen on Nixon who doesn't look like she was dressed from a mail order catalogue."

"Why thank you. I know what you mean. You'd think this place would be a fashion retailer's goldmine. It's such a cultural desert."

"They are rather dedicated to the status quo."

"At least they've done a good job keeping the planet green."

"That's all they seem to live for. That and the Library."

"Have you seen it?"

"Yeah I had a look at it the other day. Huge isn't it?"

"I suppose it keeps them busy, updating it all the time."

"If I remember correctly the message panels said they have a maintenance team of only about a thousand techs and engineers looking after the computers and the growth mechanism. Another million actuary staff input from terminals located in over a hundred information gathering agencies plugged into the Nixon population and out-planet terminals too."

"I'm sure you remembered every detail," she said, rolling her eyes upward with the suggestion of boredom. "Another drink, Mason?"

"Yes, thank you, what are you having?"

"Northern Lights."

"Make it two, then."

The bartend grinned as he served them. But this time nothing peculiar happened.

Mason decided to make his next move. He was intrigued by this woman. Or maybe it was only her name. You know, you remind me of someone I knew a very long time ago."

"Not your first girl-friend, is it?" .

"As a matter of fact, yes."

"God! I had hoped you wouldn't become boring so quickly. You're not a salesman are you, a rep for vidi-mags or something?"

Mason saw a huge opening -- the chance to redeem himself in her eyes by playing his usual trump.

"No, if I was trying to be smooth in a superficial sort of way, I would have been far more original than that, the fact is, you truly do remind me of my first girl-friend."

Jeannie rolled her eyes, "Jeesh! You've got to be more original than that."

"What would you think if I told you I'm a Creator?"

It worked. The old line was casting its magic yet again.

"A real live *creator*? Maybe *I* should celebrate with a Miner's Explosion too!"

"My first girl-friend's name was Jeannie and she changed my life. And if I remember correctly she was going to become a fashion designer. Furthermore, you'd pass for her twin."

"Clever line, Mason, but isn't it a bit too transparent?"

"Seriously..."

"I suppose you're going to tell me that if it hadn't been for Jeannie you wouldn't have become a Creator."

"Exactly. How did you know that?"

"It was just so obvious that's what you'd say next. You're not very original for a Creator," she was looking at him through a thickening veil of suspicion.

Mason had no choice but resort to deepened sincerity.

"Jeannie opened my mind to many things. Music, poetry, romance, soft things, delicate things, subtleties and joys I never knew..."

"Well your imagination is certainly working overtime now!"

"Have you ever been to Iowa?"

"Where's that?"

A lump clichéd in Mason's throat. He looked into Jeannie's eyes and saw that they were brown. "Her eyes were green."

"Were they?"

"Green flecked with gold, like a Tiger Eye." More memories came in a deluge. Was it the drink? Was it this woman? He trembled and flushed.

Suddenly, inexplicably, Jeannie got up and moved toward the exit. "I have to go." She walked quickly, almost running to the tubeway to get away. He ran after her, not thinking, just moving instinctively to follow, to not lose her.

The bartend shook his head in disbelief. This guy – said he was a creator, but he can't see a trap when it's sprung in his face. What a sucker. Oh well...

Jackson was fifty feet behind Jeannie chasing her in the crystal light of the tubeway, fifty miles above the street.

234

The explosion knocked him into the air. The tube shattered into shrapnel. Jeannie disappeared in the white flash. Ten feet of the floor was falling fifty miles. Jackson held his breath as he dropped into the vacuum. There was virtually no atmosphere at all at this height. The thought flashed through his consciousness that he might never breathe again.

He was upside down looking up at the hole in the bottom of the tubeway. His eyes fixed on familiar stars: Rigel, Arcturus, Betelgeuse, and Polaris. He knew he was going to die in the next ninety seconds when the oxygen in his lungs gave out. For some reason he thought of Atos, Dharman and Prem. How soon before he wouldn't even be able to think? Then he felt something hard rasping and burning against the inside of his right thigh. Then the same hard burning pain strained against his right ankle.

Instinctively he brought his legs together against it. A cable dangling from the wreckage! It must be a cable! Squeeze! Catch it! Crush it between my legs. Anything! Just to grab hold of something and pull myself out of here! A childhood memory flashed of rope climbing in a gym class -- so long, long ago. Sliding on rough cable. Christ it burns! Can't see it. How long is it? Will I slip off the end? Help!

The slide stopped. The pain increased. Then something tickly crawled down his face and up his nose. It crept along his dangling hands. Bubbles. Air bubbles trickling down from the blown-out tubeway. He bent his body up. Folded his legs around the precious cable. He hugged that cable with every fibre of every muscle. Won't somebody come!

The cable jerked. Voices screamed across the void, but in the near vacuum he could not hear them.

"It's okay, we've got you! Hang on!"

Jackson saw hotel staff in oxygen suits hauling up the cable. They dangled an oxygen mask toward him. He grabbed it desperately with his left hand.

235

"It's okay, we've got you, you're okay, you can let go of the cable now. It's solid floor underneath you now."

They lifted him onto a drinks trolley and wheeled him back into the Garden of Eden on the roof of the Neil Armstrong Hotel.

"Jeez, you were lucky, mister! Grabbing that poly-cable with your legs like that. That stuff is tested to a hundred tonnes per strand to hold up the tubeways -- and you put a six-inch kink in it with your legs! I ain't never seen nothing like it, you're one helluva goddam lucky guy. Hey, you're not an android are you?"

"When was the last time you saw an android cry?" Mason trembled with cold and fear.

In For Observation

Judy's face appeared on the screen at his bedside in the Neil Armstrong Memorial Hospital. "They said you tried space-walking without a suit! What happened? Bored with living?"

"There was an explosion. I don't know exactly what happened. How did you find out?"

"A message appeared on my mail screen this morning. Unsigned and anonymous. Don't know who sent it. Wasn't you then?"

"Sorry, love. No it wasn't." Jackson wondered if it could have been Atos.

"I was worried sick."

"I suppose your husband was worried about me too."

"Let's not get bitchy, Mason. Things could be better with Bruce, I admit. But as long as I'm married -- anyway enough about that. You're alive and looking well as far as I can see."

"You ought to feel it from my side. I feel dreadful. If I had been wearing an aerogel shirt or jacket I probably wouldn't have been hurt at all. Make a note to pack that stuff next time, will you? By the way, any problems?"

"The computer's got a virus, but I think she'll get over it. I've had the comp-doctor in to give it a thorough check up and she's prescribed a chip or two to cure it. "

"The computer's never been sick before. What were the symptoms?"

"Little red spots kept showing up on the screens in all kinds of files. And files kept showing up uncalled for. Like it had a mind of its own."

"Strange. Very strange."

"It was like an infection. Just kept showing up."

"Think someone's been tampering?"

"Oh no! Mason? Do you think that's it? God, I'm sorry, I never thought of that! I should have realised!"

"Well, if it was an invader, he's got what he's wanted by now."

"Sorry, Mason, truly I am."

"Don't worry. I'm getting out of here as soon as I can. I'll be back to the office on the first PanGal flight I can make, and that's a promise."

"Look after yourself, Mason. Please. There are so many jealous agencies out there wow old love to get rid of you and grab your clients.'

"And you."

Judy smiled sweetly as she disappeared off screen. Mason loved her smile. It always lifted his spirits and right now it was just what he needed. He was bruised and cold. He was also pissed off with himself at having been so gullible and easily tricked. Somebody had set him up and lured him onto the tubeway intending that he be killed in the explosion. Who the hell would want him dead? The Pirates? Had he really gone too far with his public statements? No, he considered -- it wasn't what he said but *where* he said it – on public media. But the 3000 Expansionist Elite that he had on file couldn't seriously feel threatened by little old Mason Jackson. Could they? No, not as a group, but there might be the odd individual who felt vulnerable and decided to get rid of the fly in the ointment. But who? And now somebody had infiltrated his computer system and his office files. Was there nothing left sacred to him? There was his mind, he still had that -- but even Atos & Co. had scanned every cell in his head! He felt as depressed as if he had been raped.

"Nurse Jordan? When do I get out of here? I have things to do back home."

The nurse watching the monitors was reassuring, and his pseudo southern drawl nearly had Mason in stitches. "Your life signs are stable now, Mister Jackson. But y'all had a massive shock to the system and we-all want to watch over you for a couple more hours. The way y'all bent that cable with your legs was incredible! Y'all don't look like no superman to me, but it could only have been super strength that saved y'all."

"It was life and death. People get super human strength in certain situations."

"You ought to be squashed flat fifty miles down, y'all oughta be dead."

"You sure I'm not? I don't know what death feels like, but I don't feel very healthy right now."

"With all these blips and pulses on the screens, if y'all is dead, our technician's outa her job. Now, y'all just lie back and relax. We have a couple hours to kill -- no pun intended -- why don't y'all tell me your life story or something?"

"It isn't that long."

"The bumpf I got on y'all says you're a Creator and a Resurrectee, so why don't y'all tell me about things way back when and then some? I've never met no-one one who's done the things y'all have."

"I'm not worried about boring you, I'm worried about boring me, but I suppose if you have to look after me, I at least owe you a good story."

"Now, my man, you are talkin' the good stuff."

Jackson closed his eyes as if to help him remember back through the centuries. It was a good dramatic effect. The nurse was riveted.

"Life is good for me now. But things weren't always so easy. I remember -- yes, I remember when I first decided to leave the security of a big company and strike out on my own. The first thing I knew, I was out of work."

"I can't imagine no-one being out of work."

"It doesn't happen now. But in those days it did. And it happened to me."

"Y'all get fired?"

"No, I was made redundant."

"Re-dun-dant? I don't know that word."

"It's when they don't need you anymore and they volunteer your name for unemployment."

"But this here is an ever-expanding economic universe, man!"

"With black holes in it. And I'm afraid in those days, Yukay was one of them."

"What was their problem?"

"Too much government. And too many accountants. Everybody counting the money and nobody making it. Most companies were spending between 45 and 65% of their man hours dealing with government rules and regulations."

"But making money is the only rule, man!"

"Yukay had a Value Added Tax system that was a nightmare of paperwork. Then there was National Insurance and all kinds of corporate and personal tax structures, plus regulations on export and import and manufacturing controls and standards of all kinds and a never ending system of stealth tax and multiple and compound taxes."

"Yuk!"

"Yukay."

"So how come a guy like y'all was out of work?"

"Economic depression. 'Inward expansion' they called it. The greedy industrial pirates insisted on low wages too. Big companies made it very hard for small businesses to succeed. So too did the government. Banks, controlled by the industrial pirates, gave small businesses small overdrafts and high interest rates when the little companies used their credit. Anyway, what all this was contributing to was the fact that Yukay couldn't compete in the Galactic market."

"So what were y'all doing there?"

"Advertising. And enjoying a rich and articulate culture. Yeah, they did some great advertising in those days... I didn't have a job when I arrived, though. Just landed on a vacation permit and looked for a job on the sly. When I got one, the Yukay company sponsored my work permit."

"That was lucky."

"I thought I merited their acceptance with the sheer weight of my galactic experience. Mother, Hammer and Palsey, M-H-P, seemed pretty pleased to get me. But the agency was in trouble before I joined, and before I knew it, the group owners, LIMPET, took away our franchise and rationalised us into another LIMPET outfit called Profit Point who excelled themselves in sales promotion, conference organisation and incentive schemes. But they knew bugger all about advertising."

"So y'all became their main man?"

"LIMPET out-flanked me. They had other companies who were able to handle the old MHP advertising business without having to take on the redundant MHP staff. Because I was from off-planet, they didn't even have to pay me out."

"At least they didn't kick you off the planet, man."

"Maybe they should have. There were 300 million unemployed on Yukay."

"I never heard of such a thing. Whatcha do, man?"

"I boldly went where none of those 300 million were going -- back into the interviews. But this time I wasn't hawking my off-planet portfolio. Yukay people thought their advertising was the best advertising in the galaxy -- it probably was -- so there was no point in telling them I had done better stuff elsewhere."

"So what did y'all do, man?"

"I forced them to consider how I could help them make their own brilliant advertising even better!"

"How'd y'all do that, man?"

"I used my built-in shit detector."

"What the hell is that?"

"Every good Creator has one. It's the extra sense that tells you something's wrong with a piece of work and the common sense of how to rectify it. Even though the people I was presenting myself to were the best ad experts in the whole goddam galaxy, they could still be taught a thing or three. Instead of showing them my work, I asked to see *their* work. Then I plugged my shit detector into it. I can tell you, they weren't used to having an off-planet shoot holes in their best stuff, and then suggest how to make it bullet proof on the spot!"

"So y'all got hired?"

"Not a chance. They were too proud and arrogant to allow me an elbow in. I was a real threat to every creative director on the planet. Anyway, it gave me the incentive to try my own thing. I got into sky-fi and role fantasies. It was on Yukay that I got the idea for the Wuzy Doll -- but that was a long time before I even made a prototype."

"Wow, man! You mean y'all invented the Wuzy Doll! Wait till I tell my old lady!"

It did Jackson good to bask in the glory of the Wuzy Doll. Remembering those disappointing days on Yukay left a bad taste. And one bad memory produced another as he wondered what ever happened to the real Jeannie.

"You got an old lady waitin at home for y'all?"

"No, but I got Judy, my secretary." And he thought about her blond hair and the sweet smiled that he loved. He missed her. In fact he missed a genuine relationship of any kind. How long would he go on jumping from one one-night stand to the next? Would he ever be able to make a commitment? "Say, Jordan, would you mind if I took a little nap?"

"No, man, Mr. Wuzy Creator, y'all get some shut-eye. I'll be right outside there if y'all want anything. Anything at all." Nurse Jordan strolled off to his station.

"Forever is a long, long time" Jackson said to himself as he reached for the light beside the bed and switched it off. The light stayed on. He tried the switch again. It didn't work, the light was still on. "Goddam light!"

"There's no need to swear at me."

"Atos?"

"Convenient little cover don't you think?"

"Brilliant. How long have you been here?"

"I've been with you since the alco-bar on the roof top."

"Then, the accident, you were there? You saw what happened?"

"That was no accident, you were set up."

"I thought as much. How come you didn't warn me?"

"Alcohol clouds the brain. I couldn't get through to you. And believe me, I was trying."

"Was it really Jeannie in the bar? She looked so much like her."

"She was really an android."

"I thought it was too much of a coincidence. But it was the eyes. The eyes that made me wonder. Wrong colour. Brown when they should have been green."

"The android sensed that that you sensed that something was amiss, and that's when it switched to programme B." Jackson suffered momentary confusion.

"The tubeway explosion. The Jeannie android ran off hoping you would follow her. You did of course."

"Otherwise?"

"Otherwise she would have tried another more subtle and more intimate way of killing you."

Jackson could imagine what that would have been "Well as it was I very nearly did die in the explosion and fall. Did you save me, Atos?"

"You saved yourself. I saw you fall, but there was nothing I could do to stop it."

"God, I was lucky!"

"Let's just say you functioned properly. Survival instinct 110% combined with a super rush of adrenalin at the right moment."

"A miracle."

"I don't believe in miracles. They are merely a word for a mystery that has not yet been explained. In this situation, you put the right combination of actions together at the right time. Like I said, all systems were 'go' and you saved yourself. Congratulations and well done."

"So what do I do now?"

"What do you want to do?"

"You sound like a counsellor or a shrink."

"That's the way you're using me, so that's the way I'll be until priorities change for either one of us."

"I see, okay. I want to get out of here -- I want to go back to Omicron."

"Have you got everything you came here for?"

"Yes, I think so. I've been to Earth; I've been to Iowa, New York, The Tree, The Library, and Jerusalem. And then I met you and the other bright lights, Dharman and Prem. I've been out of my body and I've nearly been killed. That about sums it up. Yes, I believe that's quite enough for now and it's time to go."

"It's not going to be easy. Whoever tried to kill you will probably try again. And I don't think Frank Laker is quite finished with you yet either."

"Then I'll have to make an end-run."

"You mean out-flank them?"

"Precisely."

"You'll have to start with young Jordan out there at the nursing station."

"The nurse is going to kill me?" Jackson's voice trembled and thinned as he spoke.

"If you let him, he's thinking about it right now."

"How do I stop him?" "It depends on what he tries."

"Well he's going to be back in here trying awfully damned soon! He said I could leave the hospital and get checked out in about two hours. If only I could get to Madame Prime."

"How do you know she's not behind all this?"

"It's all too messy for her. There's some cheap street thug behind it, not Madame Prime."

"An excellent instinct. And in fact, you're right. Madame Prime is not behind it."

"And you know who is?"

"Let's just say I am working on it."

"Then you'll help me get to Madame Prime?"

"Of course. What do you want me to do?"

"Right. I've got to think of something."

"And fast."

"Fast. That's a good suggestion. I don't know of anything faster than the Freea and mind transportation."

"Getting you out of yourself in this hospital room would cause too much commotion, Jordan would certainly be alerted and we can't risk that right now."

"Well, someone has to escort me out of here. Look, I think I have a plan. You may need some help from other Freea, but essentially, I want to send a message to Madame Prime using Freea to carry the message. Clearly I can't trust anyone anymore, public channels aren't safe.

"I think the penny has finally dropped for you, Mason."

"As far as I know, in the entire Universe, only The Freea, Judy and Madame Prime are definitely on my side. Now, here's what I want you to say..."

Battle Stations

Jackson counted off the minutes. Would Madame Prime come to his rescue? Would she be bothered? Instinct told him she would -- if she could, and if there was enough time. But who could tell when Nurse Jordan would make his move? The conspiracy had failed to kill him once; they'd be more thorough next time. Maybe they'd use more than one assassin. Maybe there was a whole team of killers waiting just out of sight for the signal to burst in and rip his heart out or whatever they intended. Paranoia, thy name is Jackson.

"Atos, tell me again what their response was?"

"Have faith, Mason, if they get here in time everything will be alright. And if they don't then we'll deal with it the best way we can. How are your legs, anyway, can you run?"

"All bruised to hell where I squeezed the cable. Rope burns on the hands hurt the most, but the salve is amazing. Look how the abrasions have nearly healed."

"Dharman tells me the escort ship is above us now."

"Madame Prime, how can I ever thank you? Can they beam me aboard?"

"If you were in a tele-booth, yes. But the nearest tele-booth is two miles down in the emergency room, where they first brought you in."

"Then how am I going to get out of here?"

"I suggest we leave that to the Navy."

So far, everything was going according to Jackson's plan. Atos had set up a relay from the Nixon to Dharman in deep space and further on to Prem who passed on Jackson's message to Madame Prime's direct line. Unless someone was tapping the Prime line (someone other than CT), the message transmission should have been safely outside the eaves-dropping capability of any opposition forces.

To make doubly sure of getting through, Prem also planted thoughts of Jackson in Madame Prime's mind, nothing specific, but enough to make her stop and wonder how he was getting along. When the distress call came through moments later, Madame Prime would be convinced she had experienced a premonition of the highest order.

"No time to elaborate. Have survived one and perhaps two assassination attempts. Next attempt imminent. Can you send military escort to extricate me from Neil Armstrong Hospital section 9407846? Otherwise I may not see you again. I would not ask you if there was any other way. Please acknowledge. PS. Beware Nurse Jordan. Signed, 485-54-0255." The message arrived just in time. Madame Prime bolted into action.

Nurse Jordan entered the room followed by a kitchen porter with a meal tray. "Thought y'all might like to have one last taste of hospital food before you leave" Jordan was grinning and jovial. Jackson still found it hard to believe the gentle giant with the ridiculous drawl could be assassin material.

"Yum-my. How did you know I was hoping you'd bring me something?" Jackson was going to play the delay as long as he could. He had no idea how soon the Navy would arrive. *If* they would arrive. He hoped the kitchen porter would be on his side if things got tough. That would make it two against one and the guy from the hospital kitchen was even bigger than Jordan.

"But first, Mr. Jackson, sir, would y'all be so kind as to autograph my Wuzy Doll?" Jordan thrust the thing under Jackson's nose with one hand. And offered a pen with the other.

"How could I possibly refuse?" Jackson pulled Wuzy's panties down and penned his initials like a seaman's tattoo across her left buttock. And kissed it for good luck.

"Thank y'all. I sure do appreciate that. Now here's your soup. Y'all eat it all, now. Ya hear? Looks better on yer chart if ya eats it all." The second man still hadn't spoken.

Maybe he didn't know how. Mason still wondered whose side the porter was on.

"Sure looks good, I'll take my time if you don't mind, and really enjoy it."

"You just do that. Take as long as you like. Ivan don't mind, do ya Ivan? He all gots to wait to take the plate back."

"Don't they have edible plates here? Or robo-chefs?" Jackson wondered how Jordan was going to explain why his dirty plate would have to be dealt with in person, by hand.

"Cut-backs. Government cut-backs. Hospital cut-backs. Centuries ago. Dis here is a very old, old hospital. They ain't never installed none of that kind of technology in dis hospital."

"I don't mind if Ivan takes the plate. It's rather quaint."

"It is, ain't it? Bringin' plates by hand. Takin' plates away by hand. It's one of the time-honoured traditions of the Neil Armstrong Hospital."

"Say this is a great soup!" Jackson sniffed the aroma. Rather like Thai Tom Yum. Jordan and Ivan looked down at him, watching the spoon go to his mouth but never going in. Where the hell was the Navy? Jackson noticed Ivan had his hands folded behind him. Both of these guys were menacing him. The kitchen porter was not a rescuer but another murderer. Was he hiding a knife? A laser? Oh shit, he didn't want to be cut. Not cut. Please. He hated blood, especially his own.

"Stay calm, they're coming." Atos whispered from the bedside lamp and into his mind.

Jordan and Ivan took a step forward. Their knees nudged the bed on both sides.

"I ain't never seen nobody take so long over a bowl of soup. I think maybe Mister Jackson here needs a little help gettin it into him, don't you, Ivan?" Just as four burly hands reached out to grab Jackson, they froze and

248

slumped to the floor, spilling the remains of the soup all over the bed sheets. And two small men in immaculate Navy uniforms stood in their places.

"Commander Ted Esworthy at your service, Mr. Jackson!" He saluted smartly."Commander Fred Esworthy at your service, Mr. Jackson!" The clone saluted just as smartly.

"We are under orders to escort you to the Quadrant Destroyer Shiva for the journey to Starbase I" they stated in perfect unison.

"Thank goodness you're here. I think they were going to kill me!"

"They weren't, but the soup probably was. Let's get you aboard the Shiva, fast."

Jackson creaked out of bed and stepped over Jordan's body. He saw a small, round and rather precise burn mark in Jordan's white jacket, just between the shoulder blades. He assumed there was one in the same place on Ivan's jacket but he didn't stop to look. "Who's behind this? Who's trying to murder me, any idea?"

"All the theatrical signs point to one of the big ad agencies. Oh, kill the light, will you, Fred?" Clone Freddie levelled his laser at the light fitting where Atos sheltered and fired.

"No! Don't!" Mason yelled too late. The light bulb was vaporised. "Atos!" he screamed in his mind.

"I'm alright, he missed me." Atos spoke back discreetly into Jackson's brain.

"You get sentimental over the light or something?" The Esworthies asked.

"No. It's okay. I guess I'm just a bit shaken up that's all." Jackson thought it best to keep silent about Atos. Besides, it was all too hard to explain. "Hooke, Ligne and Syncher. It must be HL & S. We're in competition for a very lucrative project from the Quadrant Government. A bit hush-hush so I can't tell you much about it. Christ, I didn't think Bernard Mucous would lower himself to assassinating me."

"Eliminating his only opposition must surely increase his chances by a fifty percent. It does make commercial sense."

The three men stepped into the lift and headed for the landing apron on the roof of the hospital.

"Yes, I suppose. Or perhaps it's one of the Expansionist Elite I upset in my recent cosmic interview. I could give you a list..."

"Don't give it to *us*. We don't want to know. Whoever is behind things has some pretty massive resources. The Shiva has decoded a number of wild noisy signals in this sector that suggests a co-ordinated effort to stop you from leaving this solar system."

"Is that serious?"

"It means you won't get out of here alive without authorised military assistance."

"Then thank god you're here, Commanders Esworthy."

"Somebody higher up must like you" they replied.

"At least I know I'm going to be alright."

"We didn't say that. In fact, our analysis suggests that we are in a potentially no-win situation."

"As in 'no way out'?"

"Yes. But you couldn't be in better hands" The Esworthies said confidently.

The lift stopped and the three men entered a short transparent tunnel that led across the meteor scratched roof to a small unmarked shuttle craft. "The Shiva is about fifty miles up. Strap in, we're in a hurry."

"What do you think my enemies had planned for me?"

"We believe their next plan, should you have escaped the hospital alive, which thanks to us you have achieved, was to intercept and board any Pan Gal flight taking you out of this system--"

"But before the liner jumped and left this system?"

250

"Apparently so. The chance of setting the trap in sub-hype conditions with confrontation occurring at low speed was too good a chance to miss."

"Confrontation? Are we talking guns, missiles and bombs?"

The cooperative clones grinned in confirmation.

"Shit! That is one helluva bad concept! Look, I don't want to be in any gun battles! Can't we just give them what they want? "

"What they want is *you*. So it's not an option under the orders we have been given."

They seemed genuine enough and they did rescue him from the bad guys in the hospital, but it passed through Jackson's mind that the Esworthy clones might also be imposters and maybe he shouldn't be totally trusting of them. But then, surely Atos would have warned him if they were suspect. And their uniforms seemed convincing. As did their story. In a moment he would know for sure. There would be no way of falsifying an entire Quadrant Destroyer. And once on board, well he wouldn't be able to do anything then.

Of course, if there wasn't a Navy Destroyer at the end of this shuttle trip -- well it was already too late for that and the best he could hope for was a fast rehabilitation after the Brain Drain treatments they would surely give him. For now, Mason had no choice but to trust his escorts and hope the Esworthies didn't turn out to be his captors instead of his saviours.

Suddenly it was there. The Shiva. Infinite relief! Jackson made out the official fleet markings of the Naval vessel as they approached. It was not what you would call a sleek craft, but it was not designed for battle or even recon work in atmospheric conditions. In the relative emptiness of space, speed was not a function of shape.

The Shiva bristled with weapons modules and sensor dishes, so much so that it seemed covered in a pox of convexes and concaves. There was no sign of activity as they boarded. But as soon as the door slid behind him, Jackson was aware of the rising sensation that accompanied lift-off. The Shiva was underway immediately.

The Esworthies escorted him through surprisingly broad corridors to a small observation deck overlooking a control centre humming with officers and ratings. "We are in the process of assembling a squadron of our own, though, I am afraid we will be badly outnumbered."

"Certainly we'll have superior weaponry on our side" said Jackson. "You guys are the Navy!"

"Not necessarily, "said Fred Esworthy, "The commercial fleets often have access to the same weapons as we do. In most cases, private navies cannot afford to purchase them. However, in this case, the syndicate lining up against us obviously wields enormous wealth."

By this time, Jackson was collecting his own data from the scene below. It didn't take Lord Nelson to see that the enemy fleet was already on the screens and numbered more than thirty vessels. Some of the blips were brighter than others and he wondered what that meant.

"Twenty-three vessels of our size or smaller, nine of cruiser status, Captain." A junior female commander reported.

"I can honestly say I've never had this many agencies after me in my entire career!" Jackson blurted.

The Captain below glanced up at Jackson, obviously unimpressed at what his lieutenants had brought back to his ship as cargo.

The Esworthies offered genuine consolation."Whatever you've been doing for the Leaders out here, it must be important enough to get you back to Starbase I at tremendous cost and sacrifice."

"I'm glad you said that. But I don't think Bernie Mucous at HL&S would know what to do with the information I've got anyway. His team would be too scared to use it. And without direct access to Leadership, it would all just go to waste. "

"Perhaps wasting your information would be sufficient for their purpose. And who is to know that they don't have someone in the Leadership in their pay supporting them right now?"

The Esworthies had a point. Not a nice one, but it was valid. Jackson's eyes returned to the

disciplined scene and smoothly functioning operations below. Teams of technicians, voice-controlled coloured panels on the floors, walls and ceiling, asking for information from every system aboard the ship. Fire control, navigation, scanning, decision-making, personnel, scenario projections, the lot. The Captain stood calmly at the helm in the centre of the room, his hands clasped quietly behind his back, his eyes taking in everything, his voice calm and measured as he gave a stream of commands.

"Who is our Captain?" Jackson asked his cloned companions.

"He's one of the ablest young men in Starfleet Command."

"That's Captain Shirk" They said in adulation.

Jackson wondered if he heard them right, but didn't query it. Meanwhile, things were hotting up down below.

"Let's have a look at the Agency fleet up close." Shirk ordered. The word 'agency' had not escaped Jackson's ears. The captain seemed to have little doubt that the enemy was owned, paid for and perhaps operated by an ad agency. Incredible. He'd never dreamt of such a situation. A fleet of company cars is one thing, but a private fleet of naval vessels was quite another. Things had gotten rather out of hand over the millennia.

Holograms filled a three dimensional space directly in front of the Captain. Floating like scale models of themselves, the detail of the fleet hung in the air as the Captain walked amongst the array, making a vocal record of what he saw. "What concerns me here is the presence of the 9 cruisers. Each carries ten turrets, six with Mark 2 firepower, four with Mark 3. Where in the hell they got them, I have no idea. Fire Control, may I remind you that the vulnerable area of these vessels is amidships on the top deck. I know it's a small target to hit, but our Mark 2 cannons will never penetrate the side armour and wave-shields, the turrets or the bellies. Give me looping trajectories that will hit the top decks at a perpendicular angle, no matter what spatial attitude the enemy ship is taking. Lock on targets. Now!"

Jackson saw the Captain look up to an exo-screen. What he saw gladdened him heartily. The exo-view showed the Shiva being joined by four other Crab Class Destroyers. Each, he now knew, carried six batteries of Mark 2 cannon. Three on the top half of the ship, three on the undersides. Each turret was remote-controlled from the centre where the Captain still stood. Experienced men and sophisticated computers moved the barrels and armed the explosives.

In addition to the conventional cannon and turret configurations that had been standard in the Navy for centuries, tubes full of torpedoes were concealed amidships. These were accurate to a range of 20,000 km, whilst the Mark 2 cannon could hit the mark with regularity at any distance less than 13,000 km.

Armed with UHE, (ultra-high-explosive) charges, one penetrating hit would be enough to destroy an enemy Destroyer, though it may well take as many as three to obliterate a Cruiser. The trick was to score with a penetrating hit, and that's why Captain Shirk ordered the looped trajectories. The small flat area of the top deck of the enemy ships had relatively thin armour and the wave-shields did not interlock densely there either.

Thankfully, the same was not true for the Quadrant vessels. They were clad all over with sufficient wave-shielding and metallurgical padding to stop any Mark 2 weapons from making any sort of impact, no matter what part of the ship they might hit. But Captain Shirk well knew the threat of each of the enemy Cruisers was to be respected. Each increase in Mark power reflected an exponential increase in fire power. Mark 3 was not to be engaged if at all possible. However, at the moment, that possibility did not appear to be an option.

The holographic fleet began to change its battle order. The nine Cruisers moved into a tightly knit group, fist-shaped, at the centre of a great sweeping crescent -- its gaping horns composed mostly of destroyers and corvettes ready to scoop up any damaged ship trying to slip past the cruisers.

Jackson looked at the Esworthy clones for reassurance. Once again they gave it to him. Standing to attention, intense and ready to obey any order flung at them, Jackson could see that this was just the kind of situation that training and tradition prepared crews for. Precision team work and discipline would go a long way toward evening the odds. The Mucous fleet presumably had never fought a battle of this scale before, and the mere presence of so large a formation would hamper their manoeuvrability.

"Their computers are slower than our computers!" The clones boasted.

"By how much?" Jackson begged to know.

"An almost significant milli-milli-second."

"Thanks anyway."

"And the enemy command chain will be very much slower than that. Watch and you will learn."

It was then that Jackson realised just how far apart the opposing forces were. The Naval squadron was collected about a third of the way between Nixon and Maras-space. The Mucous force was gathered in the Saturn district keeping itself between Jackson and the Titan Trans Port. Whatever the enemy fleet would do, it was clear they would do it before the ship Jackson was on could reach the Jump point at the Saturn Gate fifty million miles on the Uranus side of Saturn-space.

To a Universally known game Creator like Jackson, the control deck was fascinating, like some amazing new amusement console with blips representing make-believe fleets fighting a game scenario. Funnily enough it lacked reality. In effect, going through the Gate would be like scoring a goal. But in this case, Jackson was the football.

Of course once through the Saturn Gate, Captain Shirk could choose any of a billion or more destinations. The enemy fleet couldn't possibly know where or even when the Navy ships would re-emerge into sub-hyper space. But knowing something of Jackson's mission, it seemed probable that the Navy squadron would be headed toward the Centre. And to that end, the enemy no doubt would place a reserve force somewhere within the hundred million mile mark of Central Thought... close enough to pounce before Jackson could be safely delivered. He tried not to think about it.

The clones spoke confidently, "Don't worry, we'll get through. And when we do, we'll be in the company of Megaships."

But right now, the problem was how to get to first base, let alone home base. The Saturn Gate looked a very long way off. Captain Shirk barked orders with supreme confidence as the squadron hauled ass past Maras and shot steadily toward the Mucous formation.

"We must force the action our way" Shirk stated to his crew and the other squadron commanders via the all-ship holo system."We must make the enemy respond to us. He must react the way we want him to go.

"I will call on you and your crews for the most exacting execution of my orders. The speed with which you respond to my command will decide our fate. Is that absolutely understood?"

On each screen, each Captain snapped a smart salute to Shirk.

"There will be no coded orders; I will keep this channel open to you at all times from this moment on. For what I have in mind, it will make no difference if our messages are intercepted or not."

Lights flickered everywhere as a symphony of switches was swept into overture. If Jackson was about to die, at least it promised to be a fantastic technical spectacle.

At the rate the opposing forces were closing, the first torpedoes could be expected to be launched in just over 20 minutes. The Naval squadron approached Jupiter space and sped on.

Meanwhile, on centre stage, there had been no visible change among the holos of the enemy fleet hovering near the helm since the enemy tactical deployment was effected. Shirk stood calmly, resolutely, among the holos, his hands clasped loosely behind his back.

The enemy was still drawn up in the menacing two-horned crescent formation with the nine cruisers clustered in the centre. It looked suicidal to keep the little Navy destroyers heading toward them. The cruisers were more powerful than anything Shirk possessed and the crescent behind them would englobe the naval squadron and dissolve their ships with the combined heat of cannons and torpedoes.

Minutes followed sweaty minutes. Closer and closer the fleets crawled across the screen.

"Squadron form line abreast." Shirk said calmly.

Instantly the screen images changed on both sides. But even Jackson detected a slight hesitation in the enemy response. And that response at first seemed to present another danger. Holographs and screens showed the Mucous fleet had replied by breaking down their crescent and forming up with a line abreast of their own, sprawled a million kilometres across the path of the Navy squadron, outflanking the puny Destroyers somewhat perilously.

But the holograph revealed something else; the Mucous line abreast was in fact *two* lines, the cruisers formed up

257

in front of the smaller ships, and both lines rotating through a circle one clock-wise, and the other counter-clockwise.

Jackson thought about what Shirk might do next. If he were playing this game, Jackson thought, he'd try for one end of the enemy line, and make a run round it, perhaps laying some sort of smoke screen to make it difficult for the bulk of the fleet to follow them-- then it would be a simple footrace to the Saturn Gate. Of course, they'd have to risk getting shot in the back the whole way... depending on whether the Navy Destroyers could outrun enemy torpedoes.

"One degree starboard" Shirk ordered.

Again, there was a Mucous response in kind. Again it took a moment, yes, just a heartbeat longer to execute than the squadron manoeuvre. Of course it was a very minor deviation-- just one degree after all. But a smile had already begun to spread across Shirk's face. Or was it a smirk?

"What's he up to?" Jackson thought.

So far, the enemy had reacted tit-for-tat to each of Shirk's moves. Presumably, they had not had previous experience against a veteran Naval squadron of the line, and thought it might well confound the Navy commander if they threw his own tactics back at him. Perhaps some commanders might be rattled, but Shirk was calm and clear about what he was doing.

By Jackson's reckoning, the situation still spelled disaster. True, the enemy might decide to initiate some manoeuvres of their own, but there seemed little point. As long as the Naval squadron headed straight for them, the outcome was inevitable as the larger force englobed and swallowed up the smaller force.

"Look!" The Eswerthies leaned forward. The enemy forces flickered into life, and if the screens could be believed, the enemy vessels had just multiplied by two!

A hot blip emanated from each enemy ship. But it wasn't more ships; it was a massive weapons launch. On they came, with enormous velocity straight at the smaller Navy squadron. Down below, a ships computer reported the action in a voice nearly as calm as Shirk's, "Enemy torpedoes approaching."

Shirk, predictably, was unmoved. The hot blips reached out for the Navy Destroyers.

Steadily, directly. How could they miss? Jackson and his rescuers were headed straight into holocaust. The hot blips seemed to be on the brink of imminent collision with the Navy squadron.

Jackson was faced with the prospect of brown trousers. He looked at the others. No one else was fidgety in the least, leastwise the reliable Esworthy clones. Not a fart.

"Magnification, Lieutenant Ovaria."

Now Jackson saw why nobody was worried. The nearest blips were passing about 5,000 km off target.

"Amateurs, novices, and neophytes." The Esworthy clones harmonised beside him.

"All ahead full!" shouted Shirk.

Jackson felt the instant acceleration, and saw the squadron blips lurch forward on the map-screen. Bulkheads vibrated as ultra-drives whined into high performance, increasing in pitch to reach a high sweet steady drone of flat out power! Tora! Tora! Tora! Was this victory or suicide?

Both fleets began to enter the central circle of the map-screen. Jackson still saw no way out. It occurred to him that Shirk had all but eliminated the possibility of anyone being taken alive. How much longer before the next launch of torpedoes and the first blistering fusillade of the cannons?

"Give me real-space visual!" Shirk was crisp and decisive. He was the kind of guy you could really look up to down below. As far as Jackson could make out there was bugger-all to be seen on the real-space visual. Just the cold dark emptiness of space.

Shirk stared into the seemingly blank screen. Then, as though he sensed something imminent,

Shirk straightened and stiffened. Then he asked the impossible of his commanders--"Ninety starboard!"

Before the words completely left his lips, several things happened. First, every squadron ship screeched onto a new course absolutely perpendicular to the one they'd been travelling on. Second, for a micro-instant, Jackson was sure he saw the enemy ships on real space visual. Third, there was no doubt that the enemy had fired a full salvo from their phaser cannons.

Fourth, the blast of the combined weaponry of the enemy fleet passed harmlessly through empty space -- but only by the absolute narrowest of margins!

"The enemy fleet has changed course to heading zero-nine-zero, Captain".

The manoeuvre identically mirrored what Shirk had done. Thus the two fleets were now travelling on parallel courses at maximum speed. The Quadrant Navy squadron shot to its former starboard side, the opposing Mucous combined fleet to its former port side.

Shirk's anticipation had been uncanny. Milli-second timing had saved the Destroyer squadron from certain destruction. Everything had happened so fast, Jackson was still wondering how Shirk had managed it.

"Engineering, give me all you've got. And don't tell me we'll overload, because I'll take the chance anyway."

Shirk was gambling on getting an extra one or two percent power out of the reactor-drives. They wouldn't be able to keep this up very long, but Jackson figured Shirk knew what he was doing. And from the look of the trigger happy opposition, Jackson was even more certain that the enemy had no intention of taking prisoners.

Advertising was a very dirty business. Since a series of boardroom stabbings in the 1990's, ruthlessness had taken on an entirely new meaning in the industry. His only hope of escape lay with Shirk's abilities as a commander and tactician. The holographs and the map-screens still displayed the order of battle. The right angle line-ahead manoeuvre had gained a small but growing advantage. Though there were several small enemy ships ahead of the Navy battle line, they appeared to pose no serious threat. And the heavy cruisers in the centre of the enemy formation were slightly behind Shirk's group, but gaining speed over their own smaller vessels. Everyone watched as the enemy ships gradually resumed their original twin-horned crescent formation charging like the proverbial bull with the cruisers more or less in the middle of forming up in a line of their own. Somehow, watching it moving sideways, crab-like, wasn't nearly as threatening as when it was coming straight at you, ready to spring out in an englobing manoeuvre to surround any enemy it could grab.

As several minutes ticked away, Shirk's power overload demand was pulling them further and further away from the fearful cruisers. If every ship in the squadron could continue to

maintain this course and the speed they had now attained, eventually all the enemy destroyers and corvettes would have to give up the chase. That left only the menace of the Cruisers. But the enemy had time on their side. It was still a long way to the Gateway.

"Engineering, Captain. Generator burn-out in forty seconds if you continue to overload."

Twenty seconds ticked passively by. Shirk had replied with his silence. Then a dozen heads fixed onto the screens and holos as the Cruisers suddenly seemed to be gaining on them very quickly.

"Reverse thrust-- NOW!" Shirk shouted the command to all ships. And all ships instantly reversed thrust.

The stop was violent in the extreme. The acceleration into the opposite direction produced the most incredible jolt.

But the crew was trained for it. They stood steady, grasping rails and straps waiting to execute Shirk's next order. Meanwhile, Jackson rolled across the floor, banging and banging his shins on the legs of a table bolted to the deck.

"Space shit! We've been hit! -- Haven't we?" No one bothered to answer.

"Sixteen seconds to burn-out, Captain."

"Eliminate overload and cut to normal maximum in ten seconds."

"It may not be enough time to cool to safety levels."

"It will have to be."

The Esworthy clones helped Jackson to his feet. "An extreme emergency manoeuvre, necessary of course. Sorry you were caught unaware, but rest assured we have not been hit. Some minor internal stress damage, but nothing to worry about."

Small electrical fires glowed ominously in corners of the control arena. Sickening wisps of black smoke threatened to make Jackson vomit. It was all like a smudgy re-run of 'Voyage to the Bottom.' By the time he got back to his position, the holos had adjusted to reveal what had happened.

The enemy formation had again been caught by surprise. Apparently Shirk had waited for an indication from the enemy cruisers that they had put their own engines into overload. And while they were still actually accelerating, his reversal order had the maximum effect.

The enemy Cruisers had shot past the Navy destroyers and were still trying to sort out a change of course well beyond real space visual contact. Meanwhile, the holographs verified that all the ships in Shirk's command had executed the manoeuvre precisely and safely. The same could not be said of the enemy formation. Several mishaps had shaken their line.

Three cruisers were retiring with damage. Smoke and scorch marks marred the hulls of one other. All the remaining Cruisers had been forced to break formation to avoid collision with damaged ships and debris. But Shirk was not out of danger yet. Twenty five seconds later the remaining enemy cruisers were back in line and in hot pursuit. Indeed, the Quadrant squadron was still very much under threat in the sphere of medium range of the enemy weapons.

As the enemy fleet pulsed into overload once more, their sudden acceleration, duly noted by the entire crew of the Shiva, Shirk ordered "Full Reverse!" once more.

Again, the Mucous fleet fell about themselves in utter disarray. Two of the deadly cruisers didn't even bother to obey their own admiral's obvious order to reverse again. They just blipped into oblivion, off the screen and out of the solar system.

The Shiva groaned, rumbled, lurched and ignited into small containable fires as before, but this time even Jackson was half-expecting it and his grip on the railing didn't fail him. Shirk spoke with gleaming confidence to his cohorts aboard the Shiva and the other Navy vessels in his command. "I heartily congratulate you all on the perfect execution of Nelson's Fake Flank Movement. Set course for Saturn Gate. Maintain maximum speed."

The new heading put them at a fair distance from the pursuing cruisers, who really didn't seem to be pursuing at all anymore. Several supporting destroyers were still in a position to intercept their escape, but the dangerous cruisers were hopelessly out of position to capture, destroy or even make a telling hit on any of the Navy vessels.

But the enemy destroyers were dogged and determined. As Jackson and the crew continued to watch the map screens, about twenty-five ships persisted with the idea of regrouping and engaging through high speed pursuit.

"The bounty on you must be astronomical high for these pirates to even consider taking independent action against a highly disciplined Navy force" Ted Esworthy said.

Barrage after barrage of enemy torpedoes were leashed in the direction of Shirk's little force. After ninety seconds, Shirk was forced to order evasive action. Two torpedoes crossed and blew themselves up. Another fifty torpedoes were still closing in. Was there any way of outrunning weapons like these?

"Real space visual" Shirk ordered. Sweat beaded on every face as it became apparent that they were now travelling in the uncomfortable company of at least twenty torpedoes. Four of which were only about fifty metres from the Shiva!

"Why are they just sitting next to us like that?" Jackson asked the Esworthies" Why don't they simply swerve in and obliterate us?"

"Ah, but there's the beauty of it: our own Fire Control is now controlling them, Jackson. We have overridden the computer program guiding each torpedo with our own intercept commands and we are currently writing in a new terminal command with unbreakable coding."

Suddenly the torpedoes were gone.

"You told them to disappear?"

"No, we told them to go home."

The map-screens displayed the enemy fleet in the flight of full panic. One group of fifty torpedoes, then another and yet a third wave had reversed course and were heading straight back at the ships which fired them. Jackson watched in sheer delight and amazement as the Mucous destroyers scrambled for survival. It was no use. The torpedoes found their mark. First one, then ten, then all of the enemy destroyers exploded and were no more.

Ahead of the Shiva, an ellipse of neon blue light appeared on the map-screen. Saturn Gate.

Jackson glimpsed the famous rings, and saw a very large moon pass very close under the ship on real space visual.

"That's Titan." The Esworthies said in unison."Home free now!"

"Titan" Jackson repeated to himself. Only a matter of days ago, he had said goodbye to a girl he'd met on the Pan Galaxy flight into this System. She said she was visiting friends on Titan. "What was her name? Anna something? Annabelle? Amanda. That's it. Amanda..."

The ellipse filled the screen, and the air between Jackson and the Esworthies dazzled with kaleidoscope colours and geometric patterns. For a moment he felt intensely cold -- or was he shivering for another more ancient reason?

The real space visual showed the kaleidoscope too. Then they were through! Saturn Gate was already a thousand trillion miles behind them. Shirk had succeeded against six to one odds. They'd slipped past the Mucous trap unscathed. For the time being.

Preview

"I must say, Mr. Mucous, how thoroughly enjoyable luncheon with you and your colleagues has been."

"And we must say, Director, what an honour and a privilege it has been for us to have you here. Before you go, I wonder if you would care to see a short presentation of our thinking to date on the Entropy Project. We take great pride in our creativity here at Hooke Ligne and Syncher."

"To be honest, Mr. Mucous, that's why I accepted your invitation. I never expected to leave *without* seeing your presentation."

"A short show-reel perhaps to start the ball rolling? Just to whet your appetite?"

"That won't be necessary, Bernard. Central Thought keeps me well informed of all your new campaigns and account gains. And losses."

Mucous pretended not to here the last short comment. "Blue chips, every one, I assure you, Madame! Nothing but the leading gilt-edged industrialists at HL&S -- and our esteemed Government, of course."

"No need to crawl, Mr. Mucous, and get on with it. I also know your profits are astronomical."

"We're proud of that too. In fact we now issue numbers to potential clients waiting to get an appointment with us. They just can't wait to be able to tell their friends they got ripped off by the best in the business!"

"The Government has no intention of getting ripped off, Mucous."

"A joke of course, your Directorship. Just think of me as your good old Uncle Bernie, and jump the request queue any time you like. Just buzz me on my personal direct hotline."

Mucous nodded toward a wall and it slid away revealing a holo cube. The lights dimmed and a funny little man with a shiny balding head sat at a piano. He wore a red and white striped suit and a blue bow tie with little white stars dotting it. On top of the piano was a straw hat. He picked it up and waved to the audience with it before putting it on. The board of directors of the most powerful advertising agency in the Universe applauded. Then another little guy, equally ridiculous in the same style of red white and blue costume popped up from behind the piano. He carried a stringed instrument that one of the Board said knowingly was a 'ban-jo'. The two holo-guys accompanied each other as they spoke, played and sang.

"I hope this isn't a show-reel, Mucous. I hate advertising show-reels. They all look great but you don't know the brief they worked to or how the sales figures performed impacted the bottom line."

"Just a little pre-show warm-up, it's a tradition here at H.L. & S."

The holo-guys performed about thirty seconds of a little ditty called 'Thank Heaven For H.L.S.' As they finished they fittingly disappeared in a mushroom cloud only to be replaced by a holo-mmercial for a new cigarette that promised better performance in bed. This was followed by a squadron of stunt drivers demonstrating the manoeuvrability of the latest range of Forge Motor Company's private space shuttles. It boasted a computer that calculated your chances of surviving the day's traffic without an accident.

"I said I hate show-reels, Mr. Mucous."

Then there was an ad for some stuff that you sprayed on your hair. It rebuilt your follicles from the roots up in a single application while the canister played soothing music.

"I promise you this is not a show-reel; it's just part of a build-up. It leads somewhere important, believe me."

"Mr. Mucous, how could I not believe *you*?"

267

Bugles sounded to introduce a recruitment holo-mmercial for the armed forces of the Empire, depicting men shooting down aliens on vidi-screens, blowing up planets on weekends, and scoring with the local women on remote outpost worlds. As the last target impressively disintegrated into nothingness it was replaced by a new holo. But this was not a holo-mmercial that had hit the marketplace in the past. This was serious business.

The newly appeared holo was a single planet turning very slowly and silently in space, and it looked ominously familiar to the Director of Advertising and Marketing for Quadrant Four.

It was Earth.

Slowly rotating, the sphere was about two feet in diameter as it passed through the walls of the presentation cube and hovered in their midst over the centre of the conference table. Suddenly a spark of light appeared at the north pole of the orb. It flickered and grew. Arms, legs and even a flickering electrical head appeared. It was a state of the art holo-robo with a plasma field one-piece suit. He smiled permanently through the most perfect teeth every drawn, painted or moulded. Even if you asked him to cry, he'd smile through it. His voice programme was modelled on an obscure archival comedian named George W. Bush. Then it spoke.

"Hi! I'm Sparky, you're energetic friend, and I've come as friend to help everyone in the Universe save our most precious commodity, money!"

The sparky little flicker froze in the pose. Mucous turned to the Director. She appeared frozen too. Mucous maintained a huge grin of confident anticipation.

"Is that it?" the Director of Advertising for the entire Quadrant queried, "Is that all you've got to show me?"

"Whaddya mean is that all? Sparky's got the lot! He's got everything in the Universe going for him. We've really cracked it, Madame Director. Whaddya, think, isn't he wonderful!"

"I think I may have missed something. Can I see it again?"

So Sparky disappeared and reappeared on the North Pole, repeating his energetic money saving message.

"It's simple; I'll say that for it. Where does it go from here, Bernard?"

"That's the beauty of it, this idea has *legs*. It can go anywhere. It's got *wings!* At the end of the day, on the bottom line, the public will climb into bed with Sparky's proposition and believe that he is their genuine friend. This is an idea that will really fly!" The H.L.S. team nodded universal agreement. But the Creative Director, Marvin Fuchwitt, couldn't resist going a step too far. He opened his mouth.

"Everybody needs friends, you see, Madame. And Sparky is a harmless little guy anyone can put their trust into. First we grab them by the balls by promising money saving. Then we market a whole range of Sparky products which in itself will pay for the advertising and our fees..."

Mucous finished the paragraph before Marvin could put more than his foot in it. "What Marvin means is that this is only our preliminary thinking, but we believe we can buy the trust of people, through the sheer lovability of Sparky to such a degree, that in say twenty years time, we can ask them to make the sacrifice of their planets to help Sparky win back wasted energy."

Madame Prime was not committing herself on this.

"Think of it this way, Madame" Mucous continued in his palsy Uncle Bernie mode, "In order to make the destruction of Earth or any other planet a popular action, we need the people on our side, right?"

Madame Prime nodded in logical agreement.

"The decision has to be really popular, right?"

"'Acceptably popular' will be sufficient" she was leaning toward him now.

This was Mucous at his slimy best, getting the client's head bobbing up and down so regularly that when the sales pitch finally came, the client's head was still going up and down -- so automatically that before she knew what happened, she would be committed one hundred percent on a sound-and-vision recorded contract. The concealed cameras were rolling along and zooming in for a close-up of the final nod of approval.

"Once we have the first person convinced it's a good decision, more will follow, right?"

"Right." Madame Prime dangerously nodded again.

"And Sparky is that first precious all-important person. We've created the first domino ourselves and we will create and guide the massive chain reaction that will surely follow."

"He *is*?" It hadn't escaped Madame Prime's eyes that Sparky was a holo not a human being.

"You think saving energy is a great idea, don't you, Sparky?"

The little electric man danced and nodded enthusiastically of course. But he was not yet programmed to say anything beyond the presentation sentence about saving money.

Bernie confidently continued "Kids will adore him. Everyone will trust him. But best of all, Sparky is totally relevant to the energy saving solution. Now I'm not suggesting for a single moment that we really need to save energy, no, not a watt or a joule of it, but our persuasive little personality here will become a celebrity with a capital 'S'. People will not only love Sparky, but ultimately they will obey him because they will believe him!"

"Uh, right" Madame Prime said words she didn't really believe.

"Madame, I'm talking about a little guy you can love. A little friend you can follow. He is just so unbelievably cute. Wouldn't everyone want to take him home?"

"Uh, right."

"Kids will do anything Sparky asks. They'll kill their parents if Sparky asks them to. And embarrass others into following Sparky's sparkling example."
"Right."
"One day, after you've spent more money with us than the mint can print, Sparky will ask the people to make the ultimate sacrifice."
"He will? And what sacrifice can that possibly be, Mr. Mucous?"
"To save energy by recycling their worlds. To reduce the number of worlds using up all the energy. The logic is beautiful don't you think? Fewer worlds mean fewer users means the supply lasts longer and the rate of entropy is reduced. Sparky will have subtly led up to it so sensitively, so discreetly, so reassuringly that by the time he asks for planetary sacrifice, it won't seem such a big deal."
Prime pondered before she spoke, "An interesting approach, I admit, Mucous. You really think people all over the Universe will swallow it?"
And Bernie whispered his well practiced response, "Hooke, Ligne and Syncher, Madame."
"Mr. Mucous, I think what you're proposing here is appalling. No doubt the Universe is populated by gullible people, it must be if companies like HL&S are so successful, but this is going too far. Sparky is utterly ridiculous. Look at that silly permanent smile. And the bow legged walk."
"We can tone down the smile. We can alter the walk. Consider this as merely work in progress" Mucous was a master at back peddling when he had to.
"Sparky, 'your energetic friend', you say."
"Uh, Marve, we can change the, uh, strap line, right?"
Fuchwitt was flexible too "Yeah, maybe 'energetic' is too extreme."
"Friend. Friend. That might be too, uh, uh...."
"Friendly."

"Yeah, maybe we could be a little more aloof."

"Mr. Mucous, I've seen and heard enough. Any way you dress it up, crap is still crap. Sparky is not the solution I had hoped for. Thank you for the lunch, for your time and for not wasting any more of mine in the future. The cancellation fee is on its way. Good day."

Marve ordered Sparky to crawl under the table as Madame Prime made for the door of the presentation theatre. Mucous showed her to the lift. There were no handshakes as the Director of Advertising for the Quadrant withdrew the biggest ad brief in history.

A moment later the lift announced "Madame Prime has left the building."

Hooke Ligne & Syncher breathed a collective sigh of relief. As Bernie Mucous addressed his forlorn troops. "Jeeze I'm glad that's behind us. Where'd she come up with an insane brief like that anyway? I mean, we've got our professional pride, haven't we?"

Jump

Jackson had had enough. He asked directions to his quarters in the ship and waving the Esworthies off, slipped into his sleeping capsule. There was a VIP sign over the door and a guard remained outside. He'd leave the rest of the voyage to the crew of the Shiva. He couldn't sleep at first. The adrenalin was still pumping away. Mason tried an extra pillow but nothing seemed to help settle his mind, there was too much in it. How did all this happen?

His attention wandered back to his office and he wondered how Judy was again. It must have been Atos who alerted her. Bright spark that Atos. Was Judy safe? After the Jump, he'd enlist the Esworthies to contact her again. The Freea, himself and Judy. It came down to that. They were the only people he could trust. Everything was out of control. Plans lost. Vision blurred. Chaos theory had taken over his life. No, life was what happened while you made plans. It had always been that way. It was like a big game. Just a game. And win or lose he would keep playing. Life had been long enough anyway, he was getting tired of it. Something kept his engine running but he found it more difficult each day to stay focused and motivated. It was a target, or the lack of a target that made him depressed. Where was his life going anyway? What difference could he make in all the world, the Universe was fucked up; he'd helped fuck it up and it was all going to end in tears anyway so what was the fucking point?

The whole mad scenario was like another alien creation of his imagination. Something someone might dream up for a Wuzy Doll experience. Anyway, what were brains for? If they couldn't imagine things or plan things, they'd be a pretty useless hunk of meat.

God, here I am aboard a Navy Destroyer fighting private commercial fleets. He'd never heard of such a thing. Of

273

course lots of things happen that nobody ever gets to hear about. A key account man disappears on the way to a client meeting -- mystery agency shows up for the same appointment and wins the business, that was nothing new, but *this*. Thank Christ for Atos and the Navy, but what happens when I get back? Will I have to go into hiding?

Mason couldn't bear to think about it. He turned to the entertainment module and punched a list of contents. Nothing like a sci-fi holo to relax worn nerve endings and escape into the ether for a few hours. There was 'War of the Swirls', the life and death struggle of two warring spiral nebulae. 'Time Out', the story of a time traveller who journeys a hundred centuries into the future (been there, done that). And 'Metamorphosis', about a woman who turns herself into a beautiful butterfly. That seems a good one to fall asleep on. And with the vision running, Jackson closed his eyes and went to sleep without even watching.

Inspiration

Mason stirred from sleep. Recharged, revitalised, his earlier depression was not in evidence. Quite to the contrary he was now more determined than ever to get his thoughts properly assembled on the Entropy project. He'd make a presentation to Madame Prime as soon as he possibly could when he got back from the visit to Earth and Nixon. He borrowed a write screen from the Esworthies and set to work, often talking to himself as he thought things through.

He talked to himself as he worked, "This really has to be slick. Something with impact. Something memorable. Three dimensional, moving, reality scenarios... that kind of thing. But what's the Idea? Techniques are just bull shit without a good central Idea. What do I have to say that's _new_? Atos. The Freea. They're certainly new! But can I go that far yet? Word associations – let's see where that leads... Lights. Bright lights. See the bright lights. No, "See The Light" Good first thought. Write that one down.

"Mason, I see you're working, I'll come back another time." The bright light of Atos had entered his quarters.

"Atos! Really good to see you." The light moved and hovered above the write screen not unlike a reading lamp.

"What have I done to deserve this unexpected visit?"

"Now that immediate dangers to your life have subsided, I wondered if you had any further questions? You are central to the Entropy Project for both Freea and Humankind."

Jackson didn't like being interrupted at work, in fact once he started on something he positively hated distraction, but Atos was a different manner. He was a Light and a friend. "My time is yours, Atos. I've nothing specific to ask, but, well, I hardly understand everything about being a Freea. Suppose you tell me what's inside my head and save me the effort of asking questions."

"That is possible. But every mind is different. Some are defended with barriers. Others are totally transparent. Virtually everyone organises their store of knowledge in a different way. Though there is some natural ordering in the brain itself. Take a book. Flipping rapidly through the pages will give you a feeling for the layout and content, but you need the table of contents and an index to get more specific. No one's mind, neither human nor Freea, comes with an index or a table of contents. And believe me, it's far more interesting to experience a living story than to read it off a printed page or view it on a screen. Even the dullest personalities are more exciting in person."

"Yes, but the reality of being dull is inescapably boring." Mason squeezed in his personal point of view.

"So tell me about your most interesting moments. I'm sure a Creator has experienced a great many."

Mason launched into his memoirs. He wasn't sure why Atos wanted to hear them; he hoped he was just being friendly. He could use a friend like Atos right now. Of course the Freea were constantly gathering information and gaining fresh insights into everything and anything that mattered. Ultimately, Mason knew he himself would one day have to make the decision to try and join the Freea wandering the galaxies to the end of the Universe, or to accept the entropy of his own body and die with it on Omicron or perhaps Earth. Yes, perhaps Earth was a suitable place to die.

As he spoke to Atos, he mind worked at another inner level that considered his current situation and the way forward. He recognised some time ago that the his once Adonis like body was somewhat saggy (but not overweight) and fading into the oblivion of middle age... a time for males to endure years of lonely invisibility when women no longer looked him up and down at drinks parties -- when his eyes no longer caught the attention of an exciting woman at another table in a restaurant. True, he'd been exceptionally lucky twice on this visit to Earth. A major rarity for him these days. Amanda, a lonely and horny sex-beast on a long space-haul full of sleeping passengers. Then Alexx, a tourism officer blessed with nymphomania. But in both cases, it wasn't his looks or rippling physique they were attracted to so much as his being a Creator. If he was honest about it, for Amanda and Alexx, screwing Mason was tantamount to collecting another Brownie point toward the Girl Guide Sex Badge.

Mason told Atos about the time he went to Rabat to pitch for the Moroccan Government Tourism Authority and the client had assigned the competing agencies adjoining seats on the same aircraft. After that story, Atos had politely withdrawn from the possibility of hearing anymore of these boring memoirs and had taken himself off to meet Dharman in Quadrant Three.

"Thanks for coming; I do hope I'll see you again soon."

"Of course, Mason. Best to let you get on with your presentation now. I'll help you with Madame Prime if you like. I'll be there when you do it."

"That might be a very useful advantage. I'll hold you to it. Keep in touch. See you at Leadership Hall, Atos. Safe journey."

"See the Light, my friend."

Feeling somewhat peckish, Mason opened a snack box and re-focused on his task. "See the light, see the light." Mason had always found it ironic that he was called a *Creator* as if he was capable of conjuring something from nothing out of thin air. When so often all he did was recognise relevant associations and apply them to what he was trying to say. The idea of saying anything really new and completely original was absurd. It was virtually impossible to say something that had never been said before. And even if you invented new words and catch-phrases, they'd be gobbledy-gook to anyone who didn't

277

have exactly the safe frame of reference. As a Creator, all Mason really ever claimed to do was to say things in a *fresh* way, never a new way -- so people would think afresh about the product or service being offered.

The creative process in Jackson's mind was a much disciplined exercise. Usually he would write down the key human responses he wanted to evoke, in other words what he wanted the audience to know, think, feel and believe as a result of seeing his message. Then he would list the obvious and not so obvious associations, to be made between the product and the potential customer. Then list the ways they could be expressed or executed, crossing off the ones that were too difficult for the customer to relate to and the ones that had already been done too well by someone else. The meagre few that remained would be the focus of his final thrusts.

But today, he began with Step Two, skipping the know-think-feel-believe bit and writing 'Mother Earth' in the middle of the write screen. A moment later he scrawled 'The Mother of all intelligent life'. Those were the key emotive phrases he had instinctively pin-pointed as the basis for building his advertising campaign. But he had serious second thoughts. Such phrases would only serve to reinforce physical ties to the home planet. He might as well be writing about 'goodness', the elusive magic ingredient and undeliverable promise of virtually all twentieth century food product advertising.

Everything in those days, as now, was geared toward a better life through better technology: 'Progress is our most important product', 'Where tomorrow starts today', 'Better living through better chemistry', 'Man and machine in perfect harmony' and 'The appliance of science' had all been award winning, market-successful campaigns for the industrial giants of the age.

Faster, farther, higher, stronger, longer, thicker, thinner, deeper, newer, wider, brighter, sweeter, cheesier -- such were the Olympian ideals of the technocratic way of life man had chosen for himself! Mason turned away from the write screen. His eyes flicked around the room and landed on a black book on a small shelf beside the bunk. He almost didn't see it at all. He reached to see what it was. Gideon's Universal Bible. A perfect example of how History can get things muddled up. After countless centuries of finding their way into hotel rooms and ships cabins travelling across the galaxies, the G.U.B. had become the standard for all neo-Christians. In the much revised modern text, Gideon was himself a prophet with the Gideon Society having evolved into an elite group of apostles. Gideon was credited with the vision for spreading the Word ('in the beginning was the Word, and the Word was *expand*'). Others said Gideon was the 13th Apostle in Jesus' own time. But then not many had even heard of Jesus in these expansion oriented times. Nor Mohammed. Nor Gautama Buddha, nor Confucius, nor Lao Tze. Unless you were an ancient historian.

On an impulse, Mason opened the Bible. It fell open to the chapter on Genesis. At that moment, Jackson experienced the tingling inspiration he was looking for.

Creator

Mason imagined introducing Atos to Madame Prime, and for that matter, why not Judy, back at the office? "Hi, this is my friend, Atos, the talking light bulb" he would say. It only took him a moment to realise it was not going to be easy. They'll think I'm crazy, talking to imaginary beings, or voices in my head. But, hey, if it's real for me, it should be real for them too, shouldn't it?"

He went on to think about explaining the intricate relationships between humans and the Universe they occupied. It might take millions of words. He talked aloud again, "I don't bloody have millions of words. I've got to be succinct and right to the point or Madame Prime will simply walk away from my proposal. And I need her. Strategically, she's vital to any plans to deal with reversing entropy and saving Earth from the final bonfire. What I need is something as penetratingly powerful as an impulse beam."

He scribbled dozens more associations as he went. "Adam and Eve, Original Sin, bad news for women in the Garden of Eden, Gondwalard, Homo Freea, Africa, Antarctica, Homo Sapiens, Neanderthals, Harappa towns, Sumerians, Upanishads, Buddha, gurus, Judaism, Christ, Islam, Confucius -- what a morass! So what are we talking about here? A better life? A better death? An After Life? Death versus no death? Pathways? To the stars? To God? God becomes man? Man becomes God? What was it that Dharman said? Honour the god that dwells within you as you? Something like that. Yes. Something very much like that. Put it all together with the inspiration of Genesis and we have a tidy little play that becomes the presentation to Madame Prime. I will call it the 'Play of Consciousness'. And if she doesn't understand its implications, I'll give up and go back to my toys!"

"Discipline. I must focus and discipline and stay in the creative zone. Think of your audience as only being human, with human thoughts and emotions," he talked aloud to himself, and began to write, from his heart and from his head.

"The Beginning. That's a good place to start" And Mason Jackson began to write a story, from the very beginning.

The Play of Consciousness

In the beginning, Nothing existed. The void was the void. It consisted of nothing else. There was nothing to experience but Nothing itself. It is not surprising that Nothing saw its existence as a dead end, useless and pointless unless it did something to add to the experience. Therefore, from its own Consciousness, Nothing dreamed a Future.

In its dream, Nothing created Something, a simple Particle. The Particle was made aware of the limits of its existence, and aware of the great Nothing that surrounded it. As both subject and object, it knew itself as it knew the void, its stillness and emptiness. The Particle knew its own substance, homogeneous through the entire depth of its diameter. It measured itself equally in every direction and knew that it was a perfectly smooth perfectly round sphere, a mere speck in the vast void. Nearly void itself. As Nothing gave of itself in the Act to create the Particle, so the Particle could only give itself to the Void. To merge with the Void was to become greater than itself.

Then the Particle made a discovery. Stored within its perfect matter was perfect energy. The Particle called upon its energy to vibrate. The motion was so tiny and so fast that if you looked upon it you would not perceive it. The vibration increased until in a moment that expressed immeasurable power, the Particle embraced the Void in a perfect explosion. In a billionth of a second, the particle

281

occupied a trillion trillion trillion cubic miles of the Void. Shafts of vibrant blue energy thrust the dust of the sphere into the limitless Nothing. Outposts of the Particle scattered uniformly in every direction. For a dozen billion years the dust travelled out, continuing to vibrate with the power and energy that originally unleashed it.

By selflessness have all things been born. By selflessness shall they all return. From this Beginning we have evolved.

Primordial dust organised itself into infinite combinations. Atoms formed, then molecules, compounds, gases, liquids and solids in micro and macro shapes. A billion galaxies were conceived and a billion billion suns were born. And on at least one planet, spawned 4,600 million years ago, the inanimate became animate.

The dreamer looked down on a pool of water in a tidal basin warmed by the unclouded sun above and the molten core of the cooling planet below. The Play continued in its unstoppable sequence when a single transparent unit of something drifted against a pebble and lingered there of its own choice. The structure and composition of this unit, pulsing with the cosmic vibration, had the ability to move and its outer walls could keep its microscopic burst of energy contained inside. Four billion years ago, this little living cell was the most complex thing in the Universe.

Like the Primordial Particle, the primordial cell found no purpose in simple existence. In the next great act of selflessness, the cell sought to embrace the larger world. Within it, there could be detected the subtlest parting of its cytoplasm. A gap appeared in its inner structure as the materials polarised. The energy from within became stronger and stronger until the membrane was stretched so far there could be but one result. The cell divided into two.

The dreamer looked down again on a rain drenched gorge. The rangy beast scampered on all fours under the jungle canopy. Her mate called from a low limb in the clearing ahead. Bril screeched to say she was on her way. This was their favourite tree, full of blossom and scent and in certain seasons, food. But today they had simply come to play. Bril crouched beneath Torg, teasing him to come down. It was a trick. As soon as Torg twitched a muscle, Bril leapt into the boughs and the chase was on.

A shimmering yellow orb moved a tenth of a centimetre in the dripping wet leaves above Torg's head. As Bril saw the glint of the yellow eye, a coil of heat and energy sprang from the base of her tingling spine to the top of her flat sloping skull. But Torg was oblivious to the great green python hanging above him. Bril's voice caught in her throat as she leapt up and pushed Torg off the branch. He hit the mud with a thud, and rolled over. What he saw was beyond all his experience. The snake slithered away. Bril had landed on the ground standing fully erect on her hind legs. No ape had ever stood on their hind legs before.

The dreamer left for an eon but returned to look upon his Earth. A young man sat cross-legged in the sunshine. A warm breeze blew his red brown hair into floppy curls. He felt the sun's heat soothe his tired shoulders and aching neck. He bowed to the sun in thankfulness as the pain faded and his strength returned. It was a great time to be alive. Homo freea was at one with his world. For in those days, human kind knew what we never knew, and knew much that we have long forgotten. For one thing, they knew how very special human birth was. That of all the four billion creatures that had found life on this planet, roughly three billion, six hundred million had already become extinct. And, that of all the four billion, man, it seemed, had the best chance of survival. Like all

283

the creatures that had preceded them, Homo freea felt the inner surge of the cosmos, the energy and vibration of the Universe as it flowed through their veins, beat in their hearts and found consciousness in their brains. Homo freea was wholly aware. If a mushroom erupted from the forest floor in the middle of the night, Rajeed could feel it.

"Rajeed!"

"Gopal!"

"Come for a swim!" Gopal dived into the cool pool and surfaced with a turtle in his hands.

'Later, I'm thinking."

Gopal didn't complain. There was nothing to complain about, besides he had the turtles, fish and salamanders to talk to and play with. Nonetheless, Rajeed was not completely happy. Was this really the best of all possible worlds? His elders had said it was. Could there be more to life than this? Could he be better? Better than Gopal? Better than the people in the next valley?

Rajeed walked into the woods to be alone. He picked up a stick and smoothing off the twigs, carried it with him as he went. Two hundred yards along the trail was a clearing where the stream had cut a low cliff. He had found sharp rocks there before. Now he picked up a flat piece with a jagged edge and began to whittle away at one end of the stick until it became pointed. Rajeed ran his fingers over the point he had created and thought, "This is better."

Running back through the woods to show the pointed stick to his friend, Rajeed was so excited with his creation he accidentally stepped on the head of a cobra he had known all his life. The skull was crushed. The broken fangs *scratched the sole of Rajeed's foot and poison entered. He thought it was a briar. He never even saw his friend the cobra.*

Gopal was terrified when he saw Rajeed running to him in pain. He had never seen another human being suffer before. He had often seen people pass away and change states, but they had always done so of their own choosing. This was different. Rajeed was about to change states against his will.

"Gopal, help me! I don't want to change states. Something inside is forcing me. I'm not ready. I, I, I don't know what to do!" Rajeed's breathing lightened to fast whispers as the venom took deeper effect on the muscles of his chest.

"My eyes, Gopal, I am blind! And I cannot breathe. Tell the others."

Gopal embraced his friend and saw the inner light go from his eyes. He held Rajeed's hands tightly, and felt the pulse fade and the vibrations stop in his veins.

At this point, Mason considered how he might conclude the Play. The presentation needed to vault into the present and into the Future as it might be, and as it could be.

He could dictate the rest of the Play in sleep, what he needed now was a campaign vehicle, something tangible that Madame Prime could touch and feel. Something the entire population could relate to in their own way. That's when he thought of his own Wuzy Doll technology.

"Of course, a doll! A dramatic *new* doll. One that can fire associations with Earth and with the Play. I'll get my friends at Vision Headquarters on Malaypura, to produce the Play as a holo-series. We'll release it on holo-mags too. And I know exactly what I'm going to call the doll. And I'm going to keep it a secret until I see Madame

Prime. I won't even write it down!" he cried with relief that he had cracked it. Or had he?

"Hmm, better let this thing incubate awhile. Maybe by tomorrow I'll hate it." He stored the file marked Play Thing and put the write screen away. He stepped toward the door, then came back again, retrieved the screen, opened the Play of Consciousness file and trashed it, talking aloud to himself "Who the hell could ever relate to something like that? My crap detector nearly let me down. I'll keep the doll element, that's good, but the play seriously sucked."

It wasn't the first time in his long career that something he'd worked hard on had to be thrown away before it ever got to the client. When it was gone he felt genuine relief – and that was a sure sign he'd made the right decision in deleting the files.

The corridor outside his capsule bustled with the traffic of sailors changing shifts. Sliding back his viewport for a quick glimpse of whatever sun might be rising at the moment, he saw to his relief and surprise that they were out of the Jump and were pulling up alongside the biggest ship he had ever seen. It had to be a battlewagon.

Two hundred kilometres in diameter at least. It bristled with weaponry, screening devices and fighter ports. Landing bays held entire squadrons of cruisers, destroyers and corvettes. Then he saw the words StarBase I painted on the hull. Jackson's imagination had got carried away. It was not battlewagon, no ship could ever be that big – this was the Shiva's home port.

Until the battle with the pirate fleet, Jackson had assumed the military had nothing to do. That they were merely a show of strength, a symbol of authority that governments had always used to hold onto power. There were no enemies. No wars. No encounters of the third kind or any other kind. No external threat to Central Thought in the Universe. But now he knew there were real threats from within. Warlords, tycoons, maybe others. The future might well become very bloody indeed. As long as commercial expansion continued unchallenged, anyone who wanted more could get more without having to conquer others for it. The Universal Civilisation was politically and economically stable. Life was stable. Now the end of all that stability was more or less in sight. The Universe was more or less full. Energy resources would become valuable, not free for the taking. Resources would need to be protected as well as conserved. Perhaps starbases, battlewagons, destroyers and cruisers were still a good idea after all.

Home Delivery

From the bridge of Captain Shirk's private yacht, Jackson recognised a small reddish planet with wispy yellow-green clouds passing about a quarter million miles to starboard. He knew this to be Hesper, on the fringe of the crowded natural planet cluster that housed much of the Universal Central Government. Half an hour later, he could see a hundred artificial planets in any direction. It reminded him of New York. Instead of avenues of sky-rise office blocks, he was looking down corridors of office-planets.

Jackson was gob-smacked to be delivered in person by Captain Shirk to the Supreme Government Headquarters. But not half as stunned as when he was introduced to the Advertising Director of the Quadrant who was then further revealed to be Leader Madame Catherine Prime of the Triumvirate.

"Your Leadership, Captain Shirk, USS Destroyer Shiva, at your service, Madame Prime" Madame Prime nodded and smiled her approval. "And may I present the esteemed Creator, Mr. Mason Jackson."

"We are pleased Captain Shirk. And on behalf of the Central Government I thank you for your outstanding efforts in delivering Mr. Jackson to us in one piece, and we trust, with his mind still intact."

"I was merely performing my duty, Your Leadership."

"Your superiors tell me you were heavily outnumbered..." She found it easy to praise so competent an officer.

"All in the line of duty, I assure you" Shirk gave a snappy salute.

"Your Leadership, Madame," Jackson stepped forward. "I'd like to add my personal thanks for the services performed by Captain Shirk. Captain, I owe you my life." Mason Jackson was as sincere as it was possible for him to be as he shook Shirk's hand a final time.

"If there are no new orders, Your Leadership..."

"Order you to report aboard your yacht, Captain Shirk. And have a well-deserved holiday."

Shirk saluted, spun on his heel and left Jackson and Madame Prime on their own in the centre of the vast Leadership Hall with its glowing, flowing plasma walls.

"A great deal has happened since the first time we met in this room, Your Leadership."

"You may call me Catherine. I have looked forward to your report, Mason Jackson. Welcome back. Now, come and tell me all about it." Catherine led him toward the nebulous barrier on the left. They passed harmlessly through it, emerging into another smaller plasma-walled room; it was green with spots of tropical colours. The misty swirls of the walls and ceiling created jungled mystery, in counterpoint to Catherine's reassuring and friendly manner.

"This is a safe room, Mr. Jackson. We are completely alone, and you may say anything you wish."

"You're not going to believe everything I have to say."

"Let me sort the fantasy from the reality, I'm used to it. The most incredible things happen every day in every galaxy. Who's to say what's real and what isn't. A week in a job like this is enough to shake every belief you ever held."

"You mean like me believing you were really a government advertising director? And then finding out you are one of the Supreme Leaders of the Central Government.?"

"Yes, I think that's the kind of thing, Mason."

That she used his first name did not escape his notice. Irretrievably shipwrecked on a shoal of embarrassment, Jackson stumbled on, "I guess I should have kneeled or bowed or something, please pardon me."

"Nonsense, I'm not royalty. We don't have royalty in the Government. I am a public servant. People bow and salute because they think they should, but no Leader has ever asked for it or required it."

"You're very considerate, thank you." He was thinking that he wanted to bow to her out of sheer weight of respect. He was also thinking he was falling in love with her melodious and perfectly modulated voice. And he admired her for her control of the situation.

"Let's have your report then. It was expensive sending the Navy after you and I am yet to see the commercial value beyond your life of course." She smiled as if she was not overly serious about the remark.

"How did you know I was in danger?"

"We have our sources. And when your distress call came in we were already on our way. We could not normally have arranged a Navy pick-up like that without a far greater lead time."

"You *knew* I was in danger? I didn't know I was in danger until the bridge blew up on Nixon and I went hurtling into space!"

"Unfortunate about the bridge on Nixon blowing up and nearly taking you with it. The Esworthies were assigned to you and were on their way to look out for such things, but they were obviously too late to prevent that particular incident from happening. Truthfully, we were a little surprised your opposition actually wanted you dead. Maimed or brain-drained is standard practice in commercial skirmishing, but not murder. You had been watched for most of your journey. By my staff and by someone else's. You're familiar with Bernard Mucous I presume."

"Of course. HL&S advertising is universally known. The Destroyer Shiva had to evade the pirate fleet to get me out of Sol System. Captain Shirk said he thought it was organised by Mucous."

"That would appear to be true. But Mucous was trying to win a rather large piece of business in the process."

"Yours?"

290

"That was a side issue. Mucous was indeed working on the entropy brief that I gave you. But a syndicate of Expansionists offered him a separate deal, an exclusive package dependent upon HL&S eliminating you."

"Because of this Brief or because of the interview I gave Merry America?"

"Probably both. You certainly did not make any friends by spouting off in Cosmic Campaign."

"Mucous has made a botch of things, thanks to the Navy."

"He's fallen flat on the Brief too, but it would be inappropriate for me to tell you anymore about it."

"Shall I tell you what I've learned?"

Madame Prime indicated he should begin, Give it to me in a nutshell. Then we can move on to discuss any specific details as you wish."

"And I'd also like to talk with you about my plans relevant to the advertising brief. How are you for time?"

"Time stops for me. Proceed."

"I don't know how to make this simple, but I'll try my best. You see, I have found the answers to many of the great Universal questions. Why we are here. Where we came from. Where we should be going. How to save humanity from destroying itself. How to get more out of life. How to live perhaps forever. How to decelerate entropy. Enough so far?"

"I see what you mean. I think you've probably gone too far beyond your brief – and dabbled in areas outside your expertise, but tell me what you've learned. And try not to get overly philosophical. Now, you say you can *reverse* entropy?!"

"Not I, personally, Madame, but I know how to slow it down to its natural rate."

"That is still a by definition a reversal, and if the process could be accelerated in reverse, then who knows how long we may yet survive; and carry on. This intrigues me."

"Well, I met someone. Atos is his name. Something of a bright light. I found his help well, enlightening."

291

"He was on Earth? Our reports make no mention of an Atos."

"Yes, like me, he was just visiting."

"Where is he now? Is he an Earthling too?"

"No idea where he is at the moment, but he'll be in touch in due course. To answer your second question, he's one of the Freea, a super-evolved Earthling from an era pre-homo sapiens. In fact he is Homo Freea."

"No doubt that needs a long explanation, but please go on. It's fascinating so far."

"I would like you to meet him."

"Atos? If it's necessary I will."

"I think it will help you make sense of the things I am going to tell you. Atos was there at the beginning; he can help put it all into perspective as he did for me."

"How does Atos fit into the answers to everything, including the Entropy Question, actually?"

"The Freea are already working on a plan to reverse entropy themselves, you see -- they realised that slowing it down was a good start. And the key to that was convincing the people responsible for the acceleration."

"Everyone is responsible, Mason."

"Of course, Madame, but some are guiltier than others. And the Freea are virtually innocent."

"Quite unlikely. So what is their Answer?"

"I see it the way the Freea do. The mind, the human spirit, those are essentially the only things worth preserving. All the buildings, the homes, the objects we fill them with, the vehicles, the industries, are all superfluous."

"What a load of idealistic rubbish. You enjoy all these things as much as anyone else, perhaps even more than most. A greater hedonist I know not. You created whole planets of sheer fantasy, how can you say such things, Mason!"

"Ideas, enjoyment, feelings of all shapes, those are the benefits of life on the new plane."

"Intellectual and philosophical snobbery! Is that all you've come back with? Did you spend the night in the Israeli desert with a drug-crazed guru or something?"

"Atos is not a guru. But he has shown me another way, a higher path. It is the way of the Freea. It's not Nirvana. It's Evolution."

"It sounds more like Revolution."

"Madame, we are millennia behind schedule. The Universe on its present course is going to end far earlier than it should, but we can at least get back onto the natural course of doom. That much is still attainable. We must get started."

"And throwing out material goods is going to help us evolve, Mason? You honestly think so?"

"Such things are in the way. While we concentrate on them, we cannot focus our mental powers on real development and growth -- our ultimate manifest evolution is to outgrow our bodies and achieve a mental free-state."

"Rubbish. You want us to live in poverty? You want us to cut off supplies to billions of people on millions of worlds -- and let them die?"

"You promised to listen, Leader. You said I could say anything I wished."

"Yes, Mason, I did. You're right. I apologise. You may continue."

"You're thinking too far ahead. The end of the time-line for accomplishing a basic change in human understanding with the concomitant changes in cultural evolution is thousands of years in the future. And the changes would be handled on a voluntary basis, physical force and coercion would not be necessary"

"You propose just asking people to give up everything they own and to adopt a new life of sitting in caves contemplating their navels?"

"Well, actually, they wouldn't have navels anymore either."

"What?"

"You see, the whole thing with the Freea is that they have evolved beyond their bodies, lifted out of them, left them behind, and embraced the Cosmos in the purest sense."

"Most enlightening. I think I need some time on my own, Mason to think this through. And will you arrange for me to meet with Atos? I'll bleep your office to set up another chat in a day or two. But I must warn you that if your friend Atos cannot convince me any better than you have, well, I will be deeply disappointed."

"I'll try to raise him. Rest assured him, Madame, the last thing I want is to disappoint you in any way. I sincerely want to please you" Jackson hesitated before leaving. Madame Prime sensed he had more to say.

"And?"

"Well, Madame, I'm a bit worried that there may be further attempts on my life. You know kidnapping, torture, and murder -- things like that hurt."

"You will be safe. Trustworthy eyes, people and androids will watch you, look out for you and protect you in my name."

"Thank you very much for those reassurances ... Oh, we haven't yet talked about my advertising plans!"

"That will have to wait a little longer too."

Work In Progress

"**H**i Judy! How's it going, kid?!" Jackson opened his arms and enveloped his secretary as she ran sobbing into him. "Hey, don't get my shirt wet, will you?"

"Damn I missed you around here, Mason. Where in the hell have you been? I've been worried sick about you. Not a word, a card, a letter, nothing to let me know you survived."

"It was just one drama after another. The Navy rescued me. Then a pirate fleet attacked the Navy. You wouldn't believe it! It was incredible."

"Pirate fleets? You expect me to believe that? It's always another fantasy with you, isn't it?"

"No fantasy. I swear it's true. And I've been to see the Supreme Leadership as well."

"Honestly, you have completely blown your credibility this time. Tall tales all the time. How can I ever believe anything you tell me? Anyway it's great to have you back."

"You don't know how great is to *be* back. And I dare say you have finally had time to catch up on your shopping."

"How could I shop when I was worried sick? I'd never get a job as cushy as this again if anything happened to you!" She hugged him a little tighter.

"Hey, it's all right. I'm OK. You can let go of me now, I promise not to run out of the building for at least five minutes."

"I did everything you said about security, and as far as I can tell, we're still sealed tight again. Things have been happening though; McCosmos want an idea for another galactic re-launch of their McBurger franchise stores."

"I did the ultimate store launch for those creeps over a century ago. Nothing will ever top it."

"I think they've had a change of management."

"I don't move my bowels as often as those guys move managers. Get me the new ass-hole on the line and I'll sort this out before it gets out of control." Jackson put his bag away, marched into his inner sanctum, and sat down in the most comfortable chair in the Universe. Judy punched a few buttons and the McCosmos burger chain logo came to life on Mason's communication screen.

"Mr. Mason Jackson calling to create for Mr. Pseud." Judy announced.

Mr. Pseud popped up with a burger in his hand, chomping enthusiastically. Even so he talked at thirteen to the dozen. "Mase baby, your fee's in the mail... wait til you taste our new secret sauce. Addictive in every way. The Under Four's will be the most vulnerable. And there's a sexy hallucinogen for you ageing trendies -- no seriously, what I want to talk to you about is --"

"Crap, that's the word you're searching for isn't it? What you want to talk to me about, Pseud is crap. McBurger crap and more McRap. Anyway, I'm the leading purveyor of crap in the entire Universe at the moment, so you've come to the right place. What, pray tell, do you require of me this time, oh great and shallow Pseud, my scatological pest -- another re-launch idea? You've got it. Now listen and listen tight, you moronic asshole, the only way you're going to beat the records you already hold for mega-launches – thanks to me -- is to create a meaningful religious experience out of a visit to McCosmos."

"Wow, Mason, I think you've hit a new all-time low!"

"Yes I'm definitely digging in the dirt for this one. Now listen, this is the way I see it. Holographs, smell-o-vision, the works -- you're going to sell a billion Macroburgers a day at every location in the galaxy. What galaxy are we talking about here, anyway, Pseud?"

"I think we're scheduled for a mega event in the Malayapura Galaxy this time as a matter of fact, Jackson."

"Christ, Pseud, those people don't even like cheese! And your top profit lines all have soylent cheese slapped on them. But don't worry, as it so happens, this McMega idea is McPerfect for those McBastards, and your bastards too, Pseud. Individualism is practically unheard of in the Malayapura and McCosmos both, and humiliation is in; and what could be more humiliating than religion? So let's really give it to 'em --whaddya say Pseud, you old asshole you, let's give 'em the Second Coming of Christ, McCosmos style. They'll never know what hit 'em!

"McTastic, Jackson -- you've done it again!"

"And don't worry about a thing, they'll be eating cheese in no time -- Cheeses Christ will see to that!"

"Great, Jackson. Just what I want. Something impactful, memorable, dramatic, theatrical, something filled with deeper McMeaning."

"It's kinda like your new secret sauce, when you think about it deep enough, Pseud."

"Exactly! Yes, I see what you mean. You're amazing how did you come up with this incredible on the spot and off the cuff like that without even seeing the brief? I mean, it's spot on! You're a damned miracle worker, Mason."

"But we'll do it better than the *real* Second Coming of Christ, because we'll have Believability on our side. With the McCosmos logo stamped on everything associated with the event, the idea of the Second Coming will grow in stature. It'll be more real, more relevant, more alive, yes, and more beneficial to the seething salivating masses than it could ever have been in the biblical sense alone."

"I'm with you on that, Jackson, good buddy."

"Now, Pseud, this is important, we need a Messiah. And try as we might with technological hoopla, a talking macroburger will not come off as a Saviour of society and souls. What I propose is the power and the glory of Rollie McCosmos!"

"Really? Rollie McCosmos? Live and in person?"

"Yeah, it'll be great. Imagine it. The universally famous hamburger clown, dead for centuries, will suddenly be re-incarnated from all available archaeological data. I have a subsidiary company called Immaculate Conceptions Inc. who will do the whole thing under my control right down to building the audio-animatronics -- another significant religious link."

"Fantastic!"

"Spiritual in fact."

"Think of the spin-offs!"

"I have, Pseud, I have. Get this: Rollie will be re-incarnated as Jesus McCosmos! I see a take home doll, in fact a genuine Wuzy Doll Mk XIV pre-dressed in Rollie's clown suit -- wait for it, with optional halo attachment and a bleeding heart as standard equipment! Every man, woman and child in Malayapura will want one. And you can sell them off at a convenient self-liquidating profit price! You might even want to roll out across the Universe on this one. Pseud."

"Sheer magic, Jackson, sheer magic, baby!"

"I'll have Judy send you a costing on the whole project in a day or two."

"Thanks, Jackson. Must have lunch soon, okay?" ·

"Great. As long as it's on you and it's not a goddam macroburger."

"Anything you say, Jackson, baby."

The McCosmos emblem wiped over Pseud's piggy ketchup-and-mustard smeared face as his hand slid under his desk for another burger smothered in their new secret sauce. Jackson turned to see Judy come back into the room.

"How'd it go, Boss? Everything all right with Mr. Pseud?"

"Fine, Jude, I re-sold him on the idea of using Rollie the magic clown making yet another in-store appearance. Check our props house and see if you can dust off the robotics we used last time."

"Anything else?"

"Yeah, I was half expecting to hear an answer on the Mmorocan System Tourism ad campaign by now."

"There was an article in Cosmic Campaign saying there were four agencies pitching for the business."

"Challenging brief that's for sure. A three planet system with eleven suns. With at least six of them in the sky at any one time. You have to wear sunscreen even indoors, and you know what they wanted? They asked us to project a cool, fresh, green image of flowers, gaiety and sophistication. Spaceshit! It's the only place I know you can get a suntan indoors and at night!"

"So you're not too optimistic about getting the business, then."

"No. But telling them they were crazy was the professional thing to do. I mean, unless they change their product, they should make the most of their uniqueness. Build their identity on what they really are, damn it. All that warm wonderful sunshine they have will be worth unimaginable fortunes in times to come. Besides, I gave them a great campaign idea about everyday being a Sun Day. It's got visibility, identity, promise and simplicity. The concept can't miss in the marketplace."

"The Guillotine shaving razor thing seems to have sorted itself out. Scratchie & Scratchie picked up the account while you were away."

"Just as well. They were really squeezing me on the deadline. Anything else then?"

"One more teensie weensie item. What about that decadent lunch you promised we'd have when you got back?"

"I'm always promising to take you to lunch. This time, Judy, you're on. But I'd just like to get the feel of my inner sanctum for a few minutes on my own if you don't mind."

"Of course not, but don't be too long. Oh, I wonder if it would be okay if I had the afternoon off to go shopping? After lunch, of course. I've been stuck in this luxurious suite every single day waiting and watching for transmissions, and I'm suffering from an acute case of cabin fever. I've got to get out!"

"Sure, okay. But things are going to change around here, Jude. I'll tell you about it over lunch."

"Right, boss. Anything you say. I am here to serve." She teased.

Jackson slipped further into his contour custom made lounge chair, and flicked the lights on. It was more like a planetarium than an office. A glass floor was suspended on the equator of a spherical room with the star systems glittering on black space in every direction.

"Atos, are you there? Anywhere?" Closing his eyes, Mason focused on his breathing. Deep, long breaths. As his mind calmed, he looked into the empty space between each breath. A star map appeared as a thought. It was in the Milky Way.

"This is Mason Jackson calling Atos, come in, Atos. Atos, do you read me?" He suddenly felt quite silly as heard what he was saying. I hope Judy isn't listening. He stopped calling Atos and looked at the Malayapura Astral System. Something McAwful began to rise in his stomach.

"Mason Jackson calling Atos of the Freea."

Still nothing happened. Was this how they reached other? Was this how the Freea did it? Or did one Freea simply think of another Freea and hey presto they were in touch?

"Atos! Dharman! Prem! Atos! Is anybody there?" How in the hell am I going to contact them? I must concentrate. I must think. I must... I got it. Lift-off! I must try and achieve lift-off!"

"It's all right, Miss, we've got a pulse again."

"God! I thought he was dead!"

"I was. Sort of." Jackson blinked into consciousness.

Judy was hugging him. The medics tried to calm them both. Jackson got up.

"What the hell! You can't just get up and walk away, mister! Not when you were pronounced clinically dead twenty seconds ago!"

"Judy, get rid of these guys, will you. Look, I'm sorry; you wasted your time here. Send me a bill, no problem. I would have been alright sooner or later anyway. I can't explain, but believe me, I was coming back, I promise -- Judy, really, I was coming back to take you to lunch, remember? Didn't I promise you a decadent lunch today?"

"You promised you'd only be a few minutes. After an hour, I came in to remind you, and there you were, cold, silent and slumped in your chair. I called for an ambulance. What else was I supposed to do? Mason, I think you need a rest. Why don't you just take it easy like the medics suggested, and we'll go to lunch another day, okay? And I'll just go back to the office and go shopping another afternoon, what do you say? Okay?"

The medic was equally adamant, "You're a sick man. You had no life signs whatsoever, and I don't believe in divine intervention, even if this does look like a miracle. We'd like to take you in for a few tests and overnight observation."

"I appreciate that I've caused you all concern, and I apologise, but you cannot legally hold me here. Hell, I've been stone cold before and lived to tell the tale. I tell you what, let's make a deal. If your scanners can find anything wrong with me, here and now, you can cart me off to the hospital. Otherwise, I'm taking my secretary to lunch."

The medics and their medi-bots descended on Jackson with every piece of kit they had.

"Geezus, lady, I swear your friend was dead, now look, not a flicker or a blip on any of these graphs."

"I told ya I'm fine. Come on, Jude, I'm starved."

"Sure, Boss, I'll lock up. Sorry to call you guys down here for all this."

"You'll have to pay the bill, anyway I'm afraid."

"Like I said, no problem. At least I've had a thorough physical check-up out of it. Fancy a macroburger, Judy?"

"Barf! You promised a good, lingering, decadent lunch. Let's go to Le Chateau."

"Why not? Great suggestion." Jackson lifted his bones out of the contour chair and met Judy at the office door. The ambulance team were gone and Judy had put the info systems and security screens on auto control. They walked toward a transport station at the end of the corridor.

"Now what was all that about you smell old goat? Did you fake your death for the fun of it? And how did you do it? You had me half-scared to death if you'll pardon the pun."

"I said I was sorry, but you --"

"Look, Mason, I didn't know you working on any new illusions, I hope I didn't blow the secrecy calling in the ambulance people."

"No, hell no. If the story gets around, nobody will believe it anyway."

"That's for sure. How did you do it? You know, fake death like that?"

"All in the mind, Judy, all in the mind. But honestly, I am sorry I worried you so much. I only meant to be gone for a few minutes. I had no idea I was gone an hour."

"Gone? You were there the whole time; you just seemed to be extremely dead.'

"That's the point, my body *was* dead. But I was alive. My essence, my mind, left my body and went off to do some business."

"You've cracked, Jackson. You've finally, definitely, irretrievably cracked, flipped, gone over to the other side. You are one hopeless dreamer. One of these days God will get you for this.'

Blood Sports Forever

"Judy, I've got to go to Noddy Hemsley's place for another meeting with that loathsome bastard, Ben Airs. If you get any messages from Neil,"
"Who's Neil?"
"I thought I ..."
"No, you didn't tell me who Neil is or anything about him. This is the first I've heard of him. I certainly hope you're not starting to act strange again and go all weird and fake your death or something awful."
"Look, maybe it's time I told you a few things, Judy. So why don't you put the office on automatic and come with me, we'll talk on the way."
"Sure, Mason. That would be great, seems like you don't take me with you nearly as often as you used to."
"I'm sorry, Jude, I'll make it up to you. Just one thing though, I'd rather you weren't actually *in* the meeting."
"Oh that's nothing to worry about. Don't worry, the last thing I need is a dose of Noddy Hemsley and Ben Airs. I'm surprised either of them ever wanted to see you again after the Willysports episode. Noddy obviously survived the heart attack."
"Par for the course. He just got a new model installed. Don't know why they keep crappin' out on him. As for Airs, we're talking tough skin. Hide that mere human words cannot penetrate."
Hemsley's Hunting Lodge was on a rogue asteroid that roamed sector 186. It was not on any fixed route. The only way to get there was by private shuttle. And only then by finding its beacon frequency and homing in on it. The trip would take the better part of an hour.
"It's nice to be away with you again, Mason, even if it is for only an hour or so. We haven't really talked in ages. Not since that lunch I forced you to take me to."

"That's what I want to talk to you about, Judy. You remember the ambulance trip?"

"How could I forget it?"

"Well, I wasn't actually dead."

"I know. You faked it. The medics swore up and down that you really were a terminal case. You said so yourself."

"I said I wasn't faking my death. I wouldn't do that. I was simply out of my body for awhile, remember I said that too."

"I think you have a touch of schizophrenia" she smiled, "one part of you is here, the other isn't."

"I'm trying to be serious, Jude. What happened was that I merely left the physical side of me for a while. I came back to it in the ambulance-- when I woke up. I never intended to cause you a scare. I thought I'd be back in my office when I woke up."

"So your spirit went walkies."

"My mind, my spirit, my spark of life, call it what you will-- I checked out and went for a trip with a friend of mine."

"A girl friend, no doubt."

"I'll admit I've had the occasional girl friend over the centuries, but I've always come back to you."

"You are sweet, you old bastard."

"Jeez, Jude, you're very married, and I'm not going to break up a home by asking you to come and live with me."

"No, and I don't want you to. But sometimes I wish-- I dream--that maybe you would take me away from the melodramatic mess I'm in and we wouldn't have to work in this crazy business anymore."

"Hey, those are my lines! That's my song and dance you're plagiarising."

"I wish they were."

They sat in uneasy silence as the shuttle raced a comet through sector 47.

304

"So where *did* you go when you 'checked out' as you put it?"

"To be precise, to a globular cluster identified as NGC 1049 in the Fornax Group."

"Fornax? That's a gazillion light years from here!"

"About 800,000,000,000 anyway."

"And you went there and back in less than two hours? Come on, I'm not an idiot!"

"Which is exactly why I'm telling you all this, Judy."

"I'm sure you can see why I had to be secretive about this, Judy."

"I'm not so sure I should stick my neck out and believe you, Mason, but I do. Anybody would think I was crackers if I told them half the crap you tell me."

There was an unsettled, questioning look in her blue eyes. And Mason had the uneasy feeling that Judy was going to break into tears. He gently brushed her blonde fringe back and tried to get her to smile.

"What's the matter, what did I do now?"

"Does this out-of-body project mean you'll soon be leaving for good?"

"I haven't made up my mind yet. At the moment I have the potential to check-out permanently, but I like my body too much to leave it forever."

"I like it too, even if it is a hundred thousand years older than mine. But it's your mind that I stay with you for. Every day's a challenge with you. And every day is fun! I just know I wouldn't enjoy working for anyone else."

"I know this may sound uncharacteristically pragmatic for a hedonist like me, but well, I'm a dreamer too, Jude. And I'm not getting any younger. The body isn't everything, anyway, is it? I mean, that's what's so damned attractive about Lifting Off. You can keep your mind intact. And there's so much m ore to learn, like living on a new and higher plane."

"You really think you can do it."

"I know I can do it. And you can too, with training and the will to make the leap."

"I don't know, I have to think about it."

"There's time, well, for the present any way. And if the plans are approved, there will be a great deal of help from Central Government."

"Do you really think you'll get Government approval for a project?"

"Yes I do. It's part of the larger Entropy Project. The funding and the need to do something are already there. We'll do a pilot scheme first to demonstrate the possibilities and determine the probabilities. I have assurance from at least one top level source that trials can begin within a month. Central Thought will select the first participants."

"Congratulations then. If Central Thought is committed this far, it's as good as done! Fantastic!"

A few minutes later they arrived above Hemsley's lodge and signalled for permission to land.

Hemsley met them at the front hatch.

"Mason! Is that you? Great man! Great man! Come right down!" Noddy Hemsley was always an ebullient host.

"Governments can always u-turn I've seen it before countless times. You're in favour one week out of favour the next. And the Pirates could wreck the whole project regardless of C.T. -- Oh shit, there's Noddy grinning through the window, I've got to go now. Why don't you take our shuttle and go shopping or something, Noddy will see that I get back safely."

"Okay, boss. See you later. And thanks for the talk. You really are special to me and I wouldn't want to lose you." She touched the back of his hand, but pulled back when he reached for hers.

"And you."

The lodge was a modest dome filled with the relics of Hemsley's favourite sport. A display of subatomic machine guns in an antique glass cabinet graced a thirty metre wall. It must have been one of the last cabinets in this galactic neighbourhood to have real glass in it.

There were holo-pics of Hemsley posed with various beasts he had obliterated: a bird no larger than his hand had its head blown off. A strange, many-antlered lizard dripped yellowish blood on Hemsley's deer-stalker boots. A pheasant the size of a peacock hung limply from a tree. And there was a huge blow up of Noddy at the edge of a purple sea of wheat, having paid nearly a million credits for his place in the line of twelve thousand blood-thirsty hunters awaiting the starting signal to march across the wheat and blast anything that flew out of it.

"Hello, Mason, my good fellow, what will you have to drink?"

Jackson knew from experience he could have any brand of whisky ever made as long as it was 16 years old and labelled Old Dead Duck.

"You wouldn't have a wee dram of the Old Dead Duck in the lodge would you, Noddy? I know it's exceedingly difficult to hunt down a bottle like that these days."

"As a matter of fact, now that you mention it, I think I know just where to look. You just take a seat. Take a seat. I'll get it myself; I know just where it is."

No robo-service here. Good old Noddy handled his whiskey with personal care and absolute reverence.

"You'll have ice, and no water, right?"

"You'll join me I hope."

"I've already got one going! How are you anyway? You're looking well. Been away?"

"Me? No. I'm a slave to my office." (The wily bugger, what's he up to anyway?)

"I've got a great little job for you, my boy. Great little job on a subject that's very close to my heart, very close." He patted his bionic chest lightly as he said it.

"Not an ad campaign for Old Dead Duck? Sixteen years old?"

"Great man! Great man! The boy is quick, isn't he?" Compared to old Noddy Hemsley, Jackson was still very much a boy.

"In a way, it is about dead ducks, blood sports at least."

"Yes, I can see that blood is very close to your heart, Noddy." The pun gushed past Noddy without a nod.

"What this project is all about is the B.S.A., you see."

"How did the Boy Scouts of America get into this?"

"Where's this America? Have they got anything to shoot? Big stuff? Little stuff? Makes no difference to me. Give me a loaded gun and I'm in my element."

"America? It's on Earth. I'm sure you've never heard of the planet. Anyway no hunting there anymore, I'm afraid."

"No, Mase, you don't mind if I call you Mase once in a while? No? Good. The B.S.A. is the Blood Sports Association, of which, I am, in point of actual fact, a life member."

"Don't you mean a death member?"

Hemsley managed to cough a laugh in response. But he looked deadly serious. "The B.S.A. is responsible for the stocking and preservation of game on every habitable world we could find."

"But aren't you also the only people licensed to *shoot* game too?"

"That's very true. But of course we couldn't shoot them unless they were there in the first place."

"Yes, yes of course, I should have thought of that."

"Have another Old Dead Duck with me, my boy?"

"No thanks, I've barely sipped this one, but I'm feeling a bit chilled and this ought to warm me up some. Nice drop."

"Absolutely. A little top up always warms up the insides. Now where was I? Oh yes, the last shoot I was on, there were only five hundred of the elite shooters of the Life Member flock. There we were all lined up waiting for the

308

starter's flash -- glorious day, glorious. Brownjohn would have loved it. Bookbinder would have photographed it. Anyway, off we went, 3,000 black beaters bashing the bush ahead of us. And you'd never believe it, but we got all the way to the other end of the field, a long trek it was too, and nothing flew up. Not even an insect! Do you get my meaning, Mase? There was nothing to shoot in the whole bloody field!"

"I can imagine how disappointing that must have been for you."
"To say nothing of the expense. But that's not the point. The point is this-- the game is gone, not only from that field but from whole planets. Gone. And the public is going to notice it sooner or later, and blame *us*!"
"Do you seriously believe they might think somebody *else* shot the game to extinction?"
"That's a good angle, I like that, blame it on someone else... but I don't think so."
"What do you want me to do, Noddy?"
"Here's the brief, from the top, I mean the Top!"
"The top of the B.S.A.?"
"Yes, of course that's what I mean. I want, that is we want to get hold of a wildlife expert, you know one of those presenters from the holo-mags who goes around zoos and helps viewers spot the animals in their cages-- anyway, get one of these people and do a holo-story about how much the B.S.A. have done to preserve flocks and herds of wild things over the centuries. That ought to create a warm basis of feeling and buy us some time while we figure out what to do next."
"It's that bad, is it, Noddy?"
"Between you and me, it's disastrous. I think the game is gone entirely, wiped out last year sometime. We're still waiting for reports from the farthest corners of the Quadrant, but not a single shootable beast has been spotted for more than six months. Imagine the poor

unlucky bastard who got off the last shot and didn't even know he got the last beast."

Jackson thought of the free-flying ducks, geese, pheasants and everything else he'd seen on Earth recently, and wondered how long it would be before Noddy Hemsley's B.S.A. moved in to 'preserve' them on their members walls. At least he hadn't given the game away and told him where Earth was.

"So, Noddy, how am I expected to do a show about creatures that don't exist?""There's millions of them in film libraries, and with your Wuzy Doll technology, you've got a good manufacturing base for mass producing models -- even ones that can fly."

"Why didn't you shoot mechanical ones in the first place for Christ sake?"

"It's-it's- it's not the same."

"What you mean is they're not really alive, and they don't bleed."

"Something like that."

Jackson stared at a holo-pic of a blasted hummingbird, it was quite perplexing.

"Are you sure the public really is going to miss the game birds? I mean nobody ever sees them except the beaters and the shooters."

"That's a point."

"So why create a storm over something that may go completely unnoticed?"

"Because we are very responsible people in the B.S.A."

"I got it."

"You have? Great man! Great man!"

"Yes, Noddy, I'm afraid I have."

"Tell me!" Noddy slurped down the last of his current glass of Old Dead Duck, punctuating his excitement with another short phlegm-filled cough.

"What's your idea?"

"Expand your charter. Until now you've only shot red blooded animals. Let their number regenerate by switching your sights to animals with green, yellow, brown or black blood."

"Great man! Great Man! What a great Idea! With a capital I!""

"You could re-launch the B.S.A. as the F.S.A."

"What the hell does that mean?"

"The Fluid Sports Association. You could claim enlarged responsibility for the protection and conservation of every species in the Universe."

"Great man! I'll report immediately to the Rules Committee. I see a great new print campaign with pictures of every imaginable shape and colour running on all the major holo shows.

Jackson was suddenly washed with shame with the realisation of what he had just done--unleashing hordes of Hemsley's fellow hunters on previously un-hunted species. Why had he done it? Why, why, why? It was the nature of the business he supposed. He couldn't help himself. The Ideas just always popped out and bugger the consequences. Whenever he switched his mind into the Selling Mode, he just automatically produced ideas. A client, a problem, or a new brief-- his instinct was too strong. Winning was everything. He should have kept his mouth shut and gone away to think about it. It was too late for second thought, the deal was done.

"I hope two billion will be sufficient for your fee, Mase, my boy."

"Yes, thank you."

Mase sipped his Old Dead Duck, reasonably be satisfied with the outcome. The money didn't matter. Someday he'd probably just give it all to Judy so she could spend the rest of her life shopping. Where he was going he wouldn't need money anyway.

Time Wasters

A faint sniff of ozone reached his nostrils as he entered the dome. Glancing left, he spotted the small black pit and the tear drop of liquefied cinder brick where the wall bled from the laser wound. Mason hit the deck and crouched conspicuously in the crowd at the exit of Wuzy Enterprises. The sniper melted into obscurity from his firing position amongst a maze of market stalls two miles away.

"So much for keeping me safe, Madame!"

Mason was still furious when he stormed into Leadership Hall an hour later. Madame Prime was startled by his boisterous sudden appearance.

"Your, Leadership, pardon me if I'm not my normal smiling happy self here, but I was nearly fried by a laser in my own company headquarters. You said you'd protect me!"

"Settle down. Calm yourself, Mason. You look quite alright to me. Now what happened?"

"A sniper with a laser blade. So close under my nose I could sniff the ozone, that's what happened. The second shot creased my right arm. That's my throwing and bowling arm. It might have ruined my social life."

"Well, he missed. And the Government is pleased that Mason Jackson will live to go bowling again. I suppose you'd like a drink?"

"Wouldn't say no to that sort of offer, Your Leadership."

"Champagne then?"

"And my bodyguards on a plate please."

Madame Prime brimmed his flute with bubbly. "I have to disagree about the bodyguards. You don't know the whole story. The bodyguards did their job extremely well. I received their report on the sniper's attack about ten minutes before you arrived. They apologise for the second shot having creased your jacket. The reason you are alive

312

at all is because the assassin missed. And the reason he missed is because your very dedicated bodyguards shot him very dead as he was taking aim on you. My only regret is that we were unable to interrogate the sniper."

Mason had no course but to apologise. "I, I'm sorry, Madame Prime, I didn't know..."

"I know you're sorry, I can see that. It's all right. Sit down."

"Maybe we should share this lovely champagne with the guys who saved my life."

"The 'guys' are women and they never drink on duty."

"I would like to thank them somehow. How may I do that I wonder. A free Wuzy Doll of their choice perhaps?"

"Perhaps. I'm sure you'll find the appropriate means. I'll make sure you have their private contact numbers."

"To your health then." Mason offered the toast.

"To life!" said Madame Prime.

"Everlasting."

"I must say, Mason, I found your draft report rather amusing in its implications. I have tried to maintain an open mind about this, but I can't help but wonder whether you have considered the possibility that your alien contact, Atos..."

"With respect, Madame, Atos is not an alien; he is merely an evolved Earthling. Homo Freea predate Homo Sapiens."

"Well whatever you think and whatever Atos may appear to be to you, is it not possible that he is some sort of elaborate illusion that caused you to hallucinate so clearly and vividly that you thought the whole experience was real? Nor can we rule out the possibility of drugs." The word seemed to echo in the wall-less chamber.

"Who would take the effort to disillusion me when shooting me with a laser blade is so much easier and cheaper? And, Madame, I never take drugs. Never have, never will. Never needed them. I do get high on Life from time to time however. If it was a holographic experience,

313

it was like nothing I've ever seen and my own companies make the very best.

"I know that I went into space with Atos and his friends Dharman and Prem. I swear it to be true, Madame. I *knowingly* and willingly left my body and flew free of it."

"I can see you honestly believe you did." Madame Prime put down her glass. "You claim you can arrange a meeting with this Freea being, Atos. Is that still possible?"

"He'll be here as I promised, Your Leadership. He was somewhat apprehensive at first, but I convinced him that sooner or later we should all share the same knowledge and experience base. Did you invite your co-Leaders as I suggested?"

"No, Mason, I didn't. I do not feel it is appropriate to waste their time at such a preliminary stage of investigation. I shall be the sole judge of whether your ideas receive the Government's approval or not."

"As you wish, Madame. Atos is probably already here anyway."

"That's quite impossible. This room is the most secure site in the Universe. Not even Q-rays can penetrate the plasma walls."

"I will ask for him to join us physically in a few minutes, but if you don't mind I'd like some further reassurance about my personal security."

"The problems about your security could go one for years, Mason. If you've bucked against the system that feeds you, stepped on toes and made people squirm as you have someone among the Expansionist Elite, the 'pirates' as you call them, is likely to lash out. My staff will do the best they can, but we cannot guarantee your safety one hundred percent. Perhaps you should consider publicly re-stating your position."

"You mean a denial. A u-turn. No way! Out of the question. I don't want to be killed, but I have had a pleasantly long life, two of them in fact. I have nothing to lose by standing my ground and making my point."

314

"Or you could just leave your body and float to freedom with the Freea." Madame Prime looked askance at him, in blatant jest.

Mason wasn't so amused. "Enough is enough. Atos, would you kindly join us please?"

Immediately, in the space between Mason and Madame Prime, a pin point of bright light appeared at shoulder height and grew slowly until it was about the size of a child's fist, glowing with incandescence.

"How did you do that? I do not detect the source of your projections. No alarms have been triggered either."

"There are no projections, Madame. Atos generates his own light. Atos *is* light. Catherine, may I introduce the essence of Atos. Madame Prime, meet my friend Atos of the Freea."

In that precise moment, Madame Prime felt a gentle warmth at the base of her skull. It was extremely pleasant. Then the light spoke, "It is an honour and indeed a privilege to meet you, Your Leadership." The light twinkled as the voice spoke from within.

Madame Prime was momentarily speechless, but not yet convinced there were no tricks. "A very masterful illusion indeed! I congratulate you, Mason. I did not know you were a ventriloquist as well as a hi-tech Creator."

"Atos is not an illusion. And I am not a ventriloquist. Atos is an Ambassador of the Freea. And known in certain academic circles as the Muse of Economics."

"I extend formal greetings and salutations from the Universal Consciousness, Madame Prime."The Supreme Leader responded with a simple, "Welcome, Atos." She stared at the soft light, looking carefully for wires, and with a pen-sized laser probe, continued to scan the plasma walls and indeed the floor for hidden projectors.

"Madame, I'm sure that's hardly necessary." Mason suggested. Then he was startled as a harsh mechanical voice came out of the ether.

"My Leader, security sensors have detected an unauthorised life form in your presence. Do you wish to have the invader destroyed?"

So Atos was a *living* entity.

"No, security. We are safe. I will deal with the intruder myself as necessary." Then, looking calmly at Mason, she added, "Security has detected what I could not -- that Atos is a living being. How that can be so, I cannot guess. Perhaps there is truth in your stories after all."

"Thank you, Madame. From the beginning and through all our meetings I have told the truth as I perceived it to be."

"Thank you for keeping an open mind to the possibilities, Madame Prime," said Atos. "The way you see me now is my most natural form. It is also potentially your most natural form, even though you do not realise it yet. The light point is the most efficient form we know. It allows us to exist as free spirits."

"Which is why you call yourselves the Freea?"

"Yes. The light you see is not merely clothing, the light is our body. And as you know, light is a form of energy. As pure light, we are pure energy. But with a sentient differential. For as sentient beings we evolved into energy. Thus we are now conscious energy, and that is what makes our existence and potentially yours too, so special in this Universe."

"I see," said Madame Prime. "And it sounds as though you are something of a philosopher too."

"It is only the wisdom that comes with great age."

"But all this verbiage about the Universe and Conscious Energy. If you speak of a new religion, you're wasting your time with me. I grow weary of it easily."

"If you are not interested in my thoughts and observations, I will not force them upon you. But I am not talking about a new religion but a new matrix of social physics."

"You have told Mason of a Path of Enlightenment. That sounds like a religious phrase to me."

316

"The Path will be there when you are ready, Your Leadership. And as I said, the Path is not religious, but a very real physical route to the higher plane. The next plane of evolution for Homo Sapiens can only come through this route."

"Why would Homo Sapiens want to evolve to another plane if it isn't spiritual?"

"It depends on what you mean by spiritual. I only mean that you can find your true self and enjoy your true part of the Universe more easily as a point of Light than in the physical body you have now."

"What about you, Mason? Are you marching on the Path?" Madame turned to the man.

"I believe I am, but as Atos said, if it is of no interest to you, then there is no need to discuss it."

"I would prefer to stick to business. Shall we get on with your communication proposals then?"

"Yes, of course, Madame. If you instruct Central Thought to access Alien Creations, you will have a full copy of my report together with my personal recommendations concerning both long term and short term solutions to your brief."

"Excellent. I shall examine every thought. For the moment, would you kindly concern yourself with presenting the top lines only, Mr Jackson?"

Catherine Prime has turned decidedly icy and aloof toward him. This was all going terribly wrong Jackson thought, but a job was a job and so he launched into his proposals, "As regards the advertising specifically to your brief to persuade people that it is an acceptable option to destroy the minor planet, Earth, for fuel, I advise that such action is quite unnecessary and would be a waste of public funds.

"An acceptable answer. However we have paid you for a campaign idea and the initial execution. Your recommendation implies that such a campaign is unnecessary."

"I have nonetheless produced such an idea and its execution."

"May I see it?"

"Of course. The campaign I have produced is based on a deeper line of thought than the simplicity of the brief might command. Because I have looked beyond the brief, holistically, and have identified a greater aim. That aim is not to find new sources of fuel for increased consumption, but rather, a way to slow down consumption, even arrest it, in the long term interests of reversing Entropy."

Madame Prime raised an eyebrow.

"If we continue consuming the way we are, we will literally consume not only every planet but every star in the Universe hundreds of millions of years before they would have burned up naturally."

"I believe Central Thought touched on that fact in the Brief."

"The point is, Your Leadership, that what is needed is not an alternative fuel, but the incentive to slow down consumption."

"We all love the good life, Mason. You included."

"We can all have the *highest* quality of life, in another way."

"Do not preach to me. I am not interested in religious solutions."

"It is not religion, but a way of life. You heard Atos. I sincerely believe it is our only recourse. Our only hope against accelerating Entropy."

Madame Prime looked coldly into Mason's hopeful eyes, then at the soft glow that was Atos. She turned away from both of them and spoke loudly as if to the walls and ceiling. "I grow tired of this charade, Mason. You waste our time."

"But you haven't seen the campaign idea yet! It features a brilliant new doll!"

"One of your Wuzy things I expect. It would appear you are only interested in selling more of your toys, and not in the concerns of the Government. Leave us now. Go. And turn out your light when you leave" casting a caustic glance at Atos.

"Come on, Atos, Madame Prime obviously has better things to do today than save humanity from running down the Universe."

Yet Another Conspiracy

"**G**ood evening, Your Leadership, Madame."

"Mason, thank you for coming. May I offer you something to drink?"

"Water would be nice, thanks." Mason wondered why the mood swing? She had been really rather chilly at their last meeting and virtually offered no help at all.

"I was not aware that you were a man of such simple tastes."

"Water is something of an acquired taste, Madame Prime. Besides, I occasionally make an attempt to clean up my act."

"I'm impressed" she almost giggled so light was her tone. "Shall we sit over here then? It's been too long since we last met," she said, pouring the cool, clear, still liquid.

Mason looked up and down at his hostess. Tall, elegant, lovely in every way. Too bad she was a Leader; he'd really like to be able get to know her more personally. What was she up to? What scheme did she have in mind that necessitated this meeting? And 'far too long' since we last met? It had only been a few days.

These last few days he'd been made to feel like a banished political outcast. Indeed, in spite of the consumers who continued to buy his Wuzy Dolls and other Creations by the million and billion, he felt things were not going well, that control of things was slipping away from him. To start with, Merry America, infamous of Cosmic Campaign, reported his failure to win a large mystery brief for Government advertising just six hours before the unexpected appearance of the Sparky adverts. How did that happen? Hadn't Madame Prime said the HL & S were out of the picture? As a direct result, the whole creative industry began to look at Mason with some disdain, as a 'has been', to be shelved and forgotten indefinitely. The Cosmic reporter reported 'a strange faraway look in this man's eyes' and wondered publicly 'what he was taking these days'.

"Have you wondered why I invited you here this evening, Mason?" her eyes were firmly locked into his.

"It crossed my mind. Do you think our meeting will change my life?"

"An interesting comment. Your life? Perhaps. Perhaps not. But it's everyone else's life that I'm responsible for that concerns me at the moment."

"Spoken like a true Leader, Madame."

"Yes, a true Leader." She paused long enough to create a moment of suspense. I thought you wanted to call me Catherine, and yet you persist with referring to me formally."

"Madame, Catherine, I would dearly love to call you Catherine. And I would dearly prefer that you were not a Leader. But as you are one of the three most important people in the Universe, I hardly think it appropriate to refer to you so personally. Due respect should be observed."

"Oh, my dear, Mason. The responsibility of this office has driven me to the brink more than once. I would like to know you more personally too, but the charter of the position expressly forbids it. Though I grow weary of Leadership, I have come too far to risk everything on emotions." Madame Prime leaned forward as if to kiss him. Well that's what he thought she was doing, and for once in his life, Jackson was determined to do the right thing, to behave correctly and with propriety and not assume that there was anything happening here. So he leaned delicately back into his chair. He didn't know if that had been her intention or not, but he instinctively knew 'not this time'.

"Thank you for all your kind words, Catherine. You are very precious to me."

Then spontaneously, as if choreographed they both leaned forward and embraced. It was Catherine who spoke first. "We dare not let things go any further. Perhaps another time, another place."

"In another life."

"Yes, in another life." They held each other even closer, sharing the breath and warmth of their bodies. Eventually they sat apart and just stared into each other's eyes. Whether it was love or merely the infatuation of forbidden fruit, they would never know. Catherine spoke again, "My apologies for the sudden invitation to my villa. Things sometimes have to be done a certain way. I'm sure you understand."

"Of course, though not in this instance. You were so cold and abrupt the last time we met, and you offered me no support for the project. Couldn't you see that Atos was real? That I didn't imagine his existence? That I hadn't manufactured him with smoke and mirrors?"

"Yes, I am sorry I had to do that. But I had reasons. I invited you to my villa, my home, because is it one of the three safest places in all the Universe."

"Pardon me, Catherine, I thought the plasma walls of Leadership Hall ensured the perfect secure environment."

"Yes, but one is never *alone* in Leadership Hall. Not even me. Even if you never see the other two Leaders, they are always there. So you see I'm afraid many of the things I was forced to say to you at our last meeting were merely for the benefit of the other two Leaders."

"Then, are they your enemies?"

"Good heavens, no! But they are not amenable, as I am, to the things you propose."

"You? You would be amenable to a free-thought university? You would consider joining the Freea in a free-space existence? You can see the Higher Plane?" He hugged her spontaneously.

"Yes, yes I would" her eyes smiled consent but she pulled herself back from his embrace.

322

"That's wonderful! That's fantastic! But why?"

"Because of something I *felt*. Something about you. Something about Atos. Something genuine. I believe you. Not everything of course because I haven't experienced everything you have experienced first-hand. But essentially your ideas make good sense to me. Certainly, the way we the Universe is currently going is not the right course for the future. The whole Universe spiralled out with expansion, but now, as far as I can see, it is spiralling back down into a bottomless drain."

"Oh, Catherine, I think you really do understand."

"That much, yes. As for leaving our bodies and floating off into another existence, well, let us simply say that my interest has been piqued."

"You don't know how good this makes me feel! I didn't think anybody would ever believe me."

"Then why did you choose to tell me?"

"Basic strategy. Start from the top and work down. Jesus started from the bottom and worked up. I knew that this was so important, so revolutionary that if I was going to tell anyone it had to be the most important person I was ever likely to meet. And that person was you. "

"You flatter me. But what if I didn't buy it?"

"Then I'd revert to the common approach, but this is such an intellectual challenge, I thought I'd need a lot more time to sell it to the masses. I wish you had let me know your true assessment earlier; you have no idea how disappointed I was when you threw me out. I thought I'd misjudged you, and that really hook me. And now those stupid Sparky ads have started popping up. I thought you rejected the whole silly proposal?"

"I did. But then you came up with something better and I saw the opportunity to use Mucous to create a smokescreen. Since our last meeting, by the way, I've had CT probe Alien Creation's databanks and retrieve your report in full, with all your recommendations. Your strategy is excellent."

"You really think so?"

"Yes, don't you?"

"Well, I, uh, yes. Absolutely. But I don't see how those damnable Sparky ads are going to help."

"Stop worrying about Mucous and leave him to me. The Sparky ads are not going to hurt. And we need time, perhaps as much as five hundred years to get a meaningful flow of intellect concentrated on the problems and opportunities.

"A five hundred years? I hadn't thought of that. Uh, I could use another drink of water."

Catherine took his crystal tankard and refilled it. She filled another tankard for herself. "You know this is the first time since i was a child that I've had water without something in it!" They both had a good laugh.

"Sparky can run alongside our own Free-thought campaign. But ours will be more subtle. Applying your Wuzy Doll technology is a master-stroke, Mason. And I love the idea of creating a new doll and naming it 'Mother Earth'."

"Thank you. I thought it would work rather well. And as things relating to Earth become fashionable so to speak, Sparky hammers away with his conservation of energy message."

"It's the University that intrigues me most, however. That's the first step in becoming Freea. Tell me, Mason, is it really possible?"

"I have experienced it myself. And so can you. I have left my body, looked down upon it, travelled from Earth to Orion and back. And went back into my body and ended up here, not counting a million other events in between. But the first step has already been taken. You listened to me. You listened to Atos. And now you have clearly decided to take steps to help all mankind in this way."

"You make it sound far too important."

"It is important. And it needs someone like you to help make it happen. Will you put your name to the campaign? Can I use you as a testimonial endorsement?"

"In time, probably. Initially I will see to it that the best brains in the Universe are given Mother Earth Dolls as gifts ... from me. It should help, don't you think?"

"Excellent. No one could refuse any gift from you. Once the intellectuals begin to commune with the doll, they will open a direct channel in the meditative state to the Freea. It will be like turning a key."

"Can we get Atos to guarantee that the best teachers among the Freea will be available to contact the subtle mind of the best human subjects? Will he do that?"

"He'll be ecstatic! Of course he'll guarantee it. Every mind capable of reaching the Freea will be raised higher and higher. I can see a day, dear Catherine, when human kind will rise literally from the encumbrances of technology, leaving all their physical restrictions and demands behind, joining the ultimate life forms amongst the stars, interacting and working with the Freea to find a solution to entropy or even a bridge to the next Universe!" Mason was on his feet, punching the air with enthusiasm.

"Isn't that a little over-dramatic?" Catherine clearly wasn't used to seeing such antics.

"Sorry. I suppose it was a bit. But I am absolutely energised that now I know anything is possible. The only thing that worries me is how we're going to get support for everything and if we can speed up the process."

"Well we can't go to the private sector on this one. Security tells me they thwart at least two attempts on your life everyday now."

"They do? Catherine, I had no idea! I thought the last one was weeks ago when that sniper creased me."

"Perhaps you ought to consider joining the Freea as soon as possible, while you're still alive and capable of making the jump." She hugged him firmly.

"Maybe I should." He whispered.

"I think the only way forward now is to gain Central Government approval for the various projects that have to be implemented to see this thing through. And to obtain that, I'll have to do what now Leader has ever done before."

"What's that?"

"I'll have to be selected by CT for a second term of office."

"How will you manage that?"

"I doubt that CT will see the wisdom of our request, so we'll have to employ Atos to change a few circuits."

"Catherine, I never would have expected you to operate that way."

"Don't be naive."

"Tell me, what are you in this for? The power? The glory?"

"Gracious, no. Hasn't it ever occurred to you, Mason, that the ultimate benefit of escaping this slightly aging but hopefully appealing body still capable of some degree of restoration and preservation is *Immortality*?"

"Immortality. Unproven of course. But not *dis*proven either. The Inner Self may well be eternal. Look how long the Freea have already survived. But aside from suffering extreme accidents that cannot be foreseen, Immortality isn't something you gain, Catherine, it's something you are born with. That's what the Freea believe because that is what they have experienced. No Freea has died except when caught in natural catastrophes. They do not experience disease or degeneration."

"Really, Mason. Only God, if there is a God, is eternal."

"Precisely. *If*. And I think you should put that to the Freea for a fresh point of view. I am surprised that the thinking, highly intelligent person you so obviously are; do not question the existence of God."

"I do question, but I guess I'm hedging my bets, just in case there is some sort of Last Judgement Day when we fail to stop Entropy."

New Light

"**M**r. Jackson, there's a lady here to see you. Says she's from the Free Enterprise Corporation."

"I don't have any meetings scheduled at this time, not for at least another hour. What's her name anyway?"

"Miss P. Rem."

Mason was trying to think where he might have come across that name before.

"Uh, do you want me to spell that for you, or can you work it out for yourself?

"P–R-E-M. Says she's from the Free Enterprise Corporation. Ah, yes, why didn't you say so? Show her right in."

Prem was shown into Jackson's inner sanctum. He stood to welcome her as she entered the room, "I see you're wearing a body today, looks terrific, good choice."

"Hello, Mason. The body is an illusion, a temporary convenience that I choose from time to time. I trust the curves are sufficient for a man of your experience?"

"Perfect. Couldn't have designed you better myself."

"But you did."

"Did what?"

"Design me – in your dreams. I confess I had a peek last night."

"But it was only a dream; I didn't have dirty designs on you, Prem! Ah, but I am so flattered you came – in any form -- you could have just appeared under a lamp shade whenever you wished." He smiled widely at his own wit.

"Well, we had only met just the once, so I thought a human entrance would be more courteous."

"Thank you, Prem. That is very thoughtful of you. Have a seat."

327

Prem perched opposite him on a low standing leather looking bench.

"So, Prem, to what do I owe the pleasure of your company today?"

"I had to leave rather abruptly on our first meeting, and I was only just getting to know you. I'd like to get to know you more, if I may. Face to face, without having to be devious in any way dipping into your mind uninvited."

"I hope it's a two way exploration, then."

"Of course, and as you wish."

"I'm thinking that I could be more objective if you weren't so drop-dead beautiful."

"Should I incandesce then?"

"Why not. Illumination by any other name would be a Freea in their natural state of Light."

Prem continued to speak as she dissolved her body and shrank to the size of a small light bulb, flickering slightly as if moving unseen lips. "Are you sure you would prefer this?"

"It just kind of seems 'right and proper' that you appear to me as I saw you for the very first time."

"Right answer."

"So what do we talk about now then?" Jackson wondered aloud.

"I find I can find out more about another being if I let them do the asking."

"You mean you can tell a lot more about a person by the questions they ask."

"Equally, by the questions they don't ask. A great many adult human beings almost never ask questions of people they meet. Which often indicates they are so stupid that they think they know what they need to know – or they are just socially lazy and really don't give a damn about the person the other person."

"I agree whole heartedly..."

"So ask away – "

"I have a question that has remained unanswered since I was about six years old. I doubt that you will have an answer for it either, but if anyone could, perhaps a Freea could."

"I am intrigued by the build, so I really will try to answer it."

Jackson remembered sitting on a dock on a tranquil lake in Connecticut, Gorton's Pond he recalled the name; dangling his feet in the warm summer water and gazing at the serene liquid reflections of lazy clouds sliding across the sky. It was then, for the very first time, he realised he could not see the back of his head without a mirror. He described the scene to Prem. "And then I had a flood of questions popping up in my head. Who was I really? Why am I here? How am I here? How come I am inside this body -- and not outside it as well? Where did I come from? Am I more important than the fish in this pond or are we all the same? And then I had a most remarkable thought – that me, the fish, the pond, the grass, the trees, *everything* was made of *exactly the same stuff*. I didn't know what kind of stuff until I was about nine and found out about atoms in volume one of the set of Colliers Encyclopaedia my parents bought for me."

"It was the same way the ancient Greeks discovered atomic theory – just by making a vital connection with their own natural world." Prem listened attentively, "Then what happened?"

"It was the beginning of questioning and learning. By the time I was ten I had read all 25 volumes of the Colliers books. I never did find the answer to any of my original big questions, but it did lead me to more big questions, like were my parents really my parents and wasn't religion just mumbo-jumbo?"

"Didn't you think that the answer to all your questions must be in religion, in God, if you couldn't find it in reality, in books?"

"No, I didn't. Religion was a distraction, a waste of effort, time and money."

"What else have you learned over the centuries?"

"Perspective. People who believe in God use him as an easy answer, an unthinking answer for anything they can't answer themselves. I am not a theist!"

"Obviously."

"Prayer is a waste of time. Hope is not, but we shouldn't confuse the two. It's human to hope, and human to-try and do something about situations we may find ourselves in."

"So you don't believe in Design?"

"No. I believe in Evolution. Which is why I believe what the Freea have told me about their own past and present. In fact, I don't think you can believe in evolution and God at the same time."

"I don't think so, either, Mason."

"So the big question, bigger than 'where did I come' from and 'why am I here', has to be 'Is there God?"

"We, the Freea, have found no empirical evidence for the existence of God, if that is what you mean."

"I thought as much. So mankind was not simply created, it evolved. Human beings were not designed, they evolved."

"As I believe you know, Mason, religion is like magic. It is disconnected from science. It isn't real, it's an illusion, and a rational, thinking, perceptive, imaginative human being with a living brain can see that. That's what the Creationist Wars were about. Millions died needlessly. The real war has always been between rationalism and superstition. Science is but one form of rationalism, but religion is the most common form of superstition."

"In fact religion can exist without creationism, but creationism cannot exist without religion... but I imagine if you and Atos and Dharman appeared to the average guy in the street, they would see you as Gods."

330

"Which is exactly why we don't do it. It will take a very long time before people will be able to see us as super-humans and not super-natural."

"So, do we have to wait until the end of the Universe before the Great Debate between science and religion is finally resolved?"

"No, I can safely say no God will be revealed and no God will reveal itself, at the end of the Universe, and that we, and all other beings living at that time, will continue to be left to their own devices just as they always have been – get on with it and to deal with the situation as best they can. Live or die."

"Sounds grim."

"You mean you'd have it any other way? Like suddenly start praying to a god?"

"No, because I would still think it was a waste of time."

"Even if it was the last br4eath of your life and you had nothing left to lose by trying?"

"Hmmm. I don't know."

"Then you need more time to think, Mason."

"No, I don't. No. With my last breath I would try to evolve further. That is my own personal nature, and that is what I believe all human and all Freea must do to the end of days."

"You surprise and delight me, Mason. I had no idea you were already so far evolved."

"But I still have the doubts from childhood about not being able to see the back of my head without a mirror."

"That was about self-awareness. About realising that you are a sovereign individual, and that no one else is exactly like you."

"But it led to me feeling different about who I was, -- a feeling of being very special."

"I hope no one made you feel guilty for those sensibilities!"

"Frequently."

"Those feelings were further recognition of inner abilities. It was a sign of your innate intelligence and creativity. It takes imagination to see something extra and go outside of conventional thinking, and to be able to see through superstition, and ..."

"To be all you *can* be."

"Exactly. And that is what will allow you to evolve to your ultimate destiny among the stars."

A holo of Judy materialised facing Mason. "Mr. Jackson, your next appointment is due in twenty minutes." It was an automated reminder.

"I have a brief to read through, Prem. I hope we can continue our discussion at a later date."

"I'm sure we will someday find that we have all of eternity to discuss whatever we wish."

We used to say back on Earth that science gets the rocks and religion gets the rock of ages. Then when men made it into space, science became the study of how the heavens move and religion just carried on with how to get to heaven.

The God Hypothesis lives on, suggesting that the reality we inhabit also contains an unreal element – an entity of some sort that designed and created both the natural world and the laws of nature that make it work.

Welcome to the Club

Jackson entered the taxi shuttle craft and told the screen where he wanted to go. "Cafe Expression, please." The robo-driver obeyed immediately, hurtling out into the dense traffic. It didn't matter to Jackson that he was speaking to a computer, he always like to keep please and thank you in his everyday vocabulary. In that regard, he was a creature of habit. He also liked to treat himself every other day to a good old fashioned double espresso macchiato in a convivial cafe environment, instead of at his desk.

The shuttle went up instead of down to the street where he knew his nearest Cafe Expression was located. "I said, Cafe Espresso please." But the shuttle seemed to have a mind of its own. The next thing Jackson knew the windows darkened and he could no longer see where they were going. "Hey, what the hell's going on? I said Cafe Expression!"

A speaker panel in the ceiling, normally programmed to ask what air temperature and humidity levels he preferred, was activated, "Do not be alarmed, Mr. Jackson. You will be comfortable and safe throughout your journey."

"Who is this? Who are you? Where are you taking me?"

"I suggest you sit back and remain quiet. No harm will come to you."

"Right. Why should I believe that?"

"You have little choice. Sit still and be quiet." The voice was quite terse.

Jackson sat back, un-amused and insecure. He tried all the windows and doors but of course everything was tightly locked and he could not see out. He tried the entertainment systems and none of them worked. He had been abducted, or kidnapped if you want to call it that.

"Is it money you want?"

There was no reply from the speaker system.

"I have no family, do you realise that? If you are trying to extort my family for money you're wasting your time. You'll have to deal with me!"

Still no response. A minute later he could tell the taxi was descending, slowing down and landing. The door to the taxi opened and he was instantly grasped by two shiny black securi-bots and led into a dark room. That is, a blacked room, completely dark save for a spotlight showing on a floor about fifty yards or so in front of him. As he was led to the circle of light, a generously cushioned chair materialised and he was invited to use it, "Please make yourself comfortable Mr Jackson."

One click and Mason Jackson was released by the securi-bots. He sat in the chair and straightened his clothes. He looked around but could discern no light or colour only pitch blackness in every direction. It was disconcerting, but he composed himself and determined not to speak until spoken to.

The left side armrest opened up and a glass of champagne rose up and sparkled onto his sleeve. A disembodied voice stated, "Dom Perignon. Vintage of course."

Jackson took the flute, examined the mouche and said, "Thank you" before sipping the first scintillating mouthful. "How can I help you?"

"Very sensible of you to be cooperative."

Jackson thought it best to remain compliant, for now at least. "Why should I antagonise you when you are clearly so civilised?"

"That's what we like about you – you have powers of perception."

"You said, 'we'. Who. then are 'you'?"

"I speak for those you call the Three Thousand. Those you accuse so freely of piracy." Jackson was thinking fast, Oh shit, I am really screwed now! They've got me by the short and curlies. "OK, but do I know you? Have I actually met you?"

"No, not me personally, but you have met those who work for me, and us."

"So, what do you want?"

"It should be obvious, or at least nearly so."

"I have spoken out against you, right?"

"Yes, but that is of no concern."

"It isn't?"

"No, why should it be? Do you really think you can hurt us in any way?"

"People should be aware of how things are run so they can make informed decisions."

"But they don't. They don't make decisions any differently whether they're informed or not."

Jackson's face said it all; he was puzzled.

"You are informed and you don't behave any differently. Why do you speak against us?"

"Because you're evil and you take away control of systems and processes that influence the lives of all of us."

"Tough."

"You will never be sorry then?"

"Don't be absurd. No more than you."

"Me?"

"Look at yourself, Mr. Jackson. Your business entrepreneurial self."

"What of it? What are you getting at?"

"You accuse us of piracy and you are no different from us."

"Bull shit. What the fuck are you talking about?"

"Who do you work for?"

"Myself."

"Do you work for the Government?"

"I work on their briefs when I can."

"But you are neither their employee, nor anyone's employee are you?"

"No, and I never will be."

"Do you pay taxes?"

"Not if I can help it. My avoidance schemes are very successful."

"And so they should be."

"Do you work for the banks?"

"How do you mean?"

"Any loans?"

"No, never."

"Mortgages?"

"No, not since I was young and stupid."

"Good."

"Do you have people working for you?"

"Yes, many thousands."

"And investments?"

"Naturally, they work for me too. It goes without saying."

"Would you call yourself rich?"

"No, comfortable."

"Do you call yourself wealthy?"

"By comparison to you, probably not."

"You are a rich man, Mr. Jackson. As rich as those of us you call Pirates."

Jackson did not respond, he was thinking.

"You are, in fact, one of *us*."

"Shit, I am?"

"Yes. You have learned how to make money work for you. You have built a plethora of assets. You have very few liabilities and have amassed a great deal of wealth along the way."

Jackson still seemed stunned.

"Welcome to the club."

"What now then?"

"Nothing. We just wanted you to know. You can keep rubbishing us if you want, but you're only rubbishing yourself at the same time. You could give it all away if being a so called Pirate offends your standards, but it might be better if you just put some of your money where your mouth is. We do."

"You do? Yes. You do. Uh, good idea."

"We suggest The Universities of Free-thinking would be a worthwhile cause. We are already contributing. Use your money as well as your expertise and those programmes could expand and accelerate."

"I thought you just wanted to make more money!"

"There's only so much money you can make. After a certain point, there is no point – unless you channel your imagination and talent into new and worthwhile endeavours."

"Yes, yes of course."

"This meeting is terminated, unless of course you have questions."

"How do I get in touch with you?"

"From now on, order any taxi to take you to the Cafe Expression and someone will be here to talk again if you need to."

"Thanks. And thanks for the Dom Perignon."

"Our pleasure.

Award Luncheon

"**W**hat's this all about, Judy? I thought the Radio Federation luncheon was tomorrow?"

"I thought so too, but a reminder just came through on the mail transmitter saying it's today."

"Well check the date. Maybe the 'today' they mean is actually tomorrow."

"No, the date is today's date. Sorry about that. You still want to go?"

"Hell yes, I want to pick up my award for the best radio spot of the year in the personal gift section!"

"The whole corporation is really proud of you, Mason. Your image and reputation are restored! They're planning an avalanche of congratulatory transmissions."

"Ahh. I always did like radio. They said TV made it obsolete. They said holo-pics made it obsolete. Then they said smell-o-vision made it obsolete. Said the same thing when impulse beams came out. But they can never make the listener's imagination obsolete and that's what keeps radio alive and thriving in every corner of the Universe."

"That would be a great way to start your acceptance speech."

"Yeah, I suppose it would. Thanks for the idea. I'll do that."

"You'd best be off then, the award lunch is a full star sector away. Want me to order you a limo-shuttle? I'll look after things around here as usual."

"Why not? I can put this one on the company."

Mason sprang out of his contour chair, slipped on his jacket and flicked off the screens and lights of his private world. But before he left, he played his award winning commercial to remind himself how good it was.

It began with light, intimate piano music.

Then a deep, quietly confident male voice over:

338

"She was tall, willowy blonde and leggy.
I watched her across the piano as she slipped her hand
inside the smart leather hand bag, pulled out her slim
gold lighter, flicked it and phizzzz.
This was my chance.
I slipped my fingers around my Cricket disposable lighter.
One flick and we were flying.
Cricket. The Light Fantastic. Now at a price fantastic at
your local giftique."
(30 seconds)

"Shuttle's here, Mason."
"Thanks, Jude. See you tomorrow."
"Enjoy the applause."
"I will."
The limo-shuttle delivered Jackson to the front door of the
Cosmopolitan Hotel on Fluxton Five forty minutes before
the luncheon. He went inside expecting to meet a hundred
old mates from studios and stations around the Quadrant,
but it was not to be.
"Looks a little empty for a big event, doorman."
"Expecting a convention or something were we, sir?"
"Well, not exactly a convention, more like the annual
Radio Federation Award Luncheon."
"Tomorrow, sir. It's tomorrow."
"You know, I thought it was."
"Then why did you come today?"
"I got a special message this morning saying it was today.
I've just travelled a full star sector to get here."
"Well, you could stay. We do have a restaurant."
"And it is lunch time, nearly. Okay. Damned frustrating to
get the day wrong twice."
The doorman led Jackson behind a waterfall and into the
restaurant. There was a single table with two chairs. A fat
slob of a man sat in one. His back towards the door,
Jackson could not see the man's face, but he had a sudden
foreboding he knew who he was. The man twisted around.
His jowls sprayed slobber.

"Mucous."

"Jackson. How nice of you to be on time."

"Bernard Mucous. What are you doing here?"

"Waiting for you. I trust my driver was careful in traffic?"

"Your driver?"

"Of course. And my doorman. And my hotel."

"And the Radio lunch really is tomorrow?"

"Yes. Tomorrow."

"You tried to kill me."

"I don't do things like that."

"No, I suppose you get others to do things like that for you."

"Yes, it's much easier and cleaner that way."

"So now I'm here, you're going to try to kill me again?"

"No. Not today. You're incredibly lucky you know. And expensive. Twenty or thirty attempts so far you know."

"Not to mention a flotilla of destroyers, corvettes and cruisers."

"Shhh. We wouldn't want too many people to know about such things for obvious reasons."

The two men stared at each other nearly a minute without speaking.

"Mind if I sit down, Bernard?"

"Call me Bernie and have a seat. Have a lunch too. I can recommend the calamari to start, or sun dried tomatoes, mozzarella and avocado maybe. Then, say, penne with gorgonzola sauce, and a deep dish of tiramisu to finish off."

"Yeah, I could handle it." Bernie punched the button on the table waiter and the order was confirmed. It was going to be a delicious pig-out Italian lunch no matter what else happened.

"So why do you want to see me, Bernie? What could we possibly talk to each other about? And what do you want to kill me for? What's in it for you?"

"Me? I don't want to kill you, Mason. The idea of death makes me feel ill. Let's just have a chat and see how things go, all right?"

"Talking is free."

"But there's no such thing as a free lunch, right?"

"I've heard that before. Probably in one your ad campaigns that you stole from some poor sonofabitch trainee copywriter that was killed just because he asked to be paid for his services."

"I'll disregard your insults for the time being. And by the way, my Creative Director, Marvin Fuchwitt sends his regards. Let me get right to the point so you don't spoil your appetite with worrying whether you're going to live to the end of lunch or not. Mason, I want to make you an offer."

"An offer? Me? What kind of an offer?"

"An offer to join Hooke Ligne & Syncher."

"Screw you! Never! Why in hell would I even consider it?"

"There are always advantages in being part of something larger. Job security. Better opportunity. You name it. You write your own ticket and join HLS. I want you with us."

"You want me dead."

"Look, somebody else wanted you dead. They forced me to assist in tracking you down and eliminating you. Your interview with Cosmic Campaign made you some deadly enemies. You can't go calling universally important commercial people 'pirates' and expect to get away with it. As for me, I was promised certain large advertising accounts if I succeeded. I didn't of course, but I still might."

"So how come they didn't kill *you* for your failure?"

"These people are not barbarians, just vicious. They know I tried my best, mustered all available forces and nearly succeeded. You were just lucky, that's all. And now someone else has enlisted my help."

"Someone on my list of three thousand?"

"Could be. Very likely. Shall we exchange lists sometime?"

"Do I have a choice in this?"

"Sure, Mason. You can always say 'no'."

"No."

"You ought to reconsider." Mucous slurped his food.

"I have received new orders."

"Surprise me."

"Here's the deal. You join HLS as Intergalactic Creative Director, replacing Marvie Fuchwitt at a salary triple what he makes, and you only need to work for me one day a month and then only on projects of your own choosing. Except for the Government advertising contracts of course."

"The Government account?"

"Don't be stupid, Mason, and don't treat me like an idiot. The Entropy Brief. You know all about it. Madame Prime hated our campaign, so she obviously loved yours. We have to have it. I know our campaign is only temporary and she plans to switch to yours when she feels the time is right."

"You and who else are in the loop?"

"That's my business and mine alone."

Mason looked away, "When's the food coming? I'll give you my answer after the tiramisu. I hope they've got a decent Chianti."

"I can see you've spent too much time around old Noddy Hemsley."

"You know Noddy too, do you?"

The food came and the two rivals indulged to the full as they swapped stories about suppliers, ex-employees and implausible clients. They actually found themselves laughing together a few times and seemed to thoroughly enjoy their lunch. It was a relief to avoid the tension between them for awhile.

"I've made better tiramisu myself, but apart from that, lunch was splendid, thank you very much, Bernard."

"And have you reached a decision about joining Hooke, Ligne & Syncher?"

"I have Bernard and I'm afraid I cannot accept your offer, kind and thoughtful as it is."

"Is that your final decision?"

"I'm afraid so, Bernard."

"I will have to report your decision to my associate of course. He will not be pleased. I warn you. He will not be pleased."

"May I borrow your driver to take me home? He obviously knows the route."

"Of course. I'm sorry about your decision, I'd be extra careful if I were you. And I'd get my affairs in order too. Last will and testament, visits to grannies etcetera." Mucous snapped his fat fingers, "Doorman, will you kindly show Jackson to the limo-shuttle? Oh, and ask Margot to see me please."

If You Don't Want To Come Up With A Handful of Mud, Reach for the Stars

He hardly had time to think about it. One moment he was talking nonchalantly to Mucous' P.A., her frizzy hair one of the most frightening sights in the Quadrant, the next his life had changed forever.

Margot glared up at him, her husky voice sweet with revenge, "This is for all the promises you made and never kept. You bloody bastard!" She had plunged the scalpel-sharp blade into his back. It slashed between his ribs and reached his heart from behind. He didn't realise he'd been stabbed at first because at the same time she raised her right knee into his testicles. That pain outweighed the pain of the stab for a few moments.

He was gradually aware of a pin prick of pain in his back, then an overwhelming searing heat that seemed to reach into the middle of him. "That's a helluva knee you've got," Mason coughed dark blood.

"You told me we were going to live together, you deceitful lying sonofabitch. You hurt me. You killed me. Now I'm letting you know how it feels to be pierced through the heart -- to die."

Mason soon felt liquid gushing out of the wound; it was running down, filling his trousers. He stared at Margot, incredulous at what had happened.

"You said you'd never been so happy with anyone in your entire life. Then nothing. Silence. You never rang. You never came by. You never wrote. And whenever I tried to reach you that damned minder of yours, Judy, always said you were out." Margot was on the verge of tears but determined not to let them out. "What was wrong with me? Wasn't I good enough? What did I do to you? Nothing!"

"Who the fuck are you? You work for Mucous, OK, but we've never met before. Are you sure you've got the right guy? I'd remember your hair, it's shit. But at least I'd remember it. It's not me you want to kill it's some other guy, honestly. I don't deserve to die for whatever you think I did." Jackson grimaced with excruciating pain. He lost the strength to stand. His legs gave way. He crumpled to the pavement bleeding like a stuck pig. Mason didn't like bleeding.

The pain gave way to an increasing numbing sensation. He couldn't feel his fingers and toes any more. The blood was draining from his arteries and from his brain too.

"Bleed to death. My heart bled for you now yours is going to bleed for me. You had your good times with me and now you have to pay the price."

"A medi-bot. Please get me a medi-bot." Jackson looked up at her, pleading for his life.

"No. I don't want you to be able to hurt me again. Nor anyone else. And this is the only way I can be sure you won't. Goodbye, Jackson. Thanks for the memories."

"Margot! A medi-bot. Who the hell are you? It's not me you're after, I swear! For chrissakes, Margot, get me a medi-bot!"

"Goodbye, Jackson Howard."

"My name's not Jackson Howard, it's Mason Jackson, you stupid cow! Oh shit."

Margot hadn't heard; she was already walking away and out of his sight. Jackson crumpled from his sitting position to being fully flat on his back. A pool of blood spread around him as he stared up at the stars. Shit, what a wet sticky mess one's blood makes.

His eyes fixed on Orion. There was Rigel and Betelgeuse. He fondly remembered the visit there with Atos. Then he lost focus. Vision was soft and blurred; he could no longer make out any individual stars. "Oh no, not now." He cried, "Please, not now. I don't want to die now. Damn! Bugger! " In his dying moments he did not cry out for

God's help. He knew he wouldn't come even if he existed.

"Atos! Help me!"

As his vision blurred further and the darkness of the night spread its arms tighter around him, Jackson still fought to gain control. "Help me, Atos. Help me, Atos, quickly."

A thought bounced back, "Help yourself, Mason." It sounded like the voice of his father.

He was dizzy. His guts ached and his throat was dry. But he fought for breath and life. A distant noise was at first a distraction, but as it grew nearer it grew clearer. He could hear a chorus. Angels? No, not for him! It was a chorus of three voices he knew to be Atos, Dharman and Prem.

He focused on what they sang and joined in, "Om namah shivayah, Om namah shivayah." Over and over again he sang the chant in his consciousness, saving his breath for life. In far less than a minute Jackson managed to get control of his breathing and to clear his mind of thoughts of dying.

He found the void between his deep regular breaths and went into it. He was very weak, but the pain was drifting away -- going away behind him somewhere. He fell further into the void. There was a pin point of light ahead. No bigger than a sesame seed to begin with, but it grew wider and wider until he could see into it. "Om nama shivayah. Ommmm"

He kept going toward the pinpoint of light. There was a tunnel. Brightly illuminated. And he was going toward it. Not very far now. Atos, Prem and Dharman stood at the other end of it. Almost there. Then a thought arose in the midst of the tunnel vision. "Am I dead? Or *Canadian?*" And he heard himself manage a chuckle at the last joke he ever made in the physical world.

Mason Jackson's blood-drained body lay on the pavement outside his home on Omicron IV. It was a limp, lifeless thing that had carried him through a hundred and fifty thousand years of searching, spending, inventing and womanising. Now it was devoid of spirit or movement.

At four in the morning, the water sprinklers came on and refreshed the herbaceous outside the restaurant where he had enjoyed sumptuous Italian feast with Bernard Mucous the day before. The water played on the plants and sprayed the remains of Mason's body clean, carrying the pool of blood into the nearest drain. Dawn found him freshly washed and staring at the suns.

The New Millennium

Three beings stood in animated conversation precisely in the centre of the vast Leadership Hall. This was the innermost sanctum of the supreme heads of state of the Universal Empire. The three beings were the new Leaders selected by Central Thought and a vote of confidence by the people. This was the first day of the new millennium and the new succession of Leadership. But today a historical precedence was being set. For never in the history of the Empire had Central Thought named a Supreme Leader to a second thousand year term of office.

Today, Madame Catherine Prime commenced her historical second term. And in a matter of minutes, everything the Expansionist Empire had stood for during the last fifty thousand years would be turned on its head. Few had an idea that it would happen.

Madame Prime held the attention and admiration of the other two Supreme Leaders, Tylus and Chad. Madame Prime was tall, exquisitely elegant and moved with the same degree of exceeding grace with which she spoke. Two hundred years earlier, she had made a decision in secret to change the course of human destiny. Now, for the first time, she was prepared to speak openly with her equals about the gathering force of unseen change. With a thousand years in the supreme post already under her belt, Catherine Prime was Foremost Among Equals. In their first private conference as the new Leadership, Madame Prime confided to her co-Leaders that her private appeal for an unprecedented second term had been made to CT on a platform of Reform rather than guaranteed stability and status quo thinking.

Toward the end of her previous term in office, a popular movement had evidenced amongst the masses. A movement against higher productivity targets and innovative technology. When Madame Prime came out in favour of the Reformists, people were aghast, but people also listened. They had never heard of a Leader who was prepared to throw out established Expansionist policies and put forward fresh thinking that included putting the brakes on consumption. Catherine Prime gave inspiration to reform and free thought. She made Reform make sense. The people of the Four United Quadrants of the Total Universe gave her a mandate no one, not even the great Emperor, Chivas Regal, had been given. And Central Thought considered her position and confirmed it. The new Millennium was hers. The new Leadership called a press conference.

Tylus, Chad and Catherine stood atop a triangular column in silhouette. As the broadcast began, the light gradually shifted to the foreground, illuminating their forms and finally their faces.

"We are the Three." they said in unison. "We are Your Leadership."

The Empire's Anthem, 'Our Star Spangled Universe' swelled into the air. Tylus introduced Catherine Prime.

"I, Madame Catherine Prime, wish to make important announcements on this, the first day of the new Millennium. First, I order closed any company that markets products designed within the philosophy of planned obsolescence. Second, I order strict enforcement of the Right to Leisure Laws. The new official guideline for the working week will now be five hours in any five day period."

There was more of course, but the planned obsolescence order was the bombshell. It was a dramatic shift in government policy. Change wasn't merely in the air, it was here. It was also seen as heretical by almost every business leader in all four Quadrants. When the media asked her what she thought people were going to do with all their leisure time, Catherine Prime was quick to urge the population to start using their minds instead of their bodies. She even suggested the Government might open free-thought University courses so people could just come and think freely about anything they wanted to. Tutors could even be provided to help people get started.

"We have depended too long," the experienced Leader declared, "on the electronic resources of Central Thought. It is time we humans developed our own back-up system for the computers. There may even come a day when we no longer need such computers. And that will yield enormous energy savings."

Though no one really expected to either suffer or benefit from this new policy. people did seem to feel good about it and there was much popular support for the new programmes. After all, Sparky, their energetic friend, had long ago convinced most of the children at least, that saving energy was a rewarding feel-good experience.

Toward the end of the second Millennium of Catherine Prime's Leadership, medical science made a major breakthrough toward achieving even longer life-spans. On the 990th anniversary of the death of her friend, Mason Jackson, she addressed the people of her Universal domain, "Thanks to the dedication of our medical research teams, the human degenerative process is now nearly under our complete control. Strains of permanent blood cells, that is, blood cells that virtually never age, have for the first time been highly successful in eliminating death by natural causes."

But for Madame Prime, for whom the goal of Immortality had driven her on through nearly two thousand years of continuous Leadership, a new urgency emerged in her forward planning. What was the point of trying to live forever if the Universe was going to die first?

She had the power to move heaven and Earth. So Earth would be saved. She would see to that. So would every

350

other human habitable planet the dark dossiers had predestined for the energy fires. She could also guide things and influence decisions that would maximise the number of humans that could evolve through the universities of Freea thinking. And some day, she would join Mason Jackson among the stars.

The Last Radio Station

Atos sailed serenely toward the distant star. These days every star was distant. The kaleidoscope of swirling nebulas and spiralling galaxies, megaclusters and Magellanic star-clouds that once thrilled his travels had faded inexorably toward the terror of Entropy's last statement. Earlier in the day he found himself whistling -- quite spontaneously -- the Sparky theme song. "Energy. Energy. Remember it's not free. Energy. Energy. Save a little spark for me!"

Too little too late. Homo sapiens had never learned. Why had Homo Freea ever bothered with them? They were a lower life form and that was that.

"Come hear our song of joy..."

A new piece of music had begun to creep into his cosmic consciousness. At least his thoughts were free of that little blighter, Sparky. But 'Song of Joy'? Was he sliding into mental illness?

It was the last thing he expected to see. In fact if he had been passing another 4 cm to the right, it would have been the last thing he ever sensed in any way. Atos bounced off the ashy black transmitter with his ego thoroughly bruised but nothing else damaged. How had he missed sensing it? But whoa! It's a transmitter! This had to be the last radio station in space! He listened in awe at his discovery.

"You've been listening to the Golden Oldies. That last track was performed by the Massed Silurian Folk Singers of Galaxy 7993, Quadrant Two. And this is the station of the stars, the only station that matters, the Voice of the Cosmos. After the news, we'll be hosting the Archaeology Century, with music from the Bardaukeran Symphony introducing a travelogue to the Nazca second-hand civilisation supermarket shopping centre on the Boron Asteroid, re-created just as it was in its heyday nearly eight hundred million years ago. Imagine shopping for supermarkets from second hand civilisations -- and what a choice there was! All that and more in the next hundred years right here on Voice of the Cosmos!"

Atos didn't really have a century to spend, nobody did. Today was the day, and he wasn't about to leave his ringside seat with the news about to come on.

"And now, over to the news desk at news central..."

Atos wondered where this mythical news central place was, or even if it ever existed.

The next voice he heard seemed to reverberate as if from the bottom of canyon.

"VOICE OF THE COSMOS COSMIC NEWS TIME! NEWS AS IT HAP PENS, AFTER IT HAPPENS AND SOME TIMES

BEFORE IT HAP PENS."

Item. There is still no news from the government brain bank on the one question that matters: How can Entropy be stopped? Meanwhile, a huge computer, sponsored by the General Industries Corporation, was unveiled today, and dedicated to finding a technological solution to the problem. Already, several pet food companies have pledged their support to the project.

Item. The Vegan Galaxy hits the headlines today as the only galaxy in the universe *not* to report the loss of one of its stars in the last 24 hours. Star reporter Preedun Tome is on the spot to describe this staggering non-event. Take it away, P.T."

"Yes, I'm watching it not happen at this very moment. And it certainly is exciting I can tell you. With only 12 stars left in the Vegan Galaxy, I can assure you that our figures are accurate. Not a single star has extinguished in the last 24 hours. If there had been, I would have to report that there were now only eleven stars remaining. But happily, that is not the case. Who knows how long the Vegan Galaxy will last. 12 days? Eleven? Ten? Surely the days of Entropy are numbered now. And that really is good news, isn't it?"

"Yes, that certainly is good news, Preedun. Can you tell us how the oth--"

"Oh, oh, there it goes! Even as I speak, even as I stand here looking at the Vegan Galaxy, I can report even more news. One star has just gone pphhooot, and another is -- yes, I'm predicting-- yes, yes there we go, yes, we have it -- phhht phizzz -- another one gone. With only 10 sol-power units remaining, this Galaxy has just about seen the last of Entropy!"

"And remember, you heard it first right here on VOICE OF THE COSMOS!

"And so the reports continue to come in. Galaxy after Galaxy has become an ex-Galaxy. Space has never been darker. And it becomes increasingly difficult to look at the brighter side. But that's what we're here for, so it's back to your favourite programmes on the Archaeology Century. We want to be happy but we can't be happy till we make you happy too!"

Atos looked around for the star he was heading for. The he realised it was gone. He looked at the pocked and dented dark sides of the transmitter. It looked more like an asteroid than a manmade object. He could sense the solar batteries in its metal heart dimming with failing energy. Only the light of his own essence illuminated the shape of the transmitter against the cold dark emptiness of space. How would he meet Moron now that the rendezvous point no longer existed? As agreed, he'd look for the next nearest star and hope Moron would be there.

"Now, for your ultimate enjoyment, we have an original recording of a composition by Nehudi Janawendt first performed at the Cosmic Celebration of Mankind's Ultimate Expansion. The piece we offer is the Destiny Symphony. The composer, Janawendt, describes the emotions she experienced on that momentous occasion.

"To me, the Ultimate Expansion was the end of t h e ... dudddd."

The transmitter had died. The age of radio had gone with it. His friend, Mason, would be deeply saddened at the passing of his favourite medium. Just then, Atos sensed a distant flicker of life. Moron. Lost in space with few bearings to travel by. He homed in on the agitated life point and hurried to him.

"Atos! Where have you been? It's getting lonely out here."

"Listening to the radio."

"At a time like this? We've been summoned to the centre. Everyone's been summoned to the centre."

"This is it then."

The Last Page

"It's a pity Preadun Tome can't see this."

"Who?"

"Nothing. He never existed anyway. Just a persona-programme for a news sensing device on Voice of the Cosmos."

"Oh yeah, they'd know how to really bring this event to life."

"The death of the universe? You're sick, Moron. Sick."

"Do you guys have to make so much racket?"

"Mason, you old lecher, after all the work you did to expand the Free population, I knew you'd be one of the first here!"

"Everybody's here. This is the last page. The end of the sentience. I wouldn't miss it. Hey, where else would I go? Where can anyone go? The Universe is empty except for us, here and now."

"And the biggest most powerful computer in the history of the Universe."

"Have you no faith in General Industries? They make wonderful computers.""Well I don't have much faith in them being able to find a market for their computers after today!"

Billions of Freea gathered and englobed the last sun that still burned feebly at what was now the centre of the universe. An elite free thinking minority, just a few million minds -- started rolling a giant thought wave around the single sun's equator: "Ask the question. Ask the question. Ask the question."

Mason felt himself become swept up in it and knew what it was like to be but a single molecule of water in a tidal wave. On the other hand, the General Industries Corporation computer was only a little larger than a double-decker macroburger, about the size of a human brain, but it contained all the accumulated knowledge of the universe. The body-less souls asked the burning

356

question fusing their minds as one, uttering the question together, "How can Entropy be reversed?"

The hamburger groaned under the strain. No response. No one was surprised.

"Can the universe be restarted after it dies?"

"ONE QUESTION AT A TIME, PLEASE" This was not a very understanding computer. It obviously lacked social graces. Then it glowed. It moaned. It hummed. It threatened to explode. It gave its final reply. "INSUFFICIENT DATA FOR MEANINGFUL ANSWER."

Mason Jackson was still plugged into the universal consciousness as they received the shock reply. Well that was it. The ultimate failure of human technology. Homo sapiens had bombed out. It was up to them now, the Freea. They were the only hope left in the entire Void. It was show time!

The response was spontaneous and it surprised even the brightest intellects of Atos, Dharman and Prem. Every one of the billion billion beings knew instinctively what had to be done -- this was their moment. This was what they were here for. All the training of millions of years, the mind expansion, the Lift-offs, the Universities of Free Thought, the efforts of the Freea supported by millions of Homo Sapiens who had elevated themselves sufficiently to leave their bodies behind and join them in free space.

The collective super-heightened consciousness of the Freea welded the mass into a single entity of such power, such force, and such knowledge that the G.I.C. computer was obliterated by the sheer presence of it. The heavens glowed with the combined auras of the billions. And as the last sun silently died to grey ash, a new radiance, brighter than the universe had ever known -- shone bravely in the cold vast emptiness of space.

"Let there be light! Let there be light!" The Freea billions boldly sang!

But they could not sustain it. Jackson felt himself straining to the limits. Felt Atos, Dharman and Prem. Catherine, Moron, and Judy, -- all of them were pushing too with all their might and will and skill. Jackson's awareness was on the point of bursting. But it was no use. The collective radiance was fading. How could they presume to --?

"No! No! It must not go out! We can do it! Push! Try harder!"

But even the glow of the last sun was gone. Then a thought struck the minds. The suns were gone, the planets, the asteroids, the dust and gases were gone, but the Universe wasn't. Atos, Dharman, Mason, Catherine and billions of other points of light, were still there. Their nodes of pure energy still intact, functioning and in total harmony with each other and the space they occupied.

"What are we going to do now, then?" Mason asked Atos.

"We still have each other." he calmly replied, apparently content to live in empty space forever and ever. "Indeed, it's the end of the universe and I don't see anyone praying."

"That, Atos, is because we are the highest beings that have ever existed. Not only that, but you have given me an idea!" And with that thought, Mason's light shone brighter and brighter with all the force and brilliance he could muster. And he began connecting with others – Atos, Prem, Dharman, Catherine.

"Honour the light that dwells within you as you!!" Mason screamed into the Void! His words were swept on a typhoon of self-awareness throughout the billions of the Universal Consciousness. Individually, each being of the vast assemblage had reached self-perfection as evolved Freea beings. And as they united in spirit and common recognition, they came together. The closer they came, the brighter their collective light became. Closer and closer until each touched another. And from the Many came the One. The One was all there was. All knowledge, all energy, all light, all that the Universe held burst forth and began to fill the Universe anew.

Epilogue

An eon had passed. "And now, Atos, just where do you think this has gotten us?" The bulb of light known to the Universal Consciousness as Oron sent out a tentacle of thought across the exciting newborn Universe in search of his eternal friend. New worlds and galaxies were coming into being hour by hour. It was a stupendous display of creation. Or in this case, re-creation.

Immediately a reply came in the physical form of his light-hearted companion who was physically indistinguishable from himself. Atos spoke calmly, "In the physical world there was no questioning of the 'How' and 'Why' until the Greeks. In the Christian world, and indeed in every world supporting religious life, the answer was 'God did it'. And then, with the explosive forces of science and technology came new philosophies."

"I fear you digress, Atos. All I wish to know is, are we any further along toward knowing what is certain than we were at the start back on Page One?"

"Ah, what provides absolute certainty? Reality? What is 'real'? Philosophy can merely comment on society and science. Both disciplines are fundamentally unstable. There is no philosophy founded on certainty."

"But there is philosophy based on knowledge."

"Oh, yes. But first ask yourself, 'How do you know that you Know?' And you are left all over again with uncertainty."

"Surely, after a hundred billion years, everything can now be explained by a combination of History and Science."

"A man named Marx, from an early physical world, said that. Referring I suppose to the belief that even if the world itself is not certain or stable, then perhaps at least the tools by which we study are stable and certain."

"Then you imply, Atos, that the tools are *not stable*?"

"It has never been proven that they are."

"You mean to tell me, Atos that throughout the eons of History there are no patterns?"

"Within temporary cycles, yes. But nothing by which we can predict the future with absolute certainty. There is always a chance that things will not turn out as they seem. Chaos is always a factor. That there will be Chaos is the only certainty."

"Until your last thought, Oron. Until your last thought."

"Then, even with only one absurdly dim and dying sun in all the Universe smouldering into oblivion before our eyes, you still think there is a chance that we may yet find a way to reverse Entropy?"

"What's the point? Why bother? It is obviously part of the natural order of things and as long as we have the power to ride along with it and see us through the end of the Universe time after time, then there are no ends, only beginnings."

"I find that somewhat exciting."

Deadline

"Well, Atos, what did you think of our ideas?"
"I like the bit where the Navy squadron out-manoeuvred the pirate fleet. It had me sitting on the edge of my asteroid."
"And the central character, Mason?"
"I wouldn't say he was a waste of space, but he certainly provided an unusual choice as the chief catalyst. A robotics engineer, a genetic physicist perhaps but an advertising man? Not what I'd call hero material. That's a fetch too far." "He wasn't intended to be so much a hero as a comment. In fact I rather thought it made the presence of all the other bullshit so much more plausible. In all seriousness I was attempting to make a statement about the futility of man's effort to change the outcome of *anything*, and advertising seemed a potent environment for getting that kind of message across."
"I'm not sure that's what I got out of it. My holistic analyser tells me this approach lands entirely too low on the probability scale. I don't think it's a realistic enough scenario. Especially as we will be faced with the problem of Entropy soon enough in real time. Sorry, I think your Plan B ought to be filed under 'W' for wishful thinking."
"Too exciting for you then? Not quite conservative enough? You are such a boring piece of shit."
"I'm afraid that's the way the Chairman will look at it. Still, I'd like to congratulate you on making an excellent presentation. There's a lot more you could have done on the getting the technology side more plausible and frankly more up to date, but then you are a Certified Dreamer and not really a tech guy. However we appreciate all the hard work that went into it. "
"About twelve thousand hours, actually."

"I'm sorry we won't be able to pay you, Oron. You do realise it's corporate policy not to pay for creative work, we expect that to come as part and parcel of the service."
Over a hundred thousand words screamed in pain as Oron dumped Plan B into the Trash.
"Yes of course. If, you uh, aren't too rushed for time, my assistant will reset the programmes to the default settings while I set the scene for a quick run-through of Plan C."
"That's very kind. Perhaps another time? Must dash."
"No problem, Atos. Another time, as you say. Eons before Entropy really begins to bite."
"Exactly. We really have to crack on with the E-Question urgently. Gotta go. Deadline. Sorry. Let's do lunch some time. Ciao."